THE CAVE OF RÚIN ÁRSA

Thunder on the Moor Series
Thunder on the Moor
Ride with the Moonlight
Shake Loose the Border

The Cross of Ciarán Series
The Cross of Ciarán
The Book of Carraig

www.andrea-matthews.com

Facebook Page: Andrea Matthews Historical Romance
Twitter: Andrea Matthews Author @AMatthewsAuthor
Instagram: andreamatthewshistoricromance

THE CAVE OF RÚIN ÁRSA

Andrea Matthews

Inez M. Foster

The Cave of Rúin Ársa

This is a work of fiction. All characters and events in this publication, other than those clearly in the public domain, are products of the author's imagination or are used fictitiously and are not to be construed as real. Any resemblance to real persons, living or dead, is purely coincidental.

Cover designed by Jenny Quinlan, Historical Fiction Book Covers

ISBN 978-1-7333375-6-4 (Pbk)

Inez M. Foster
New York

Website: www.andrea-matthews.com
Facebook Page: www.facebook.com/andreamatthewshistoricalromance
Twitter: www.twitter.com/AMatthewsAuthor
Instagram: www.instagram.com/andreamatthewshistoricromance

To my friends who followed me from first draft to published book

Go raibh maith agaibh, mo chairde

CHAPTER 1

Aodhán Donnelly cursed under his breath as the therapist demanded he take a few more steps. All right, he wasn't demanding, more like encouraging, but it still raised Aodhán's dander. The doctors all said he was making wonderful progress, so why did he feel so frustrated?

Oh, I don't know, maybe because Niamh has refused to sleep with you until you make more of an effort. Sweat was pouring off his brow. How much more of an effort could he make? Still, he'd only taken six steps, and that was with him hanging on to both railings for dear life.

Not until ye can walk to me without any help, she'd said late one night before kissing him on the forehead. He knew she was afraid of hurting him somehow, but shit . . .

"Ye're making fine progress," the therapist said. "We'll have ye up and about in no time at all."

Bull shit! Aodhán flopped back down in the wheelchair to wait for Niamh's brother, Duffy, to pick him up. What the heck was wrong with him? In fifteen hundred years, he'd never even known a woman's touch until the night of

1

Ciarán's wedding. As a chosen child of the goddess, charged with caring for the creatures of the sky, such carnal knowledge had been forbidden him. But then he'd awaken in this century and fallen hopelessly in love with Niamh. They'd only lain together once before the world came crashing down around him, though even that was enough to whet his appetite for the beautiful chestnut-haired *cailín*, who now looked at him as more of an invalid than a lover. "Shit!"

"What's that?" Niamh snuck up behind him and kissed the top of his head. Not what he needed kissed at the moment. He slumped farther down in the chair.

"Aren't we a ray o' sunshine this morning?" She wheeled him out of the hospital toward the car.

"Where's Duffy? I thought he was to pick me up this morning."

"He was, but I decided to play hooky and come get ye meself. Though if I'd known ye'd be in such a foul mood, I wouldn't have wasted me time." They'd reached the car, and she opened the door, letting down the wheelchair's right arm. He sat for a moment, scowling at her. "Well, go on, then," she said. "D'ye think a wee girl like meself is going to be lifting the likes o' ye into the car? Yer therapist suggested 'twould be good for ye to be doing it yerself."

"Did he now?" He grumbled but lifted himself onto the seat. If the therapist meant to consult with her about his condition, he might recommend another type of physical exercise, one that would be a bit more pleasant.

After loading up his chariot, Niamh got in behind the wheel. "What has ye so prickly now? The doctor says ye're doing better than expected."

"D'ye truly want to know what it is that's bothering me?" he said.

She turned to face him, a tender smile crossing her lips. "O' course I do, darlin'. Maybe 'tis something I can be helping ye with."

"Oh, there's no doubt o' that, but sure ye'll not be obliging me."

She folded her arms across her breast, one eyebrow lifted in a defiant challenge. "Well, what is it, then? Get it off yer chest."

"I just want to feel ye next to me. Is that so much to ask?"

"I'm next to ye now, but it doesn't seem to be doing ye much good."

"'Tis not what I meant, and ye know it. I love ye, Niamh. I want to hold ye in me arms as I close me eyes at night, to know ye're safe in me embrace, to feel yer breath warming me heart."

"But it wouldn't be all ye wanted, now would it? And ye're still healing. D'ye like being in that chair, having folk wait on ye, then?" Aodhán could hear the tension in her voice, see it in the flair of her gorgeous blue-gray eyes. He could get lost in those eyes. Wanted to. "For God's sake, Aodhán. I nearly lost ye."

"And I ye as well. Or have ye forgotten that?"

"O' course I haven't." She reached out and touched his hand, her voice softening. "God's given us a second chance, and I don't want to be blowing it just because ye're getting a wee bit horny."

"A third chance for me, I'm thinking." He let his mouth crook up a bit at the corner, knowing full well it would display a dimple. "But what does it mean to be *a bit horny*?" He touched the top of his head, searching for some sort of pointed protrusions, and she laughed.

"It means ye're feeling the need o' some intimate stimulation."

"Well, if that's what it means, there's no wee bit about it." He broke into a full-fledged grin and lifted her hand so he could kiss her palm.

"Just pack those dimples o' yers away. They'll not be doing ye any good today." Leaning over, she gave him a kiss on the mouth, deep and warm, before pulling back. "That's all ye'll be getting for now, so ye'd best savor it. Besides, could ye imagine what me brother would do if he caught us together?"

"We could be finding a place o' our own. I saw a wee cottage advertised, not far from Mrs. Byrne's."

"Ye did, did ye? Well, I reckon 'tis probably taken by now and all."

"How d'ye know unless ye take a look? Can ye not at least do that for me, seeing as ye'll not be offering anything else to divert me attention?"

She rolled her eyes but headed off in the direction of the cottage he'd spoken about. Though they rode in silence for a while, Aodhán could almost hear her mind working. He tried to slip inside, but it was like entering a room with twenty people all talking at once. Only one thought rang out clearly. *Pick up milk on the way home.* He should have paid more attention to Domnall's lessons all those centuries ago. Finally, she took a deep breath and spoke.

"Duffy would never stand for us moving in together. Ye know that. Besides, there's me reputation to think o'."

But he'd already considered that excuse and had his answer ready, though he had to bite his lip to keep from grinning again. "Ye'd just be there to tend the handicapped. After all, what can a poor invalid lad like meself be doing?"

Niamh frowned. "Ye're impossible, ye know that?"

"I do, but 'tis part o' me charm, is it not?" Before he could say anything else, she pulled up in front of the cottage, and he grimaced. "Needs a wee bit more work than I was expecting."

"D'ye think?" They sat for a minute, staring at the dilapidated cottage. "And I doubt it has more than two rooms in it."

"As long as 'tis a bedroom and a kitchen, 'twould do me well enough."

Niamh slapped him on the arm and laughed before pulling back on the road and heading home. "'Tis all for the good. The best place for us right now is with Duffy. There's always someone home if ye need anything, and yer room is on the first floor."

"What I need Duffy can't be giving me." He slouched down in the seat and crossed his arms.

"Nor can I at the moment, so cool yer jets, darlin'." Her lips quirked up on one side and her eyes twinkled, causing Aodhán to grip the car seat. Dear God, didn't she know what that sweet smile did to him? He wasn't exactly sure what *cool yer jets* meant, but he could hazard a guess.

He turned to stare out the window, trying desperately to suppress the heat that had rushed into his cheeks. What he needed right now was a dip in the lake, but that wasn't going to happen either. Niamh would never hear of it. Blowing out a long breath, he wiped a hand across his mouth.

What was happening to him? He'd dealt with women before, back in the fifth century, when he was a priest of the *túath*, yet never had he felt such a yearning for one. True, he wanted to lay with her, to join with her in carnal bliss, but it went far beyond that. He had lost his heart to this perky little nymph with alluring eyes and tiny turned-up nose. That was what made his need for her so intense.

They pulled up in front of Duffy's cottage, and, giving him another deep kiss that nearly sent him over the edge, Niamh jumped out of the car, a twinkle in her eye.

"Shit!" he said. Tomorrow he was going to walk more than six steps, even if it took all day. He was tired of being stuck in one place, especially when Niamh was in another.

****

Niamh walked into the house to find her sister-in-law cleaning up the breakfast dishes. "Good morning to ye, darlin'," Fionnuala said. She put the plates in the sink and wiped her hands on her apron. "I don't suppose ye remembered the milk?"

"Oh no! I'll go back out and get it."

Fionnuala laughed. "Don't be worrying yerself about it. I'll give Duffy a call and ask him to pick some up on his way home from work." She glanced down the hallway. "Should I be making a plate up for himself?"

"Ye may as well go ahead." Niamh knew whatever Aodhán's disposition, he wouldn't turn down Fionnuala's cooking. "Don't be waiting on an answer from him, though. He's in a right mood this morning and all."

Aodhán pulled up to the table and frowned, though he didn't contradict her.

"Sure, 'tis just because he had naught but a cup o' tea and a piece o' toast before he left this morning. The poor lad's just hungry."

Niamh let out a barking laugh. "Oh, he is that all right, but 'twill take more than a fry-up to satisfy him." Fionnuala tried to hide a smile, but Niamh could see the twinkle in her eye. "And don't ye be encouraging him. Ye know what Duffy would say."

Fionnuala bent down to get some rashers out of the fridge, chuckling to herself.

"Go on, then," Niamh said. "What is it ye find so funny?"

"D'ye truly think yer brother's never had the same thing on his mind as this one does?" She nodded toward Aodhán, and his cheeks flushed a lovely shade of red.

"I suppose he did, judging from the amount o' wee ones that are running about, but I doubt he'd be seeing it the same when it came to me."

Fionnuala nodded, standing for a moment with the egg carton in her hand. "Ordinarily, I'd say ye were right, but after all the two o' ye have been through, sure, he may not be as hard to get round as ye think." Aodhán looked up, the spark of hope shining in his eyes, so Fionnuala continued. "Depending on what it is ye're talking about, that is."

A flicker of sympathy touched Niamh's heart at the sight of Aodhán's shoulders physically dropping a few inches. Fionnuala must have noticed too because, after cracking a few eggs in the frying pan, she turned back to face them.

"Well, what is it ye're wanting to ask him, then?"

"Go on," Niamh said. She sat next to Aodhán and bit into a piece of dry toast. She had been so excited about going to pick him up she had forgotten to eat herself.

"Shall I make yerself a plate as well?" Fionnuala asked. Her sister-in-law had an uncanny knack of picking up on the slightest hint.

"That would be grand, thank ye." She turned back to Aodhán. "Are ye just going to sit there like ye've lost the gift o' speech?"

Aodhán shifted uncomfortably in his wheelchair. Maybe it was mean to put him on the spot like that, but after the mood he'd been in that morning, she thought he deserved to squirm for a bit.

"'Tis naught important," he said. "I just thought that I saw this wee cottage and Well, it doesn't matter, does it, because the place was a wreck."

Fionnuala put a steaming plate of rashers, hash browns, and eggs down in front of him. "So ye're wanting to move in together, then. D'ye think it wise, being ye're still recuperating and all?"

"O' course 'tis not wise," Niamh said, "but then he's not using his brain to think, now is he?"

"Men rarely do." Fionnuala chuckled and put another plate down in front of Niamh.

"'Tis not like that at all," Aodhán said, his cheeks darkening to an even deeper shade. Niamh rolled her eyes and popped a piece of bacon in her mouth. "All right, maybe it is a bit," he said, "but 'tis more than that."

Shaking his head, he frowned and looked down at his plate, pushing the food around with his fork. He looked so much like a wounded little boy, lost and alone, with no one to love him, that a ripple of guilt washed over Niamh. Perhaps she had carried it too far. She placed her hand on his and gave it a gentle squeeze. "I want to be with ye too, but we need to be getting ye well first. That tree could have killed ye."

"I know that, *a chuisle*, but it didn't, and me heart aches for the feel o' ye."

Fionnuala cleared her throat, the hint of a smile slipping across her lips, and Aodhán went all red again. "Well, if ye're wanting to know what I think, Niamh is right—for now. That's not to say 'twill be the same two or three weeks down the road. Put some o' that yearning ye're feeling into getting yerself on yer feet, then we'll all put our heads together and handle Duffy Flynn."

She sat and poured herself a cup of tea. "Now eat up so I can get the dishes done before 'tis time for lunch."

Niamh looked to Aodhán, and he smiled. That was all the encouragement she needed. "Fionnuala makes sense, darlin'. I'm scared to death I'd hurt ye right now, cause ye to have some sort o' relapse. I couldn't bear the thought o' it."

"'Tis all right, a ghrá. I'm sorry for being in such a foul mood this morning 'Tis just taking so much longer than I ever expected. Six steps was all I could manage, and I dared not let go o' the railings for fear I'd fall and end up having to start all over again."

Niamh's heart was breaking. She reached out and brushed the tawny curls out of his dazzling blue eyes. She could stare into them for hours and never get bored. Didn't he know how much she wanted to be with him as well, to feel his breath upon her neck, his touch against her naked flesh? "Just try to be patient, *a ghrá*. We'll get through this together."

"Will ye wheel me outside for a bit?"

Niamh sat back, surprised. "Are ye daft? 'Tis freezing out there."

"Don't be troubling yerselves." Fionnuala got up and patted Aodhán on the shoulder. "I'm off to make the beds. The kitchen is all yers."

Aodhán's cheeks flushed again. Niamh didn't think she'd seen him blush that much in the entire time she'd known him. Albeit that was only a few months.

"'Tis not exactly the way I'd imagined this," he said. "I was planning to wait till Ciarán was off on his honeymoon and things had settled down, but then " He sighed. "I can't even get down on me knee."

Was he going to ask what she thought he was? A jolt of pure joy surged through her body, but no. Maybe that wasn't it at all. She had to calm down. She cleared her throat. "What were ye planning on doing?"

"Ye're going to make me work for this one, aren't ye?" His eyes twinkled with a warmth that had been missing all morning.

"Probably," she said. "If ye're about to be asking what I'm hoping "

He reached in his pocket and pulled out a ring, a beautiful little trinket with a diamond set between two rubies—her birthstone. "Will ye marry me, *a chuisle*? When I'm able to walk down the aisle, o' course."

Tears welled up in her eyes. Did he have any doubt what her answer would be? He must have, for the light in his eyes had dimmed just a bit. Well, she'd make sure she whisked away every trace of doubt that reared its ugly head.

"I'd wheel ye down the aisle and marry ye today if ye wanted me to." She sat on his lap, wrapping her arms around his neck and kissing him long and deep. When they finally separated, he was grinning from ear to ear.

"I'll take it that's a yes, then." He slipped the ring on her finger and kissed her again, his lips soft and firm against hers, his arms wrapped tight around her waist.

They probably would have stayed like that for hours if a tiny voice hadn't interrupted. "Auntie Niamh," Kathleen said, "why are ye sitting on Uncle Aodhán's lap?"

"I'm thinking they're celebrating, darlin'." Fionnuala came down the hall carrying a bundle of sheets. "Well, am I right, then?"

Niamh nodded. Unable to keep the grin from spreading across her face, she jumped up to show her sister-in-law the ring. Had they been on a romantic island, with champagne and roses strewn about, she couldn't have been happier. That was the sweetest proposal she could have imagined, and she wouldn't have had it any other way.

"So when's the wedding?" Fionnuala asked.

"September," Aodhán said, "if Niamh's agreeable. I've got something to work toward now. And if I put me mind to it, I should be able to dance at our wedding without any trouble."

"September it is," Niamh said. How did he know she'd always dreamed of being a September bride? Had he slipped into her mind to retrieve the information? If so, she didn't care, for she trusted him with her entire being.

CHAPTER 2

Manhattan, New York, USA – December 1967

Ciarán stared at the letter and grumbled. What was Aodhán thinking? He flopped down in his favorite chair, resting his forearms on his knees as he scanned the short missive again. Part of him could understand it, he supposed. His brother had nearly lost Niamh just two months before. But did he have to make the wedding so soon?

An icy chill clutched his heart whenever he remembered that day in early October. They'd nearly all died at the hands of Bradaigh, a fifth-century serial killer who had somehow managed to survive fifteen hundred years, much the same as he and Aodhán had.

"I thought you'd be happy for them." Caitlin pulled him up from the chair and straightened his tie. "You're not going to pout all through Christmas dinner, are you?

"O' course not. I'm thrilled for them." Grabbing his jacket from the closet, he helped Caitlin with her coat.

She wasn't really showing much yet, but the knowledge that she was carrying his children caused him to smile every time he looked at her. He only hoped her uncle didn't notice the little bump that had appeared in the last week. Having only been married in October, she shouldn't be showing at all. Of course, they had let the cart get ahead of the horse just a bit, as Father Dennis would say.

"What's bothering you, then?" She picked up one of the shopping bags filled with presents and headed for the elevator.

"'Tis his timing, that's all. Sure, he could have waited a few more months, what with the babes coming and all."

"Good Lord! I hope I've had them by next September."

He frowned, not really in the mood for her teasing. "I know that, but they'll still be wee things, now won't they?"

They got in the cab, and after telling the driver to head for St. Monica's, she sat back and took his hand. "They'll probably be almost four months old by then, maybe even older since twins tend to come early. Doctor Smith says that's old enough to fly."

"I don't like the whole idea o' it."

"The whole idea of what?" She frowned for a moment before her brow relaxed and a twinkle lit her emerald-green eyes. "You don't want them going on the plane." She shook her head and laughed. "That's it, isn't it?"

"And what if it is? They won't be able to fend for themselves. What if something should happen? How am I to see to ye and the two wee ones as well?"

Caitlin's expression softened. "I know you don't like flying, but it really is far safer than getting in a car. Don't pass your fears on to your children."

"I've no intention o' doing that. Still, if he could wait till the following spring, they'd be that much older, walking maybe. At four months old, we can't exactly be strapping them into a seat, now can we?"

"We'll manage. Just like everyone else, so stop worrying. How is Aodhán getting on with his therapy? At least he'll be with Niamh and her family for Christmas."

The thought of how his brother had been crushed beneath a tree felled by Bradaigh's power caused his stomach to clench. He'd thought for sure he'd lost him that day. "Ye know Aodhán. He'd say he was doing grand, whether he was or not. Niamh, however, added a little note at the end. She says the doctors are optimistic that he'll walk again. He's doing his therapy, though she had to tell him she'd not wed him if he didn't."

"That doesn't sound like Aodhán. He's usually so conscientious. Now if it were you "

Ciarán tried to stifle a smile. "Sure, ye're not saying I'm a disagreeable patient?"

"You, my love, are a pain in the arse." She kissed him on the cheek, climbing over him to exit the cab.

He paid the driver and followed her out, hurrying up the church steps. "Find us a seat, and I'll put these in the sacristy until after Mass." Taking the packages, he hurried down the side aisle and slipped through the small door that led to the room behind the altar.

"Ah, good, ye're here," Father Michael said. "Go see Anthony Bertolini. He's short an usher, and ye're just the man for the job. Merry Christmas, lad."

"Thank ye, Father. Is it all right if we leave these here?" He lifted the two shopping bags.

"O' course. Now ye'd best be getting yerself out there before poor Mr. Bertolini has a panic attack."

He turned to leave, but before he did, Michael grabbed him by the arm. "How's me niece this morning?"

THE CAVE OF RÚIN ÁRSA

"Much better. The morning sickness seems to have ended. At least she hasn't had any for three days now."

"Ah, that's good, poor thing. Well, what are ye waiting for? Off with ye now."

Ciarán shook his head and smiled before ducking through the door and hurrying toward the back of the church. There was no use in pointing out it was Michael himself who had held him up in the first place. He barely got halfway down the aisle when Father Dennis caught him by the arm.

"You'd better get up to the choir loft. Ned keeps asking if you're here yet. You have a solo, don't you?"

"Sweet Brigid!" Ciarán exclaimed, eliciting a frown from Dennis. "Sorry, force o' habit." There were certain aspects of his former life he just couldn't seem to rid himself of, and that was one of them. Appearing to call on the goddess Brigid didn't go over well with his new family, though, especially when he was standing in church.

"I'll assume you were referring to Saint Brigid," Dennis said, rubbing a finger under his nose to hide his smile.

"Are ye trying to get me to lie in church as well?" Ciarán said.

"Point taken." Dennis laughed and grasped his shoulder. "What has you so flustered anyway?"

"Michael's asked me to lend a hand with the ushering. Seems we're short one, and Mr. Bertolini is . . ." He frowned, trying to recall Michael's words.

"Freaking out?" Dennis said.

"If ye say so. Is that the same as having . . . a panic attack?"

"Pretty much." Dennis nodded toward the back of the church, and they both started walking in that direction.

"But why does that have you so upset? You've ushered before."

"Not when I'm to be singing a solo in the choir at the same time."

"Oh, right. That could present a problem." Dennis stopped for a moment, deep in thought, so Ciarán stepped out of the aisle and waited. "You go on up to the choir loft," Dennis finally said. "I'll get one of the other parishioners to help with the ushering."

"Are ye sure? I wouldn't want Michael to be upset with me." In truth, he'd rather usher any day than stand up there in the loft and sing by himself for all to hear. No matter how good everyone said he was, his stomach still insisted on protesting.

"Don't worry, it's probably just slipped his mind. Besides, Mr. Svenson just came in. He'll be happy to get a break from his family. Between his wife's nagging about one thing or another and his kid's whining over having to sit quietly, it's a wonder he has any hair left at all. Now get going before Ned comes down and drags you up there."

Ciarán glanced back down the aisle. "Caitlin . . ."

"I'll tell her on my way to the sacristy." He rolled his eyes and nodded up the spiral staircase that led to the choir.

Ciarán nodded and turned to head up the stairs, but Dennis stopped him, squeezing his shoulder. "You've nothing to be nervous about, you know. You've got the voice of an angel. I wouldn't lie to you, little brother."

Ciarán couldn't help but chuckle. At six years his senior, Dennis really had become like an older brother to him, even though technically Ciarán had fifteen hundred years on him. "I know ye'd never lie to me. That's true enough, but it doesn't say much for yer musical taste, now does it?"

Dennis laughed, giving him a fraternal slap on the back before taking off toward the Svensons' pew. Like it or not, Ciarán was going to have to sing. Mr. Svenson was already hurrying down the aisle to the aid of Mr. Bertolini. O holy night, indeed! More like O holy morning! Lord help him!

****

"'Twas beautiful!" Mary Monaghan greeted Ciarán at the foot of the choir loft stairs, sniffling and holding a hankie to her nose. "If I didn't know better, I'd have sworn an angel had come to serenade us."

Caitlin kissed him on the cheek. "I don't know about that, but it was beautiful, as usual."

Mary blew her nose a final time before stuffing the tissue back in her handbag. "Of course, an angel wouldn't give me quite as much *agida* as you do."

"Agi . . . what?" Ciarán scratched his head.

"Heartburn," Caitlin said, her emerald eyes gleaming with laughter. "She means you can be a pain in the . . . butt."

Ciarán gasped in mock indignation. "A Mathair!"

Mary chuckled. "Honorary or not, you wouldn't be a son of mine if you weren't a pain in the tuchus." She headed for the church doors. "Now get a move on. Dinner's at one, on the dot. Don't be late."

"I'd best be getting the presents, then," Ciarán said to Caitlin. "Ye'll want to be getting there early, I suppose." He stole a quick kiss and headed back for the sacristy, but he hadn't gone three steps when a gaggle of ladies gathered around him like he was some kind of movie star.

"You had me on the verge of tears," one of the ladies said.

"Such a lovely voice," said another, causing the heat that had rushed to his cheeks to rise another degree or two.

"Just like my Jimmy," Mrs. O'Toole said. "He was tall and dark haired just like you, and such a voice." She shook her head, her eyes drifting away. "He was from Ireland as well. Did you know that?"

Ciarán looked down at the tiny gray-haired woman. She must have been ninety if she was a day, and yet her cheeks were still smooth and touched with a hint of pink. "No, I didn't."

"Oh, you would have gotten on with him. Everyone loved my Jimmy. Are you sure you didn't know him?" she asked.

"Now you know he didn't, Molly." Dennis came up from behind and wrapped the old lady's hand around his arm. "Ciarán would have been an infant back then."

She flashed a sweet smile, her cheeks darkening a bit. "Of course, you're right. That was silly of me. I'd best hurry along. Patty's youngest is supposed to be picking me up, and Lord knows he doesn't have my Jimmy's patience."

"I'll take her, Father," one of the other ladies said. "Come on now, Molly. Sometimes I think you keep the poor boy waiting just to aggravate him."

They walked down the aisle, and Dennis smiled. "After all these years, she still misses him."

"How long has her husband been gone?" Ciarán asked as they headed back toward the sacristy.

"Must be thirty years now, I expect. I can't really say for sure. I was only six or so at the time he passed, but that's what I've been told."

"Ah, right," Ciarán said. "Ye weren't born to yer priesthood like I was to mine."

"I thought Ruadhán didn't send for you until you were seven?"

"He didn't, but me destiny was always set. I was a child o' the goddess. There could be no other course for me. But back to Mrs. O'Toole. 'Tis grand how she still speaks o' him that way after all these years."

"I asked her once why she never remarried. She would have only been about sixty when he died. Do you know what she said?"

Ciarán shook his head, curious as to what this spunky little lady's response might have been.

"*I've had the best,* she said, *why would I want anyone else?*"

Ciarán's throat constricted, and tears rushed to his eyes. It was so touching. He'd have to take her arm and walk her out next time he saw her. Maybe it would bring back a memory of her Jimmy. Blowing out a deep breath, he reached for the shopping bags.

"Tugs at your heartstrings, doesn't it?" Dennis said.

Caitlin poked her head through the doorway. "Are you ready yet? Not to rush you, but with the holiday traffic, it will take us at least an hour to get to Mary's. And you know how my bladder is lately."

Ciarán nodded and picked up the bags. "We'll be seeing ye at Mary's in a bit, then," he said to Dennis before he and Caitlin strolled back down the now empty church aisle. As he walked, listening to her heels click on the marble floor, Caitlin grabbed onto his arm. A warmth spread through his heart. He couldn't help but wonder if Caitlin would remember him as fondly as Mrs. O'Toole remembered her Jimmy.

****

Mary Monaghan's son, Tiernan, shook Ciarán's hand when he and Caitlin arrived at her home a little while later. Though Mary had been a surrogate mother to Ciarán since he'd first woken from his fifteen-hundred-year long sleep and stumbled into the rectory the previous year, Ciarán had not been fond of her youngest son, Tiernan. Sibling rivalry? More likely the fact that the man had paid Caitlin an exorbitant amount of attention during last year's holiday season.

"Congratulations," Tiernan said, "and no hard feelings?"

"I beg yer pardon?" Ciarán said. Had his dislike of the man been that obvious? He shrugged inwardly. Caitlin had indicated it might have been.

"Last Thanksgiving," the man said, a comfortable smile on his face. "I could see how Cait looked at you, so I thought I'd give it one last try."

Ciarán narrowed his eyes, letting a smile twitch in the corner of his mouth. "So I wasn't being paranoid."

"Heck no, but with someone as fine as Caitlin, you can't blame a guy for giving it one last shot."

"And what about now?" Ciarán asked. Somehow he found the man genuine. Perhaps he had judged him too quickly, jealous of the attention Caitlin had shown him. After all, the guy was Mary Monaghan's son.

"Are you out of your mind? Aside from the fact that the church doesn't look kindly on such behavior, my mother would skin me alive. Besides, what kind of a man flirts with his brother's wife?"

Ciarán frowned. Were he and Tiernan talking about the same thing? "I was speaking about Caitlin."

"So was I." The man's smile broadened, brightening the sparkle in his eyes. "Since Ma's made you her honorary son, you're one of the family now, whether you like it or not."

Ciarán liked it fine, but he wondered how his new brothers felt about it. Almost as if Tiernan could read his mind, he patted Ciarán on the back and laughed.

"Don't worry, we're all cool with it. You're not the first—or the last, I'd wager. But don't think you're borrowing my new jacket." Tiernan laughed again and nodded toward the living room. "We'd best get in there or they'll all think we're up to something."

"Are you usually?" Ciarán had an idea that he and Tiernan just might be good friends. And the knowledge that Mary's sons weren't offended by their mother including him as one of her own warmed his heart.

"Of course," he said. Father Bill came down the stairs and gave a shy nod before heading for the living room. Tiernan greeted him with a cheery "Merry Christmas" and waited for him to be out of earshot before speaking again. "Though we all know enough not to speak in front of Father Bill. The poor man can't help himself. The words just spew from his lips like water over a cliff."

Ciarán nodded in agreement. "Ye go ahead. I have to check with Caitlin about something first." *Like just how much everyone knows about me.* He walked into the kitchen to find five women flitting around the room, each seeming to know what they were doing. Caitlin kissed his cheek as she grabbed a pitcher of cream from the refrigerator.

"Out!" she said. "Unless you don't want to be eating until midnight."

"Just a quick question. Do Mary's sons know . . . about me, I mean?"

She cast a glance in the direction of the kitchen table, where Mary and her daughters-in-law were diligently at work. "Not that I know of, why?"

"Something Tiernan said about not telling Father Bill anything."

Caitlin sighed, her eyes brightening just a touch. "I doubt he was talking about our secret. The fact is no one tells Father Bill anything. For the life of him, he can't seem to keep a secret. I feel sorry for the poor man."

"And Father Mike lets him take confession?"

"Oh, that's the one thing he has no problem keeping to himself, no matter what. I remember a big commotion a while back when the police came to the rectory, asking him questions about a local thug. He wouldn't budge. Almost went to jail over it."

Ciarán scratched the back of his head. He didn't quite see the difference. "I'm not sure I understand."

"One is a sacred oath, I suppose. Haven't you ever made a vow that was more solemn than any other, one you'd be ashamed to break?"

Ciarán swallowed hard, the memory of how he'd betrayed his goddess burning his cheeks. "I have, and I broke that vow for the love of a woman."

Tears welled up in Caitlin's eyes, and she rested her hand against his cheek, brushing back a strand of hair. "Oh, Ciarán, I'm sorry. I didn't mean . . . There was more to it than that. Circumstances you never foresaw."

"'Tis all right, darlin'. I don't regret me decision. I'd lost faith in the very entity I'd made the vow to, so . . ." He shrugged. "Father Bill won't be facing the same dilemma, now will he?"

"I certainly hope not."

Ciarán smiled and kissed her on the lips. "Ye'd best get back or Mary will be having me head in that roasting pan o' hers."

He walked down the hallway and up the stairs until he was safely ensconced in the bathroom. Putting the toilet lid down, he sat, his head in his hands. Images darted through his brain like flashes of lightning. His arms around Aisling, loving her, trying to protect her from a vengeful priesthood. The dagger being driven into her chest. His father, Domnall, a high priest, pleading with him to forsake her. The chief priest Ruadhán's angry eyes glaring as they dragged Ciarán away to Tuamaí Dearmadta, the Forgotten Tombs.

Ciarán had betrayed the goddess of his *túath* and so had been entombed alive, his fate to be left in her hands. Taking a deep breath, he stood and leaned on the sink. But the vow had all been based on lies; even Domnall had hidden his true identity from him. He couldn't imagine not telling his own children he was their father. And yet his heart ached for the pain he had brought upon him.

There were times he wondered what had become of him and of Ruadhán. Had they been buried in the Hills of ár Sinsear, like their fathers before them? They would have never had converted to the Christian faith. He was certain Ruadhán would have died before he did that.

His thoughts returned to Aisling again, the beautiful woman he'd taken as his wife. He'd barely known her, and still her memory held a small corner in his heart. Would that love have grown like Mrs. O'Toole's had they been given the chance? Only God knew the answer to that. One thing he knew for sure: God had granted him a new life, a new love, and he had no intention of wasting it brooding over the past.

"Ciarán," Father Michael called up the stairs. "Have ye fallen in, son?"

Ciarán shook his head, chuckling, sending up a prayer of thanksgiving for all he now had. "No, Father, I'll be down in a minute." And brushing his fingers through his hair to make himself presentable, he headed down to resume his new life.

CHAPTER 3

Ruadhán drifted in and out of sleep, visions crowding his thoughts and skewing reality. He blinked to clear his eyes but caught only glimpses of darkness and a heavy mist. Where was he? The answer hovered near the edge of his consciousness, just out of reach. Though he strained to catch it, the draw of sleep enticed him back into its warm embrace.

He'd taken the elixir, placed himself in the goddess's care. How long ago had that been? His eyes drooped once more, his vision fading. He was still so tired, yet his mind raced as he sought to unravel the events that had brought him to this place.

Sleep, my faithful one. The words of the goddess calmed his frantic thoughts, caressing him with their soothing touch, and he abandoned himself to their allure once more.

****

The warmth of the early afternoon sun warmed Ruadhán's shoulders. He always enjoyed Domnall's company, even if he didn't necessarily like what he had to say.

"Much of the *túath* has chosen to follow this new religion," Domnall said. "Soon they will have no need for us unless we learn to adapt."

"I will not betray the goddess," Ruadhán said. "And what of you, *mo chara*? Will you follow the path chosen by your favored students and bow to their god?"

Sorrow glistened in Domnall's eyes. "My sons stood firm, even knowing what lay ahead of them. I do not think I would have had such strength. Fortunately, I am not faced with such a dilemma. Or am I?"

Ruadhán spread his hands apart, indicating the empty grove. "It does not appear so." Though his reply was lighthearted, his friend's words infuriated him. But what did it matter now? Six years had passed since he'd entombed the rogue priests, and even he had to admit Domnall was right about the *túath*. Only yesterday Killian had informed him they would no longer be taking part in the Beltane celebrations. Lughnasa and Samhain would surely be next.

"Do as you must," he said, "become one of their priests. As for myself, I will place my fate in the hands of the goddess of our *túath*."

Domnall frowned and grabbed Ruadhán's shoulder. "Surely you do not mean to drink the Elixir of Suain Cráite. To do so will bring about a long and painful death."

"Only if the goddess so chooses. Do you forget what you learned in your youth so quickly, or have you simply lost all faith in her? Go, follow your sons in their treachery."

"It does not matter what I believe. The elixir is reserved for those who have betrayed the goddess, not for those seeking an escape from this world. She will not be pleased with your actions."

"Would you have me betray her instead, as you have? If so, then I would deserve no less than Tuamaí Dearmadta."

"You need not betray her, *mo chara*. You have a wealth of knowledge to pass on to the generations to come. Tell them of her if you will, but do not condemn yourself to certain death."

"And how long before these Christians forbid me to speak of her, forbid me to teach her ways and honor her?"

"Their beliefs are not so different from our own. They preach of love and kindness, of the sacredness of all around us."

"But not of our goddess. No, I will give myself into her hands, and she will rescue me from any torment. When the time is right, she will call for me once more."

"Please, Ruadhán! Give these Christians a chance. Speak to Padraig. He is a gentle man, not adverse to listening to the thoughts of others. Are you to surrender so easily?"

Ruadhán barked a laugh. "Is that what you think I would be doing?"

"What else if you drink the elixir and seal yourself in a cave to die? Stay in this world and fight to preserve her memory. Die fighting for her, not withering away in agony." Domnall squeezed his arm tighter. "Please, *mo chara*, I do not wish to lose your friendship."

Ruadhán sighed, reaching out to touch his friend's arm. "We each do what we must, *mo chara*. But I will wait a while longer to make my decision. The lady will guide me along the right path and come for me when it is time."

When it is time. The thought played through his memory like a tune that could not be forgotten, his mind drifting in and out of a misty slumber. She would wake him—*when it was time.*

****

The first thing to penetrate Ruadhán's consciousness was the constant drip of water over his right shoulder. He blinked to clear the sleep from his eyes and spotted a thin shaft of light peeking through a crevice in the rocks. That hadn't been there when he sealed the cave. The air was far warmer than he'd remembered it as well.

Sitting up, he grabbed the edge of the altar, steadying himself and allowing his head to settle. The burial shroud was damp, and puddles of water encircled the stone on which he sat. Could the small drip running down the wall have caused it?

He fell to his knees on the dampened ground. "What is it you have need of, my lady? For if you have awakened me, it is your will." Standing once more, he bowed his head, summoning his energy until his fingertips tingled. Then, directing a surge of power toward the large stone that blocked his tomb, he released it, pushing the boulder aside.

There was still a chill in the air, and the buds were not yet blooming on the nearby gorse and hawthorn bushes. *Surely it was after Imbolc. Around Ostara perhaps?* He stretched and breathed in the fresh, clean air, the morning dew still new on the ground. But how long had he slept?

Slipping down along a path, he hid behind a boulder, awed by the sights he beheld. Machines of metal rumbled along the trails at great speeds while houses of wood and stone dotted the countryside. The men were garbed in tight-fitting *triubhas*, longer and broader at the bottom than any he'd ever seen before. And the women's *léinte* were above their knees and showed far more than any man should see. What sort of world was this the goddess of his *túath* had sent him to? He shook his head to clear his thoughts. *And who am I to question her edicts?*

Taking another deep breath, he returned to the cave, shifting back the boulder with a wave of his hand. Whatever her plan, she would guide him in what needed to be done. Clearly, he could not appear in the village dressed as he was. Whatever time he had awaken in, it was far from his own. Tonight, as the villagers slept, he would slip down and relieve them of their washing. Then he would explore the village. A thought occurred to him, and his hand sprang to his cheek. He would need to mix an ointment of some sort to cover his priestly mark. No sense announcing his station until he had a chance to assess the situation.

His stomach growled. How long had it been since he had eaten? He would rest a bit more, until the sun set to herald a new day, before heading down the hillside to gather the clothing. Then as the moon rose to its zenith, he would forage for some sustenance and other items he might need. It would be safe enough within the cave until he got his bearings. Though his powers were a bit rusty, he still possessed enough skill to conceal his presence and accomplish what he must.

Checking the items he had brought to the cave with him, he slipped the Scian na Lúin in his girdle, removing his priestly collar and the circlet he still wore around his head. His task would require stealth, so he shed his robe and cloak, folding them neatly next to the Cup of Cheartais and the rest of his small collection of sacred accoutrements. For now, he would rest and await the lady's instructions.

Releasing a weary sigh, he closed his eyes once more, thoughts of the past and the oath he'd sworn to his goddess utmost on his mind. He was still so tired. The lingering effects of the elixir at work, no doubt. A fog was descending over his mind, images of long ago beckoning him to join them, and so he drifted off once more.

****

Ruadhán gazed out across the green valley and tranquil lake he'd known since his youth. Domnall had not been wrong. The world was changing, faith in the goddess of their *túath* faltering, being replaced by belief in this new Christian god. Many of his priests had already left the fold, beguiled into becoming Christian priests or monks. The rest were regarded as nothing more than poets or bards.

Domnall came to stand beside him once more. They had been friends since childhood, and he had always held the man's opinion in high regard, but he feared they had come to an impasse. "I have no heart to argue with you over this, *mo seanchara*," Ruadhán said. "We must both do what we believe in our hearts. I should be angry with you, but I do not wish to part with ill feelings between us."

"We have faced a lot together, have we not?" Domnall said. He leaned up against one of the tall stones that surrounded the sacred altar.

Ruadhán couldn't keep a smile from blossoming on his face. "That we have. Some good and others . . ." He shrugged. "I only did what was required by law."

"I know that." Domnall sighed. "Though I think perhaps you took greater pleasure administering it in some cases than you did in others."

"You speak of your . . . students, Ciarán and Aodhán."

"They were my sons." Domnall too gazed out across the tranquil lake, his eyes glistening with tears. "Can you not admit that even now?"

"They belonged to the goddess. You were nothing more than her consort, her guardian, there to serve her, but you have chosen to turn your back on her."

"Can you still believe that? A goddess mother whose seed joins with that of her sons to create yet another child, one of who will do the same." Domnall shook his head. "Moira was their mother, and I took her from them."

"Moira was a vessel to bear the goddess's child, and she was well rewarded for her service."

"I loved her, Ruadhán, with all my heart, yet I did not have Ciarán's courage. And so I took her life as required by law. That is a sorrow I must bear."

"Was it courage or lust that guided Ciarán's actions?" Ruadhán said. The thought of bestowing such a noble quality on the fallen priest still angered him. But, as usual, his friend remained calm, no matter the tempest raging within him.

"A bit of both, I suspect. Lust may have drawn him in, but one word from his lips and he could have taken her that Beltane, saved himself, yet he refused."

"Fool that he was. Instead, he sacrificed all he could have been, and for what? A night's pleasure?"

"Or an eternity of happiness with her by his side."

"Do not be blinded by the rogue's treachery. Ciarán betrayed his goddess mother, not for courage or love, but for the lust of a woman that had not been sanctified." Ruadhán couldn't keep his voice from rising. "His punishment was far more lenient than he deserved."

"And Aodhán?" Domnall pushed away from the column, his hands clutched at his sides. "He sought no woman."

"Sweet Brigid, *a shagart*! The children he took belonged to the goddess."

31

"They belonged to his brother!"

Ruadhán turned and strode toward the water, its gentle waves lapping along the bank. He had to calm himself, lest the last words he spoke to his friend would be bitter and filled with contempt. He didn't want their time together to end that way.

"Let us not fight, *a seanchara.*" Domnall walked up beside him and placed a hand on his shoulder. "What is done is done."

"There was a time we saw things through the same prism." Ruadhán continued to stare out across the crystal water. "Now the glass is cracked and shattered into so many pieces it is difficult to see anything at all."

"Join us, then. At least hear what Padraig has to say."

"I have heard his words, and many align with our own beliefs, but there is one demand I cannot obey. When I became a priest, I pledged myself to the goddess of our *túath*. I cannot now abandon her."

"What will you do? The village no longer has need of our priesthood."

Ruadhán knew where his duty lay. But he must tell no one, least of all his dearest friend, lest they try to stop him.

"I could travel the land, singing ballads of the great battles fought by the old gods." He chuckled. "Your priests still permit them, I hear, though they look on them as nothing more than myths to entertain." Domnall frowned, and Ruadhán laughed out loud. "Do not look so troubled. I was a fair bard once, if you recall."

"I do recall. Master Ailbe lamented the day you were taken into the *filidh*. He was convinced he'd lost his best bard."

"And so he had."

The two men laughed. Ruadhán savored the memory for a moment, recalling the brotherhood he'd shared with Domnall, but he could not dwell on the past. "I will manage. Do not concern yourself."

"We are no longer young men, able to roam the countryside unfettered by aching muscles and creaking bones."

"Speak for yourself, *a chara*. My muscles do not ache. Perhaps you should have joined me on my morning walks."

"Walks indeed. You went no farther than that small copse of elder trees, where you rested until an hour's time had passed."

Ruadhán shrugged. "I was exercising my mind." He nodded toward the gnarled branches of hawthorn and blackthorn that formed the entrance to the sacred grove. "Come, let us go before the sun sets and a new day is upon us. Share one last meal with me before I leave you."

"I will miss you, my friend," Domnall said.

"We will meet again one day. I am certain of that. Whether it is in Tir na nÓg or the heaven you speak of, only time will tell."

He led the way through the tunnel. His heart ached at all he was leaving behind, but it was for the best. He would join his friend for one last meal, then be about his task. The goddess of his *túath* would expect no less.

CHAPTER 4

Caitlin sat curled up on the love seat, staring out the window at the latest blast of snow. The holidays had rushed by, as they always did, and March had come in like a lion with no hint of the lamb in sight. Since she was six months pregnant, Ciarán had suggested she not chance going out to work, and Daniel had wholeheartedly concurred. Instead, she sat with a book on her lap, completely bored. At least it wouldn't be too long before the twins were born. The doctor said she probably wouldn't go beyond thirty-six or thirty-seven weeks.

A little arm caused her stomach to roll, and she smiled, wondering which tyke it was. If someone had told her a year ago that she'd enjoy the feel of a small living creature poking around in her stomach, she would have thought it was gross. Funny how much she loved the feel of them now, especially when Ciarán cuddled up next to her in bed with his hand on her stomach. Of course, that usually led to something else, which made her smile even more, and the twins never seemed to object to Mommy and Daddy having a little fun.

THE CAVE OF RÚIN ÁRSA

She looked back down at her book. God, it was making her horny, but as big as she was, it was getting a bit awkward. Still, they managed to find a way. A key rattled in the door, and she threw down her book, running into the small hallway. Ciarán looked up, grinning when she wrapped her arms around his neck.

"Happy to see me, are ye?" he said.

"No, just bored." She gave him a long, hard kiss on the lips, pressing her tongue against his.

He dropped the bags of groceries on the floor and wrapped his arms around her. "Ye've been reading another romance, haven't ye?" He nuzzled against her neck, nipping at her earlobe, his fingers slipping under her blouse and beneath her bra. "I'll be needing to put the ice cream away first, though."

"Ooh, ice cream?"

He lifted an eyebrow and chuckled. "Ye'd prefer the ice cream, then?"

"Only if you were wearing it in certain, tender parts."

"That's not going to happen. 'Tis bloody freezing." He bent to pick up the groceries, then headed to the kitchen to put them away, though he left the ice cream on the counter and grabbed a bowl.

"That will be dessert." She shoved the frozen carton in the freezer and turned back to Ciarán.

"I thought I was dessert." He took her in his arms and kissed her again, his tongue circling hers, teasing the promise of so much more. Finally, he lifted her and carried her to the bed, laying her gently on the blankets before lifting her blouse and rubbing her stomach.

"Is it still safe enough? I don't one to harm ye or the wee ones."

"The doctor says they're well protected, and it's fine, so . . ."

Ciarán grinned and, dropping his paints to the floor, climbed in next to her.

"Still no underwear?" She laughed as he helped her off with her clothes.

"'Twould be a waste o' time, now wouldn't it?" he said.

His head ducked under the covers, and she moaned, a wave of delight touching her core. "It certainly would."

****

Ciarán smiled down at his wife the next morning. They never did get supper, let alone ice cream. He pushed aside a stray lock of hair, the color of autumn and warm September days. God, he loved her, and now she was carrying his children, a symbol of the love that filled his heart every time he looked at her.

He sat up and pulled on his jeans, trying not to wake her. Was it only two years ago that he'd knelt before the goddess of their *túath*, a chosen son of their order, destined to father her children? *Just two years and yet centuries away as well.* All that he'd gone through, all the shame and horror the tomb had brought, was a small price to pay for this. Leaning over, he placed a gentle kiss on Caitlin's forehead, smiling as she snuggled farther beneath the blankets.

Though he would have loved to join her, he had to get some studying in before heading off to work. He owed it to Father Mike. The priest had gone out on a limb for him, invoking his longtime friendship with the president of Columbia to help Ciarán earn his degrees. After his initial shock, the man had agreed, a testament to his regard for Michael. He did have a few stipulations, however. After all, this was a big favor, and he wanted to make sure Ciarán was deserving of the risk.

First, Ciarán had to pass the man's evaluation. Clearly, in spite of his fondness for the priest, he was skeptical of Ciarán's learning ability. And second, each and every class had to be completed under his personal tutelage. If he performed as well as Michael had suggested, the man would make sure the degrees were added to the university's files.

Ciarán couldn't help but smile fondly at Michael's audacity when it came to him and Aodhán. The priest had actually chuckled when he told him about the look on his friend's face when he asked if he would do the same for Aodhán—long distance, of course—so that he could enroll in a doctoral program at Trinity College.

"Are ye sure ye can trust the man?" Ciarán had asked.

"With me life," Michael had said. "Just as ye'd trust Aodhán." No more needed to be said, though he did wonder what that bond was.

Ciarán shot a glance toward the bedroom, then sighed and headed for the living room, book in hand. Domnall would surely chide him for taking three months to get a bachelor's degree, not to mention another four weeks for his master's. And he was still only halfway through his PhD in archaeology. He was far more skilled than that and should have completed all three courses within a matter of weeks. It had been part of his training. Only those who could master their memory, retaining large amounts of information in no more than a few days, could move on to the priesthood. And he had done that, hadn't he?

He slumped down on the couch with his book, determined to do better, but the early morning sun shining through the window warmed his shoulders, and try as he might to fight it, he could feel his eyes growing heavier by the second.

****

Domnall frowned, his cerulean-blue eyes intense with disappointment, and Ciarán hung his head, avoiding his teacher's stare.

"You have had that volume two days hence," the high priest said. "And yet you still know but half of it. Are you pleased with your progress?"

"No, master." Ciarán could feel the heat rising in his cheeks. He knew well why he hadn't already conquered the tome, and to his shame, it had nothing to do with his learning ability.

"Then why do you not study harder?"

"But there is so much in the world to absorb, master, and not just that which comes from books."

Domnall chuckled. "You have been letting yourself become distracted again by that which is around you."

"But should I not develop an appreciation of that as well?"

"Of course, but for each thing there is a proper time and place. You are young yet, and your mind needs to be developed to reach its full capacity. Only then can you truly comprehend that which surrounds you."

Ciarán sighed. "But I do not wish to understand it, master. I just wish to enjoy it." At this, Domnall chuckled, and Ciarán relaxed a bit. "Perhaps I am not meant for the priesthood."

The high priest rested his hand on Ciarán's shoulder and gazed deep into his eyes. "Do not ever doubt your abilities, *a leanbh*. You were blessed by the goddess with great gifts, but you must learn how to put them to use. Now put aside yesterday's lesson."

"But I have not yet completed it, master. I do not wish to fail."

"Am I not the one who assigns your lessons?"

"You are, master, but . . ."

A smile crossed Domnall's bearded face. "Then do not question my decrees. I have a more important lesson for you today."

"I am sorry, master. What is it you wish me to study?"

Domnall drew a scroll from his satchel and handed it to Ciarán. "I want you to study this scroll while I bathe in the river. When I am finished, you are to recite it to me word by word. If you do not succeed, I will give you another scroll of the same length, which you will be instructed to learn while I go about some other small task. Until you have succeeded, there will be no morning meal."

"But, master, it will not take you more than a few moments to bathe, and the scroll is quite long."

"If you keep your mind on the scroll, *a leanbh*, and not on the rippling of the water or the song of the bird, you will achieve your goal. There will be time for those things later. For now, you'd best be about your task. Remember, *a mhic*, keep your mind on the tome before you."

****

The words were still echoing in his head as he straightened up on the couch and stretched. He'd been dreaming again. But Domnall did have a point. He had been distracted of late, between his work at the museum and Caitlin and the prospect of becoming a father. In his defense, though, Caitlin would distract even the most gifted high priest. That wasn't helping him now, though, was it? Domnall was right, he'd have to work harder on his concentration.

At least Daniel had acknowledged his work on last year's dig, so the internship was under his belt, as Father Dennis would say. And if he put his nose to the grindstone, to coin another of Dennis's idioms, he should be able to complete his PhD by the end of the month or mid-April at the latest. Not as quickly as Domnall would have liked, but it would have to do. So what if it took a day or two longer to master the course work?

Grabbing his shirt and the book on archaeological theory he'd been attempting to study, he stood up and padded into the kitchen. They may have been two naughty little children and gone to bed without supper, but they were going to have breakfast. Much to everyone's surprise, himself included, he'd become quite a cook and enjoyed puttering around in the kitchen—as long as he didn't have to clean up the mess.

"Do I smell bacon and eggs?" Caitlin shuffled into the kitchen and sat down at the table, licking her lips.

"Is that look of desire for me or my culinary skills?" Ciarán said.

"No offense, but at the moment the bacon has my undivided attention. Fionn and Aisling have been beating out a frantic tattoo this morning. I think they know we missed supper last night and went straight for dessert, and I don't mean the ice cream."

He put some bacon and eggs on her plate with a nice mound of hash browns. "I've got some waffles on the griddle as well."

"What about you? You've got to be starving."

"I'm just waiting for the waffles." He put a second plate down for himself before filling another with the golden-brown squares and sitting down across from her.

"Won't you be late for work?" Caitlin's brow creased, and a faraway look filled her eyes.

"Ye miss being there, don't ye?"

She sighed, rubbing her stomach absentmindedly. "Yes and no. I miss the discovery and research, but then I think about Fionn and Aisling, and I can't even remember what my life was like before them. But they're not quite here yet, so I get bored, especially now with the weather being so miserable. I can't even go out for a walk." Taking another bite, she narrowed her eyes and looked up at him. A beautiful shade of emerald adorned them this morning. "You didn't answer my question. Won't you be late for work?"

"No, I don't have to be in until ten. There's a meeting, so Daniel said 'twould be a waste o' time starting anything before."

"What's the meeting about?" She'd started on the waffles and was pouring a sickly amount of syrup over them.

"I'm not really sure, technical stuff, I'm thinking." Did he just out and out lie to her? No, it was dealing with the *technicalities* of going on another dig, and since he'd never been to one of their meetings before, he could honestly say he wasn't sure what they'd be discussing. He was stretching it a bit, to be sure, but under the circumstances, he thought it best.

Of course, he wouldn't be going along on the dig this time either, but still . . . Best not to say anything about it if he didn't need to.

She bit off a piece of bacon, letting the other half hang in the air. "Have they said anything about going back to the excavation site this year?"

Shit! Might as well just get it over with. "That might be what they're wanting to discuss this morning. But I won't be going. I'm to stay here to take charge of the artifacts as they come in."

Her lips tweaked into a playful smile. "You can relax. I realize I won't be able to go, but I'd still like to know what's happening with it."

"I just didn't want to upset ye. I understand how much it means to ye."

"These two little guys mean a whole lot more." She let out a big burp and giggled. "Sorry, I don't know where that came from." Grabbing another waffle, she doused it with syrup and then looked at his plate. "You going to eat that bacon?"

He lifted an eyebrow. Where on earth was she putting it all?

"What? I burped, so now I have room for more. It must be Fionn. No daughter of mine would eat this much."

"But a son o' mine would?" He ran a finger under his nose to stifle a laugh and thanked God for her once more.

"Um, yes!" she said, grabbing his bacon and biting off a piece. "Like father, like son. Now don't you have some studying to do?"

****

Ciarán could barely keep his eyes open at the meeting that morning, not that he regretted one minute of lost sleep. He must have been drifting off, though, because Steve

Pendleton, one of the team's specialists and its resident doctor, gave him a nudge.

"Not much sleep last night?" The man lifted an eyebrow, a smirk etched across his face.

"Caitlin's taken to snoring o' late."

"Is that what they're calling it now?"

Ignoring his friend, Ciarán tried to concentrate on what the site's director, Daniel Lambert, was saying. Even if he wasn't going to be accompanying them this year, he still needed to know what they had planned.

"We'll not be doing any further excavations on the caves," Daniel said, "though we will check them out to make sure nothing's amiss. We will, however, be continuing the excavation along the lake and possibly in the cave where the book was found."

"The Cave o' Rúin Ársa?" Ciarán said. "I doubt ye'll be finding much else in there."

"And how would you know that?" the newest member of the team asked. Russell Bridges was a recently graduated archaeologist who was convinced his degree had been accompanied by twenty-five years of experience or more. "You were a simple digger last year, weren't you?"

Daniel's eyebrow shot up, and he turned his stern professor's gaze on the young man. Ciarán cringed, remembering receiving a similar look when he had taken an unauthorized dive the year before. Daniel had a calm demeanor, but when riled, a lion came to life.

"Mr. Donnelly has a degree from Columbia," he said. "Something you'd do well to remember, young man."

If the truth be told, Ciarán had a hard time remembering it himself. Though he didn't quite have his PhD yet. He wondered again what the bond was between Father Mike and his friend at the university. The priest had friends in the most unlikely places, loyal ones who could keep a secret, thankfully, but then he did have an entire life before Ciarán met him.

All this talk of degrees reminded him, he had his thesis, *The Importance of Mythological Objects and Legends in Celtic Culture,* due at the end of next week. A subject he knew quite well, fortunately.

Russell squirmed in his seat. "I meant nothing by it, Professor."

The heck he didn't. Ciarán cast a quick look in Steve's direction, knowing if he actually met his eyes, the two of them would burst out laughing.

"Then what did ye mean, lad?" The professor took his pipe out of his pocket and calmly stuffed some tobacco in the bowl.

"Um . . . uh . . . simply that . . . well, we don't really know much about it, do we?"

Ciarán gave him a sympathetic smile. "I suppose not, but tradition says 'twas seen as a place to house a book of ancient secrets and a portal to Tír na nÓg. As such, 'tis not likely it would be used for the storing o' knickknacks." He shifted his gaze back to Daniel. "Most o' the other sacred items would have been kept either within the temple itself or in the residence o' the chief priest."

"The locations of which we have yet to locate," Daniel said, "so we will be keeping our eyes open for them as well." Daniel lit his pipe, taking a few puffs before speaking again. "I do wish you and Caitlin were going with us again this year."

"I'm sure we'll be fine, Professor," Russell said. "It is why you hired me, after all." Steve snorted, and the young man glared at him.

"I assure you, Mr. Bridges," Daniel said, "I did not hire you to replace the Donnellys. They both have years of knowledge and experience under their belts. Fortunately, we'll mostly be going over areas we've already started to excavate, and Mr. Donnelly's brother will be there to assist us in any new discoveries."

"Aodhán?" Ciarán said, unable to keep a smile from breaking out on his lips. "He didn't mention it. 'Twill be good for him to get back to work."

"He assured me he's quite recovered from his accident." Daniel frowned. "I don't want to put the lad in any danger of a relapse."

"Not to worry, Professor. Niamh won't be letting him take any chances. From what I've heard, he's getting round quite well, though he may have to take the hills a bit slower than he used to for a while."

"I'll keep that in mind. Luckily, he's not as thickheaded as you." Daniel smiled. "If there's nothing else, we'll be leaving a week from Friday." Everyone got up and started to exit the room, but Daniel latched on to Ciarán's arm, holding him back. "How is Caitlin taking all this?"

"Surprisingly well." Daniel narrowed his eyes, causing Ciarán to laugh. "I know. Sure, I expected an argument meself, but she truly seems content with where she is in her life. She's looking forward to being a mother."

"I'm glad." He sighed, clearly relieved. "Will she be helping you with the cataloguing?"

"She will, as much as she can, though it won't be long now until she'll have other things on her mind."

"I must stop over and see her before we leave."

"Ye were waiting to make sure I told her before ye did, weren't ye? I never took ye for such a coward, Daniel."

The professor chuckled. "Yes, well, I've seen her at her worse, and that's one tempest I choose to avoid."

"I'll have to admit ye're right about that. I've been on the windward side o' more than one o' those storms."

Daniel patted him on the back. "Yes, lad, I suppose you have."

****

By the next week, the snow had finally melted away, and taking pity on Caitlin's growing boredom, Ciarán had dropped her off at the rectory for the day.

"You're coming to dinner on Easter, aren't you?" Mary finished dishing out a bowl of her famous chili soup for Caitlin and sat down across from her at the kitchen table.

"Of course, I wouldn't miss it." Caitlin had spent many a holiday with Mary and her family after her parents had died, so the woman was more than just the rectory's housekeeper. Not to mention that she'd practically adopted Ciarán and now considered him one of her boys.

"Looks like Dermot might be making it this year as well, though Liam and his family will be going to his in-laws. It's only fair, though I'm not going to pretend I won't miss them."

"Of course you will. I'm so glad Ciarán seems to be getting along with everyone this year. I thought he was going to punch Tiernan out the Thanksgiving before last. Not that he had any right. We'd only been dating a few weeks. This past holiday season was much better."

"Well, I like all my boys to get along." Mary got up and busied herself at the sink.

"Wait a minute," Caitlin said. How had she not seen it before? She'd known Tiernan for years, and that

Thanksgiving had been the first time he'd laid the flirting on that heavily. "You put Tiernan up to it, didn't you? To make Ciarán jealous."

"Well, lord help us, someone had to light a fire under that boy's britches. Honestly, such hemming and hawing when anyone with eyes in their head could see you two belonged together. And now look . . ." She grabbed a tissue from her pocket and blew her nose. "Two more grandbabies on the way."

"Two more hungry grandbabies." Caitlin held up her empty bowl and smiled.

"I see they take after their father." Mary took the bowl, ladling some more of the beefy soup into it, and passed it back to Caitlin. "I'll pack some up for you to take home for dinner."

"Would you? Ciarán really misses your cooking."

She gave a mock scowl. "Then maybe he should bring you by a bit more often. In fact, why don't you both just stay for supper tonight?"

"That'll be nice, but could you still pack us a doggie bag?" She gave a big grin that caused Mary to laugh.

"And why hasn't the lad been stopping by more often?" Father Michael had just walked in the room and kissed her on the head before sitting at the table. "'Twill just be me this afternoon, Mary. Dennis has started his baseball camp, and Bill's off visiting an old family friend."

"Would have been nice if someone told me. Now what am I supposed to do with all this extra chili?"

"Doggie bag?" Caitlin grinned.

"I doubt there'll be much left after dinner tonight," Michael said. "Between Ciarán and Dennis, ye'll be lucky if there's a drop left in the pot."

"Then maybe I'd better make some extra," Mary said. "Can't have my boys going hungry."

"What's the lad been up to anyway?" Michael asked.

"He's been studying a lot, working on his PhD now. Thank you for that, by the way. They're also getting things ready for the dig at the end of the week."

Mary spun around from the stove, waving her wooden spoon in Caitlin's direction. "Don't tell me you two are planning to go along on another excavation. Have you lost your minds?"

"Calm down, Mary, neither of us is going, but the rest of the team is. Ciarán just has to take care of the preparations."

Father Mike touched her hand. "There will always be other digs, darlin'."

"I'm okay, really. The truth is, after almost losing Ciarán last year, I'm content to sit this one out and just be a normal family. Besides, with the amount of kicking these two are doing, they'll be wanting out before long."

"Well, twins do tend to come early, but you should have a few months yet."

"A few," Caitlin said, "but the doctor says it really could be anytime now." She slurped up some soup, not only because it was good, but because it meant she wouldn't have to say anything more about when she was due. Neither her Uncle Mike nor Mary had any idea that particular horse had already been out of the gate when they got married. Hopefully, she wouldn't go into labor too early or she'd have a lot of explaining to do.

CHAPTER 5

D'ye think ye're well enough to be helping out with that dig?" Niamh bit her lip. Aodhán knew she still didn't like the idea of him tramping up into the hills. He was walking fairly well, but his back still pained him a bit, and she picked up on every flinch and groan.

"I'm fine, darlin'. The doctor gave me a clean bill o' health, now didn't he?" He kissed her forehead, eliciting a smile.

"Don't try to be plying yer charms on me, Aodhán Donnelly. I see well enough how ye wince when ye get up from a chair."

"Now what would ye be expecting a fifteen-hundred-year-old man to be doing, *a chuisle*?"

"Don't be giving me any o' yer blarney either. Ye're barely over thirty."

"And how d'ye know that, may I ask?" He sat down and pulled her onto his knee.

"Caitlin told me. 'Tis how I knew to give ye such a grand birthday present this past February."

"I'll have to be thanking her, then. But be that as it may, while me back still bothers me from time to time, the

49

doctor says 'tis naught to worry over. In fact, he said a bit o' exercise would be good for it." Niamh frowned, and he took her hand, weaving his fingers with hers. "'Twill pass in time as well, *a ghrá*, so there's no need for ye to fret. Besides, as long as me important parts are working, 'tis all that matters."

"Is it, then? Let me brother find out what ye've been up to with yer *important* parts and he'll be taking the cleaver to them."

"Then ye'd best not be telling him, I reckon."

She slapped him playfully on the chest. "Ye're a wee scut, ye are." Her lips pressed against his, sending an ache down to his toes that had nothing to do with his injury.

"While we're on the subject o' me being brazen," he said when she finally sat back. "I've had a word with Duffy about us getting a place o' our own."

"Ye didn't!" Niamh got up, the hint of disapproval clear in her tone. She walked away and looked out the window, not saying another word, but Aodhán had learned to keep quiet and wait her out. At last, she turned back around. "And what did he say, then?"

"Well, he's not keen on the idea, I'll grant ye that, but I told him about that wee cottage we found and how we wouldn't likely be able to move in right away at any rate."

The corner of her mouth quirked up, a sparkle lighting her eyes. "Ye really like that dilapidated old cottage, don't ye?"

"I do, and 'tis far bigger inside than we thought, with room for expansion. Not to mention 'tis close to Duffy and to Mrs. Byrne's and the excavation sites. I think 'twill make a grand home for us once 'tis fixed up a bit."

"And where will we be getting the money to pay for it, then, not to mention the work that'll need to be done?"

"Daniel's been paying me to do some cataloguing, and he and Michael have added in their wedding presents, and with the money I've earned doing bits and bobs for Mrs. Byrne . . . 'Twill be tight, I know, but . . ."

She put her hands on her hips, her mouth dropping open. "Does the whole county know about this, then?"

"Not quite, but I have talked to the bank, and they're willing to give me a mortgage." He hesitated for a moment, not sure now was the time to tell her, but in for a penny . . . "Daniel's hired me on year-round as one o' his site specialists."

"A site specialist? But won't ye being needing a degree for that?"

"Sure, I thought so, but he said not to be worrying meself over it, that 'twas all in the works."

"What exactly does that mean?"

"I'm not sure, but 'tis a grand position, and it means I'd be close to home most days."

"And where would ye be the other days?" She was frowning again and biting her nails. This was not going the way he'd hoped.

"It'll mean driving to Dublin two days a week, but—"

"Dublin! That's a three-hour drive at the least, and I'll be in school, so I'll not be able to go with ye. Did ye even think o' speaking to me about all this before ye made yer decision?"

He stood up, trying to hide a wince when a sharp pain dug into his back. "I haven't made me decision, and I'm speaking to ye now. 'Tis what I'd like to do, but if ye don't want me to, I'll look into something else. No doubt Mrs. Byrne will be needing a handyman now and again, and I can hire on with one o' the fishing charters."

"Don't be so pathetic." She walked over and wrapped her arms around his waist, resting her head against his shoulder. "'Tis a grand plan. I just wish ye didn't have to go all the way to Dublin."

"Well, 'tis no set days as yet, and 'twill only be when I'm not here working on the dig. We can at least give it a go, can't we?"

"I suppose we can, though I wouldn't be getting yer hopes up about me moving in before the wedding."

"We'll see about that when the time comes." He squeezed her to himself, breathing in the scent of clean linen and fresh dew. "But as no one's home at the moment . . ."

"Fionnuala's just gone for the messages, hasn't she? She'll be back any minute."

"It will not take me much longer than that. I've been thinking about ye all day." But the words had barely left his lips when a pack of children came running in the house.

"Mamaí brought us all some sweets, Uncle Aodhán," seven-year-old Kathleen Flynn said. "Would ye like one?"

"Thank ye, darlin'," he said, though the little girl had no sooner run off than he leaned over and whispered in Niamh's ear. "'Tis not the sweet I had in mind."

"Maybe not," Niamh said, kissing his cheek, "but 'tis the only one ye'll be getting this afternoon."

****

Though Aodhán had protested at first, he finally conceded to Niamh's demand that Ryan Gerraghty, Professor Lambert's best digger, accompany him up to the hills the next morning. Daniel had asked him to check on Tuamaí Dearmadta and make sure no one had been poking around.

The last thing they needed was another rogue priest waking from a fifteen-hundred-year-long sleep.

A chill ran through him as he walked up to his former tomb, the cave sealed once again with a large boulder. Memories crashed over his mind like the surf upon a rocky shore, spraying its salty foam throughout his body. He leaned against the entry stone, trying to anchor himself in the present and drive the tide of past events back out to sea.

Relinquish them! He could hear Ruadhán's angry words echoing in his ears as if he stood beside him.

"Are you all right?" Ryan's voice broke through the mist that had engulfed his thoughts.

"I'm fine." Aodhán forced a smile onto his lips, though the terror of that day fifteen hundred years before was not going to be that easily dissipated.

"Maybe we should head back down. Niamh would never forgive me if you did any damage to yourself. This has been quite a hike."

That did break through the haze a bit, and he laughed. "'Tis naught to do with me legs. They're grand. A long-buried memory just flashed through me head. It took me by surprise is all. I've not thought about that day for quite a while."

"The day they put you in there." Ryan nodded toward the cave. "It must have been horrific."

Aodhán's head snapped up, forgetting for the moment that Ryan had been one of the original archaeologists at the hillfort that day he and Ciarán fought Bradaigh. He took a breath and shook his head to rid himself of the traumatic experience's distant echo, though that of the cave was no better. "'Twas not the most pleasant day o' me life." He grinned and checked the seal around the ancient tomb. "No sign o' anyone trying to get in."

Ryan bent down to look at the etching on the stone. Since they had wanted to reseal the caves after removing the occupants, Professor Lambert had ordered the original boulders be left in situ, mysterious messages and all. "I get what this first bit means now. Betrayer of his goddess mother, life without death, and so on, but this Latin still has me puzzled. Do you know who wrote it? Or etched it, I should say. *Salvete Frater . . . sit habitas in Christo.* Hail brother . . . may you live in Christ."

"I've no idea, but ye can be sure I'm not the author. I barely had time to take a breath before they sealed me up, let alone ask them to be waiting an hour or so while I carved a blessing into the rock. I'm glad someone did, though."

"The same phrase was found on Ciarán's tomb. Who would have known about your entombment, though? I thought these were the Forgotten Tombs."

Aodhán chuckled and led the way over to the tomb that had been his brother's. "Have ye ever tried telling a group a people to forget they saw something?"

"I get your point, but why would someone within your priesthood have written a Christian blessing?"

"I don't suppose they would, although from what I can gather, many o' the pagan priests eventually became Christians themselves."

"And if they did, I imagine they might have felt a pang of regret for what they'd taken part in here. That could explain it."

Aodhán shrugged. "Maybe so, though I think they'd be more concerned with retaining what little they could o' their former lives. Having a new god wouldn't present a problem in itself, but insulting the goddess by carving a Christian sentiment into the tombs o' those who'd been condemned by her was another issue indeed."

"It could have been done in secret."

"And it could have been done years later by men who had nothing to do with the priesthood. We've no way o' knowing, now do we?"

Ryan frowned. "No, I suppose not, but as an archaeologist, it's my job to search for explanations."

"Ah, well, ye'll never have the answers to everything, so ye'd best just accept it and move on."

"Right then, let's check Bradaigh's tomb so we can get back home. It looks like a storm is brewing off to the east."

Aodhán followed Ryan's gaze and nodded. Clouds were forming a dark umbrella, and the wind had whipped up. The last thing he wanted to hear was Niamh scolding him for coming home soaked to the bone.

****

Try as he might, he couldn't get that dreadful day out of his mind. Even safe and warm in Duffy's house, the storm kept at bay by the sturdy walls that surrounded him, the memory kept forcing its way into his thoughts. The pounding rain sounded like hoofbeats, chasing him down, their relentless riders intent on his capture.

He slid farther under the covers, fighting off the veil of sleep that was descending upon him, but his eyelids were growing heavier by the minute. Once he succumbed to their weight and surrendered to Tír na Haislinge, he would no longer have any control over his thoughts. He blinked and rubbed the sand away, trying to concentrate on Niamh and the life they planned to build together. Perhaps if he was thinking of her as sleep overtook him, she would be the one giving form to his dreams. No longer able to fight the compulsion to slip into that world of shadows and unbidden memories, he let out a weary sigh and drifted off.

"Halt!" the voice called out to him, and he stopped, his horse pawing the ground as he turned to face the approaching riders. He recognized them immediately as the elite group of *filidh* chosen to keep order within the priesthood. They answered only to Ruadhán, and once given a command, they did not stop until their duty had been carried out.

Taking a deep breath, he reached over, patting his horse's neck. There was no use trying to ignore their instructions. "What is it you want, Giolla?"

"What have you done with the children, priest?" The man rode up next to him, grabbing the reins from his hands.

Once again, Aodhán knew it was pointless to deny the allegation. His fate had been sealed the moment he had taken Bréanainn from the compound. He could, however, buy some time for Aisling's brother to get the children farther away.

"What children is it you speak of?"

"Do not play your games with me, Aodhán. The high council wishes to see you now, and you will not dare to evade their questions so easily."

"Then let us go to them at once and waste neither your time nor mine with your petty accusations."

The man scanned the horizon. "My time is to be spent searching for them, so it is no trouble at all. I will ask again: Where have you taken them? And remember as you answer, priest, the goddess does not look kindly on those who speak untrue."

"Then I have nothing to fear, for I do not know where the children are at this moment."

"You play games with your words, but I will have the truth."

Aodhán had known the man since childhood, and fortunately he was nowhere near as intelligent as he thought. With that in mind, Aodhán cast a furtive look to the east. He had set the children off on the road south with Aisling's brother, Niall, then taken a roundabout way to return, so it made the subtle hint all the more feasible.

Giolla fell for it at once, a self-satisfied grin spreading across his lips. Calling two of his underlings, he directed them to take Aodhán back to compound so he could ride off to the east in search of the children. "I will retrieve them, and you shall be subjected to the full extent of the lady's wrath. You cannot escape your fate, but you can show the goddess of our *túath* that you repent your actions. Tell me where I may find them, and she may bring you a quick death."

This time Aodhán avoided looking to the east but pressed his lips firmly together in defiance, once again suggesting that it was indeed the direction they went. Giolla cursed under his breath and grabbed him by the arm, squeezing it tightly, but Aodhán yanked it away. "Do not lay a hand upon me, cleric. I am a chosen child of the goddess, named as a guardian for her creatures of the air."

"Then you are well acquainted with the law and will go peacefully with Uaithne and Ruairí while I ride to the east to retrieve your brother's charges."

Aodhán breathed a sigh of relief, though for Giolla's benefit he threw another troubled glance to the east. He had managed to send him away from the children's true path. "I will go with your men, but unless they too wish to feel the goddess's wrath, no one will lay another hand on me."

"My men and I are not hindered by such a *geis* when in pursuit of one who has been summoned before the high priests. You should know that well."

"Do not quote the law to me, cleric. You only do this job because you failed to pass the trials of the priesthood."

Giolla clenched his fist around Aodhán's reins. "Perhaps they should rethink the trials, then, if they allow such as you to pass."

Aodhán couldn't help but chuckle. "You may be right, but that will not change who I am, nor will it allow your entry to my station."

Giolla growled and threw the reins to Ruarí. "You two guide our *chosen priest* back to Ruadhán. I'll take the rest of the men and head east in search of the children. It should be easy enough to catch up with them. The eldest has but eight years."

Aodhán didn't resist, but instead said a quick prayer to his new God that Ciarán's children were well on their way south to the Christian enclave in Mumhan. He trusted Aisling's brother to see them delivered safely. As for Ciarán, there was nothing he could do to save his friend. Ciarán had sealed his fate far beyond anyone's help.

All Aodhán could do now was assure that the children were removed from Ruadhán's supervision and see that they knew God. For that, he was willing to sacrifice himself as well.

He watched as that fool Giolla headed east toward the mountains. He would find nothing there, nor would he find Niall's path to the south. Aodhán had made sure to obscure the trail behind them, leaving little sign of his passing.

"Let us go, priest." Ruairí tugged on Aodhán's reins. "We'll see how stubborn you are when Ruadhán forces you to drink from the Cup of Cheartais."

"You have already determined my fate, cleric?" Aodhán grabbed his reins from Ruairí's hands, and Uaithne took hold of him, earning one of Aodhán's scathing stares. "Do not attempt to place your hand on me again. I have powers you cannot even comprehend."

"Ruadhán awaits you." Uaithne let his hand drop, but Aodhán knew the man would not hesitate to knock him from his horse if he resisted. Regardless of Aodhán's threats, the cleric would be firm in his belief that he was doing the goddess's work.

"And I will deliver myself into his hands. I do not need your assistance."

Uaithne cast a glance in Ruairí's direction before giving a curt nod. "You do not lack courage. I will give you that."

"It is not courage, Uaithne, but knowing what I must do, regardless of my fears."

"Is that not what true courage is?" Ruairí said before motioning for Aodhán to start down the road. And yet, somehow, Aodhán did not feel very courageous.

****

Aodhán woke to find himself staring at a small crack in the ceiling. He would have to tell Duffy about that. The early morning sun highlighted the room in shades of mauve and gray. Or was it the curtains? Remnants of his dream lingered in his thoughts, causing his stomach to turn. At least he hadn't replayed the entombment ceremony itself. He always felt like throwing up after one of those nightmares—and did on occasion. No, this dream was more about the children's escape.

He turned with a sigh, remembering as he did that Niamh would not be beside him. Duffy's house, Duffy's rules. How many times had he heard that? Which was exactly why he wanted to move into their cottage. But while Duffy pretended to be supportive, Aodhán had no doubt he'd be bribing the workers to take their time.

"We'll see about that." Sitting up, he winced as pain ran up his back, and he sat for a moment to catch his breath. A reminder of why he couldn't be doing the work himself just yet, he supposed. A lark sang outside his window in agreement, and Aodhán grumbled at it.

"Don't be giving me that. Sure, ye're not sleeping alone every night. I'd be singing this morning too if I'd spent the wee hours snuggling up next to Niamh." He lay back down and pulled the blanket over his head. Just a few more months.

CHAPTER 6

The moon had been high, its light casting long, mystical shadows when Ruadhán had roused himself once more and made yet another trip down the hillside to gather the things he needed. Now he sat back in the cave before a small fire, frowning as he shifted through the clothing he'd pilfered over the last few days, or was it weeks? He really had no way of knowing how long he'd slept between each trip.

He picked up a small white piece of cloth and threw it to the side, opting to study it later. Instead, he tugged on a pair of heavy woven *triubhas* and pulled a knitted *léine* over his head. Such constrictive garments. The short hose were of the type the Saxons used, though they would not come very far up his legs. Having peeked through one of the cottage windows, he'd discovered how they were to be worn and slipped them on under a pair of laced *broga*.

No one seemed to wear cloaks or robes, but rather heavy overgarments of wool or other material that had sleeves. He'd have to make another visit down the hill and locate one, he supposed, as well as some coin to pay for the things he couldn't manage to acquire otherwise.

Under ordinary circumstances, he would think such actions wrong, punishable by stiff fines or perhaps even banishment. But these were not ordinary circumstances in any sense of the word. The goddess would forgive his unsavory deeds, considering the situation. After all, she would not have set him on this path if she did not understand what would be required.

Letting out a deep sigh, he dug into the food he had appropriated at an inn of some sort: a loaf of sliced bread and some kind of roasted beast and cheese. It was quite delicious and brought to mind the many celebrations he'd once taken part in.

His belly full at last, he leaned back against the stone wall. The task the goddess had bestowed upon him, whatever that was, would not be easy, and he was no longer a young man. He didn't even recognize the language they spoke, though it did have familiar aspects about it. Something else he would have to learn, but if the goddess had awakened him, she must have a purpose. Though others had failed her in the past, he would not.

After all, even a novice priest could misdirect another's attention and plant a notion in their mind. And he was no mere beginner, to be sure. He would lurk about below, listening to conversations, trying to interpret what each phrase meant. Not a simple task, true, but he had learned to speak the tongue of the Saxons that way. Come the morning, he would venture out and begin his mission in this new world. His only hope was that the goddess of his *túath* would not be long in revealing what that mission was.

For now, however, he needed to sleep. His eyes were getting heavy and his mind clouded. Could it even now be the remnants of the elixir? He supposed it could. After all, they'd never had anyone to question on its effects. One thing he was sure of, if he meant to interact with the inhabitants of this new time, he would need to have all his wits about him. Stretching, he gathered up the remaining food, wrapping it in a small cloth and laying it beside his small collection of items. The hard burial slab did not look very welcoming, but he'd slept on worse.

Resting back on the cold stone, he pulled his cloak over himself and closed his eyes, letting his mind drift back through the centuries, back to the world he'd left behind.

****

Ruadhán moved with stealth around the small hut he'd called his home for the last thirty years. As chief priest, he was afforded his own accommodations, but in truth he sometimes missed the fellowship of the communal living quarters where he had spent a good portion of his life. He had been just under forty when the old chief Ailbe had died and Ruadhán had been chosen as the new one. It pained him when he thought of how he had failed the position entrusted to him, but more than that, he had failed his goddess. Were he still a mere priest, he could join his friends and travel the countryside as a bard, telling tales of great adventures and holding on to his beliefs. But he was their chief priest, and a higher price was demanded of him.

While those that still remained in the compound slept the peaceful slumber of innocence and no responsibility, Ruadhán set about gathering up the sacred treasures. The Cup of Cheartais sat on his bedside table, next to a flask that held the Elixir of Suain Cráite, the draught he would need for the ceremony. He had committed that formula and many others to his memory long ago. There was no doubt in his mind as to its efficacy. A chill of fear ran through him, but he implored the goddess for courage and continued collecting the items he would take with him.

The Scian na Lúin, of course. The goddess had asked it as payment from Fionn Mac Cumhaill himself, a sliver of his own spear, its power so deadly that one scratch would end in death. Ruadhán had never removed it from its sheath, but he would take it with him. Who knew what deeds the goddess might call on him to perform? If need be, he would use it to protect her legacy.

He slipped it in his girdle and gazed back at the table. His ring of wisdom, Fáinne Na Eagna, sat beside the flickering lamp. Forged in the Well of Knowledge itself, it was crafted of the finest gold. Picking it up, he gazed at the name hidden within the secret compartment—Cian, the son of Carraig, birthed to the goddess to rule after his father. All who inherited such a ring were born from his direct line, one of each generation always destined to rule as chief priest. Domnall had received such a ring as well, bestowed upon him by their father, Ailbe.

Ruadhán shook his head. No, Ailbe was not their father. He was merely the goddess's consort, and yet . . . had it not been his seed the goddess had blessed? Domnall was the eldest and should have been chosen as high priest, but he had no wish of such responsibility, and so the goddess had bestowed the honor on Ruadhán. He huffed a laugh. No wonder Ciarán had been so reckless. And yet both he and Aodhán had received a ring as well, marked with the seal of Cian.

"And they never knew," he said to himself, for the knowledge came not with the bestowing of the ring, but with the acceptance into the high priesthood. "Ciarán might have been chief priest one day had he remained loyal to his goddess mother." He shook his head again, regret and anger mixing in a turbulent stew. Such a waste.

Breathing in the damp evening air, he placed the ring on his finger and frowned, his anger surging to the fore as a realization occurred to him. Ciarán had not been wearing his ring when they'd placed him in the tomb. Had he done the honorable thing and returned it to his goddess mother? Or had he given it to Bréanainn? But why would he have done either? *Because he knew he was about to betray all he had ever believed, no doubt.*

Fury flared in his bowels once more. The ring was a sacred item, not to be awarded to one who would soon be taught their mother was nothing more than a hollow myth. Even Domnall had returned his ring once he had made the decision to follow their new god. And as was prescribed by law, it had been returned to the lake, to the mother from whence it came. Perhaps he should seek the boy out before joining the goddess in Tír na nÓg.

No, my faithful one, it is but a ring. You must escape this place until the time when we can reign again.

A calmness overcame him as the goddess's words echoed through his mind, a soft whisper, like the gentle breeze on a spring morning. He touched his own ring, remembering his duty, and reached for the shroud he had prepared, the Veil of Cinniúna, folding it before placing it in the satchel that sat on his pallet.

Turning, he gazed in the looking glass that hung over a basin of water. A beam of moonlight flashed off the silver collar that covered most of his chest. His hair was nearly all white now—more of a gray, really. The last six years had been hard on him. He straightened the silver circlet on his head, adjusting it so the emblem of his station was centered. It was time. But as he leaned over to retrieve his satchel, a frightening thought occurred to him. What of the Book of Carraig?

The law was firm on the subject. It must never be removed from the Cave of Rúin Ársa. To do so would bring the wrath of the goddess down upon the offender. But how could he leave it undefended?

Have no fear, mo mhic dílis. *No one will be able to find the entrance, and should some man stumble upon it, he will rue the day he challenged my power.*

Ruadhán nodded and tightened his girdle around his waist. "Of course, my lady." The Cave of Rúin Ársa was indeed well hidden, far more secure than the tombs in the Hills of ár Sinsear. And who better to guard it than the goddess herself?

Walking outside, he scanned the compound, quiet now in the still of the midnight hour. He waited silently as the moon started its descent, its ethereal glow casting the small, round wicker structures in shades of cobalt and silver. A raven cried off in the distance, a message from his goddess. It was time for him to put his plan in motion.

Without another thought, he slipped into the wee hours, making his way toward the Hills of ár Sinsear. He would endure the same fate as those sealed in Tuamaí Dearmadta, the Forgotten Tombs, but unlike them, he would not await the judgment of his goddess. Instead, she would watch over and preserve him until she had need of him again. A shiver ran through him as he entered one of the frigid caves. Undeterred by the numbing cold, he lit the four torches that surrounded the limestone burial slab before using his powers to shift the large boulder across the tomb's entrance. There was no turning back now. The deed was nearly done.

Laying the Scian na Lúin at the base of the altar, he took up the Cup of Cheartais and placed it on the smooth limestone surface. He pulled the stop from his leather flask and carefully poured the deep red elixir he'd prepared himself. A wave of panic gripped his bowels, but he took a deep, calming breath, knowing his lady would save him from the torments the elixir inflicted upon those destined to be entombed alive for their betrayals. After all, he was doing this because of his loyalty. No, she would lull him into a peaceful sleep until she called on him once more.

He drank deep of the liquid, its effects washing over him almost at once. Fearful he may collapse on the packed earth floor beneath him, he lay back on the limestone altar, covering himself with the sparkling shroud. His body clenched, the goblet dropping from his hands. Was he even breathing anymore? Misty shapes swam around him, calling his name, and he gripped the altar beneath him. Had his lady abandoned him? But no, she was there.

One of the shapes drew closer, touching his cheek. She was as beautiful as he'd always imagined her.

Sleep, my faithful servant, she said, her voice no more than a whisper. And so he did.

****

Ruadhán bolted up with a gasp, trying desperately to catch his breath. His eyes darted around the darkened chamber as he tried to gain his bearings and distinguish his dreams from reality. But had it been a dream? More like a vivid memory. He scrubbed a hand across his face and tried to calm his racing heart. The goddess had lulled him into a peaceful sleep, just as he had expected, and she had reawakened him to serve her, though he still had no idea what it was she wished him to do.

His stomach grumbled, and he rose from the burial slab to retrieve the small package of food he'd lain next to his other treasures. He'd need to make another visit to the village and develop a plan about where to go from there. It would be difficult until the goddess apprised him of her needs, but he would move forward as best he could. With the lady's help, he would spend the next few weeks learning their language and gaining a feeling for the land. Perhaps by then the goddess would send him some hint to guide his steps.

CHAPTER 7

Ciarán stared into the darkness, a cold breeze drifting over his sweaty body. A torch flickered to life at his right foot, then another at his left. Though he tried to rise, he was chained to the cold, hard surface of his funeral pyre. A wave of panic shot through his soul. Had it all been a dream: Caitlin, Father Mike, his unborn children?

The torches flickered, and Ruadhán appeared between them, his face crushed into a furious mask. "You have taken what belongs to the goddess of our *túath*, *a shagart*, and now you must return them."

Domnall's voice echoed from the side, concealed in the shadows. "What did you expect, *a mhic*. Tell him what you have done with them, and perhaps he will not come for the others."

"What others? Who are you talking about?"

Caitlin appeared on his left, the light of the torch illuminating her upper body and the two infants she held in her arms. Tears were streaming down her face, hate in her eyes as she gazed at him. "This is all your fault." The children disappeared from her arms, replaced by a dagger that pierced her heart. "Your fault," she uttered. She reached out to him, her hands covered in blood.

Ciarán turned toward Ruadhán, who now held the infants in his arms. "No!" Ciarán tried to sit up, to reach for his children, but he couldn't move. Domnall shook his head, taking him by the shoulders. "Ciarán! Ciarán!"

"No! I beg of you, *a Athair*. Ask that he spare them."

"Ciarán!"

He struggled against Domnall's hold, blinking to clear the haze from his eyes, and Caitlin's face came into focus. She was sitting over him, holding him down.

"Ciarán, wake up. You're just having another dream."

His heart was racing, his body covered with sweat, the small nightstand lamp the only light in the room, save for the glow of the streetlight that filtered through the venetian blinds. He took a deep breath and let it out, slow and steady. "A dream," he said, his voice no more than a whisper. Looking up at Caitlin, he touched her cheek. "Why are ye straddling me?"

"Because even with the twins' extra weight, you're far too strong for me to hold down any other way, and this was iffy." She flashed him a smile that made everything all right. "You were thrashing around like a fish out of water. It was either this or be knocked out of bed on my behind."

"It was now, was it? Well, unless you mean to do something productive while you're up there, ye can get off now."

Her eyes sparkled a deep mistletoe in the lamplight. "Are you all right? You were scaring me this time. You looked wide awake, the way you did the night before Bradaigh attacked the school. And you kept begging someone to *spare them*. Who were you talking to?"

"'Twas nothing, *a chuisle*, just a bad dream."

She scooted down to his side and rested her head on his shoulder. "Do you want to talk about it?"

Resting his hand on her swelling stomach, he shook his head. "I'm not sure I even want to remember it." Not a complete lie—he didn't want to. "D'ye recall yer dreams when ye wake?" Okay, now he was embellishing his non-lie. Michael had taught him well.

"No, not usually. I suppose that's for the best, especially when they're as terrifying as yours seemed."

But Ciarán did remember, and it sent a shiver through his body so cold it felt as if ice water were running through his veins. He wanted to speak to Father Mike about it, but how to do that without alerting Caitlin? Just before Easter, the doctor had suggested she take a leave from work, and staying home was making her antsy.

Instead, he held her tight and kissed her forehead, though he lay awake for the rest of the night, wondering what his dream meant or if it meant anything at all. No, he knew better than that. He may not always interpret his dreams correctly, but they definitely meant something. It was one of the talents that had been cultivated in him as a child of the goddess so many centuries before. That life was long behind him now, fifteen centuries to be exact, but the gifts remained, though sometimes he thought they were more of a burden.

Still tired when he headed for work the next morning, he managed to stay awake in spite of the day's boring agenda. As much as he hated to admit it, he realized cataloguing artifacts was just as important as discovering them. That didn't mean he had to enjoy it, and so he was more than happy to leave the stuffy room at one o'clock.

May had warmed the air with a fragrant perfume, and since Caitlin had gone on maternity leave, he'd taken to meeting her for lunch in the park whenever the weather permitted. "D'ye think ye should be out walking about by yerself?" he asked as he met her on the museum's steps. "The doctor said ye could go into labor anytime now. Ye won't go nine months with twins."

"I *was* in the room when the doctor told us, you know." She laced her fingers in his and leaned against his arm. "I haven't even had a tiny cramp today. If I do, I'll grab a cab and head straight home or to the hospital, whichever is called for."

"And how would I know?" He stopped walking and turned to face her. "I think ye should go stay at the rectory while I'm at work." She opened her mouth to speak, but he bent over and silenced her with a kiss. "'Twill ease me mind. Me stomach's been in knots all day."

"Ciarán, you can't keep me in some kind of gilded cage. You couldn't protect Aisling, and that weighs on your mind. I get that. But this isn't the fifth century. There are telephones, and I doubt any Celtic priests are roaming around looking to sacrifice me."

"Don't even be joking about that. We don't know who else is buried in those caves or who survived."

"And we're not going to be poking around to find out, so stop dredging up old ghosts. The caves are off-limits. Even if someone did start snooping around, it took us two and a half days to get those tombs open, so we'd have plenty of warning. Aodhán said he and Ryan had been up to check on them, and everything is quiet."

"'Tis good to know, but there are far more tangible dangers I'm worried about as well." They started to walk again, though he was sure his next words were not going to go over well. "I was thinking, after the babes are born and all, maybe we should be looking for a place on the Island."

"The Island? What about the museum?" Though they kept walking, he could feel the tension in her grip. "It'd be close to two hours each way, every day, not to mention the cost."

"True, but 'twould be worth it, don't ye think? The wee ones would have a yard to play in and rooms o' their own."

"But we hardly see each other as it is. And what about Father Mike and Mary?"

"Sure, we'll still come to visit, and there'll be no stopping them from coming out to see us as well." This was going to cause an argument, but he'd have to face it at some point. Better to get it over with. So much for their pleasant afternoon. "And as for the traveling, I was thinking about that. Ye know how much I enjoy the digs, but the cataloguing bits . . . Now, that I've finished all me degrees, I've decided to look for something else. I applied for a job at a university out east, on Long Island, and they've asked me to come in for an interview."

This time it was Caitlin who stopped walking. She spun around to face him, her eyes flashing a deep forest green. "You what! We've never even talked about it."

"I've tried, but every time I bring it up, ye change the subject."

"And what does that tell you?"

"That ye're more concerned about digging round in the dirt than ye are about yer own children." The words had no sooner left his mouth than he regretted them. The look on her face was like a spear to his heart. "Cait, I didn't mean that." But it was too late. She was already walking out of the park toward Fifth Avenue.

He ran after her, but she pulled away, her jaw set firm and her eyes glaring darker than he'd ever seen them. "Don't! I'll see you at home tonight . . . maybe!"

A jolt of panic gripped his bowels. He had to stop letting his dreams control his life, or he may not have one worth worrying over. Casting a quick look toward the museum, he made his decision. He'd call them later and apologize, say something about Caitlin having contractions and it being false labor. God forgive him, but he couldn't let Caitlin just walk away. Under the circumstances, he'd be no good at work anyway.

She was sitting on the sofa, gazing out the window when he entered their apartment. *"Ta bron orm, a chuisle."*

"Stop! Your sweet Irish tongue isn't going to work this time. Not only did you sneak around behind my back, planning our lives, but you don't think I'm a fit mother for your children. You knew who I was when you married me, which is more than I can say."

"I told ye who I was before we were wed."

"No, Ciarán! I *discovered* who you were. Did you ever have any intention of telling me, or was it just that you got caught? What else don't I know? You've been hiding things from the moment we met, and I've just been letting it go. I can't believe I fell for another lying bastard. Well, no more. I think maybe you should sleep on the couch from now on. It's hard for me to get comfortable with anyone else in the bed."

Caitlin was glaring at him, her eyes a mist-covered forest, but he wasn't going anywhere. "Fine, then, I'll sleep on the couch, if 'tis what ye want. Just don't be comparing me to yer old boyfriends. I've no intention o' abandoning ye, no matter how stubborn ye are."

"Whatever. Just stay out of my way."

She flicked the TV on to some inane soap opera where everyone was sleeping with everyone else and opened the latest PD James mystery. How she could read and watch that talking box at the same time amazed him. Probably figuring out the best way to poison him as well. He slipped into his office, which was in the process of being transformed into a nursery, and called the museum, lying through his teeth. He said a prayer of contrition afterward and peeked in at Caitlin. She had a bowl of ice cream in her lap now too.

Best if he stayed in here. She needed her space, and he needed to get some work done. He owed Daniel that much. Logic told him she couldn't stay angry forever. Then again, last time it took him nearly getting killed to soften her up. Hopefully, he wouldn't have to go that far again. Ruffling the hair on the back of his head, he pulled over a list of artifacts that had just come into the museum, though he really couldn't concentrate.

He should have listened to Father Mike about the whole thing, but as usual, he just plowed ahead without thinking it through. God, he hated accession numbers. Disgusted with himself, he shoved the ledger aside and lay down on the small sofa. His legs hung over the side, causing his feet to dangle, but he didn't care. Exhaustion was creeping up on him, too many nights of vivid dreams he'd spend the day trying to forget.

****

Ciarán walked into the small village, two priestly guards by his side. He didn't expect any trouble, but on occasion a child's grandparent had been known to protest. Once more, young boys would be chosen for the priesthood, and while most parents could decide for themselves whether or not to send their sons to the selection ceremony, there was to be no such choice for the children of the goddess.

Bréanainn was Ciarán's first born. Seven years before, his mother had been honored for her service to the goddess and sent to Tír na nÓg, while the child had been given over to the care of his grandfather, Killian. Now it was time for him to be reclaimed by the priesthood.

Ciarán nodded a greeting to Killian. "Where is Bréanainn? I must take him to the great hall for the feast."

"You must drug him and drag him off to your priesthood, you mean." Killian's eyes flared with intense hatred, though Ciarán couldn't understand why. It was an honor to be chosen. As his son, Bréanainn's place in the priesthood was all but guaranteed.

"The drink we give is only to ease their minds."

"It will wipe their minds clear of all but what you choose to fill it with, priest. Do you think I don't know what goes on in there?"

"'Tis best that they see the priesthood as their home if their powers are to grow strong."

"And what if he does not possess those powers?"

"He is a child of the goddess. There is no doubt he will be gifted, for she has granted those talents herself."

"Bréanainn is my daughter's child, and yours, may the god's help him." He nearly spat the last words, and Ciarán took a breath, trying to calm the anger that was growing in his chest.

"He is a child of the goddess. Your daughter was but a human vessel in which he could grow and flourish."

"Why, Ciarán? You loved Órfhlaith as a child. We had even talked of your marrying when you were of age. Of course, that was before I knew who you were. Let me take Bréanainn away from here. No one will miss one small child."

Ciarán shook his head, unable to believe the blasphemous words that spilled from the man's mouth. No wonder he whispered them. "You will tell me where I can find my charge, old man. I will not let your selfish needs keep him from the honors that are his."

"Is there a problem, master?" one of the guards asked.

Killian bowed his head, his eyes glazed with tears. "You will find him down by the fairy well. Once a month he goes there to tie ribbons and pray for the return of his parents."

Ciarán held up his hand to the guards, staying them. "And so his prayers shall be answered this day."

"Will they? The way yours were answered? Do you even remember Fionn?"

Ciarán frowned. Why was he supposed to remember that old man who sold his vegetables to the priesthood? "I'll be going to get Bréanainn now." He looked over his shoulder. "Do I need to leave these men to guard you?"

"What is it you think I will do? You will have him no matter, and I have other grandchildren to think of. But I will ask one question of you."

"I will answer if I am permitted."

"Does your heart hold no love for the boy at all?"

The question nearly took Ciarán's breath away. It had pained him to stay away these past seven years, but it was his duty, prescribed by the law, and it was for the good of the child. Ciarán had done no more than offer a seed for the goddess to breathe life into. She was the child's mother, the priesthood his family, and yet a joy sprang in his heart at the thought of having the boy close.

"It does," Ciarán said, his voice so low that none but Killian could hear. "I will watch over him and guard him."

Killian nodded. "Then I suppose I must be satisfied with that."

A deep mist engulfed Ciarán, swirling around his body, draining it of all energy. The scene shifted to a time when it was he who was being taken away. His feet scuffed along the ground as they dragged him up to Tuamaí Dearmadta. He was too weak to fight them off, his mind clouded, his limbs heavy and limp. Caitlin stood at the entrance, tears streaming down her cheeks, their two infants held in her arms.

"They're going to take them, Ciarán. Do something. I can't fight them off. I'm not strong enough yet."

But he could barely keep his head aloft. Domnall stood beside her. "We have to take them, my son. You know it is for the best."

"That's them, master." The cleric Dáire stood next to Ruadhán, pointing a finger at the infants Caitlin held. "Ciarán's illicit spawn." A look of satisfaction crossed his thin lips, his watery eyes filled with glee. "You'll pay now."

Ruadhán looked down at Ciarán. "You owe them to me for what you have taken."

Ciarán tried to lash out, but his arms were so heavy, his knees were numb, and rain was falling on his face. No, not rain. He blinked, Caitlin's face coming into view, the tears running down her cheeks as she strained to hold his arms down.

"I can't take any more of this," she said between sobs. "What if you hit the babies while I'm trying to hold you down? This isn't about moving to Long Island or another job or a yard for the kids, is it?"

Ciarán sat up and rubbed his throbbing head. Pins and needles pricked both legs from hanging over the arm of the sofa, but now that they were resting on the floor, the feeling was returning. He sat with his forearms on his knees, staring into nothingness—or was it the past? Caitlin sat beside him, blowing her nose and waiting patiently. Her tears had tasted of salt, and he savored it for a moment before speaking.

"I'm not sure what any of it means, but Ruadhán is always there. Ye are as well, with the babes, and he takes them from ye, saying I owe them to him."

"Why would you owe our children to him?"

"Because Aodhán took me fifth-century children and hid them away, didn't he? I know it makes no sense, that he's been dead for centuries, but I just can't rid me mind o' it."

"Maybe you're just afraid of being a parent. I am too. We'll do it together, just like every other couple. But why the sudden urge to move to Long Island? Is it to get away from a long-dead chief priest or because you think it will make you a better parent?"

A smile tugged at the corner of his mouth. "A bit o' both, I suppose. I couldn't protect me wife or me children back then. And what if Ruadhán does wake, just as we did? Sure, he'd learn o' the museum soon enough and the Celt ye brought there. He'd figure it all out and come looking for us."

"Ciarán." Her eyes softened, and she touched his cheek. "Would Ruadhán have done anything to betray your goddess?"

"Sweet Brigid! He'd have died first."

"Then there's no chance he'll be waking, is there? He'd have died a natural death and been buried in the Hills of ár Sinsear."

He knew she was right, and yet there was a nagging itch in his gut that he couldn't quite rid himself of. "Would he, though? Christianity was spreading, wasn't it? I can't see him becoming a monk or roaming the countryside as a bard. There's no telling where he's been laid to rest."

Caitlin frowned. "So what do you think happened to him?"

"I've no idea. Became some kind o' hermit, maybe." He grinned, attempting to insert a bit of humor in the conversation. "I'm being ridiculous, I know, but ye o' all people understand how me dreams work. I don't always get their meaning right, but they do have a meaning."

"And guilt about leaving your children back then and fear about not being a good father now could be that meaning."

He released a soft chuckle. How had he ever found such a wise woman? "I suppose it could, but me dream's not the only reason I want to move to the Island. In truth, the more I think about it, the more I like the idea. The houses do have big yards, and the wee ones could play in the streets, and we could even have a pool, if ye like. Almost like a lake in yer own garden. There's fresh air and trees." He stopped for a moment, considering what it really was that appealed to him about it. "But most o' all, it reminds me more o' home."

"Why didn't you ever say anything?"

"Ye'd change the subject every time I'd hint at it. Besides, I know how much ye love the museum, and ye're right, 'twould be near a two-hour train ride for ye each way. 'Tis not like I meant to keep it from ye. I was just building up the courage to broach the subject."

"Do you really think I'd put my job before my children?" Her chin quivered, and she breathed in a stunted sob.

He wiped a tear that had escaped down her cheek and pressed his forehead against hers. "No, *a chuisle*, and it was cruel o' me to say such a thing. Ye'll make a grand *mamaí*. I can see it in the way ye rub yer belly, soothing them, protecting them."

"Actually, I've been thinking I might not go back to the museum or to teaching, at least not on a daily basis. The truth is, after spending almost eight months carrying them around with me, I don't think I want to leave them behind and go off to work every day." He opened his mouth to protest, but this time it was her who stifled his words with a kiss.

"But ye worked so hard to get where you are," he said when she finally released his lips.

"And I won't be giving that up. I can still go on digs and do research papers. That's the beauty of what I do. I can always find a way to do it and be with my children as well. Besides, considering their father is an artifact, it would be good for them to have an interest in archaeology."

Ciarán laughed. "I never meant to hurt ye, *a ghrá*. Ye know that, don't ye?"

"I do, and I should never have compared you to Kyle."

Ciarán pulled her up to his lap, and she wrapped her arms around his neck, leaning against him. "That was hitting below the belt."

"From the feel of things down there, the blow didn't damage any sensitive parts, but you realize it is terribly awkward at the moment. You may have to take care of things yourself, especially since I've been cramping a bit."

"What?" Ciarán jumped up as best he could with her in his arms and carried her to the bedroom, depositing her softly on the bed. "I'll call the doctor. No, a cab first."

"Ciarán!" She pulled him down by her side. "They come and go, and they're miles apart and not severe. I'll let you know when they get bad. For the moment, I'm fine."

"But ye're not even eight months."

"How many times have we talked about this? Twins usually come early. It's nothing to worry about, though the longer I can wait, the better."

Ciarán nodded, pulling her close. "Ye'll not be waiting too late, will ye? I've never delivered a baby before, let alone two o' them at once."

"I promise I won't wait too late. Though I think you might be right about going to the rectory during the day. Just in case." She gasped, and Ciarán stiffened.

"Calm down, that was just Fionn giving me a good kick in the kidneys."

"Fionn again, was it? Ye know Aisling's mine as well."

"What's that supposed to mean?" Caitlin pulled back to look at him, a smile dancing on her lips.

"Any daughter o' mine will be holding her own, so don't be surprised if 'tis wee Aisling that's giving ye a good nudge now and then as well."

CHAPTER 8

Dia duit! Ruadhán stood with a long pole, casting the line out into the lake, all the while listening to voices that came and went. Fly-fishing, they called what he was doing, but he was more interested in catching the words of those who passed within his perimeter than in the fish that swam beneath him.

Dia is Muire duit! Another voice answered the first. While the words were strange, they did have a familiar ring to them. It was a greeting of some kind, asking the gods to be with someone, but who was Mary? The goddess of their *túath*, perhaps. And yet, would they be so bold as to invoke her name?

For the past few weeks, he'd placed himself in various locations, entering the minds of those who wandered into his sphere. Without them even knowing it, they would explain this *English* to him or the *Irish*, whichever the case may be. Learning two languages at once could cause confusion, but he was up to the challenge. It would help stimulate his sluggish mind. Besides, the second was very similar to his own tongue. It was difficult at first, as any task worth accomplishing would be, but little by little it came easier, so that within two weeks he understood most of what was said.

Hmpf! For an old man, his mind was still crisp and quick. The bones, however, were another story, though he continued to take a brisk walk every morning and climb up and down to the ancient tombs without too much trouble. And if anything, his powers were more potent than ever.

Returning to the cave, as he had every morning for the past few weeks, he leaned his fishing pole against the wall and grinned down at the basket he carried. He'd have a hearty meal later this evening while he reviewed the information gathered during the day. He had to admit some of it did puzzle him. The crumpled parchment he'd taken from one of the houses a few nights before, for example. It was apparently money, but even stranger was the fact that they seemed to put more value on it than they did the coin he'd been gathering. Yes, this was certainly proving to be an unusual world.

Taking the fish from his basket, he placed it in a box filled with ice and grabbed some bread for his lunch. He gazed out the cave entrance at the blue sky and took a bite of his bread and crushed berries, contemplating his predicament while he wiped the gooey, sweet remnants from his lips. Nearly three weeks had passed, and still he did not know why the goddess had awoken him.

The sound of voices carried through the air, catching his attention. They seemed to be coming from the direction of Tuamaí Dearmadta, though why anyone would be wandering over there, he had no idea. His curiosity getting the better of him, he scurried across the hillside and slipped behind a large boulder so he could listen and get a peek at what was going on.

"Why can't we excavate another cave?" a young man with unremarkable features and dull yellow hair asked. "Surely if there were three, there must be others."

"Because the site has been declared off-limits to all but a select few," a sandy-haired young man said, a major cleric, no doubt. Perhaps even a novice priest. "And you're not one of them," the man added.

"And I suppose you are," the younger man said.

Ruadhán scowled. Clearly, no more than a minor cleric, and the jealous sort, just like Dáire and Godfraidh had been. While their deceits and treachery had been helpful at first, in the end the priesthood had seen the scoundrels condemned to Tuamaí Dearmadta. A sudden realization caused a shiver to rack his body. Had they opened any of the tombs? Sweet Brigid, there were wicked men entombed there. But surely the goddess of their *túath* would not allow them to live the way she had him. He had not betrayed her, but had chosen the tomb rather than forsake her name.

He would chance a look later, when the sun sank low in the sky and they all went for their evening meal. They didn't seem to have any guards posted. It should be safe enough. An older man had joined them, one with a trimmed beard and smoking pipe. Clearly, he must be a high priest of some sort, though his clothes did not signify such, with patches sewn to the elbows of his multicolored tunic—or jacket, as the locals called it.

"Should we get Aodhán up to take another look?" the sandy-haired man asked.

"No, I don't think Niamh would thank us for dragging him up here again," the elder priest said, "and as long as there's no sign they've been disturbed, there's really no need."

Aodhán? Surely it was no more than a coincidence. Ruadhán watched the three men head back down the hillside and up the road. A thrush sang out in the distance, and he relaxed a bit. Their priest had indicated they had not been disturbed. Besides, what havoc would Aodhán raise anyway? Timid and shy, he had only acted out of loyalty to his brother, unaware of the skills he held himself. But his brother—Ciarán—now there was a force to be reckoned with.

Ciarán had barely touched the extent of his powers. Sadly, he had chosen to betray his goddess mother and so had ended all hope of advancement. That Christian nymph had seduced him, dragged him off the road he was meant to travel. And because of that, Aodhán had acted recklessly and spirited away the children Ciarán had fathered, the goddess's children. For such betrayals, there could be no other consequence for either.

The bearded man's response had calmed him, but perhaps he should wander through the village and see why they were concerned about the tombs in the first place. Had the goddess placed guardians over them throughout the years? Was that who these men were? If so, perhaps he should speak to them, tell them who he was. Not just yet, however.

Determined to discover more about the caves, he returned to his fishing site and, after a quick greeting, sat off by himself and began exploring the minds of two older men, one a Christian priest, it seemed. So Padraig's religion had survived, while Ruadhán's priesthood had died out. Perhaps that's why the goddess had called upon him after all these years. First, though, he must learn more about his enemy . . . Dearmid McDonald, a serial murderer, had been put in his grave by two brothers—Ciarán and Aodhán Donnelly! No, it couldn't be them.

He searched the Christian priest's mind a bit deeper. Not Dearmid, but Bradaigh. How could this be? Had all three been awakened? And even if they had, how could two fledgling priests defeat a high priest as powerful as Bradaigh? The potential existed, to be sure, but . . . The Book of Carraig!

No! Not even they would dare enter the Cave of Rúin Ársa. Then again, Ciarán had ventured within its precincts as a mere bard and dragged Aodhán with him. Ruadhán clenched his fists. He had to see for himself, see if the fallen priests' tombs had indeed been disturbed. A bell rattled, and he cast a glance over his shoulder. A young man on the two-wheeled contraption the locals called a bicycle came to a stop just feet away, and fury flared in Ruadhán's bowels. There was no longer any reason to check the tombs. He would know Aodhán's piercing blue eyes anywhere. And if he survived, there was no doubt Ciarán would not be far behind.

His instincts urged him to return to his cave, lest he be recognized, but he needed to learn more. Pulling his collar up around his ears, he slanted his hat a bit more and turned so that his back faced the small group of men. Oblivious to the small tug on his fishing pole, he directed all his attention to the conversation going on not five feet behind him between Aodhán and the small group of villagers.

Ciarán lived in a place called New York with his wife. Ruadhán could feel the heat rising in his cheeks. Once again, the upstart had taken an unsanctified woman to himself. No wonder the goddess had awoken him. This was an affront to her station. His fists still clenched, he breathed out a long, slow breath to quell the anger and not draw attention to himself. It was better they did not know he was there just yet. But the next thing he heard caused him to bolt from the lakeside to keep from unleashing his wrath upon the men gathered there.

"Ciarán's to be a father anytime now," Aodhán said, "a boy and a girl, they reckon."

Fury tore through Ruadhán's body. He could stand to listen to no more. Reeling in his fishing line, he closed his tackle box and headed back to the Hills of ár Sinsear. So great was his anger that his hands were shaking when he entered his cave, and he fell to his knees in prayer. "How am I to vindicate you, my lady?" Peace descended on him as he prayed, calming his body and clearing his mind. It would not do to act rashly. From what he understood, he had slept for fifteen hundred years—another few months would matter little.

He would require a disguise of sorts if he meant to live amongst them. Fortunately, he didn't possess any unique qualities, not like Ciarán and Aodhán. Those distinctive blue eyes, their irises rimmed in midnight, stood out, just as Domnall's had. A thought occurred to him, and he sat back against the altar, smearing some of the delicious *jam* on a piece of bread. A funny name for the substance, but many words were odd to him here.

Taking a bite, he brought his thoughts back to the issue at hand. Domnall had passed his remarkable eye coloring on to Ciarán and Aodhán. Perhaps the man he'd seen was simply a descendant of Ciarán's. Aodhán had stolen his children away, after all, to be raised as Christians, no doubt. And it was traditional to repeat certain names within a family unit. Had they not done that within the *túath*?

Sighing, he made his decision. There was nothing else for it. Just before dark, he would have to traverse the hills and enter the precincts of Tuamaí Dearmadta. If the seals on their tombs had been broken, then Ciarán and Aodhán truly lived again, just as he did. He could not allow that to go unchecked.

****

Ruadhán watched as the sun sank close to the horizon before hurrying across the hilly ground to Tuamaí Dearmadta. How many had he seen entombed there? Had they all arisen or just the three he had heard mentioned? If the individuals they spoke of were indeed his rogue priests, Bradaigh was dead. He supposed he should be grateful to Ciarán and Aodhán for that, but even that good deed could not erase their transgressions.

He breathed a sighed of relief as he came to the tombs, for they were still sealed. Or were they? Something was not right. He moved closer, tracing his finger around the edge of the boulder for the sacred seal of the priesthood. Only the chief priest knew of the secret marks placed across the stones, and if opened, only he would know how to align them again.

His fingers skimmed the marking on the boulder, and his heart sank, for it did not align with the one carved into the hillside. They had been disturbed. By whom or when, he did not care. It was a great sacrilege nonetheless. Concentrating all his energy against the boulder that blocked the entrance, he shifted the large rock and entered the darkened cave. A snap of his fingers caused a ball of fire to hover just above his head, sending a bright light throughout the cave.

Sweet Brigid! Who had done such a thing? Those men he had heard talking that morning, no doubt. But why?

They had seemed to be protecting the tombs. Maybe others had broken in, and so they had set guards to see nothing more was taken. Releasing the hounds too late for them to catch the scent, he feared, for there was nothing left to salvage. Even the altar stone had been removed.

Collecting himself, he scoured the hillside, checking each sealed tomb. As chief priest, he knew where each one was and what their crimes had been. Perhaps that's what the gray-haired elder meant by seeing nothing else was disturbed. He supposed he should be grateful they had only opened three, yet the fact that they had disturbed any caused his blood to boil. Now he would have to act on the goddess's behalf and see the two remaining occupants were returned to their graves.

He scratched his beard. *Patience, Ruadhán.* First, he would travel to a larger town where he would be unknown. There, he could transform himself, learn all he needed to know. Once he was ready, he would return and plant himself in their midst, though they would never suspect.

Time and patience, my loyal son. The goddess of the lake, of his *túath*, whispered the words sweetly. *I know you will not fail me.*

Returning to his cave, he prepared to leave. He folded up his ceremonial robes, placing them on the burial slab with care. It would not do to be found with any of his priestly accoutrements, save one. He sheathed the sacred Scian na Lúin, placing it at the bottom of the large satchel he'd acquired. Should someone identify him before he was ready, it might become necessary. Though he hoped he would not need to use it, he would not hesitate if the need arose. The rest, including the Cup of Cheartais and his burial shroud, he wrapped in his robes. They could all be retrieved later the from the hidden repository in the wall of his burial chamber.

A sudden thought caused Ruadhán's stomach to clench. The Book of Carraig! He had left it unprotected, had not saved it from the unsanctified hands of two rogue priests, for how else could they have defeated Bradaigh? Had they discovered the secret of the shrouds as well? But no, interpreting the meaning of one small passage to overcome Bradaigh was one thing; it would take far more concentration to decrypt the rest of the book. Talent neither of them had likely developed.

Lifting the bag, he walked to the entrance of his cave but stopped for a moment. Perhaps he should check the Cave of Rúin Arsa, make sure they had not removed the book.

Do not trouble yourself over it for now, my loyal son. You did right to leave the sacred book in its sanctuary. It is as I wished.

Once again, the goddess had eased his mind. Whether Ciarán had violated the Cave of Rúin Ársa or not, one thing was certain. He would know the location of the book before he returned the miscreants to their tombs. With a deep conviction, he waved his hand, closing the boulder back over the entrance to his burial tomb, and mounting the two-wheeled contraption they called a bicycle, he headed for a town they called Castlebar.

CHAPTER 9

Ciarán sat at work, finding it increasingly difficult to concentrate. He'd assessed the same torc three times now, staring at the phone, waiting for it to ring. It had been six days since Caitlin had experienced the cramping. False labor pains, the doctor called them. But it could be any day now. He pressed his fingers against his eyelids, then shook his head before picking up the same torc yet again.

The next thing he knew, a snort woke him, and he sat up, blinking. He rubbed an indentation on his cheek, indicating he'd obviously dozed off on the infamous torc. Steve snickered, and Ciarán looked over to see him shaking his head, an impish smile on his lips. At least he hadn't lectured him about sleeping on the job. Thankfully, Daniel had already gone on ahead to Ireland with most of the team.

Lack of sleep was impairing his cognitive ability. Of course, the impending birth of his children and Caitlin's health wasn't the only thing on his mind. Without thinking about the repercussions, he'd already made a down payment on that house on Long Island and signed the loan papers. In his defense, he thought Caitlin would be pleased.

It looked just like she'd described her childhood home, and she always seemed so happy when she talked about that. Of course, in retrospect, he realized how it might seem like he was cutting her out of the decision. Foolish of him, knowing how independent and headstrong she was.

And then there was the job at the university. They'd needed an answer right away. Granted it was a bit of a drive from the house, but not too far. Better than the near two-hour ride from the museum. God, what had he been thinking? He'd planned their whole lives out and not even consulted her. If she'd been upset about him simply looking into it without mentioning it, wait till she found out the entire thing had already been signed and sealed. No question, she was going to be furious, and rightfully so. Now, to make matters worse, he kept having those accursed dreams. He sat back in his desk chair and tried to massage away the ache in his temples.

"You want to talk about it?" Steve said as he put a fresh cup of coffee in front of him.

Ciarán started to shake his head. What he wanted was to talk to Father Mike, but that was nigh on impossible with Caitlin coming along all the time. He doubted even the confessional would be sacrosanct at the moment. She'd become very protective of him in the last few weeks, like a mother hen, he supposed.

Steve had assured Ciarán it would pass when he had shared his concerns with the man one afternoon. What the heck? It wasn't like he'd never confided in the doctor before. He'd been the first to discover Ciarán was actually their fifteen-hundred-year-old missing Celt, after all, and he'd never told a soul unless he checked with Ciarán first. Why not confess his secrets to him now?

"I don't know what I'm going to do."

"About what? You'll be a great father. I've seen you with Duffy's kids."

Ciarán couldn't help but let a smile quirk his lips at the thought of Duffy Flynn and his family. Aside from Mrs. Byrne, they'd been the first of his countrymen he'd met after returning to Ireland the previous year. They'd given him a ride to church that first morning, flagging him down as he'd walked from Mrs. Byrne's bed and breakfast. Needless to say, they'd been friends ever since, and he adored the entire family.

"I hope ye're right, but 'tis the least o' me troubles at the moment. Caitlin may leave me when she finds out what I've done."

"Caitlin's a good Catholic girl. She's not going to divorce you."

"Maybe not, but she could try to get an annulment, or worse yet, insist I sleep in another room and treat me like nothing more than a boarder."

Steve's eyes widened. "Dear God, what did you do that's so bad you can't charm your way out of it?"

"I bought that house out on Long Island, and then to make matters worse, I took the teaching job at the university."

Without saying a word, Steve sat beside Ciarán's desk, his brow furrowed. After a moment, he looked up. "And she's going to leave you because . . . ?"

"I didn't speak to her about it first, and when I mentioned the idea last Wednesday, just mentioned it, mind ye, she . . . blew her stack. At least I think that's the term Father Dennis would use. She was furious."

"Ah!" Steve relaxed back in his chair. "So you mean you still haven't told her?"

"I tried to, but when she got so upset with no more than the idea o' it . . ." Ciarán shrugged.

"And why was it you went behind her back in the first place?"

"I didn't mean to, not like that anyway. 'Tis just, after all she went through last year, I thought 'twould be a grand surprise for her. She told me about where she lived as a wee *cailín*, and she always like it at Mrs. B's so much . . ."

"Where's the house located?"

Ciarán pulled an envelope out of his pants pocket with a picture of the house and the address. Pushing it over to Steve, he rubbed his eyes again.

"Have you been getting any sleep?" Steve asked before picking up the picture. "Nice house."

"She'll hate it, and she'll hate me more for not telling her."

Steve put the picture down and cocked his head to the side. "I'll ask again. Have you been sleeping properly?"

Ciarán sighed. If he was going to ask Steve for help, he'd have to be completely honest. "No, I've been having dreams. Bad ones. Ruadhán shows up with either Domnall or this little weasel of a cleric named Dáire, and he rips me children out of Caitlin's arms. He says I owe them to him."

"It sounds like your fear of being a father, of having responsibility for two new lives, is manifesting itself in some sort of guilt over leaving your fifth-century children to fend for themselves."

"And ye sound like a psychiatrist. I thought ye were more o' a surgeon?"

"I've had my own ghosts to deal with, and don't ask me to explain. We're not talking about me now."

"Funny how we never are."

Steve grinned. "One day, maybe."

"I suppose ye're right," Ciarán said, "but only partially. Me dreams tend to have a bit o' truth in them as well, at least the ones like this. A hint o' something that's to come."

"What do you mean?"

"Before Bradaigh attacked Caitlin, I'd been having a dream o' her lying on an altar, with him as the presiding priest."

"And then she was attacked." Steve scrubbed a hand across his mouth. "Could just be coincidence. You were falling in love with Caitlin."

"And if that was the only time it had happened, I might agree with ye, but it's happened all me life." He got up and went to pour himself another cup of coffee, spiking it with whiskey this time before returning to his seat and setting another cup down before Steve. The doctor lifted his eyebrow. "What?" Ciarán said. "'Tis well after twelve."

"Look, Ciarán, Ruadhán is long dead. Do you think he's going to wake in one of those caves of yours and come back to claim your children? How is he going to do that? None of the caves are being excavated. And even if he did somehow reappear, how would he know you had survived, let alone that your . . ." he nodded down to Ciarán's crotch, " . . . was still working. Besides, when you dreamed of Bradaigh attacking Caitlin, only part of it came true. Caitlin was attacked, but not on an altar, and you saved her."

"So me kids are in danger, just not the way I'm thinking. That makes me feel so much better."

"Or maybe you think you're the danger because you're scared to death of being a father."

Ciarán took a long drink and swallowed. Steve wasn't completely wrong. "What if me inexperience harms them?"

"Your kids aren't harmed in the dream. Someone is taking them away from you. I hate to break the news to you, but you will lose them in some ways as they get older. I went through a period where I didn't think my father knew anything. They'll come back eventually, though, because I know you. You'll be there for them and love them. That's what counts."

"How could ye think yer father knew nothing?"

"You're trying to tell me you never rebelled?"

"I did, to be sure, but I always knew Domnall would find out the truth in the end. Me stupidity was in thinking that I could fool him the next time."

"See, not so different."

Ciarán took another long drink and put the cup down, staring into it. Even if he accepted Steve's reasoning about his dream, he still had another problem. "Suppose ye're right there, that still doesn't explain what to do about the house."

"Oh no!" Steve stood up and drained his cup, patting Ciarán on the back before heading for the door. "You're truly screwed there."

Ciarán groaned. What had he expected the man to say? Placing his elbows on the desk, he rested his face in his upturned palms. A moment later, he felt Steve's hand on his shoulder again, and he looked up.

"Look, kiddo, just come clean with her. Explain everything. Why you did it. Then say you're sorry and offer to sell it. She may be angry for a while, but she'll get over it. I haven't steered you wrong yet, have I?"

"What happened the day your wife died?"

"I'm not ready to part with my demons just yet, but when I am, you'll be the first to know."

****

"You what!" Caitlin stood spellbound, her fists clenched in anger, her eyes glowing a deep green. "You paid for it."

"The down payment. I had to take a loan out for the rest." Ciarán twisted the ring on his left finger. He felt like it was getting tighter by the minute. "I thought ye'd be pleased." He readied himself for the onslaught, but instead of anger, she just shook her head.

"I always dreamed it was something we'd do together, after the babies were born. Something we'd do as a family." She slumped down on the bed, and he went to sit beside her, but as soon as he did, she got up and walked into the living room.

"I'm sorry," he said. "I didn't think."

"No, you never do."

"What's that supposed to mean?" Ciarán could feel his own temper rising. He hadn't meant to be selfish or bossy. How was he supposed to know what she wanted? It wasn't like he'd had a family to teach him all the little nuances of married life. His ancient priesthood didn't worry about houses or jobs, let alone whether or not someone liked what they did. Rules were rules, and they'd lived by them . . . until he hadn't.

"You don't think about what anyone else wants. The first day we arrived in Ireland, you wanted to go exploring, but did you even consider how it might worry me? No! When you discovered the location of Aisling's body, you wanted to see her, and so you made the dive, even though you weren't authorized. You never stopped to take into account what such a rash act might mean for Daniel or the dig. Do you ever once take a moment to contemplate how your actions might affect someone else? How long would you have gone on with the charade if I hadn't noticed those tattoos and realized you were my missing priest?"

"I was going to tell you that night, but you didn't want anything to ruin the moment."

"After you slept with me, you mean."

"I'll sell the bloody house, then, and tell the university I've changed me mind."

"University? You took the job as well? Have you told the museum?"

"I have. Or am I not allowed to decide what career I want either? Sitting in that stuffy office day after day is stifling. The digs are grand, and I understand the need o' recording it all, but 'tis not for me. I was trained to impart knowledge, to guide me charges along their path." He cursed under his breath. "Ye're as bad as Ruadhán, making demands and telling me what I can and cannot do based on what ye want."

"I didn't want to make the decision," she said, her voice no more than a whisper. "I just wanted to be part of something that was going to affect my life."

This was bad. She hadn't even raised her voice, and somehow that made it all the worse. Ciarán took a breath to calm himself, but he couldn't stop the angry words that forced their way from his lips. "Ye mean like ye deciding ye'd be dragging me children along on digs."

"You bastard! My parents did, and I turned out fine."

"Did ye now? Well, ye could have fooled me. Ye're nothing but a spoiled brat; even yer Uncle Mike will tell ye that."

That was it. He knew he'd gone too far the moment the words left his lips, but he couldn't seem to stop himself. All he wanted to do was make her happy, and this was the thanks he got. Her face had turned a crimson red. And he held his breath waiting for the proverbial axe to fall. It did, though not the way he expected, for she still didn't raise her voice.

"Maybe we just need a little time apart."

"I'm not going anywhere without me children." He stood firm. Guilt still nagged at him from the knowledge he'd left his fifth-century children behind when he'd betrayed the goddess and been entombed alive.

"Your children! Carry them for nine months, did you?"

"The doctor doesn't think 'twill be more than eight months, remember, not with ye carrying twins." Even he had to admit that just sounded stupid.

"Right, well, when you can pop out your breast and produce milk, maybe we'll talk about that aspect of it, but for now, they're our children. Besides, I'm not kicking you out. This is your home too. But I do think we need a little time apart, even if it's just in separate rooms."

"Not even pretending 'tis because it's awkward for ye to sleep with anyone this time, then?"

"No, I just don't want to see you right now. I'm too angry."

Ciarán knew it was pointless to argue, not when she was this furious. Every other word out of his mouth made him sound more idiotic, and she dug her heels in even further. It would be best if he went, for now. St. Monica's wasn't that far away, and he always knew he had a bed there. Besides, he needed to talk to Father Mike before he let his mouth say anything else that wasn't in his heart. The weeks of worry and sleepless nights had taken their toll, making his temper short and his reasoning clouded.

He walked past Caitlin, back into the bedroom, and threw a few things in a bag. "I'm angry and hurt as well. I just wanted to surprise ye. Sorry if I muddled it up, but I'm sort o' learning as I go. Maybe ye're right, though, we both need some time to think." Kissing her cheek, he headed for the door, but she just stood there, glaring at him, her eyes filled with tears. "I'll be at the rectory if ye need me. Ye will call if ye do?"

"Of course I will."

He opened the door but stopped a moment, without turning around. "Did ye ever think that, with all ye're going through, I might have just wanted to be doing something nice for ye?" With that, he closed the door behind him.

****

The latch had no sooner clicked shut than Caitlin slumped down on the couch, grabbing one of the pillows to herself and sobbing into its soft crevices. She must have cried herself to sleep at some point, for her back was stiffer than usual, and her left arm was numb from being stuffed under the pillow. A kick to her side told her she was right. The twins seemed to get feisty after ten. She looked around the room, remembering the argument that had driven Ciarán to the rectory, and she started to cry again.

Why was she making such a big deal of this? Memories, that's why. She remembered going with their parents to find their little house. The excitement of seeing the backyard and of having her own bedroom. Ciarán had robbed her of that, and she resented him for it.

But how was he to know? He should have asked, that's how. Her anger flared again, and she stomped into the bedroom. A piece of paper hit her foot. Without thinking she bent to pick it up. It was a picture of the house he'd bought. Their house. And it was perfect. Tears started flowing down her cheeks again. She sat on the bed, staring at the black-and-white picture a moment before flipping it over: four bedrooms, den, unfinished attic, eat-in kitchen, dining room, two baths, one-third of an acre treed property—thirty thousand dollars! Where had he gotten a down payment for that?

She jumped up, running over to the dresser, and grabbed their savings account book from the drawer, her brow creasing as she looked at the balance. Nothing had changed. Now she really did wonder where he'd gotten the money. Had he been doing anything illegal, selling artifacts, fencing them?

After putting the book back in the drawer, she turned to look at the clock. Two in the morning. She couldn't call the rectory now, not unless she was in labor. Drifting back into the living room, she cuddled up on the sofa and grabbed her pillow again. Her sobs came deep and fast until she'd cried herself out, and she lay down, pulling the throw blanket over her legs. No, Ciarán cared too much about the artifacts. He'd never sell them. Believing in her husband, she shifted onto her side and dozed off to sleep.

****

"Caitlin?" Father Michael opened the door, his gray hair sticking up at angles. "Has she had the wee ones?"

"No, Father." Ciarán twisted his mouth, ashamed of his outburst. "We had an argument and thought it best to spend a bit o' time apart."

"That wee lass threw ye out?" He scratched the back of his head and motioned him in. "Ye'd best come into the parlor, then."

Ciarán sat in his favorite green chair and stared into the empty fireplace while Michael poured them both a drink. "No, I left by mutual agreement. I thought it best to give her a wee bit o' space, and I needed to be speaking with yerself."

"Tell me what happened, then."

Somehow the whiskey didn't even seem that appealing. "I told her about the house and me taking the job at the university. She said I was selfish and only thought o' meself."

"Did she even look at the place?"

Ciarán shook his head and downed the whiskey. "She feels like I'm making all the decisions. That I expect her just to go along with whatever I say." He looked up at the priest. "I know ye told me 'twas a bad idea, but I'm not, am I? Making all the decisions?"

Michael shrugged. "Ye meant well by it, though I expect she had her own thoughts on the subject. She's not had a real home o' her own since she was twelve. All the decisions were made by others, mostly men and most without ever consulting her."

"Her brother?"

Father Mike nodded. "Daniel and I tried to watch over her, but Grady was her legal guardian after their parents died. He was about twenty-three at the time and planned on heading out to California. Their parents asked him to put it off. They wanted him to join them on one last dig before he went out on his own."

"Was he an archaeologist as well?"

"Of a sort, but he preferred working in the museum to the actual digging. He was in conservation. Still is, I suppose."

"Why don't he and Caitlin speak?"

"I'll be getting to that. 'Tis not as if ye'll be going anywhere tonight, now is it?" Ciarán shook his head, so Michael continued. "He and his parents had a huge argument over it that night, and it made them late for an important dinner. They were to be honored by some archaeological association or another. The last words they said before they went rushing out o' the house was that they'd speak more on it later."

"Only later never came," Ciarán said, sensing what was coming.

"No, they died in a car crash on their way to the awards dinner. Grady blamed himself at first. Their argument had caused them to be running late, which in turn caused them to go rushing off to the dinner. If he'd only agreed to consider going on the dig, perhaps they'd still be alive. But then, after a bit, he began to see it differently and shifted the blame to his parents, saying it was their own fault. He began to argue that if they hadn't made such a big deal about him going on another dig with them, they wouldn't have been rushing at all. 'Twas the grief talking, o' course, but Caitlin didn't see it that way."

"Caitlin blamed him."

"Not at first. Not until he started saying 'twas their fault. He dropped her off with me one night, said to find her a good boarding school, then headed for California. Being a priest, I couldn't very well be keeping a young girl here at the rectory, and Mary already had a houseful. It wouldn't have been right to saddle her with another. So I did as he asked and found a good school. Mary took her for vacations and such, but for the most part she grew up in Sacred Heart."

"Did she hold ye responsible for it?"

"Caitlin, no! She's always been a sensible girl—at least she was till she met you." He pushed down his glasses and looked over the frames, though a smile played on his lips. "Grady would check in with me from time to time to see how she was faring. And when he put the house up for sale, he made sure to put her half in a trust fund, though she couldn't access it until she was twenty-five. He never did call her, though. She was hurt and angry, and so she never bothered with him again either."

"And now I'm making all the decisions and not even letting her choose her own house."

"Something like that. Ye're not the only one with ghosts from yer past, ye know." Michael stood up and stretched. "But there's nothing more ye can do about it tonight, so up to bed with ye and get some sleep. Things will look better in the morning."

CHAPTER 10

The sun had barely risen when Caitlin heard the key in the door. She sat up, still holding the picture in her hand. Ciarán walked in the door, stopping short when he saw her sitting on the sofa, the blanket thrown over her legs.

"I need to be getting ready for work," he said. "I'll try not to take too long."

"You couldn't have gotten much sleep," Caitlin said.

For one long moment, they stood staring at one another. Had she truly driven him away? A tear trickled down her cheek. No, she could see the pain in his eyes. The next thing she knew, she was running into his arms, sobbing into his shoulder, mumbling incoherent nonsense, but he held her tight, and that was all that mattered. A kick from little Fionn—or wee Aisling—finally caused them to separate. They pulled apart, and he wiped the tears from her face.

"I'm sorry, Cait. Ye're right. I should have discussed it with ye first. I'll be asking the real estate agent to put the house back on the market. I should be able to make enough to get me down payment back."

"Don't you dare." She was still holding the picture in her hand. "I love the house, but I have to ask—and please don't lie to me—how did you afford the down payment?"

"I sold me torc."

"Oh, Ciarán, no. That's the only thing you have from your father. Where is it? I'll go pick it up. We've got enough money in our savings to cover it, I think."

"No, 'tis fine. I gave it as collateral to Daniel. He didn't want to take it, o' course, but I insisted we'd pay him back. I only borrowed half o' it anyway. Yer uncle was paying me a bit while I was his handyman at the rectory, and Daniel offered me a good salary for working with ye at the dig last spring. I don't really need much, so . . ." He shrugged.

"When can we go see it?"

"It needs a wee bit o' work and all, but I figure I can handle most o' it meself, though the lads have offered to give me a hand as well. And it has a grand yard in the back, with room for a swimming pool one day, if ye like."

She loved the way his deep blue eyes sparkled when he was excited, but they still had more to discuss. Pressing her lips to his, she stopped him from talking with a kiss. It appeared to be becoming a habit of theirs lately, but neither of them seemed to mind. "Now about your job," she said when she finally pulled back, her senses still tingling from the feel of his tongue caressing hers.

"'Tis no worry. Sure, we can commute to the museum. The railroad's not far from the house, and we can leave the car there while we're working and all."

"But it's not what you want."

He hesitated a moment. "I like sharing what I know with others, Cait. Seeing the excitement in their eyes when I show them a piece o' history. The museum did say we'd still be part o' the digs, and when ye're ready, yer position as supervisor will be waiting for ye."

"Then that's what you should do. As for me . . . I really did mean it about not being sure about leaving these little guys to go back to work . . . not for a while anyway."

"But ye love it so much. I know how hard ye worked to make a name for yerself."

She laughed, happy to be in his arms once more. "Don't worry. Daniel's not going let anyone forget I'm still the best archaeologist in the field, whether it's true or not. We'll go on the digs, with the kids if it's all right with you. And I've already started a research paper on what we know of the missing Celts."

His eyes widened, and she laughed again, kissing his cheek. "Don't worry, I'm not going to reveal your secret. And there's a bunch of other articles I've been wanting to write, but they just kept getting put off, so what better time to do it?"

"Are ye sure, Cait? I don't know why I said all those horrible things. Ye're going to make a grand mother. I've no doubt o' it."

"And that's what I want to be right now, first and foremost, and you should do what you want too." She kissed him long and hard on the lips, then pulled back. "So when do I get to see the house?" she asked again. "And when are we moving in? I think we need to wait until after the babies are born at this point, don't you? It would be silly to start looking for a new doctor this late. Besides, I really do like Dr. Smith. I will have to find a pediatrician for Fionn and Aisling, though. How are the schools? I know it's a ways off yet, but . . ."

This time it was Ciarán who stopped her with a kiss. A long, deep one that practically made her toes curl. Maybe it wasn't so bad having an argument now and then, just so they could make up. He lifted her in his arms and carried her into their bed, brushing back her hair and leaving soft kisses on her forehead, nose, and cheeks. It went no further, however, for her stomach clenched in a contraction like none she'd had up to that point, and her breath caught as she grabbed her stomach.

"Ciarán! Either our children don't want this going any further or they're ready to come out."

"But 'tis barely eight months."

She rolled her eyes. "How many times do the doctor and I have to remind you? Twins usually come early, and eight months is perfectly normal."

"Maybe 'tis just a cramp."

She held her breath as another contraction squeezed her insides. "That was no cramp."

He called for a cab, grabbed her suitcase, and they headed for the elevator. "'Tis a good thing we had that argument."

"Why is that?" she managed to squeak out when another contraction clenched her womb.

He'd already picked her up and held her against his chest. "We didn't have to take time dressing, now did we?"

"I suppose not." She wrapped her arms around his neck, her heart bursting with love for him. He always made her laugh just when she needed it most.

The cab was waiting, but a man was standing beside it, arguing that the driver needed to take *him* somewhere. Ciarán apparently had no patience for such nonsense and opened the door, pushing the man out of the way.

"Hey, I was here first," the man said.

He sat Caitlin down on the seat. "I called it, ye daft fool. Can't ye see me wife's in labor?"

The man stumbled back, but the driver wasn't so sure. "Hey, look, she's not going to have it in my cab, is she?"

"Seriously!" Ciarán got in and slammed the door shut. "Don't be worrying yerself about it. I'm a doctor. But step on it."

"All right, then."

Caitlin smiled at him. "Ye're getting quite good at picking up on Father Dennis's idioms."

"'Tis true, but that particular one I heard in an old movie. It seemed appropriate."

She leaned over and whispered in his ear. "And when did you become a doctor."

"Do I not have a doctorate from Columbia University?" He grinned and held her close to himself just as another contraction caught her breath.

****

Ciarán held Caitlin's hand while another contraction racked her weary body. He pressed some ice to her lips, and she smiled. "I'm so sorry I did this to ye."

Caitlin breathed out a long breath and laughed. "I seem to recall this being a joint venture. This *is* how babies are born, you know. I thought you wanted children."

"O' course I do. I just didn't realize 'twas going to cause ye so much pain."

"Haven't you ever seen one born before?"

Ciarán threw a glance behind him, but the nurse had stepped out of the room for a moment. "'Twasn't part o' the curriculum, now was it? I just planted the seed and didn't return till after the babe was born."

Caitlin's eyes darkened a bit, but it seemed to be more out of sympathy. "And you never saw the mother again?"

While Caitlin knew some of what he'd been through, he'd not gone into all the details. He swallowed before speaking, trying to bury the ache that clutched his heart each time he thought of it. "Not until I went to fetch her for the ceremony."

"What ceremony?" The answer must have shown on his face, for she continued. "Oh, that ceremony." She reached up to touch his face. "I'm sorry I brought those memories up. Let's return to happier ones. Like the fun we had making these little guys."

He couldn't keep the smile from breaking out on his face. God, he'd never experienced anything like it before. It went beyond mere physical pleasure—not that he didn't enjoy every moment of that as well, but there was a joy that filled his soul when he lay with her. He lifted her hand to his lips, rubbing them gently over her knuckles. And now the living proof of that love was about to enter the world.

She squeezed his hand again as the pain reached a peak, then eased down the other side. "Mary says you forget it after you see the babies. I suppose she must be right since she did it five times."

"She usually is." He bent over and kissed her forehead just as the doctor came in.

"Let's take a look, shall we?" He grunted, then looked up at the two of them. A pleasant man with a neatly trimmed mustache, he sat back on his stool and sighed. "Things aren't preceding the way I'd hoped," he said, his voice calm and steady. "Both babies are breech, but many times at least one will turn itself around, causing the second to do the same after the first is birthed. I'm afraid these two little tykes are being stubborn, though, and are determined to come out feet first."

"Figures my kids would want to jump in feet first," Caitlin said, and the doctor laughed. "They must take after their father."

But Ciarán didn't see anything funny about it. "So what will ye do, then?"

"I'll have to do a Cesarean section. We'll make an incision in your wife's womb and take the children out that way."

Ciarán could feel the blood draining from his face, the horrors of his dreams racing through his mind. "I know what it is," he said, trying to keep his voice from trembling. He'd read about C-sections and the dangers that went with them, but he'd also read about breech births. "There's a risk involved."

The doctor rested his hand on Ciarán's arm, his voice and expression as calm as ever. "There's risk in every birth, son, but it's extremely low, and in this case, she and the babies are in more danger from a natural birth than they are from a C-section."

"It'll be fine, Ciarán." Caitlin gripped his hand, squeezing tight, tears coming to her eyes as she curled up in pain, and then it eased. When she spoke again, there was a fire in her tone he knew all too well "And truthfully, at this point, I don't care how they get them out, just as long as they do it."

Ciarán opened his mouth, determined to discuss the alternatives with her, but her eyes flashed a deep forest green, and she pointed a warning finger in his direction. "Listen, you Irish son of a bitch. Dare to go against me on this and I'll pull your testicles out through your nose. Do you understand me?"

Ciarán's eyes widened at Caitlin's foul language and the thought of how much pain such an act would cause.

Without another moment's hesitation, he gave a quick nod of assent to the doctor, who had covered his mouth, clearly to stifle a laugh. Though Ciarán had faced Caitlin's wrath on more than one occasion, he'd never seen it reach that height before. One thing he knew for sure: she was not about to brook any argument.

"You'll have to sign some consent forms," the doctor said.

"What kind o' forms?"

Caitlin was in the throws of another contraction but reached up, grabbing Ciarán's shirt until his face was inches from her. "Just sign them."

He swallowed again, giving the doctor another nod, his words seemingly having deserted him. Given her state of mind, he couldn't be sure Caitlin wouldn't act on her previous threat. The thought caused him to wish he'd opted to give Father Dennis's tighty-whities a try.

"There's a father's waiting room outside." The doctor's lips twitched as he obviously tried to suppress a grin. "Why don't I have the nurse bring you the papers there?"

Caitlin narrowed her eyes in warning. "I'll sign them," he said, "but I'm not going anywhere."

The doctor started to speak, but Caitlin cut him off. "The hell you're not, you bastard!" She pushed up on her arms and looked on the verge of jumping out of the bed and throttling him. "Now get your ass the fuck out of here so they can get these kids out of me."

Ciarán's mouth dropped, but she was squeezing his hand so hard he thought maybe he'd best do as she asked. Yet as he stood to leave, she reached up and touched his cheek, the contraction having past once more. "I didn't mean to curse at you. I'll be fine."

He returned her smile and kissed her on the forehead. "I know that, *a chuisle*." Then he hurried from the room before another contraction hit.

"Do they all get like that?" Ciarán asked the doctor, who had followed him into the hallway.

He laughed. "She was rather tame, considering. You know that threat she made?" Ciarán blew out a long breath, nodding, and the doctor shrugged. "I can't say for sure, not having experienced it firsthand myself, but from what I understand, that's a pretty close description of what giving birth feels like."

Ciarán couldn't suppress a cringe. "Women must be very brave creatures, going through it time and again and all."

The doctor chuckled and patted him on the back. "I believe they are."

"She'll be all right, won't she?"

"There's no guarantee with anything," Dr. Smith said, "but I can assure you that I do at least a dozen of these a month and have had no problems yet. We'll notify you as soon as your children are born. You can take a peek at them in the nursery while we get Caitlin settled in a room. And don't worry; you won't be the only one wearing a hole in the carpet."

"Pacing, ye mean," Ciarán said, recalling one of Dennis's idioms.

The man smiled and nodded down the hallway before he returned to Caitlin. Ciarán took a deep breath and, rubbing his sweaty hands on his pants, headed in that direction.

There was a waiting room just like the doctor said, occupied mainly with men like himself, pacing back and forth, biting their nails, or staring into space. Dear Lord, was that what he looked like?

"Mr. Donnelly?" a nurse called, and he turned toward her.

"That would be me." A jolt of panic surged through his body. "Is me wife all right?"

"She's fine, sir. You just have to sign these forms in case anything should happen where a choice needs to be made between the mother or the children."

"A choice? What sort of a choice?"

"It's just procedure, Mr. Donnelly. Nothing to worry yourself over."

"What if I don't sign? Are ye just going to leave her there? How can ye expect me to be choosing between me wife and me children?"

"What is it, son?" Father Mike came out of nowhere, his calm voice soothing Ciarán's frazzled nerves, if only a small bit.

"They want me to choose who they should save if something goes wrong—me wife or me children. How can they expect me to make such a decision, and why would anything be going wrong in the first place?"

"What's going on here?" Mary said.

Ciarán turned to see Father Dennis and Steve were with them as well. Where had they all come from? But before he could voice his query, the nurse spoke up.

"Do you know Mr. Donnelly?"

"Oh, you've never met my adopted son, have you, Mabel?" Mary replied. "Now what's this all about?"

"Just procedure," the nurse said. "The babies are breech, so the doctor needs to do a C-section."

"Let me handle this." Mary turned to Ciarán, thrusting the clipboard against his chest. "Now you listen here. Two of my daughters-in-law have had C-sections, and they think they're the best thing since sliced bread. You sign that paper and let these fine folks get on with birthing your babies."

Ciarán hesitated, and the nurse whispered something in Mary's ear, causing a smile to cross her face.

"I just might have to carry out your wife's threat if you don't," she said, still smiling, but then her eyes narrowed and the smile dropped away. "Only I won't be nearly as gentle. Now sign those papers before you lose all three of them."

Ciarán signed the form, knowing better than to argue with Mary, though it was still tearing him apart inside.

"'Twill be fine, lad," Father Mike said. "Now why don't ye come over here and calm yerself down?"

Ciarán cast a look toward Caitlin's room before nodding and going to sit with his family. "Ye've adopted me, then?" he said to Mary, though she'd informed him of such months before. At the moment, he never needed to hear it more, to know this no-nonsense woman had his best interests at heart, to realize he wasn't left alone in a strange new time to face everything by himself.

"'Course, I have, sweetheart. You're like one of my own. After all, I've seen all your bare butts, now haven't I? Sat in more than one waiting room as well, so you can trust me when I say they'll be calling you to take a look at those sweet little things of yours in no time at all. Then after you go see your wife, you can come with us back to the rectory."

"I'm staying with her."

"Good Lord, all that girl's going to want is rest." She pinched Ciarán's cheek. "And as charming as this handsome Irish face of yours is, that's going to win out in this case. So you're going to go to the rectory and get some sleep, and I'll have a nice breakfast for you come morning."

Ciarán frowned, but he nodded and sat back in one of the chairs. "How long have ye been here?"

"Most of the day," Father Dennis said. "That little nurse ye were giving such a hard time has been keeping Michael up-to-date."

"I didn't notice ye. Ye should have let me know ye were here."

"I'm surprised you found the waiting room at all, let alone noticed who was in it." Dennis twisted his mouth, clearly trying to prevent a smile from breaking out. "You looked like you were in a bit of a trance when you walked in here."

"I suppose I was." He kept glancing down the hall. "Why is it taking so long?"

"Lord help us," Mary said. "It's only been ten minutes. What do you think, they just pop her open, grab the kids, and zip her back up? Sit back and relax."

"There can be complications, ye know," Ciarán said. "I've been reading up on it and all."

"'Course there can," Mary said, "but that's true of anything, even a natural birth. Since you've been reading up on it, you must have come across that as well." She looked at him pointedly, then took his hand. "Now stop your fretting and have a little faith."

"Ye might try speaking to Michael as well." Ciarán smiled over at the priest. "I'm sure he's looked down that hallway as much as I have in the last ten minutes."

"I heard that, lad. I'm simply excited about having some wee ones about for a change. 'Twill liven the place up."

An hour and a half later, the doctor came down the hall, and Ciarán rose, his heart shooting up into his throat.

"Do you want to see your children?" the man said, a broad smile on his face.

"Are they all right, then? And Caitlin? When can I see her?"

"You have a handsome boy and a beautiful girl, and they're both fine. Just over six pounds, both of them."

"Six pounds—that's small, isn't it?"

"Not really. It's within normal range and actually quite big for twins. As for Caitlin, she's exhausted, but that's to be expected. She's doing well, and they're getting her settled in her room. Now go see your children, and by then Caitlin should be ready to see you."

Ciarán stared at the two little souls lying in the nursery, one in a pink cap and one in blue. His eyes teared over, and he wondered how he'd never felt this overwhelming emotion when he'd seen his fifth-century children. *Because they never let me feel anything for them. They were the goddess's, not mine.* He swallowed the lump in his throat, wishing he could hold Fionn and Aisling in his arms and press them to himself, wanting to assure them he'd keep them safe and warm. But most of all, to let them know he was their father and always would be.

"If you'd like to come with me now, I'll take you to Mrs. Donnelly," the nurse said. "But you can't stay long. Having a baby is exhausting, and she needs a good night's sleep. You do as well," she added.

"No fear there," he said with a smile. "Me *mamaí* will be making sure of that." He cast a huge grin in Mary's direction, all the worries of the past few months evaporating as if they had never existed. He was home, with his family, and happier than he'd ever been.

CHAPTER 11

Caitlin watched her husband nestle their daughter into the double stroller they'd received at her baby shower. She really was lucky to have found him. Not only was he handsome in the extreme, with thick raven-black hair and deep blue eyes that darkened to a midnight blue at the edge of his irises, he was gentle and brave as well. And he had a heart the size of Texas. Okay, so he did have a bit of a backstory, but she loved teaching him about the twentieth century. For the most part, he embraced it—except for planes. They'd been across the ocean twice now, and he'd upchucked his lunch and most of his stomach both times.

He turned to take Fionn from her arms and smiled. And how could she forget that smile? It would melt an ice cube in the Yukon. Best of all, he was completely hers. He may have betrayed his goddess fifteen hundred years ago, but he'd never cheat on her. Of that she felt sure. Besides, just let some woman try to steal him. She'd send her from here to Canarsie.

Ciarán reached for her hand. "Ready," he said.

She nodded and inched out of the car. It wasn't easy with a series of stitches up her belly, but she leaned on

Ciarán and straightened up. At least she wasn't walking crouched over like a ninety-year-old woman anymore. Managing the steps to her apartment building, however, was another story, one which seemed to leave Ciarán in a dilemma.

"I can do this," she said. "It's been over a week. The doctor said not to keep going up and down the stairs, but going up once will be fine."

Their neighbor Mrs. Krauss was just coming down the steps. "Oh, they're finally home. Such beautiful babies, but then what else would they be with you two for parents?"

"Thank you, Sophie," Caitlin said.

"But you do have a bit of a problem, don't you?" She looked up at Ciarán, and his brow crinkled. "Mr. Krauss and I had the same problem after my Herbert was born." Aisling was starting to fuss, and Sophie sat down on the steps, tickling her under the chin. You get your wife up the stoop. I'll watch over the little ones while you do."

Ciarán hesitated, but the woman smiled. "Go on. I'm not going to run off with them, and Caitlin's going to need those big strong arms of yours to help her up. My Henry used to have arms like those, God rest his soul."

Caitlin tugged at Ciarán's shirt. "It was only a dream, and she's right. I'm not sure I can navigate those steps without a little help."

He nodded, scooping her up in his arms and hurrying up the front steps, though she noticed his eyes kept flicking back to the twins. No doubt he'd leave her stranded there if their neighbor made any move away from the building. Perhaps she should be a little jealous, but the truth was she'd do the same if their roles were reversed. In fact, his attendance to their needs made him all the more endearing.

Letting her down by the elevator, he darted back down the outside steps, taking a moment to charm Mrs. Krauss and thank her for watching the twins. The older woman laughed and tapped him on the arm. Ciarán bent over, checking the twins were secure before lifting the carriage and carrying it up the stoop to the safety of the building's foyer. From there on, it was easy going.

"I took next week off." Ciarán tucked Fionn in his bassinet before checking on Aisling once more. "After that, I'm thinking we should get someone to help out until you're feeling better."

"I'm feeling fine." Caitlin stretched out her legs on the love seat, glad to be home.

Ciarán sat on the other end, lifting her bare feet onto his lap and massaging them. "The doctor said no bending, no lifting, no pushing, no pulling for six to eight weeks."

"I don't think the twins count." God, he gave a good foot massage. "I am breastfeeding them, you know."

"And I'll see ye have them when they grow hungry or any other time ye're wanting to hold them, but ye'll not be lifting them yerself."

"If you think I'm sitting on this sofa like Cleopatra for the next eight weeks, you're out of your thickheaded Irish mind." With that, she put her feet on the floor and pushed herself off the couch.

"What are ye doing, now?"

"Getting something to eat. I'm hungry. Do you mind?"

"I do. 'Tis more than just yerself ye've got to be thinking o' now, so sit down and tell me what it is ye're wanting."

She rolled her eyes and plopped back on the couch. "Pizza and maybe some garlic knots." Ciarán grabbed his wallet, then cast his eyes in the twins' direction. "They're not going anywhere," she said.

"Not unless ye take it in yer head to pick them up."

"Then ye'd better get going while they're asleep."

He frowned, obviously debating whether he should go or not. Instead, he headed toward the bedroom.

"Hey, what about my pizza?"

"They deliver. I'm going to call. Are ye wanting anything else?"

"No." Caitlin scrunched her face up in disappointment, but Ciarán had no sooner left the room than Caitlin got up and stood by the bassinets. "Your daddy thinks he can outsmart me. Silly man. I do worry that he's going to have a nervous breakdown if he doesn't stop fussing over us, though." Aisling stuck her hand in her mouth and started sucking away. "Oh, are you hungry, sweetheart?" Caitlin reached down and picked up her daughter, sitting in the rocking chair beside the bassinet and baring her breast. The baby latched on and was happily sucking away when Ciarán returned. Caitlin smiled up at him as he entered the room, but his blue eyes flared with silver specks. He was not happy.

"Did ye not hear what the doctor said? Ye're not to be doing any lifting."

"She's barely six pounds! My jeans probably weigh more than she does. Stop being so ridiculous."

"That settles it. I'm having a woman come and sit with ye while I'm at work."

"The hell you are! I'm not an invalid, and I don't want someone else taking care of my children when I'm perfectly capable."

"No, ye'd rather die and leave us all behind."

"Stop being so dramatic. I was hardly dying." She held Aisling over her shoulder to pat her back, but when the infant let out a burp, Ciarán insisted on laying her back in the bassinet.

"D'ye want Fionn as well?" He had his back to her, staring down at their son.

"Does he look like he's hungry?"

"He's eating his fist." He lifted the baby in his arms and kissed his head.

Caitlin watched how tender he was. Something more was going on in that gorgeous head of his, though, something more than just being protective of her and the children, but he was keeping it to himself. If he had a flaw, that was certainly it. He bottled everything up inside, believing he could deal with it and shelter those he loved.

"It's those dreams, isn't it? I hoped once the babies came, they would stop."

"I'm sorry, *a chuisle*." He laid Fionn in her arms and sat on the edge of the bed. "'Tis more than that. What if I screw it all up? They're so small and depending on me to keep them safe. What if I can't?"

"Then no one can. You'd give your life for them. I know that. But you need to stay around if you want to protect them."

"I'm not going anywhere."

"You're going to make yourself sick if you don't stop this nonsense. And it all leads back to those silly dreams, doesn't it?"

Ciarán got up and walked over to the window, staring at the street below. "I can't control me dreams."

"No, but you can control how much impact they have on your life."

"Ye're right" He spun around, smiling before he came over to give her a kiss on the forehead. "I am going to pamper ye a bit, though . . . if ye don't mind." He cast a glance down at their newborn son. "Ye've given me two grand gifts. 'Tis only fair I give ye a little service in return."

"Hmmm, we're going to have to wait a few weeks for the real servicing."

Ciarán's eyebrows lifted, the dimples in his cheeks deepening. "Mrs. Donnelly! Are ye suggesting I pay with me body?"

"Right from the tip of your tongue." She grinned up at him, and a twinkle lit the silver specks in his eyes.

"I can start that bit right now." He leaned over, but their lips had barely touched when a tiny screech rose from Aisling's bassinet, and Ciarán rested his forehead against Caitlin's. "Maybe not just yet. She can't be hungry again already, can she?"

"No, but she might need her diaper changed."

He jumped up. "Ah, I can do that. I've been practicing on a doll, under the auspices of Mary Monaghan."

"Well, you can't do better than that." As if to concur, Fionn let out a burp that was way too big for a child his size, and Caitlin and Ciarán laughed so hard tears were running down their cheeks.

****

Ciarán caught a glimpse of Father Michael as they pulled up to the church. He was already dressed in his white vestments, greeting the families of the other children who were to be christened that day, but he slipped away the moment he caught sight of them. Mary was there as well, in her best Sunday pillbox hat and yellow suit. The rest of the

Monaghans stood off to the side while she and Father Mike took charge of the twins. Father Dennis and Steve were there as well, grinning from ear to ear. If only Aodhán and Niamh had been able to come . . . and Daniel . . . and all of his Irish family. He shook his head, happy for the family he did have around him.

At least Father Mike had agreed they could still have Aodhán and Niamh as the godparents, even though they weren't here. Father Dennis and Mary would stand as their proxies or something like that. He didn't care what it was called as long as it was possible.

Caitlin stepped out of the cab and beamed up at him. He didn't think he'd ever seen her look so radiant. She wore a pretty gingham two-piece suit, with ruffles just under the elbows, and a light blue pillbox hat on her head. Her cheeks were blushed with the slightest touch of pink, and her lips were dabbed with a matching color that shone and looked good enough to eat.

Father Mike handed Aisling to Dennis. "Much as I'd love to stay, we do have other wee ones being brought into the fold today, so I'd best get to greeting their families as well."

Aisling reached up and touched Dennis on the chin, causing the man to smile. "Hello there, sweetheart. You remember your Uncle Dennis, don't you?"

"Come on, then, Mrs. Monaghan," Steve said, "let someone else have a go." Mary frowned, relinquishing Fionn, but not before giving the child a kiss on the forehead.

Ciarán felt something warm and gentle tug at his heart. They were his family, a real one, and they all cared about each other, even Tiernan Monaghan. They'd become good friends the previous Christmas, and that friendship had only grown around Easter, when Caitlin had informed Ciarán of Mary's scheme to make him jealous that first Christmas after he'd awoken. It had worked, and he could kiss Mary for it.

"We'd best be getting these babies inside," Mary finally said. "I've reserved the front rows on the right." Ciarán went to take Fionn from Dennis, but Mary nudged him away. "Never mind, Fionn. We'll take care of them. You just concentrate on getting your wife inside."

"I'm fine, Mary," Caitlin said.

It had been six weeks since the births, and Ciarán knew she was getting weary of reminding everyone she didn't need to be pampered anymore. Regardless, she let him take her arm and escort her into church.

Ciarán headed toward the front of the church as Mary had instructed, but the pews looked pretty crowded to him. He supposed they would be with all the Monaghans present. They'd probably left the first row empty, though. He smiled and kissed Caitlin on the cheek as they hurried down the aisle, Mary on his heels with Fionn. But as he got closer, he realized the front row was occupied as well. He began to turn back toward Mary to ask directions, but as he did, the man in the first pew shifted to face him, a broad grin crossing his face.

"Aodhán!" Ciarán had to control himself to keep from shouting. Without thinking, he grabbed his brother into a hug, then pulled back to wipe away a tear that had escaped. "What are ye doing here?"

"Ye want us to leave, then?" Aodhán said, sniffling back his own emotion.

"God, no! I mean . . . I didn't think ye could make it."

"Ye didn't think we'd be missing such a grand occasion, now did ye?" Niamh stuck her head around Aodhán's shoulder, her eyes sparkling with mischief.

Ciarán could barely contain his joy, but when he looked back to the surrounding pews, his heart swelled so he thought it would burst. Not only the Monaghans were there, but Mrs. Byrne and Daniel as well, along with the Flynns—little Kathleen practically jumping up and down with glee. Ryan and Chris were there as well, and even Father Seamus.

He swallowed to hold back the tears, but Caitlin had no such inhibitions. Happy tears slid down her cheeks as she tried to hug them all, but Mary bustled them into the front pew just in time. Bells rang as Father Michael came in, followed by his fellow priests. Panic rose in Ciarán's throat, momentarily replacing the joy. *Where is Fionn?* A quick look to the side calmed his fears, for Aodhán and Niamh held the twins, secure in their arms, as well they should, given they were to be their godparents.

Another tear snuck down his cheek, but he didn't wipe it away. He cherished it, for it represented the happiness that filled his heart, and he said an earnest prayer of thanksgiving for all the gifts he'd been granted.

****

Caitlin and Ciarán held their sleeping twins while Father Michael began the ceremony. "What names have ye given yer children?"

Ciarán's voice shook, and Caitlin wondered if he was recalling his own baptism fifteen hundred years ago, or if he was just overwhelmed by the small bundle he held, the same as she was. And yet somehow they both managed to say the names they'd chosen.

"What do ye ask o' God's Church for yer children?"

A warmth suffused her heart as they replied, "Baptism."

"In asking for baptism for yer children . . ." Father Michael continued.

Ciarán bent over and kissed her on the head. Further prayers were said until at last it was time for the actual baptism. Tears of happiness filled Caitlin's eyes as she and Ciarán carried their children to the baptismal font, followed by Aodhán and Niamh. Father Mike beamed at them, his eyes twinkling, and Caitlin was sure she could her Mary sniffling in the crowd of parishioners.

Once again, Father Michael spoke. "Is it yer will, therefore, that Fionn Michael should receive baptism in the faith o' the Church, which we have all professed with ye?"

Ciarán smiled, squeezing her hand, and they replied that it was. Fionn blinked as Michael poured water over his head but didn't seem too bothered by it all. Then Father Michael turned to their daughter and asked the same question of them, to which they replied that they did.

Aisling sighed in her sleep and grasped her father's finger as Father Michael poured the water over her head.

"Aisling Marie, I baptize ye in the name o' the Father . . . and o' the Son . . . and o' the Holy Spirit. Blessed be God, who chose ye in Christ."

Caitlin gazed down at the wonderful little beings they held in their arms. She hadn't really thought about it while she was pregnant. First, she had been so sick, and then she couldn't seem to get comfortable, and they were busy getting ready for them. But now, in the quiet of the moment, in this holy place, with her husband standing next to her and the babies in their arms, it washed over her like a gentle summer breeze, engulfing her with its warmth and contentment. They were neither her nor Ciarán, and yet they were both of them a true testament to their love—no matter what the future may bring.

The christening party was at Mary's, and Caitlin would have thought that Ciarán was indeed one of her sons, the way she fussed over the babies, bragging what good-looking children they were and how well behaved. And Uncle Mike! Not having any children of his own, Caitlin was his family, and this afternoon he was outdoing Mary for bragging rights.

At last, Ciarán and Caitlin were able to slip away to a quiet corner of the small backyard at Mary's Queens home. Caitlin leaned back against his shoulder, melting in the warmth of his embrace, utterly exhausted.

"Do you think anyone would notice if we took a small nap?"

"I won't be telling if ye don't. Why d'ye think I wandered out to this bench, strategically located behind that hyacinth bush?" He leaned back against the tree that held up the wooden bench.

She could feel the grin on his face and cuddled deeper into his shoulder "I knew it wasn't just your ancient good looks that won me over."

"Hmm, how d'ye know 'twasn't some spell I put ye under?"

"Well, if it was, kindly keep that information to yourself. I'm enjoying it."

A chuckle rumbled in his chest, and he let out a relaxed sigh. "As ye wish," he said, though she could hear his voice drifting off.

She woke to find herself sitting on the ground, Ciarán bent over, his elbows on his knees, his hands raking through his hair. "What happened? Are you all right?"

"'Tis nothing. Just another dream. 'Twas Ruadhán, standing next to that bush, and he held the twins. Ye and I were tied to the tree, and he just watched us, laughing as we struggled to get free, but we couldn't."

"It was just a dream." Caitlin got up, brushing off her suit, and sat back down on the bench. "You know that, right?" She touched his cheek, and he managed a weak smile.

"I want to believe that's all it is, but ye know how me dreams work."

"Not exactly spot on, though I get your meaning." She scrunched her face up, and he let out the hint of a laugh. "But Ruadhán's dead, has been for about fifteen hundred years, I imagine. So what do you think they mean?"

He shook his head, leaning back against the tree once more and taking her hand in his. "I don't know, but I'm not getting any sleep between them and the wee ones."

Caitlin sat up straighter so she could look at him. "Okay, so maybe we need to analyze the ones we know you've had. You dreamed about Bradaigh attacking me, only it wasn't me at first, it was Aisling."

"Until I fell in love with ye, then 'twas yerself I saw."

"And when was that?" She grinned at him, and his cerulean-blue eyes sparkled with mischief.

"As soon as I bloody opened that rectory door, wasn't it, ye wee nymph."

She giggled and squeezed his hand. "I might have been fighting it, but that's when I fell in love with you as well, you know."

"Did ye now?" He kissed her on the lips, his mouth warm and soft. "But that's not solving me dreams, now is it?"

"No, you're right. So you saw Bradaigh killing me, but in reality all he got to do was fondle me a bit. And while he hurt you, it wasn't a mortal wound, thank God. Though it was touch and go for a while."

He frowned. "But he would have killed ye if I hadn't come along when I did. What is it Tiernan says, it was his MO."

She touched his cheek, glad he and Tiernan had become such friends. "But that's just it. You did come along. And the dream you had on our honeymoon warned you there was danger, but what else did you see?"

"I don't remember much about it. I just knew something was wrong and I had to get back to Mrs. Byrne's."

"Well, whatever it was, you stopped him again, so it didn't turn out the way it was in your dream."

"Niamh might not completely agree with ye there."

"Actually, I think she would. Though I'm afraid as far as she's concerned it was Aodhán that was really her knight in shining armor."

"We weren't allowed to wear any sort o' armor." He grinned, and Caitlin could feel the tension draining from his muscular frame.

"Besides, don't you have a lot of dreams about your past? Maybe that's it. Weren't your fifth-century children taken away by Ruadhán?"

"I do have dreams o' me past, but 'twasn't Ruadhán who took me children from me. 'Twas I who took them from their mothers and handed them over to their grandfathers. Bréanainn was seven before I went back for him, and even then 'twas I who took him from Killian, his grandfather."

"Then that's it!" she said. "In those seven years, you didn't get to see them, did you?"

Ciarán bit his bottom lip. "So ye're thinking 'tis that loss I'm reliving, as it were?"

"Maybe. It was Ruadhán who saw that you abided by the rules, right?"

He tilted his head back and forth a few times, obviously considering her explanation, before finally letting a smile tug his cheek. "I suppose it could be, especially seeing there's no way Ruadhán betrayed the goddess and got himself entombed alive."

"Meaning that he isn't about to wake up in the twentieth century."

"I didn't know 'twas such a wise woman I was marrying." He had just bent to kiss her again when a wail went up from the other side of the bushes and Father Dennis came around them, holding one very unhappy Aisling.

"I think she might be hungry." He handed her over to Caitlin, then scurried away.

"Coward!" Ciarán called after him. "Now if me little darlings would just sleep through the night, we might actually have a normal night's rest."

Caitlin laughed. "Good luck with that. Everyone keeps telling me this is the easy part."

Ciarán's expression reflected mock horror. "Then Lord help us." He put his arm around her, letting Aisling grasp his finger, and watched lovingly as she fed their daughter.

CHAPTER 12

Ruadhán gazed at the stone pedestal that had once held the Book of Carraig. Heat rushed up his neck to the tip of his ears, and his hands trembled with anger. Could it be true? He had no doubt that rebellious upstart and his brother had dared to enter the Cave of Rúin Ársa, but to remove the sacred book from its confines as well? It was a sacrilege. Ruadhán was stunned the goddess had not stricken them down on the spot.

He clenched his fists, trying to calm the fury bubbling up in his gut. True, they had been a special gift from the goddess—two born as one, but that dark-haired Ciarán had always been the rebellious sort, far too inquisitive for his own good. To think there was a time Ruadhán feared the younger twin, Aodhán, would hold him back. In the end, it was he that had been led astray by Ciarán. And yet it appeared the goddess had seen fit to let them live, forgiven them their treachery?

Sitting on a nearby boulder, he closed his eyes and let his mind clear. No, not the goddess of their *túath*, but another jealous goddess perhaps . . . or this new god of theirs. That was possible, he supposed. And now his goddess had awakened him to set things right. The question was how.

First, he must make certain that it was true, and that the twentieth-century Ciarán and Aodhán the villagers spoke of were indeed his wayward priests. After all, it was possible they weren't. As he'd already conjectured, they could simply be Ciarán's descendants. And as for the empty tombs . . . His fifth-century betrayers may have already been dead when the caves were opened, or perhaps the goddess had whisked them away to the otherworld. He gave an incredulous grunt. Along with their burial slabs and sacred candles as well? Highly unlikely.

He rubbed his newly shaved chin, deep in thought. From what he could gather at the inn he'd been staying at in Castlebar, Ciarán and Aodhán had confronted a serial killer over this way last year and succeeded in ending his reign of terror. Ruadhán had no doubt it was his reprobate high priest, Bradaigh. That was easily gleaned from Father Seamus's cluttered mind even before he headed for Castlebar, but the fact that Ciarán and Aodhán been able to overcome him was surprising. His power was far greater than theirs. But then, of course, they had absconded with the Book of Carraig. Clearly, Ciarán had managed to decipher the meaning of a certain passage that referred to the power of the triad.

He shook his head. Together, he and Aodhán would have been a formidable force. There was no question why the goddess had chosen them. If they had only used their skills *for her* instead of to betray her. Ruadhán sighed, quelling the fury that continued to rumble in his stomach, or was it hunger this time?

Patience, the lady whispered to him.

With a shake of his head, he reached down and picked up his satchel, taking out the food he'd brought with him. The twentieth century! He had so much more to learn. At least he'd mastered their language and form of dress. It felt odd without his beard, though it was for the best. Should he come face-to-face with one of the little miscreants, he wouldn't want them to recognize him, not at first anyway. They wouldn't be expecting him to survive, that was certain, so he did have that on his side. At worst, he might need to block their minds, though he couldn't be sure how effective that would be. If his fifth-century recreants had indeed survived, their powers would have as well, and even as fledgling priests they had commanded considerable skill. Nowhere near his, of course, but strong enough to be a hindrance to his plans.

He frowned and touched the torc around his neck. It was such a shame. Ciarán could easily have reached the high priesthood one day, maybe even assumed his own role as chief priest. Instead, the man had chosen to betray his goddess and violate her holy precinct. Rage filled his heart once more. Perhaps *he* should simply strike the pair of them down before they could even realize who he was. But what of the sacred book? No, he must bide his time.

"Patience," he said, the word whispered on the morning dew. "They will pay for the desecration they have wrought."

While in Castlebar, he'd also learned a good deal more about the white-haired guardian he'd seen after he'd first awoken. An archaeologist, one who studied the past through excavation and the study of artifacts, the book of words said. One of the locals had referred to him as Professor Daniel Lambert. In time, he would make his acquaintance, but not just yet, and not up at the tombs. No sense tempting fate.

It appeared the man had been keeping an eye on Tuamaí Dearmadta, assuring no one further violated the site. He laughed to himself. Ciarán was probably afraid someone would discover who he was and seal him back inside. That was an idea, only this time he'd make sure no one could unseal it. For now, however, he was simply grateful he wouldn't have to deal with any additional renegade priests roaming the countryside.

It was still early in the morning, the sun just barely above the horizon, so all was quiet save the sound of birdsong. Ruadhán took a deep breath, savoring the freshness of the crisp summer air, and unwrapped his breakfast: eggs and a delicious delicacy called bacon between two pieces of bread. He had always sensed Ciarán would be trouble, but what was it about the man that caused him to despise him so?

Did he resent the priest's talents? It was obvious he possessed far more skill than he should have as a neophyte priest. No, he would have taken pleasure preparing him for his own position. Perhaps he was angered by the attention Domnall paid him and his brother? He shook his head. Then why not feel the same animosity toward Aodhán? It was something more, something he'd buried for years, centuries as it turned out, but what?

He took a bite of his sandwich, relishing the smoky taste of the meat, and thought deeper. Domnall was his best friend. Did he begrudge him the joy the young priest brought him? No, in fact, he wished he'd had the chance to know such a relationship himself. But that was at the core of his resentment, wasn't it?

He opened the small carton of orange juice and took a drink. As much as he cared for Domnall, he had never truly forgiven him for shirking his responsibility. The position of chief priest should have been Domnall's. Ailbe had groomed him for it since his birth, and he was the eldest, not that their position of birth really mattered. It would ultimately be the decision of the Ancient Ones. Domnall had never given them the chance, though, had he?

Putting down his drink, Ruadhán starred into the darkened cave. But his indignation went even deeper. Ailbe had been chosen as a guardian of the goddess, and so he had given her sons, himself and Domnall being two of them. That honor too had been offered to Domnall. But while he had scorned the position of chief priest, he had been more than willing to accept that appointment, relegating Ruadhán to caring for the creatures of the sea.

Ruadhán hadn't really minded that. He could remain a priest and take a wife, but when Domnall had rejected the chief priesthood as well, all Ruadhán's hopes of a family had been crushed. Within a month, he had been elevated to high priest and set on the path to become chief priest himself. Domnall had never even considered the ramifications of his refusal for anyone else. Twice he had blocked Ruadhán's way to having a child of his own.

He took another bite of his sandwich. And Ciarán was just like Domnall: reckless and headstrong, and yes, selfish. Somewhere along the line, he had forgiven Domnall, become content in his position, but a seed of resentment still lingered. Ciarán reminded him of all Domnall had denied him. Had Ciarán not done the same? Had his betrayal not altered all their lives in one way or another?

The seed of an idea was forming in his brain. A way he might yet have his own children. Children with the goddess, but how? The kernel was mired in a boggy summer fog, a fairy dream.

Grunting an oath, he shoved the rest of the sandwich in his mouth and, picking up his satchel, entered the Cave of Rúin Ársa. He would see Ciarán paid for his dismissive behavior and for the betrayal of all Ruadhán held dear. But for now, he'd check the sacred precincts to make sure the secret compartment hewn into the stone had not been compromised. Ciarán may have entered to steal the Book of Carraig, but even he wouldn't know of this hidden sanctum deep within the recesses of the cave.

Moving to the edge of the vast chasm that yawned at the rear of the cavernous chamber, he inched his way to the right, stepping out on a ledge concealed by the cave wall itself and the blackness of the abyss. He bent down, shifting the stone at its base, and snapped his fingers to light a flame that illuminated the interior of the compartment. Thank the goddess, the ceremonial items were still there, including the ornamental Lann na Leorghnimh, the Blade of Atonement and the sacred Claíomh na Ailbe, the Sword of Ailbe. He retrieved the Cup of Cheartais from his satchel along with the Veil of Cinniúna and placed them inside the small recess.

He would keep his personal accoutrements, along with the Scian na Lúin, tucked up in the loft of the cottage he'd just purchased. It was laughable how effortless it had been to arrange for a well-appointed bank account and history for himself. These men were so easily manipulated. By the time they noticed anything was amiss, he would be well on his way. Given what he now knew, however, Ciarán might not be so easily influenced, but as for the rest . . .

Ruadhán rubbed his chin again. Between the elimination of his beard and long hair, along with the addition of the eye adornment they called *glasses*, surely he wouldn't be recognized. He didn't have those hypnotic blue eyes like Domnall and his two youngest sons, didn't stand out in a crowd the way they had. The thought brought his old friend's image to mind. In spite of the hint of resentment he still nurtured toward him, Ruadhán missed his brother. If only Domnall had remained loyal to the goddess as the new religion swept the land, they might be here together.

So he could do all in his power to protect his traitorous sons? Ruadhán grunted as he put the stone back in place, concealing the hidden niche once more. No, Domnall had forsaken the goddess. She had chosen Ruadhán for a reason. He let out a weary sign. But how to best serve her?

Patience, mo mhac dílis, the goddess whispered again. *All in good time.*

As you wish, my lady. He snapped his fingers and extinguished the flame still burning at his side. With a sigh, his knees creaking, he stood and made his way back out of the cave, waving his hand to roll the enormous entrance stone back into place. *But I cannot act unless I know what it is you want of me.*

Patience, and all will be revealed, the voice of the goddess echoed once more.

****

Ruadhán's new home was quite different from the one he'd known back in the fifth century. At the time, he thought it had been quite comfortable, but he had to admit, the furnishing of his new abode far surpassed it. He sat back in the cushioned chair, drinking a glass of something they called Guinness—an excellent brew regardless of its name.

A soft summer breeze blew in through the window, carrying the scent of fresh morning dew and the nutty aroma of the *aiteann* that sat just outside his door, its yellow flowers almost always in bloom. It brought back the memory of Ostara and the Beltane celebrations that he'd so loved and was a sign of hope and light in the darkest of times. Ruadhán smiled to himself. The goddess was sending him a message. All would be well again if he just had patience.

Tomorrow he would put his plan in motion by acquainting himself with the white-haired chief of the archaeologists, Professor Daniel Lambert. Once he got to know him, he could better assess the situation and slowly ingratiate himself with Aodhán. He'd need to be careful there, for he was still unsure if he had changed his looks enough to fool the young priest.

He stood and gazed into the looking glass by the door and chuckled as he recalled the look on the barber's face when he'd gone to get his hair cut in Castlebar. Though he'd attempted to remove some of the lime-touched locks himself, he hadn't done a very good job, and it looked as if someone had taken a cleaver to it.

What on earth did ye do to yerself? the man had said. *Did ye just dunk bits o' yer hair into a bottle o' bleach, then try to hack it off?*

It was an experiment, Ruadhán had replied. *One that didn't turn out very well.*

Fortunately, the man had accepted his explanation and had done an excellent job of repairing what he called *the damage.* While he was there, he'd had the young man shave his beard as well, and when finished went to purchase a pair of glasses.

He touched his cheek and sighed. Never had he thought he'd seek to conceal his priestly mark, but under the circumstances he knew the goddess would approve. Though he'd mixed up a lotion that successfully covered the triskele on his cheek, he would have to use clothing to conceal the remaining tattoos. To that end, he'd stopped in a small clothing shop in Castlebar. A sweet *cailín* had happily suggested some thin long-sleeved *léine* for the summer when he'd mentioned he wanted to hide the scars he'd received during the war. After reading about World War II, he thought that would be a suitable explanation. It appeared it was.

The next step had been to establish himself as a respected member of the community, a retired teacher from Dublin, looking forward to enjoying his leisure time. The trip to Dublin had been tiring but necessary if he hoped to acquire a believable identity. Back in his time, such an endeavor would have been far easier, but after a bit of digging around he'd discovered an adequate subject. The man who called himself Cormac McGuire was leaving the next day for his planned retirement in a place called California. Having now discovered its location, he determined it was far enough away so no one would be able to challenge his identity.

Now all that was left was to make the acquaintance of Professor Lambert and Aodhán Donnelly, as he called himself. Between the two of them, Ruadhán would be able to learn more about Ciarán. Perhaps the lady would let him know what her intentions were by then.

****

Aodhán grumbled as Niamh nudged his shoulder, rolling over and pulling up the covers she'd yanked off him just moments before.

"'Tis time to get up, darlin'." She leaned over, running her fingers over his bare shoulder as she whispered in his ear. "Ye've got to be meeting with Daniel this morning."

"Sure, they'll all be staying in bed a bit longer as well." The flight had sent his internal clock into chaos, and he hadn't fallen asleep till just before dawn.

"I told ye not to be taking a nap when we got home, now didn't I? None of us did, only yerself, and now ye're paying for it. And don't be looking to me for sympathy. I doubt ye'll find any from Professor Lambert either, so ye'd best be getting up. I'm off to the school." She gave him a peck on the cheek, then headed for the bedroom door, stopping just before leaving. "And don't be going back to sleep."

"All right, I won't." He sat up just in time to see her head down the stairs. She wasn't wrong. That nap he'd taken had thrown everything off. Well, it wasn't the first time he'd functioned on two or three hours' sleep. Blinking, he stared out the window, listening to the sweet song of a robin and trying to keep his eyes from closing again. The sun's rays shone through the sheer curtains, warming his body and carrying him away to another time, centuries before.

****

Aodhán frowned at his brother as they knelt on the lake shore. His knees were sore, and he could barely keep his eyes open, though he knew falling asleep would only bring more punishment. Ciarán knelt beside him, his eyes on the distant shore, and Aodhán gave him a sharp nudge on the shoulder.

"You were sleeping, were you not?" Aodhán pressed his lips together, but if the truth be known, he was in awe of his brother's ability to appear awake while deep in slumber.

"What?" Ciarán said. "Of course not. How could one be awake and asleep at the same time?"

"I do not know. Perhaps you will tell me one day." Ciarán opened his mouth to comment, but Aodhán narrowed his eyes. "Do not lie to me, brother. Master Ruadhán may not have caught on to your trick, but I know you far too well. I do not begrudge you the skill. I only wish I could master it as well."

Ciarán grinned. "It is the only time I bother to practice *dercad*. So you see, I am doing something that would please Master Domnall."

"It would not please him to know you were doing it while you were to be contemplating what you have done wrong." Aodhán frowned at his friend, but as usual, it did no good.

"Is *dercad* not deep contemplation?"

"It is not meant for that, and you know it. Besides, you are not contemplating anything while you sleep."

"I am sorry, my friend. It was rude of me to leave you alone to bear our punishment, especially since it was because of me we were so chastised."

"I knew what you were about." Aodhán shifted his knees on the sandy dirt. "'Tis my own fault and myself I am angry at, not you."

"It really is easy to do," Ciarán said. "Just stare out across the lake and let it's tranquil waves carry you away."

"But if we are caught, we will receive thrice the penalty."

"We will not be caught unless you decide to confess all to Master Ruadhán."

"I would never betray you, brother, but he will find out just the same. He always does."

"Ciarán!" a voice echoed throughout the lakeside grove. They had been found out. "Did you think you could escape my wrath?"

"I did not, master. Am I not kneeling here within the lady's grove, doing homage to her?"

"I am well aware of your gifts, Ciarán, and your ability to feign your state of being. Just as you have convinced Domnall that you sleep when your mind is set on wandering the countryside as soon as he leaves your presence, so too can you feign your wakefulness."

Ciarán shot a wounded glance in Aodhán's direction, but it was not him who answered.

Ruadhán let out a hearty laugh. "Your friend did not tell me. He did not need to. You give yourself away by the lack of concern in your eyes when punishment is inflicted. Even now there is a sparkle of humor there, a glint of superiority that makes you think you have outsmarted me, but you have not. You shall kneel here, within the temple of your goddess, until I see true sorrow in those eyes of yours. They may charm Domnall, just as he uses his own to win the favor of others, but they will not lure me into your web of deception."

The man sat on the ground and spread an array of delicious morsels before him. "And do not think of attempting to deceive me again. I will be here beside you to assure you do not sleep until the sun sets to herald yet another day."

"But the sun has just set, master."

"It has." Ruadhán chucked a piece of cheese in his mouth and grinned. "As you have slept through your first punishment, I have chosen to extend it for yet another period." Turning to Aodhán, he frowned. "As for you! You kept his secret and thus are just as guilty."

"No!" Ciarán said. "He did not know, master. And only guessed moments before you appeared."

Ruadhán peered into Ciarán's tear-filled eyes. "So that is what it takes to elicit the proper reaction from you." He threw a glance in Aodhán's direction. "You shall share in my judgment and kneel beside your brother till the sun sets once more."

"Please, master," Ciarán said. "I will do twice the time you have decreed, but do not punish another for my transgressions."

"Silence!" Ruadhán's voice echoed throughout the grove. "Aodhán could have spoken the moment I walked into the grove, but he chose not to. Now kneel, the two of you, and be thankful you are not yet priests. Your loyalty is first and foremost to your goddess and her priesthood. This will serve as a lesson to you both."

"I am sorry, *mo chara*." A tear ran down Ciarán's cheek, and he hung his head as he knelt back on the dew dampened ground.

A mist had started to fall, making their situation all the more miserable, and Aodhán hesitated. Master Ruadhán was not being fair. Whether Ciarán had slept or not, they had still spent the last twelve hours kneeling on the scratchy lakeshore.

"Aodhán!" Ruadhán grabbed him by the arm, his tone stern and unforgiving. "Accept the consequences of your transgressions or see yourself banished from the priesthood and your *túath*." Ruadhán tightened his grip, green and yellow sparks igniting in his hazel eyes. "Do not defy me, bard!"

"I am sorry, Master Ruadhán. We did not mean to escape our punishment."

****

"Aodhán!" A hand shook him again, but the voice was soft, not the harsh tones of the chief priest. He blinked to clear his vision.

"What are ye talking about?" Niamh said. "It wasn't a punishment, and ye've no one to blame but yerself for not wanting to be getting up." She kissed him on the cheek and he sat up, grinning, the feel of her lips gently jolting him back to the present.

"Now that'll be waking me up. If ye could do it a time or two more, maybe on the lips this time, I'm sure I'll not be drifting off again."

"Ye drift off again," Niamh said, "and 'twill be a bucket o' water I'll be dumping over yer head. Now up with ye. I've got to be off to work, and ye do as well."

He tousled his hair and threw his legs over the edge of the bed. "I'm up, though I can't say I want to be."

"Hmm, maybe ye'll listen me next time we go to the States. What were ye dreaming about anyway, and who's Ruadhán?"

"Our chief priest, and he was scolding Ciarán and I for being in trouble again." He held up his hand to cut her off. "And don't be asking what we were in trouble for. Only the Lord above knows. We were always being reprimanded for one thing or the other."

"Did he beat ye, then, this Ruadhán?"

"Beat us? I only wish we would have gotten off that easily. No, we'd be made to kneel before the lake, praying for hours on end to the lake goddess until she determined we'd repented enough, or we'd be given some odious chore day after day on end until she felt we'd done enough penance."

"And who judged when she was satisfied?"

Aodhán laughed. "Ruadhán, o' course. I'm not sure he really cared for either of us, though he seemed fond o' Domnall."

"Yer father, ye mean."

Aodhán nodded, stretching as he rubbed the back of his neck. "I haven't thought about Ruadhán in a good while, though Ciarán confided he'd been dreaming o' him a good bit o' late."

"And what does that mean?" Fear shot through Niamh's eyes. "Ye'll not have to be going up against another o' them, will ye?"

Aodhán pulled her down on his lap. "There's no need for ye to be worrying that sweet head o' yers. To begin with, Ruadhán wasn't a wicked man. He was just trying to teach us right from wrong."

"Are ye sure o' that? From the way ye were calling out, 'tis not the impression I got."

Aodhán kissed her forehead. "I was no more than eleven or twelve at the time and probably more annoyed that I couldn't be off playing than anything else. As for having to face Ruadhán again, 'tis not likely to happen. He would never have been condemned to Tuamaí Dearmadta, so he'll not be waking up, now will he?"

"And why not? Ye spoke of some ancient tombs where the other priests were buried. Suppose he's in one of them?"

"The Hills of ár Sinsear? Unlike Ciarán and I, the priests laid to rest there were already dead when they were interred, so there's no chance they'll be waking up."

"Then why the dreams?"

"They're naught but dreams, *a chuisle*, so rest easy." Aodhán kissed her on the lips this time, savoring the sweet taste of mint on her breath and wishing they could both go back to bed. Reluctantly, he finally pulled away, the deep kiss becoming a peck and then nothing more than a brush of his lips. "Now off with ye, or I'll not be responsible for what happens next."

She gave him another quick peck, then hurried down the stairs, but as Aodhán headed for the bathroom, he asked himself the same question that Niamh had asked. Why the dreams? Shaking the thought from his head, he stepped into the shower. It wasn't like he'd never dreamed about his old life before. They were memories and bound to come to the fore while he slept from time to time. But that wasn't really what was worrying him.

Rinsing himself off, he stepped out of the shower and gazed in the mirror as he dried himself off. He'd need to shave. An image appeared in the mist, and he spun around, but of course no one was there. Perhaps he was giving too much weight to Ciarán's dreams, and yet . . .

Ciarán, you have a gift. He recalled sitting before Domnall one morning, the man's voice calm and gentle as he spoke. *Your dreams hold meaning. You have the gift as well, Aodhán, but yours will not be as intense as Ciarán's. Do not ignore them, but do not be ruled by them either. They are not the future, but a guide to warn you of what might lie ahead and to help you make the right choices.*

Ciarán had said his dreams were vivid, images that showed Ruadhán taking away his children. But how could that be? Aodhán closed his eyes, returning to that morning so many years before and listening for his father's voice once more.

But be on guard how you interpret them, mo mhic, for their meaning will not always be clear.

That had to be it. Ciarán was interpreting them all wrong. He did tend to jump into things with both feet, which could be good at times, but not always. Lathering up his face, Aodhán picked up the razor and shaved, feeling much more at peace with it all. Even Ciarán did have normal dreams from time to time. They might not mean anything at all. He was probably just afraid of failing to be a good father to the twins.

Aodhán dried off his face and chuckled. That would never happen. One thing he was sure of: Ciarán would make a wonderful father. He hoped he would as well one day.

CHAPTER 13

Ciarán still wasn't completely comfortable with operating this twentieth-century vehicle, but it wouldn't look very good for his wife to be driving him to his new job. The university had been a bit skeptical about him not being able to start until the spring semester, but he'd managed to smooth things over by taking a summer class and promising to sponsor an archaeology club.

He blew out a long breath as he pulled into his parking spot and turned the monstrous vehicle off. What had he been thinking? Having to drive to work every day was the least of his worries. He'd never be able to hold up this charade. Oh, he'd done the coursework, all right, and achieved a doctorate from Columbia University in ancient Irish studies. But the only experience he had in front of students was fifteen hundred years ago.

"If they ask anything about modern Ireland, just say it really isn't your field," Daniel had counseled him. "You're a specialist, a seasoned archaeologist concentrating in ancient Ireland. That is your field. Don't stray from it, and you'll be fine."

He rubbed his forehead, willing away the dull ache that was growing there. *It's not the first time ye've faced a class.* "No, but 'tis the first time in this new century," he said in a whisper. Well, sitting here thinking about it wasn't helping. Grabbing the leather satchel Caitlin had bought him for the occasion, he slipped out of the car and headed for the humanities building, where they'd given him his own office.

"Professor Donnelly?" a young man said as he reached for the doorknob.

"I am," Ciarán said. "How may I help ye?"

"Brian Sweeney, sir. I'm to be your teaching assistant."

"Teaching assistant?" Nobody had mentioned anything about this to Ciarán.

"Yes, sir. They should have sent you a letter."

Shit! Ciarán had given them his new address, figuring they should be settled by now, but with the twins being born and the baptism and his family all being here, it hadn't happened yet. "Ah, I've not been able to move out here yet, so . . ."

"You never got the letter." The man seemed disheartened and rubbed his hands on his pressed slacks.

"Never mind, then. Perhaps ye can just be telling me what it said."

A pleasant grin crossed the young man's face. "Yes, sir. I'm a senior, majoring in history, and plan to continue for my master's degree. I'm especially interested in ancient Ireland. My ancestors came during the Potato Famine, and someday I'd like to return to Mayo and see where they lived. I was especially attracted to the position because of your archaeological experience. It's what I'd like to do ultimately, but I know I have a lot to learn before I can be of any real value to an expedition run by someone like Professor Lambert."

"And ye're hoping I can teach ye all ye'll be needing to know."

"Yes, sir!" The man's eyebrows lifted. "Well, at least a good portion of it. I've read everything I can find about the altar you discovered and the artifacts in the lake, though I have to say I can't understand why you were just a digger."

"I came to the expedition late, so I took what Professor Lambert had to offer. 'Tis the first lesson I'll be teaching ye. If ye're truly thirsting for knowledge and experience, ye won't be expecting to start at the top."

"Oh no, sir. It's why I took the position with you." The man seemed to have realized what he'd said, for he clamped his lips shut.

"Instead of trying to get a place on Professor Lambert's team, ye mean." Ciarán had to press his own lips together to keep from laughing. At least the man was honest.

"Yes, sir." Brian sighed, probably certain he'd just lost the position.

Maybe he should have let him suffer a bit, but Ciarán actually felt sorry for the man. After all, he had spoken the truth. "Well, I'll be glad to have ye, then."

"You will?" His eyes widened again. "I mean, you're not angry about . . ." He shrugged.

"Of course not. Professor Lambert is the best in the field. But ye'll have to be paying yer dues first and make him take notice . . . and not be expecting to start as anything above a digger when the opportunity presents itself." Ciarán smiled and opened the office door, quite proud of himself for using one of Father Dennis's idioms appropriately.

"Is that how you got a position, sir?"

"Me?" Ciarán stifled a chuckle. If he only knew. "No, but I'd advise ye against the path I took."

"Oh, what was that, sir?"

"I slept with his site manager." When the boy's eyes became so big Ciarán feared they'd pop from their sockets, he rested a hand on the boy's shoulder. "I married her, lad. She's me wife."

"Oh, of course, Professor O'Connell." He shook his head. "I mean, Donnelly."

"Calm yerself, lad. She goes by either, and I'm not the type to be concerned over such as that. If ye can settle yerself, and not act like ye're walking on eggshells when ye're around me, ye've got the job." Ciarán grinned again. Two of his friend's idioms in one conversation. Dennis would be proud.

"Yes, sir." He put his books down on the small desk across from Ciarán's. "This just really means a lot to me. I've wanted to be an archaeologist for as long as I can remember." He scratched his head, hesitating a moment before speaking again. "Can I ask you something, sir?"

"'Tis the only thing to do if ye're expecting an answer."

"I read that Professor Lambert opened the dig again this year. Didn't you and Professor O'Con—Donnelly want to go with him?"

"We've newborn twins, and as much as we both love digging for artifacts in Ireland, we love them more."

"Oh, congratulations, sir. I didn't read anything about that."

"We're not exactly newsworthy, are we? 'Tis not as if I was one of those missing priests come back to life."

Ciarán sat behind his desk, and Brian scooted his chair up close. "You know, there are rumors about you and your brother being just that."

"Dead priests?" A year ago, the thought of such a tale would have terrified him, but with all the safeguards

Michael and Daniel had put in place, he felt far more secure this summer. "Do I look as if I've passed on? Sure, the wee ones have been keeping me up at night, but I didn't think I looked that bad."

"No, sir, I didn't mean to imply . . ."

"Ye're going to have to relax a bit if we're to work together, Mr. Sweeney."

"Yes, sir, I'm just nervous. I don't want to blow this."

Ciarán's mind raced. Blow this? Right, make a mess of something. "No worries, lad. I'll let ye know if ye're heading down the wrong path." Three in a row. He really was getting the knack of this idiom stuff.

"Should we head to the classroom? It's just downstairs."

Ciarán wiped his hands on his pants. "I have to admit I'm a bit nervous meself. I haven't taught anyone in a . . . few years."

"You've taught before, sir?"

"Just the wee ones, a while back, before I had me doctorate. 'Twill be a little different here, I expect."

"I would imagine so. This is a graduate class."

Crap. What did that mean? "Masters, then?" He hoped they weren't doctorate students.

"Yes, sir. This is the Irish Mythology class. Your Intro to Archaeology is an undergrad class at 12:15."

"Well, best be getting to it, then."

****

Ruadhán had gathered the ingredients he needed from the indoor market in Castlebar before setting out for his new cottage on the shores of Lough Beltra. Now he stood in his kitchen, blending them together into a thick paste. Though he would have preferred to use his own ingredients, picked fresh on the day of use, this boxed potion was what the merchant suggested when he inquired. Sighing fondly, he recalled the days when his potions were in high demand. He remembered most of them by heart, though he had to admit he had no idea what was in this concoction. Taking a quick whiff, he pulled back, his eyes watering. Certainly not fresh.

Looking at the box once more, he began to read the ingredients. Amino . . . Could it be Latin? No, he would recognize that. He tried to think what the strange words might refer to. Lime was used on a regular basis to lighten darker hair, and while berries were used to blacken eyebrows, he couldn't recall anyone using them on their hair.

No matter, whatever was in the foul-smelling preparation, it needed to be done. Sighing, he rubbed the thickened compound through his graying hair. If he meant to keep his identity hidden from his former priests, he would have to use all means at his disposal, like it or not.

He allowed the mixture to soak into his thick strands of hair while he cleaned up, then he stepped into the indoor waterfall to rinse the dark mixture away. The warm water eased his weary bones, and he sat in the large pottery tub for a few moments, savoring the feel of the droplets against his back. When he was done, he rinsed one last time before stepping out to see how his experiment had worked.

Wiping the mist away from the looking glass, he gave a satisfied nod. While more of the hair had turned black, strands of white were still mixed in here and there, though nowhere near as many as there were originally. It resembled the hair of the merchant in Castlebar where he'd purchased the ingredients. Maybe it was indeed what men here did. Regardless, he no longer resembled the chief priest

Ruadhán that his wayward priests might recognize. He rubbed his clean-shaven face once more, still unable to get used to it, and placed the faux glasses on, checking again to make sure his priestly sign was well hidden. The only thing left to do was test it out, but where?

The fishing charters were a popular spot, but Aodhán didn't seem to frequent them. Then again, even when a young bard, the spoiled whelp had turned his nose up at fish. Domnall had indulged the two of them far too much, and he had been rewarded with the disgrace and shame they'd brought down upon him.

Ruadhán clenched his fists and stared into the mirror. Patience! The goddess would lead him where he needed to be. Taking a deep breath to compose himself, he headed out the front door. It was a lovely afternoon, not as hot as it had been earlier. A gentle breeze blew off the lake, and with it the blessings of the goddess, for he'd no sooner reached his gate than the sandy-haired archaeologist walked by with none other than his treacherous priest Aodhán.

"Good afternoon to ye," he said, clearing his mind of all thoughts of his former life.

"Good afternoon," the sandy-haired one said, though Aodhán frowned.

Ruadhán worked fast, quickly sending a misleading thought into his former priest's head before he could form any of his own. "I'm new to the area, just retired from teaching, and was wondering if ye could be telling me where I might find a good hiking trail." He looked to Aodhán, pressing the seed he'd planted deep into the man's mind. "Are ye all right, lad? Is it something I said?"

Aodhán smiled and shook his head. "No, I'm sorry for staring. 'Tis just, for a moment, there was something familiar about ye."

"Perhaps ye were a student o' mine? Did ye go to school in Dublin?"

"I'm afraid not." He hesitated a moment, causing Ruadhán to chuckle to himself. "That is to say, I don't recall having ye for one o' me professors. Were ye at Trinity College?"

The little upstart had prepared a story for himself, even if he had almost forgotten an integral part of it. Domnall had taught him well, after all. "I wasn't, but ye know what they say. We Irish all look alike. Cut from the same cloth, I suppose. Me da used to claim we were descended from some ancient Irish priests."

"Did he now? I wouldn't know about that. I can't trace me ancestry back before me father."

I'll bet ye can't, ye wee scoundrel. "Really? Aren't ye one o' them archaeologists, then? I'd have thought ye'd have a long lineage."

"I study bones o' the ancient peoples and sherds o' pottery, not me own genealogy. Though me da did try to encourage it. Me brother, Ciarán, might be knowing more about that."

"Well then, I hope ye have luck with it. Could ye be telling me, though, what the best hiking trail might be through the hills?"

"There are a few actually," the sandy-haired one said. "If you stop by the B&B down the road, Mrs. Byrne will be able to set you up."

"Now, ye'll not be Irish born."

"No," the man laughed. "Queens County, New York."

"Ah," Ruadhán said as if it meant something to him. "I'll be on me way, then. Thank ye again for the help."

So his wayward priests had indeed survived, and one of them was right here before him. His mind was stronger than he remembered it. He would have to be careful if he meant to conceal his identity. Another seed, planted in the man's treacherous mind, but what? Being a high priest, he would have no descendants of his own, but he did have a few sisters.

Ruadhán grinned as he sauntered down the road. They still weren't powerful enough to outsmart him.

****

Aodhán stared after the man, his brow furrowed. He'd seemed so familiar, and yet . . . Shaking his head, he turned and walked down the path toward the sacred grove.

"What is it?" Ryan asked. "You look like someone just walked over your grave and ye came face-to-face with him."

Aodhán stopped and sat on one of the low stone walls that lined the road. "'Tis almost as if I did, and yet 'tis not possible."

Ryan joined him, stretching his feet out as he propped himself on the fence. "Who did you think it was?"

"'Twas only for a moment, and then the resemblance seemed to pass. Ye remember Ciarán and I speaking o' the chief priest Ruadhán?"

"The one that sealed you in the cave?"

Aodhán nodded, rubbing the back of his neck as he stared in the direction the man had gone.

"Hmpf! I always imagine him with long white hair and a beard." Ryan laughed, clearly trying to lighten the moment, and Aodhán joined in.

"And ye imagined right, though 'twas more what ye might be calling salt and pepper. But it can't be. And even if it were possible that Ruadhán betrayed the goddess and somehow got himself buried alive in Tuamaí Dearmadta, which 'tis not, the man really doesn't look anything like Ruadhán. There's just a resemblance o' sorts, the way ye can tell Caitlin and Father Mike are related."

"Maybe it's a descendant of this Ruadhán, then."

"That's not possible either. As a chief priest, he was forbidden to have relations with a woman, let alone marry one and father children."

"Maybe he had a little nooky going on the side." Ryan laughed and Aodhán chuckled, rolling his eyes.

"Ye didn't know Ruadhán. He was by the book. Domnall would bend the rules now and again, but not Ruadhán. Me father was able to convince him to go easy on occasion, but if a punishment was due, it was delivered."

"So no chance he had a few little Ruadháns running around."

"I'm afraid not."

"What about a brother or sister? He must have had a mother and father, and they probably had a few other children."

"He was a chosen child, but that means his father was as well. While he definitely had brothers and sisters, they would have been . . . Unless . . . No. They would have been children of the goddess, 'tis true, but it didn't necessarily follow that they'd be chosen as guardians or for the high priesthood. Not all the goddess's children were so honored."

Ryan scratched his head. "And what does that mean?"

"That once they attained the priesthood, they could marry."

"But you just said they couldn't marry?"

"High priests couldn't. Yer everyday run o' the mill priest could, as long as they weren't chosen as a guardian."

"Well, there you go, then. That guy's a descendant of one of this Ruadhán's brothers or sisters."

Aodhán released a weary sigh. He supposed Ryan was right. The whole thing was so mind-boggling. He'd be glad when Ciarán arrived so he could get a look at the man. In the meantime, he'd promised Daniel he'd check around Tuamaí Dearmadta once more and make sure the tombs were still secure. The professor had also asked if he'd map out any additional tombs he came across and copy the inscriptions they held, so he'd better get to it.

"Will you be all right climbing up there?" Ryan said.

A smile pulled at the corner of Aodhán's mouth. Niamh had likely cornered the man. "Don't be worrying yerself. 'Tis not yer responsibility."

"Maybe not, but if you have a relapse, it's my head Niamh will have."

"She might that, but so long as 'tis yer head and not mine, I'm thinking I'll chance it."

Ryan groaned and followed him up the trail. "Then since my head's on the line, maybe I'll just join you."

"Aren't ye supposed to be working down by that lakeside grove Ciarán came across last year?"

"I am, but I'm far more afraid of Niamh than I am of Professor Lambert. Besides, he'll understand when I explain. So do you think seeing your burial site again might spark a memory as to where some of the others are?"

"Oh, I'm sure 'twill spark a memory all right, but it won't be the kind that'll be helping me find any o' the other tombs."

CHAPTER 14

What are you doing up?' Niamh asked.

Aodhán took her hand and pulled her down on his lap. "I think Ciarán's been sending me a message." He looked out the window, across the lake toward the hills. Niamh was not going to like this.

"What kind of a message? I didn't hear the phone ring."

"Sure, 'tis not the kind I was talking about." She definitely wasn't going to be happy about this.

"Don't be telling me ye still have that thing going on where ye can hear each other's thoughts, with an ocean between ye and all?"

"Not exactly, 'tis more o' a feeling, really."

Niamh sprang up, her hands on her hips, her soft blue-gray eyes narrowed to conceal the storm that was brewing in them. "And what is it ye have a feeling he wants ye to be doing?"

"'Tis something I've been thinking o' looking into meself as well, ever since I met that man down the road a ways asking about the hiking trails. There was something so familiar about him."

"Ye're going to go searching for this Ruadhán, aren't ye? And yerself not out o' the hospital but a few months."

"It's been seven months, and I'm fine."

"Still, 'tis no reason for ye to be tempting fate." She stormed over to the bed, sitting down as tears flooded her cheeks.

"I'm not planning to open any tombs, just have a look at the names is all. I'll take Ryan with me if it'll make ye feel better."

"Why are ye still so worried about him? Ye said he wouldn't have been buried alive, that he'd never betray yer goddess."

"And I stand by that, but I just want to have a look to make sure." He got up and walked over to the bed, touching her cheek. "I'll be careful."

"Do as ye will, then." She pulled a tissue from her robe pocket and blew her nose. "Never mind that I'll be worried sick about ye."

He went to kiss her cheek, but she pushed him away and headed for the bathroom. "Where are ye going? 'Tis only three in the morning."

She stopped short and spun around. "Oh, that's grand, isn't it? Ye can take off wandering round the hills, with only God knows what up there, but I can't even go to the jacks without yer approval."

"Don't be an eejit. 'Tis not what I meant at all."

"I'm an eejit now, am I? Well perhaps I should just be gathering me things and go back to Duffy's. At least he doesn't brush aside me concerns as if they were o' no consequence at all."

She was pulling on her sweater when Aodhán took her by the shoulders and pressed her back down on the bed. "D'ye want to tell me what's really bothering ye?"

"What if this Ruadhán is up there? Ye barely survived Bradaigh, and that with Ciarán at yer side. And this one's the chief priest or something, isn't he? He'd be far stronger than Bradaigh."

"I'm just going to have a look round, see if his tomb is there."

"And if ye find 'tis open and the body gone?"

"I don't know, but ye can be sure I'd be talking it over with ye first. Besides, I told ye 'tis fair sure Ruadhán never betrayed the goddess. I don't think he was capable of it. And even if he did, he was the chief priest. Who was going to be challenging his word, let alone see him entombed alive?"

"I know ye're right, but I just keep thinking of ye laying in that hospital bed." She wrapped her arms around his neck, pressing him against her chest, but he pulled back.

"I almost lost ye that day as well, if ye recall."

"Ye're the only reason I can forget what happened. Each time ye hold me close and touch me soul, a bit more o' the memory is driven away."

Aodhán had been kneeling before her, but he moved up to the bed, slipping his hand beneath her sweater. "Ye were dressing so fast ye forgot to put on a bra."

"Maybe I didn't forget it at all," she said, a mischievous smirk touching her open lips.

They were full and ripe and waiting for him to taste of them, and so he obliged. Pulling the sweater over her head, he laid her back on the bed and kissed her. "I don't mean to make ye fret, *a chuisle*, but 'tis something I need to be doing." He brushed back her hair and trailed his kisses down her neck. "I swear to ye I will be careful, though."

She sighed as his tongue found its way to her breast. "I know that, but I can't help worrying over ye." A gasp of pleasure rang from her lips. "Ye do know how to take me mind off things. I'll give ye that."

Aodhán wrapped her legs around his waist, and she arched her back. "Not quite yet, *a ghrá*." He slid his hand along her thigh, her breath quickening as each pass teased more intimacy. How could he have lived twenty-nine years without discovering the pure pleasure that could be found in a woman's tender touch? Moving from one breast to the other, he suckled at her nipples, and they peaked beneath his tongue, sending a thrill of excitement to his core. She controlled his happiness, and he was more than willing to place it in her care. But first, he would pleasure her as well.

Slowly, he slipped down along her body until her thighs caressed his neck, and she knotted her fingers in his hair, purring softly as his tongue probed deep within her. She pressed against his neck, and he sucked harder and deeper, her purrs becoming moans of delight.

His heart raced, her sweet nectar touching his tongue and sending a throbbing ache down his thighs. Unable to resist any longer, he slid up her to meet her lips, slipping within her and pressing himself against her hips. She rose to meet him, her fingers entwined in his hair, her lips caressing his in a feverish rhythm until at last a bolt of ecstasy shook his body as their souls embraced.

"Sweet Brigid, *a chuisle*. If ye asked me never to leave yer arms, I'd spend me life right here."

"Hmm, 'twould be a grand idea, but not practical, I fear. We'd not be able to afford the bed."

Aodhán laid back against the pillow, feeling happier and more content than he would have ever thought possible. Slipping his arm beneath her, he nudged her against his shoulder. "I suppose ye're right. 'Tis a pity, that. Sure, I'd not be wandering round the hills if I could."

"Well then, maybe we can come up with a compromise."

He chuckled. "I'm fairly certain I'd come out on the losing end o' that deal, so unless ye plan to spend yer life in this bed, I'll be searching those hills for Ruadhán's tomb."

"And what if I refuse to let ye into me bed again if ye do?"

"First, 'tis not in yer nature to be so cruel, and second, 'tis something I have to do, and ye know it. I promised to be careful. Ye have to trust me on that, *a chuisle*."

She groaned before leaning her head back to kiss his cheek. "I do. 'Tis just I love ye so much I can't bear the thought o' losing ye."

"Ye are me life, darlin'. I have no intention o' doing anything foolish, but 'tis something I feel the need to explore. If Ruadhán is wandering round out there, it might put ye at risk, and I'll not allow that."

"And how's that? Sure, he's not a pervert like that Braddaigh was, is he?"

"No, that he's not, but he may have an issue or two to settle with me, and Ciarán for that matter, and that could put anyone we love at risk as well. I'll not take that chance, not without doing everything I can to stop him."

Niamh pulled away and rolled on her side. "So ye do mean to confront him."

"Niamh!" He rolled her back toward him. Thank God she didn't resist, though he could see the tears glistening in her eyes, the dim moonlight reflecting off them like two bottomless lakes. "We're getting ahead o' ourselves. There's nothing to even hint that he is alive. In fact, the odds are against it. So don't be worrying yerself over it needlessly."

She nodded and snuggled back against his shoulder, yet as she drifted off to sleep, Aodhán couldn't quell the nagging suspicion that, against all logic, Ruadhán had somehow survived.

****

Caitlin looked up as Ciarán came out of his makeshift office, stuck in a corner of their bedroom. Caitlin's old office now housed the nursery, so for the time being it was about the only space available in the small apartment.

"Have you got your lesson plan ready for tomorrow?"

"I have," he said as he swiped a cookie from the tray on the kitchen counter and shoved it in his mouth.

"Hey! I just made those."

He nearly choked and spit what was left in his mouth out in a napkin. "Sorry, I didn't know ye'd been baking again."

"What's that supposed to mean?" Caitlin narrowed her eyes, her hands placed firmly on her hips.

"Ye know I love ye dearly, *a chuisle*, but yer cooking leaves a lot to be desired. Though I have to admit that bit I tasted wasn't bad at all."

"Well, for your information, I've been taking lessons from Mary. I never had time before, but I'm really enjoying it."

Ciarán grabbed another cookie and shoved half of it in his mouth before heading for the refrigerator for the carton of milk.

"Use a glass!" Caitlin shook her head as Ciarán's mouth widened into a grin.

"I'm famished. Are there any hamburgers left?"

"Wrapped in the tinfoil on the second self, next to the potato salad. And use a plate."

"Sure, I'm not certain what a mother would be sounding like, never really having known one, but I'm thinking you've figured it out."

"Very funny. Just for that, you can bring two plates." She sank down on the stool next to him and sighed. "I'm exhausted, but I think I have pretty much everything packed for the weekend, and the movers will handle the rest."

"I never worried about such a thing before. What I needed I carried on me back, and there was always a bed waiting for me wherever I went. Ye've a lot o' . . . things . . . in this century."

"And you're telling me nobody in the fifth century had a lot of . . . things?"

"I suppose they did. I went to Tara once, and there was a lot there. But I was naught more than a lowly priest, so I didn't need much."

"Uncle Mike doesn't have a lot of *things* either. I mean, the furniture at the rectory belongs to the church, so it's just his clothes and vestments and a few odds and ends. The church provides the rest."

"So we aren't all that different, then, except for who it was we were worshiping."

Caitlin frowned and plopped some coleslaw on her plate. "I don't think our religion would sanction sacrificing the mothers of his children, nor his fathering any for that matter."

"No, I don't suppose it does." He flipped the hamburger on the griddle and shrugged. "It was all I knew, and ye see what questioning the priesthood's precepts got me. D'ye think the Lord will ever forgive me?"

Caitlin slipped off the stool and walked over to put her arms around his waist and kiss his cheek. "Of course I do.

He's given you a second chance, and for the moment they're sleeping peacefully.

"That they are." He turned off the stove and wrapped his arms around her. "So d'ye think we might be starting on another, then?" He leaned down to kiss her neck, sending a pleasant chill down her spine, but before Caitlin could answer a cry echoed from the nursery.

"Hmmm, hold that thought." She shoved a spoon of potato salad in her mouth and headed for the bedroom. "And keep a burger warm for me, will you? If one's awake, it won't be long before the other wants feeding as well."

"Sure, I will, but don't be forgetting their father needs some attention as well." His distinctive cerulean eyes sparkled with delight.

"Does he?" Her stomach grumbled, and she laughed. "Well, I'm afraid he's going to have to wait until I've eaten, or I may not have the strength to satisfy him."

"'Twill not be taking much effort," he called after her, causing her to chuckle as she lifted Fionn from his bassinet.

****

Aodhán made his way up the hill toward the Tombs of the Ancient Ones. What had he been thinking? That the entrance stones would just present themselves to him? Grasses and moss, bushes, and the occasional tree covered what was once a series of tombs cut into the hillside.

"Just what are we supposed to be looking for?" Ryan asked. "We're a bit off track for the tombs, aren't we?"

"We would be if we were looking for Tuamaí Dearmadta, but the criminal element weren't the only ones to be buried beneath these hills. The priests were as well, with honors and all."

"So are you telling me they might wake up as well?" Ryan rubbed a finger under his nose and chuckled. "Colonel Fitzcairn won't be pleased to hear that."

"He's naught to worry over. These men would have been long dead when they were buried. I just want to see if I can find some o' the tombs."

"Like your father's, you mean?"

"It would be nice to know where he was laid to rest, but I'm looking for another as well. One who has been visiting me dreams a bit too much o' late."

"And you want to make sure he really is still sleeping peacefully."

A smile tickled the corner of Aodhán's lips. Though still a graduate student, Ryan picked things up without too much explanation, especially once their identity had been revealed to him. "Something like that, I suppose. Thanks for coming with me. Niamh's not at all happy about me rummaging round up here."

"My pleasure. I'm always sure of an interesting afternoon when you or Ciarán are involved. What do you hope to find, though? Whatever tombs there might be seem to be pretty well hidden."

"'Tis no doubt ye're right; still I thought I'd be taking a look round."

Ryan trudged ahead through some high grass and pushed a few bushes aside. "Could you be looking for something like this?"

Aodhán's heart sped up as he walked over to the stone and reached out to touch the series of carved lines. Trying to stifle the excitement building in his chest, he took his time to make sure he got it right. "Carraig," he finally said, taking a deep breath. Memories of his childhood assaulted his senses.

"The original . . . um, founder . . . of your priesthood."

Aodhán nodded, though a cold chill brought goosebumps to his skin, even with the warmth of the sun. "I remember the first time Domnall showed us this. I couldn't think clear enough to read it, but Ciarán did. The day took a disconcerting turn not long after."

"What does it say?"

"*First of the high priests. Teacher of all those to come.* Funny how easy it is to remember something when you've been embarrassed into it."

"That's one way to learn, I suppose. What happened later that made the day so unforgettable?"

"After we left the Hills of ár Sinsear with its Tombs of the Ancient Ones, Domnall led us to Tuamaí Dearmadta and sealed us inside one."

"What? How did you manage to escape from that?"

"He let us out again, after what seemed an eternity but probably wasn't more than twenty minutes or so. He said he wanted us to realize how horrid such a death could be."

"That worked out well, didn't it?"

Aodhán laughed. "I suppose it did, ultimately. I wouldn't be here with Niamh if it hadn't, though I have to say as frightening as that lesson was, it paled in comparison to the real thing." He looked over the hillside, to where it was likely other tombs were, and his stomach clenched upon seeing a stone where the vegetation seemed to have been disturbed. "Let's be taking a look over there."

"It's a tomb all right." Ryan ran his fingers around the edge of the stone. "Though it doesn't seem to be sealed as well as the others we found."

"They wouldn't be worrying about the occupants of these getting out, now would they? Still . . . Step back for a minute. And if anyone asks, ye didn't see a thing."

Ryan stayed his arm for a moment. "You can't think you'll be able to open this without anyone finding out, not to mention the trouble we'll be in for disturbing another one in the first place. They're off-limits, remember."

"Tuamaí Dearmadta are, but no one said anything about the Hills of ár Sinsear."

"You think just like your brother. Act first, pretending you didn't know, then ask forgiveness later."

"Only if we're discovered." Aodhán flashed a big grin. "Now stand back while I concentrate. I've not tried anything like this in a while."

"You're not going to blow it up or something, are you?"

Aodhán cast a glance in his direction and chuckled. "Is that what ye think I'm about? Calm yerself. That's more me brother's style. I'm just going to move it. If that doesn't work, then I'll be blowing it up."

"What!" Ryan's eyes widened, but then he must have heard Aodhán snickering. "Very funny. Let's just get on with it, shall we?"

Aodhán hadn't been joking about the need to concentrate, though. He hadn't exactly been called on to use his powers all that much in the twentieth century, at least not since he and Ciarán had faced Bradaigh almost a year before. Taking a deep breath, he stretched out his hand, his fingers tingling as he focused his energy there, then with a swift wave of his hand, the large boulder moved slowly to the side. Without saying a word, he picked up a small branch, gazing at its end to light it afire.

"Unreal! I mean, I caught a bit of what you did up at the hillfort with Bradaigh, but . . ." He shook his head, letting out a long sigh. "Remind me not to get on your wrong side."

Aodhán frowned. "And which side would that be? Me left, I suppose, since I'm right-handed."

Ryan bit his bottom lip, obviously attempting to stifle a laugh.

Groaning, Aodhán walked into the cave. He'd clearly taken something too literally again and would have to ask Niamh later what being on one's wrong side meant. For the moment, though, he had more important things to discover. As he peered into the flickering light, a bright beam pierced the darkness from behind him, and he spun around. "Shit!" he said. "Why didn't ye just tell me ye had one o' yer torches instead o' asking me riddles about which is me wrong side?"

"To be fair, you never asked, but as to the so-called riddle, your wrong side means the part of you that gets angry at something or somebody. Being I don't want to be wearing one of your fireballs, I'm not going to give you any reason to be annoyed with me—be on your wrong side. Get it?"

"Not really, but ye've no need to be worrying yerself. We were cautioned to control our anger and use our powers only when there was no other alternative."

"Like Bradaigh did, you mean?"

Aodhán stamped the branch out in the dirt. "Does everyone from this time use their abilities for the good o' mankind?"

"Point taken. You really should start carrying a light around with you, though. Archaeology 101."

Aodhán squished up his face, reminded of the paper he had due next week, and grabbed the extra flashlight from Ryan. *Archaeology 101? Another misleading term, no doubt, probably for someone who doesn't use common sense.* Well, he hadn't in this case.

He didn't know what he'd been expecting, but the cave was bare except for an altar that sat in its center and four tall candlesticks that stood one at each corner. There were no bones or funerary objects scattered about. Clearly, it had never been used as a tomb, and yet . . . the candles had been burned all the way down. He could still see the remnants of wax caked on the holders.

"What is it?" Ryan asked.

Was he just making something out of nothing, the way he had as a child? Ciarán would have said he was inviting trouble where none existed. "Nothing. It looks as if they just rolled the stone over without ever using it. If I remember right, they never did leave them open. I suppose they didn't want us exploring too much."

"Makes sense, I guess. It's not as cold in here as it was in the other tombs either. Maybe that's why they never used it?"

"I suppose it might be the reason, though there seems to be a fissure of some sort up there." He pointed up toward the ceiling where a long, thin opening was letting a ray of sunshine seep through.

"Good thing no one was in here, then, or we might have had another priest on our hands."

Aodhán slapped Ryan on the back. "Not to fear, *a chara.* Those buried here had already gone on to Tír na nÓg when they were sealed inside. The most we would have found was a few withered bones and a trinket or two."

"So not what you were looking for, then?"

He shrugged. "It doesn't appear like it was ever used, so not much help either way. Let's be getting on with it, then, and see if we can find some inscriptions."

Ryan led the way out, and though Aodhán followed, he threw one last glance back at the altar. Something about the melted wax on the candleholders still bothered him. *Stop letting yer imagination run away with ye.* Surely they'd been used for another ceremony first and whoever was charged with cleaning them hadn't removed all the wax. Lucky for them, the holders were never needed again. Neither Ruadhán nor Domnall would have been pleased, and that was never good.

CHAPTER 15

"I've been meaning to show ye something," Fionnuala set two pieces of birthday cake down before Aodhán and Niamh before hurrying off to the bedroom.

Aodhán scratched his head. Could she have stumbled across an artifact? No, probably just something she wanted to pass on to Niamh for their wedding. He looked in her direction, but she just shrugged, as did Duffy, who was in the middle of shoving a piece of his birthday cake into his mouth.

Swallowing the cake, he took a drink of Guinness. "Ye can't be thinking she tells me everything that flits through that wonderful mind o' hers, now can ye?"

"I thought ye might have an idea in the instance," Aodhán said.

"Well, he wouldn't." Fionnuala sat down next to her husband, a small package in her hand.

"For me, is it?" Duffy said, a broad grin breaking out on his face.

"Ye'll be getting yer present later tonight, I'm thinking." A twinkle lit her deep blue eyes, and Duffy's grin widened. "This is the ring me father gave to me. I wanted Aodhán to have a look and see if it really is as old as me da always said."

"Let's have a peek, then." Aodhán was happy to give her an appraisal. Duffy and Fionnuala had gone out of their way to befriend both him and Ciarán and had never once betrayed their secrets. The moment he took the ring in his hand, however, he could literally feel the blood draining from his face. "Who is it ye say gave this to ye?"

"Me da, but are ye all right? The color's all but gone from yer face."

"Just tell me the tale yer da told ye, if ye wouldn't mind."

"Supposedly, the ring's been passed down in me family for centuries, from eldest son to eldest son."

"And how did ye end up with it, then?"

"Me da only had seven daughters, me being the eldest, so it was passed on to me instead. Legend has it that each of those receiving it has been named Fionn, but I've no idea why. Regardless, though I was a girl, me da decided to name me Fionnuala, just in case, I imagine. Me ma came from a family of girls, and me da had but one brother, the rest all being *cailíns* as well. I don't suppose the odds were in his favor for having a lad. So is there anything to his tale, then?"

"I should say there is." Aodhán swallowed, still shocked that the ring could have survived so long and that one small boy had remembered his instructions and started a tradition that remained in effect through the twentieth century.

"Well, how old is it, then? Have ye any idea who me ancestor might have been? We used to guess as wee lasses. I thought it might be from the sixteenth century or so."

"'Tis from the fifth century—the year 419 AD by me reckoning. It was given to Ciarán by our father, Domnall."

A confusion of voices reached Aodhán's ears. He didn't know whether to laugh or shout for them all to be quiet. His own thoughts were spinning out of control, and his stomach was a potpourri of emotions.

Duffy must have seen something of his distress, for he stood up and spoke, his voice quiet but firm. "'Tis enough o' yer questions. Give the lad a moment to digest it all, then I'm sure he'll be explaining it to us." He gazed into Aodhán's eyes, a slight twitch of humor in the corner of his mouth. "Ye will be, now won't ye, lad?"

"I suppose I'd best be about it, though I can't say I understand it all meself."

"Start at the beginning, then," Niamh said, resting a calming hand on his arm. "Take as long as ye need."

Closing his eyes for a moment, he let his mind drift back, centuries before, to the sacred grove and a quiet ceremony set amidst the Beltane celebrations.

****

"I can't believe we are to be clerics," Aodhán said, "even if it is only at a minor rank."

Ciarán smiled and shook his head. "I know of no one who is a child of the goddess who has not at least attained this rank. It is what lies ahead that has me troubled."

"I did not think there was anything that troubled you."

"I will admit there is little that does, but I had hoped to rise to the priesthood one day. They say one must have self-control to achieve the position, however, and I fear I may fail in that regard."

"You will not fail if you put your mind to it." Domnall's voice broke into their conversation, calm yet firm, as it usually was.

"I do try, master," Ciarán said, "but the world is full of such wonder; I grow impatient at times."

"You grow curious, *a leanbh*, and think you should have all the answers you seek, whether it be beyond your status or not. That is not the way of the world, and you must learn to control your impulses."

"I will do my best, master."

"I have no doubt you will try, but let us not dwell on such things. Today you leave behind the life of a bard and enter the ollam as minor clerics. With this elevation in station comes additional duties and obligations. During the next few years, you will learn discipline and sacrifice. You will now be able to attend some ceremonies, if invited, and be able to cast satires—under supervision, of course."

"What if we speak in error, master?" Aodhán asked.

"That is why you shall not cast one without guidance." Domnall's cerulean eyes darkened, a sure sign a warning was in the offing. "Retribution for infractions, even minor ones, will be far greater now that you are no longer mere bards." He cast a glance in Ciarán's direction. "Do you both understand that, *a mhic*?"

"We do, Master Domnall," they both said in unison, though Aodhán was fairly sure it had registered with him far more than it had with his friend.

Domnall nodded, a smile breaking out on his lips. "But those are lessons for another day. Today will celebrate your entry into the ollam. When you were children, you were marked on your cheek with a sign that you were destined for the priesthood. Now you will be painted with a band of spirals around the upper arm of your dominant hand. It will signify the power that lies in the priesthood. Should you use it for wicked deeds, you must return what is no longer yours."

Aodhán's eyes widened, but it was Ciarán who spoke. "You mean we will lose our arms?"

"Did I not just inform you the penalties for your transgressions shall be far more serious now?"

"But if our bodies are so marred, we will be looked down upon and shunned."

"So you had best think before you act, *a leanbh*. I have a gift for you both. As your master teacher, this will identify you as my charges. No other priest, save Master Ruadhán, may punish you or instruct you in any deed or lesson."

Domnall put a golden ring on each of their hands. "Wear this on the fourth finger of your right hand. It will help center your power in casting satires and keep your mind on the deed at hand."

Aodhán looked down at the golden band. Polished stone from the hills of *Conmaicne Mara* framed a golden triquetra, while the band meshed three types of metal: gold, silver, and bronze.

"Thank you, master."

"I've never come across any like it before," Ciarán said, equally pleased with the gift.

"The ring is designed for each student by their master. I am glad you are pleased by them. You will find three letters carved inside, written in ogham. They represent faith, loyalty, and honor. I expect no less from either of you."

****

"And neither o' ye kept yer pledge?" Niamh said, jarring Aodhán back to the present.

"I don't suppose we did, and yet I don't think he was any less proud o' us."

"He sounds like a man who taught his sons to be following their consciences, no matter where it led them."

Aodhán gave a quick bob of his head, swallowing the lump that had appeared in his throat. "Even though we didn't know him as such until just before our deaths, he was a good father."

"D'ye still have his ring?" Niamh asked.

"I do, though with all the secrecy about who we are, I thought I'd best be keeping it locked up at home."

"But how did I end up with Ciarán's, then?" Fionnuala asked. "And why doesn't he still have it, the same as ye do yers? Don't tell me one o' me ancestors robbed it from his grave. There were a few unsavory characters in me family tree."

Aodhán had to suppress a laugh. "I don't think that's what happened."

"I don't suppose we'll ever find out how it all came about," Duffy said, "but I'm thinking we should be giving it back to Ciarán, eh, *a chuisle*?"

"O' course we should," Fionnuala said. "I just wish we knew more about how me ancestors came by it. Ye know, what the real story was? How is it he wasn't wearing it when Caitlin came across his tomb? It seems so important to ye."

"Ye remember what the etching inside said?"

"Faith, loyalty, and honor," Duffy said.

Aodhán nodded. "Ciarán took the words seriously, but after he met Aisling, he could no longer be keeping them, not the way Domnall would be expecting him to. Just before he went to be wed, he took the ring off and gave it to me, asking that I give it to Breánainn should things not go according to plan."

"He was afraid he'd be found out, wasn't he?" Fionnuala pulled a hankie from her pocket and blew her nose. "'Tis just so sad to think o' all he risked for love."

Duffy rolled his eyes, smiling as Fionnuala slapped his arm playfully. "Go on, then, lad. He took the ring off and gave it to ye."

"His plan was to take the children away after he and Aisling were wed, but as ye know, things didn't quite play out that way. Aisling was sacrificed and Ciarán sealed in Tuamaí Dearmadta. There was only one thing I could do."

"Ye carried the wee ones away for him," Niamh said.

"It wasn't a hard decision to make. I'd been listening to Padraig meself and had started believing in this new god he spoke o', and Ciarán . . . I think somewhere deep inside, I knew he was me brother even before Domnall told me. I had to get his children away, make sure they grew up in the faith their father had chosen."

"And that's what got yerself sealed in that tomb, then," Duffy said.

"It is, though I don't regret a minute o' it." Aodhán smiled and took Niamh's hand.

"'Tis grand," Fionnula said, "but d'ye think we might be getting back to the ring?"

"I did what Ciarán had asked. I gave it to Breánainn and told him that Ciarán was his father."

"How did the lad take that?" Duffy asked.

"Not all that well. He wanted to go back and ask his master himself. O' course, he couldn't be doing that, now could he? So I told him what the engraving meant and that since Ciarán was his da, he needed to do as he asked. The lad was only eight years old, but he was strong like his father. Just before he left, I told him he should pass it on to his eldest son and tell him to do the same so that his father's memory would be carried down through the generations." Aodhán shrugged. "I'm thinking that's exactly what happened."

No one spoke for a moment, but finally Fionnuala cleared her throat and took a deep breath. "Are ye telling me, in yer roundabout way, that Ciarán Donnelly is me ancestor?"

"I believe he is."

"Sure, ye're joking. Me father probably found it somewhere."

Duffy was frowning, tapping her arm. "Tell the lad what yer maiden name was, *a chuisle*."

"McKieran, but what does that . . . Oh!"

"Son o' Ciarán?" Aodhán huffed a small laugh. "The wee lad did remember all I'd told him. There's something more, though. I didn't remember till I woke up in this century, but Ciarán and I had spent the first seven years o' our lives with our maternal grandfather. His name was Fionn."

"Glory to God!" Duffy said. "How on earth . . . ?"

"I don't know how Breánainn found out, but I'm thinking he must have visited the village at some time when he was older, asking questions, perhaps. They would have known, maybe even told him. The inscriptions on our tombs . . . Ryan was asking about them, and I have to say I wondered meself a bit."

"About why ye were entombed, ye mean?" Niamh said.

"No, the second bit, the Latin. *Hail brother. May you live in Christ.*"

"Ye're thinking maybe Breánainn came back later and etched it there?" Niamh said.

"He would have been raised as a Christian. If not him, then maybe his son."

"So Uncle Ciarán is really me grandda?" Timothy said from the hallway.

"And how long have ye been there, lad?" Duffy asked, his expression belying the sternness in his voice, though by the boy's response, it didn't fool him.

"A while," Timothy said, ducking his head as if in contrition, which was as convincing as the harshness in Duffy's voice. "Don't worry, I know we can't be telling anyone about who Uncle Ciarán and Uncle Aodhán really are."

"And what do ye know o' that, then?" Fionnuala asked.

"I was at the school when that bad man was there last year. I heard what everyone was talking about at Mrs. Byrne's. I'm not a baby."

"No, that ye're not." Fionnuala motioned the boy over to her, and she put her arm around his shoulders. "But ye're right. Ye can't be telling anybody about it."

"Not even about Uncle Ciarán being me great . . . great . . . great . . ." Timothy stopped and scratched his head. "How many greats would it be?"

"A good deal, I'm sure," Duffy said. "So best if ye just keep calling him Uncle Ciarán, then, eh?"

"What would that make Aisling and Fionn to me?" the boy asked.

"I'm not sure," Aodhán said. "I suppose they'd be yer great . . . great . . . however many greats it is . . . auntie and uncle, wouldn't it?"

"But ye'll be telling everyone they're yer cousins there as well," Fionnuala cautioned the boy.

Timothy sighed. "Yes, Mamaí, but how come ye didn't name me Fionn? Wasn't that part o' what ye were supposed to do?"

"Oh, well . . . I suppose it was, but . . ." Fionnuala shrugged. "Fionn Flynn sounded a bit like a tongue twister or something. I just couldn't do that to ye, tradition or not."

"'Twas a wise decision," Aodhán said.

"Shouldn't we be calling Ciarán, then?" Fionnuala said. "Sure, he'll want to be knowing he has descendants living and breathing right here in Ireland, and 'tis not only meself and the wee ones, ye know. I have six sisters and cousins and . . ."

"I'm sure ye're right," Aodhán said, "but I'm thinking it's something we should be doing face-to-face, not over the telephone. He'll be here for the wedding before ye know it."

"Right ye are." Fionnuala couldn't keep the excitement from her face. "And everyone will be at the wedding as well, so we can tell them altogether."

"No!" Aodhán, Niamh, Duffy, and even Timothy echoed in unison, though it was Timothy who explained their reaction.

"Ye can't be telling anyone, Mamaí. They don't know about Uncle Ciarán."

Fionnuala's shoulders drooped. "Right ye are. Well, that's a bit of a letdown, isn't it?"

"Now ye know how I feel," Timothy said.

Aodhán couldn't help but chuckle. Out of the mouths of babes.

CHAPTER 16

Ye want this one in the bedroom, do ye not, *a chuisle?*" Without waiting for an answer, Ciarán pointed toward the correct room. At least he thought it was the right room. Why on earth had they bought such a big house? He stared out the back window. He did like the yard.

Trees surrounded the perimeter, just in front of a wooden palisade like some of the old hillforts might have had. And except for a square area of wooden slats outside the sliding doors, the rest was covered with soft green grass, the way the Ireland of his youth had been. There was a nice piece of land in front of the shelter as well, mostly grass with some blue and yellow flowers and a few more trees, oak and maple, he thought, with one large fir tree.

A seed of joy burst open in his stomach. For the first time since he'd awakened, he could truly say he felt like he was home. He cherished the sensation for a moment, taking Fionn from Caitlin's arms as she rushed into the house to catch one of the moving men.

"No, that goes over there in the dining room."

"So, *a leanbh*," he said to his son. "What do ye say we go out back and stay out o' yer *mama's* way?" Sitting down on the grass and leaning against a tree, he spread out his legs and bounced Fionn on his lap, much to his son's delight. "Ye'll have a grand bedchamber, with room for ye to play. Yer sister will as well, though I think yer *mamaí* wants to be keeping ye together for a bit longer."

The small boy smiled at Ciarán, laughing and cooing while he reached out to grab at his cross and his nose alternatively. His eyes sparkled with curiosity, the same deep cerulean eyes that Ciarán and Aodhán had inherited from their father, Domnall.

"I wish ye could have known yer *seanathair*. He was a good man, and a good father to yer Uncle Aodhán and I, even if we didn't know it at the time. We were never scared of him, even when he was firm with us. And ye should never be afraid of me either, *a leanbh*. I would die before I hurt ye."

Fionn laughed, trying to push himself up on his tiny legs.

"Ciarán?" Caitlin called from the house, and Ciarán sighed.

"I suppose our small repose is over for now, *a mhic*." Standing up, he cradled his son against his chest and went inside. "What is it, darlin'? I thought to be staying out o' yer way for a bit."

Caitlin kissed his cheek. "You are sweet, but I have to feed the twins, moving men or not. I don't want to throw their schedules off."

"What is it ye want me to do, then?"

"The boxes are all marked. Just see they put them in the right rooms, or you'll be the one moving them later. The big bedroom is ours, the green one Aisling's and the blue one Fionn's." There's not much for upstairs at the moment except that one bookcase and the sectional."

"The what?" Ciarán scratched his head. He'd gone shopping with her for some of the furniture but pretty well left it up to her as he'd never been used to anything more than a narrow pallet and perhaps a small bedside table, though that was changing rapidly.

"The big sofa that came in sections. The blue one with little flowers on it."

"Right, that goes upstairs, does it?"

Caitlin laughed as she headed for the bathroom with Aisling. "With all the in and out, I figure this is the quietest room in the house at the moment."

"Couldn't we just close one o' the bedroom doors?"

"We could, but then the furniture would end up sitting outside it, blocking the path, and you'd end up—"

"Never mind," he said, kissing her on the forehead. "Let me know when ye're ready for Fionn, then, eh."

He walked out to the front yard, ready to steer the men in the right direction, when he heard someone say his name, though it was one he wasn't quite used to hearing yet.

"Professor Donnelly?"

He knew the man, an undergraduate . . . *Think, Ciarán* . . . "Mr. Palmieri, is it?"

"Yes, sir, Frank. My father owns the moving company, so I give him a hand on the weekends to make some money and help pay my way through school."

"'Tis admirable o' ye."

The young man shrugged. "I don't know about that, but he is coughing up most of the money for college, so . . ." He shrugged again. "Besides, it saves him having to pay someone else a full salary."

"Still, 'tis kind o' ye."

Frank smiled at Fionn, and the child whimpered, causing the young man to pull back. "I'm sorry, sir. Babies don't seem to like me."

"I'm thinking they're not too fond o' anyone at this age, save those they've come to know, so no worries. Give it a bit, and he'll warm to ye. Me wife says it's all quite normal." Fionn peeked up from his father's chest. "See, he's sizing ye up, he is."

An older man called Frank's name. "I'd better get back to work." He ran off toward his father, clearly explaining why he was having a conversation with the house owner when he should have been moving furniture, for a moment later the older man came over.

"Giovanni Palmieri," he said, putting out his hand for Ciarán to shake. It had taken him a while to get used to the gesture, but after two years in the twentieth century, he responded accordingly. "Frankie tells me you're his professor. The lad wants to be an archaeologist or something. I hope I'm not wasting my money. Told him he'd need to have a backup, though, so he's taking education classes as well."

"Most archaeologists do teach as well now and again, so 'tis wise advice."

The man straightened up. "Yeah, well, thanks. You wouldn't mind mentioning it to him, will you? He thinks I want him to take over my business, but I don't. I want something more for him, and if this archaeology stuff is what he wants, then I'll support him all the way. Just want him to be able to have a comfortable life for himself while he's at it. You'll want the same for your boy, won't you?"

"I will," Ciarán said. "I hope he's as amenable to me advice as yer son is to yers."

"He is?" A smile broke out on Giovanni's face. "Well, good. I'd best get back to moving this furniture for you. You'll want to sleep in your own bed tonight."

"I would that. Thank ye."

"No problem. You just point us in the right direction, and we'll see everything gets put where you like."

"So, Fionn, are ye going to be listening to yer da when ye get older, or will ye bring me grief like I did me own da?" He kissed Fionn on the top of his head, letting his mind drift off, and the world seemed to drop away. He looked up to see Domnall standing before him.

"My grief was for what you had to go through, *a mhic*, not what you brought upon me."

Domnall smiled at Fionn, but he didn't whimper. Then again, this was Ciarán's vision, not his son's. But then the child smiled at his grandfather. Could he see the man as well?

"He is your child, Ciarán. Did you think he would inherit none of your talents? But do not trouble yourself over such things now. He has much growing to do before that time comes, and you will teach him well, as I taught you."

"Mr. Donnelly?" A voice broke through the fog, and Ciarán turned to see Giovanni Palmieri smiling at him. "Drifting off, eh? I don't expect you get much sleep with two little ones."

Ciarán scrubbed a hand across his face. "Not much, I'm afraid, but ye'll be wanting to know where to put that, will ye not?" He smiled and walked back into the house. "Up against that far wall would be grand."

When the man walked away, Ciarán bent over and whispered in Fionn's tiny ear. "So I'm thinking I might want to be speaking with yer grandfather a bit after we're all settled in tonight. See just what it is I should be expecting, eh."

As if in answer, Fionn laughed and grabbed Ciarán's ear.

****

"Did you think he would inherit none of your talents?" Domnall said again later that night.

The children were asleep, and Caitlin had joined them moments later, nodding off in the rocking chair that sat in the nursery. Ciarán took the moment of silence to slip outside and settle himself beneath his favorite tree and stare up at the star-filled sky. Closing his eyes, he let himself drift away into *dercad*, and, as expected, Domnall had appeared.

"How do you always know what it is that troubles me?"

Domnall chuckled. "There could be a number of explanations for that. Some might say I am only a creation of your own mind. Others, that being from the otherworld, I would surely be aware of what worries you. What is it you say, my son?"

Ciarán smiled. "I do not know anymore, Father. My old beliefs keep clashing with my new, and I cannot always find a way to reconcile them."

"What need is there to do so? Aside from who it is you believe in, of course."

"I'm talking to my father who died fifteen hundred years ago as if it were an everyday occurrence."

"Have I not heard others talking to their dead ancestors at your cemeteries and such?"

"Most don't actually see them, though."

Domnall shrugged. "Who's to say? Now what is it that is really troubling you?"

"I've survived fifteen hundred years to father a child."

"It is as your Lord and God has ordained. Do you not have faith in that? Your Father Michael would take issue if you didn't."

Ciarán laughed. "It is not that I have concerns over, but what kind of a father I will make."

"Ah, now we get to the crux of the matter. Go on."

"As you say, the wee ones are bound to inherit some of my *talents*, as you put it. Father Mike calls them gifts."

"An even more appropriate term, I think. But why does that trouble you?"

"I had you to teach me how to control them, to instill a conscience deep within me. Fionn and Aisling will have only me. What if I fail?"

"You will not, *a mhic*. I have taught you well."

"And even under your tutelage, I gave you little to be proud of."

"*Bhí mé bródúil asat i gcónai, a mhic.*" Domnall looked down at him, a gentle smile spreading across his lips. "Besides, your Father Mike is a good man. He will keep you in line where my lessons fail." With that, he turned and walked away, disappearing into the mist.

Only the stars appeared above, the sound of crickets answering his still unspoken questions. Ciarán wiped the tears that had risen unbidden in his eyes and listened to the sound of peace and serenity. Little bugs Caitlin called fireflies lit the air around him, adding to the sense of tranquility that was engulfing him. He was just drifting off when Caitlin appeared.

"What are you doing out here?" She sat beside him and rested her head against his shoulder.

"Just relaxing a bit." He wrapped his arm around her, pulling her into his embrace, and his heart swelled with joy.

"I think this is me favorite spot. 'Tis like I'm back in the forests o' me youth, and yet I have yerself and the wee ones here with me."

"The way it might have been back then if . . ."

"No, *a chuisle*. 'Tis not what I meant. I loved Aisling and me children. I always will, but 'twould never have been like this. I'm thinking Father Mike is right. Things work out the way they're meant to, even if we can't always figure out the why o' it."

"But you lost Aisling and had to leave your children behind."

"Sure, I don't understand it all, but if I'd not been placed in that tomb, me children likely would have been raised in the priesthood, not as Christians. And I never would have met ye or fathered those two wee hooligans in that nursery."

"That's true." She cuddled closer into his caress, her lips just inches from his when a small wail rose from the nursery followed in short order by another. Caitlin gave him a quick kiss on the lips before getting up. "You take Aisling this time since Fionn woke first."

Ciarán got up and scratched the back of his head. "How can ye tell?"

"You mean you can't?" She chuckled and hurried into the house.

****

Ruadhán walked into the Christian church. Surely his goddess would understand the need of his attendance there. Aodhán seemed to spend a lot of time with a certain family, so perhaps he could get closer by befriending them. He'd been watching for the last few weeks, and they always

THE CAVE OF RÚIN ÁRSA

seemed to attend this service. What more appropriate place to strike up a natural conversation?

He entered the bench next to them and nodded to the woman. As he did, a wave of excitement ran through him. She had those distinctive blue eyes. He sat for a moment, trying to calm himself. Surely others could have inherited those eyes, though he had to admit he had never seen them in anyone else, save Domnall and his two youngest sons. Though how could it be?

Ciarán's three children, that's how! Without doubt they had married, brought children into the world. But how could he be sure? And did Ciarán know of it? Of course he must. Ruadhán would have to search her mind, but he needed to be careful, not alert her. Suppose she possessed some of Ciarán's skills as well?

The service was ending, but for some reason many of the parishioners seemed to be mulling around, the blue-eyed nymph with them.

"Is there something going on?" he asked. "I've only been here a few weeks and haven't gotten to know the place that well yet."

"There's to be a picnic this afternoon," the woman said. "Why don't ye come along? 'Twill give ye a chance to get acquainted with everyone."

"Thank ye, I think I will, then."

"Ye bought that wee cottage close to the lake, did ye not?" the woman's mate said.

"I did that. After nearly fifty years o' teaching, I thought 'twas about time I started enjoying a life o' leisure. Besides that, things have changed so much from the time I was a young lad."

"True enough. Well, welcome to ye. Duffy Flynn's the name. This is me wife, Fionnuala, and the wee ones, Timothy, Kathleen, Patrick, and Brigid."

"Glad to meet ye all. I knew this would be a fine place to settle. Cormac McGuire's the name."

"Pleased to meet ye," Duffy said. "Why don't ye come sit with me family for the picnic? They can be a bit rowdy, but . . ."

"Well, children will be children."

"That was the adults I was speaking o'." Duffy laughed and clapped Ruadhán on the back in a friendly gesture.

"All the better." This was going to be easier than he imagined. Now if he could just manage to muddle Aodhán's mind enough so that he wouldn't be recognized, his plan would be well on his way. Of course, his changed appearance and the likelihood of him surviving to this century would make it all the easier; still, he didn't want any lingering suspicion. Not just yet anyway.

He stifled his disgust as Aodhán and his woman came toward the large blanket they had seated themselves on. Treacherous little snipe, taking a woman when he'd been chosen as a guardian. A wave of anger coursed through him, and he had all he could do to stamp out the fire.

Be patient, my loyal son. 'Tis not yet the time.

Taking a deep breath, he planted the seed in Aodhán's brain—a descendant of one of Ruadhán's brothers, perhaps—before reaching up and taking the man's hand in greeting.

Aodhán frowned but quickly recovered himself and took Ruadhán's offered hand after being introduced by Fionnuala Flynn. "I think we met down by the lake a few weeks back."

"Ah, so we did. That Mrs. Byrne o' yers gave me a grand hiking trail."

His renegade priest shook his head as if trying to clear his thoughts and smiled. "I'm glad she could be helping ye."

"That she did." Ruadhán returned his smile, a sense of victory settling in his gut. His seed had sprouted, to be sure, and the traitorous priest hadn't even realized it. "Ye're one o' these archaeologists, are ye not?" He needed to turn the conversation to Ciarán somehow so he could slip into Fionnuala's mind.

"He is," Niamh said, "along with his brother, Ciarán, and quite good at it, they are."

"No better than any other," Aodhán said.

Ruadhán could barely contain himself. Still the more modest of the brothers to be sure. He picked up a delightful little pastry and bit into it, staring out across the field while letting his mind slip into Fionnoala's. And there it was. It was too good to be true. Fionnuala Flynn and her brood were indeed descendants of his feckless priest, now known as Ciarán Donnelly. This was proving to be quite a productive afternoon.

CHAPTER 17

A Athair?" The voice was soft but deep, a hint of affection in its tone.

Ciarán blinked to clear the sleep from his eyes and see who was speaking. A handsome dark-haired man gazed down at him, his youthful face graced by a heartfelt smile.

"Who are ye?" Ciarán said. "And what are ye doing in me bedroom?" He cast a glance over to Caitlin, but she still seemed to be sleeping soundly.

"Do you not recognize me, a Athair?"

"Fionn, but . . ." Ciarán threw his legs over the side of the bed and sat up, shaking his head to clear the sleep fog that still clouded his head. "No, 'tis just a dream, isn't it? And ye must be me idea of what Bréanainn would look like had I seen him grown."

The man shrugged. "Or perhaps I am who you speak of."

"Donmall's put ye up to this, hasn't he? Would ye prefer I speak the Gaelic, then?"

"No, I understand your English, but do as you wish. As to Grandfather, he had no part in this. I met him but once after you were entombed, for I was raised as a Christian in Mumhan, but surely you know that."

Ciarán decided to switch to Gaelic. It just felt right somehow. "I don't *know* anything. Aodhán said he sent you there, that is true, but I've no way of being sure you stayed there. Ruadhán could have found you and brought you back to the priesthood."

"He did not, but then you've studied history. Surely you've figured out the priesthood was dissolved but a few years after you were . . . laid to rest."

"There was no rest about it, but I have read of Ireland's conversion. There was little on the individual *túath* however."

"I suppose not."

"So why have you come? Surely, you would have known little of me. And try to keep your grandfather's riddles to a minimum."

The man's forehead crinkled. "I will do my best to tell you what I can, though you may indeed see my words as one of these riddles you speak of. As for knowing you, 'tis true, I recall little about the time we spent together. My uncle spoke to me of you before he left us, though. I recalled his words and honored them. Perhaps not at first, but after, when I embraced my new God. And I tell you now, Ruadhán is still a danger, not only to yourself, but to those who came after me."

"Fionn and Aisling, you mean."

"You fear for your children, and well you should, but it is not the newborns who are in danger."

"What are you talking about, then? Get to the point so I can go back to sleep."

"As you wish, Father. Ruadhán will not be looking to my new brother or sister, but there are others who share your blood, who carry your name. It is they who are in danger."

"Then who? I've no other children in this time, and you must surely be well beyond harm."

The young man sighed. "Seanathair was right. You've not been listening." He shook his head, though a smile played across his lips.

Ciarán lifted an eyebrow. "A bit impudent, aren't you?"

"Perhaps I am more like yourself than I care to admit." His smile broke into a full-blown grin, his eyes reflecting his good humor. "You have let this new century soften your senses, a Athair, and your skills are not as sharp as they should be. Do not forsake the gifts of your past for the material pleasures of the present.

"You may not know Domnall well, but you certainly sound like him."

The young man shrugged. "I think perhaps it is in the blood, as is your answer. Take care, Father. Do not forget us." With a tender smile, he turned and walked away into the gathering mist.

"Bréanainn!" Ciáran called out, rising to run after him, and a sudden pain shot through his knees.

"Ciáran!" A distant voice called. "What are you doing?" Someone was slapping his face. "Ciáran! Are you all right?"

He blinked his eyes for the second time that night, only this time it was Caitlin who came into focus, kneeling beside him, her forehead creased in worry. "What happened?" he said.

"That's what I want to know. You shot up out of bed, like you were going after someone, and fell on all fours. You must have been dreaming again."

Ciáran sat back, leaning against the bed frame, and rubbed his forehead. It had seemed so real. He thought he'd been waking up then too. What if he was still dreaming? But then Caitlin slipped down beside him and kissed his cheek. No, he was awake.

"You called out for Bréanainn," Caitlin said. "Wasn't that one of your son's names?"

He nodded. "Me eldest. Ruadhán had already marked him for the priesthood before Aodhán took him away."

"And you were dreaming about him? Why?"

"I haven't stopped loving Fionn, if that's were ye're thinking." He got up, grabbing his pants from the chair and slipping them on. Why had he said that?

Caitlin's eyes narrowed, but more out of concern than anger or suspicions, he thought. "Why would I think you had?"

"Well, what did ye mean, then, asking why I'd been dreaming about him?" For some reason, he was angry, though he couldn't pin down why.

Pulling on her bathrobe, she reached out and touched his cheek, clearly sensing his muddled sense of mind. "Only that your dreams usually mean something. It's quite natural that you should dream of the children you've left behind."

"Become a psychologist, have we?" Why was he being so short with her? He put his head in his hands and scrubbed them across his face.

Because ye don't understand any o' it. Talk to her, ye daft fool.

He sat on the bed and rested back on his arms. Was Aodhán speaking to him now as well? No matter who it was, the voice was right.

"Maybe I'd better go check on the kids." Caitlin squeezed his shoulder and turned, but Ciarán grabbed her arm and pulled her back in front of him.

"I'm sorry, *a chuisle*. I didn't mean to snap at ye. 'Tis just I don't understand a bit o' it."

"Do you want to tell me about it?" She peeked at him from the corner of her eyes, the hint of a smile tweaking her lips.

"I do." He flattened the blankets beside him in invitation, and she sat down, rubbing his neck to ease the tension that had built there. "'Twas Breanainn right enough, but I've no idea what he was going on about."

"What did he say exactly?"

"That I needn't worry about Fionn or Aisling being in danger, but that Ruadhán was a threat to the others."

Caitlin's eyes narrowed again, though this time they remained a bright emerald. "Is there something you need to tell me about—another family, perhaps?"

"Don't be daft." He couldn't stop his lips from quivering into a smile. She always knew how to calm him after one of his jarring dreams. "I have me hands full enough with yerself and yer two wee sidekicks."

"Hmmm, so what do you think it all meant, then?" She hesitated for a moment, clearly reluctant to say what was on her mind. "Do you think Ruadhán may have found them in spite of all Aodhán's precautions? Or at least maybe that's what your heart fears."

"I suppose that could be it. The thought has crossed me mind from time to time, but why think o' it now?" He shook his head, discarding the thought. "'Tis not like I could do anything about it."

"No, but if it's been on your mind, you might dream about it, wonder what happened to them and if Ruadhán caught up to them. It must be awful, not knowing for sure."

He kissed her forehead and wrapped his arm around her shoulders. "No, Aodhán saw them safe to Mumhan. I have to believe that."

"Well, if Aodhán said he did, then I'm sure that's what happened."

He frowned, feeling there was a gentle insult in there somewhere. "Meaning he can be trusted to get the deed done, while I . . ."

Caitlin got up, chuckling as she kissed his forehead. "My, you are prickly this morning. Meaning you've each got your own virtues. However, I've no doubt you would have accomplished the same were your roles reversed. It's perfectly normal for you to wonder what became of them, but I'm certain their lives continued just as you and Aodhán hoped. That they became Christians and grew up to marry and have children of their own. If they were anything like their father, they definitely would have had children."

Ciarán tugged on his T-shirt and stood, pulling her to himself. "Now what is it ye mean by that?"

"What are you thinking about doing right now?"

"Oh, that? Well, I suppose they would have had a few, then."

"Try to think of them that way. Aodhán feels sure they did escape Ruadhán. Maybe you even have a descendant or two out there."

"I have wondered about that, ye know, though I don't suppose I'll ever find out. 'Tis nice just thinking about it."

She kissed him long and hard on the mouth, and he hugged her tighter. "See," she said after releasing his lips. "That was probably all on your mind, and so it manifested itself in a dream. Ruadhán is long gone. He would never have betrayed the goddess the way Bradaigh did. You told me that yourself. You also said sometimes it's just your own subconscious reminding you what you should already know."

"I don't recall ever saying anything like that."

Caitlin shrugged. "A loose interpretation."

"But what did he mean by the others? Was he talking about Áine or Daibheid? And why dream about it now? Sure, I haven't thought about it all in a while?"

"How should I know? It's your brain." A cry rose from the nursery, and Caitlin gave him a quick peck on the cheek. "The point is the only thing you have to worry about right now is getting ready to pick Fionn up when he wakes."

"I don't care what ye implied the other day. Ye can't possibly be telling me ye know one from the other just by their cries."

"Okay, I won't, but don't be surprised when it's Fionn you're left holding."

Ciarán scrunched up his face and followed her into the brightly lit room. She'd just picked up the crying child when the other started to fuss. Smiling at the wiggling bundle of life, he bent over and lifted the three-month-old to himself.

Caitlin sat in the rocking chair and grinned up at them. "Well, which one is it?"

Groaning, he grabbed a thin blanket and walked out into the sunlit backyard. How could she tell?

****

Ciáran sat beneath his favorite tree once more, Fionn resting against his chest with a pacifier in his mouth. It was almost as if the child knew he would have to wait a bit before being fed.

"Ye'll have to be waking up first if ye don't want to wait for yer breakfast, *a leanbh*." The child looked up at him,

202

grinning around his pacifier, and Ciárán got the impression Fionn might like these quiet moments with him. *Don't be daft. He's not old enough to be figuring that out yet.* But Fionn snuggled closer into his chest, and Ciárán told himself he just might.

"Even *your* child is not that bright, *a mhic.*"

Ciárán looked up to see Domnall resting comfortably against another tree. "I don't recall summoning you, a Athair. Or have you taken to just appearing whenever the spirit moves you?"

Fionn lifted his head and smiled, reaching in his grandfather's direction.

"Don't tell me he has summoned you himself. He's naught but a few months old."

Domnall chuckled. "Not quite yet, though he can see me, just as you can. Children are always more open to things beyond their understanding than adults are."

"So tell me, Father, what are you? Some kind of ghost sent to haunt me? A spiritual guide to help me along the way? Or merely a figment of my overactive imagination?"

"That, my rebellious son, is for you to decide. It always has been."

"Another riddle! Do you ever speak plainly?"

"My meanings are always clear. It is you who turn them into conundrums."

Fionn was dozing against his chest, so he tried not to disturb him as he shifted to a more comfortable position. "What is it you have to tell me today, then?"

"I once told you to look to the living for your answers; my advice remains the same, though you may think one has passed on."

'Ruadhán? Are you saying he does still live? But how? He would never have betrayed the goddess."

"No, never, and therein lies the answer you seek."

"Another riddle! Just say what you mean, please, Father. My head is muddled in this new world."

"Then you must find time to clear your mind. Do not let the gifts you were given fall into disuse. You have the answers you need."

Fionn stirred, and once more Domnall faded into the mist, only this time it was a glimmering ray of early morning sunshine that hit Ciarán and his son in the face. He shifted once more so it wouldn't wake Fionn and let out a long sigh, hissing an accusation after his father. "More riddles, as usual, a Athair."

"What's that?" Caitlin sat down next to Ciarán and swapped children, Fionn waking immediately at the feel of his mother's touch. "Another disgruntled conversation with your father?"

"Is it that obvious?" He leaned Aisling up against his shoulder, and she let out a burp a sailor would have been proud of. Neither of them could stifle their laughter. "That's me wee *cailín*."

"She must get it from you because I would never . . ." A pink blush rose in Caitlin's cheeks, causing Ciarán to laugh even harder and prompting her to smack him across the arm. "Well, not often anyway."

"O' course not. Now what makes ye think I was talking to me father?"

"Generally, that's who you're conversing with when I find you staring into space and mumbling to yourself."

"The way you do with Father Mike, ye mean?" He cradled Aisling in his arms, resting his head against the tree as he smiled over at his wife.

"He's usually right, though."

"True enough, but he's also a living, breathing man. I can't be saying for sure what me father is."

"Maybe he's a combination of things. You need him, and he comes. Does it really matter how?"

"I suppose not. Father Mike always says all things are possible with God." He sighed. "But me father wasn't a Christian."

Caitlin laughed again. "And you think that matters? You weren't either. Besides, who's to say he didn't become one in time? Many a pagan priest ended their lives as Christians."

"They did, 'tis true." He gazed out across the yard and kissed his daughter's head. Something was tickling the edge of his mind, dashing in and out of view, but he couldn't quite catch it.

"What are you thinking?"

"I'm not sure. I'll have to mull it over a bit. It's there, but I just can't catch hold o' it."

Caitlin got up, grinning down at him. "Well then, in the meantime, the kids are asleep, we're awake, and it's Saturday."

It didn't take a minute for Ciarán to catch her meaning. "So it is. I'm thinking maybe we should warm our sheets a bit. Sure, they must be feeling neglected."

"Right." Caitlin grinned as she headed for the house. "It's the sheets that are feeling neglected. And who knows, it might even nudge those shadows at the edge of your consciousness out into the open."

"I doubt that, *a ghrá*. 'Twill not be me brain I'll be employing."

"Exactly, maybe it just needs a little diversion."

****

"Aodhán?" Ciarán's voice poked at Aodhán's consciousness. "Can ye hear me?"

"What are ye doing in me dream, brother? Leave me be, and if ye've something to say, use that contraption everyone talks into." Aodhán rolled over, trying to regain snippets of his previous dream, the one that involved Niamh touching him in ways he had only imagined.

"'Tis important, *a dhearthái*! Ye can return to yer sexual fantasies later."

"Can ye not just phone me?

"I'm not sure what it is I would say. It only comes to me in me dreams."

"Ye've been speaking to *ár athair* again, have ye?"

"Have ye checked the caves for Ruadhán's grave?"

"I have, but I've no luck yet. Why? What has Domnall told ye?"

Ciarán grumbled. "He never really tells me anything, now does he, but he seemed to imply that Ruadhán might have somehow survived."

"Ruadhán? Sure, ye're daft. Ye know he'd never betray the goddess." Aodhán shifted yet again, trying to block Ciarán and retrieve the alluring Niamh of his dreams, but Ciarán grabbed his shoulder, spinning him around to stare into his eyes. The deep blue sparkled, causing Aodhán to wonder if it really was a dream.

"O' course 'tis still a dream. D'ye think I've managed to pop across the ocean for a wee visit in the middle o' the night?"

Aodhán frowned, annoyed by his brother's sarcasm. "Get on with it, then. How did Ruadhán manage to survive? He would have been dead when they buried him, not half-alive."

"I don't know, but ye need to think on how such a thing might've come about."

"And why are ye not thinking on it yerself? Me mind's full o' Niamh and our wedding."

"And I've barely had a good night's sleep in three months. Sometimes I feel like I'm walking around in a fog, so I figure between the two of us . . ."

"Two heads better than one, then, as Father Dennis would say."

"Does he? I'll have to remember that one, but in the meantime . . . ye need think on how such a thing could be."

"There was something, though I don't know how it can be anything. There was a cave in the Hills of ár Sinsear that had a fissure in the upper wall. It didn't appear used except that the candles had been burned down to the stands."

"Why would anyone have been burning the candles if it were never used?"

"Sure, I don't know, now do I, but there's no sign o' anyone being there other than that."

"Just another part o' Domnall's puzzle, I suppose."

"Most likely." He groaned as he felt Niamh's hand rub his back. "Can I be going now? Seems me dreams o' Niamh are about to become reality."

"Ye'd best be about it, then, but keep all I've said in mind. God be with ye, *a dheartháir.*"

Niamh snuggled into his shoulder and ran a hand up his inner thigh. "Sweet Brigid, sure he must be, for I'm about to get as close to heaven as I can on this earth."

CHAPTER 18

Aodhán stood staring at the wax-covered candleholder. Why on earth had they allowed sacred candles to burn down until not even stubs were left? Had the tomb been occupied, it would be understandable, but in an empty tomb . . .

"Those candlesticks still bothering you?" Ryan looked at the narrow crevice in the upper part of the stone wall. "I'm more curious about when this happened. It's still damp."

"Recently, most likely. There was a good bit o' rain this spring, even for Ireland."

"That's true. I got back to Mrs. B's soaked to the bone on more occasions than I care to remember. Tell me, though, why are those candles so important again?"

"Sacred candles were only placed in a tomb with a body. Not only were they considered the property o' the goddess, but they were no doubt too expensive to waste as well. And yet, I see no signs o' a burial. There's no bones, or even dust, and no burial shroud, let alone some o' the artifacts that might have been buried with them. Since only high priests and guardians were interred in this area, there should be some grand examples of jewelry, not to mention tokens o' their station, sacred items that had been bestowed upon them . . ." He shook his head. "It just doesn't make any sense."

"Maybe the tomb was robbed years ago."

"Swept up the remains o' the body as well, did they?"

"Maybe other archaeologists?"

"And kept such a find to themselves?"

"Hmm, not likely." He frowned, staring at the limestone burial slab for a moment before speaking again. "Maybe they thought someone was dead, but then he woke. They might have been so shocked they would have forgotten about the candles and just sealed the cave back up again. There are diseases that could mimic death, especially back then."

"Feasible, I suppose, but it is a bit far-fetched."

"More far-fetched than your corpse waking up, gathering his things together, and leaving his tomb clean as a whistle? Even Ciarán didn't do that."

"No, but Ruadhán might, especially if he were trying to hide his identity."

"Ruadhán? Your chief priest? You think he was buried alive? Because that's the only way he might have survived."

"No, he was a stickler for rules and would have died before betraying the goddess."

"Still, it would explain things. He'd know the rituals, how to see someone entombed alive."

"But why? It was a punishment. He would have believed that those so entombed would suffer for all eternity."

"A lot of his priests were likely becoming Christians. Maybe he saw himself as having failed the goddess and deserving of such a punishment."

Aodhán couldn't restrain a smile from tugging at the corner of his mouth. "Domnall, perhaps, but Ruadhán was not likely to take blame on himself."

Ryan shrugged and brushed his dust-covered hands on his pants. "Just a theory. If you've seen everything you want here, we'd best seal it back up and get going. Chris found two more tombs just east of here, a Lughaidh and an Éibhear."

Aodhán nodded, and with a wave of his hand, the boulder rolled back into place. "Eibear was one o' the elder high priests, in what ye might call retirement nowadays, but I don't know o' Lughaidh. Before me time most likely."

"Should we open them up, then?" Chris asked as Aodhán and Ryan approached the next tomb.

"No!" Aodhán said, so sharply he stunned the two youngest men. "Sorry, but that wasn't me purpose in searching for the tombs. Besides, we're not to be excavating any more tombs, remember."

"That was over on the other site, where the notorious priests are," Chris said with a grin.

"I beg yer pardon, but I was one o' those notorious priests, and I take exception to that moniker."

"Oh, I didn't mean anything by it, sir. It's just . . . well . . . these tombs here wouldn't be included in the restrictions, now would they?"

"I'm not so sure about that," Ryan said. "I'll have to check with the professor. For now, cover them back up as best you can. Maybe take a few photos and mark the spots on a map."

Chris made no attempt to hide his disappointment. "But didn't you open that one over there?"

"There was no name on that one, so it wasn't technically a tomb," Aodhán said.

"For two guys who just learned English a year ago, you and Ciarán certainly know how to use semantics to get around things." Chris sighed. "So we're really never going to excavate the others, are we?"

"I'd prefer we didn't," Aodhán said. "Leave them to rest in peace. There's nothing their tombs can tell us that Ciarán and I haven't already revealed."

Chris nodded, heading off to replace the foliage that had covered the entrance stones, but Ryan sat on a boulder next to Aodhán. "Just because we haven't found him doesn't mean he isn't here."

"I know that. I'd just be feeling a whole lot more comfortable if we did." He walked a few steps away and stared out over the valley toward the lake. How much should he tell Ryan? It wasn't for fear the man would reveal his secret. He had proved himself many times over on that count. But he hadn't even told Ciarán about Fionnuala yet. As for his dreams . . . anyone in their right mind would think he'd lost his. Then again, he hated worrying Niamh about them anymore than he already had.

Ryan took out a breath mint and popped it in his mouth. "Whenever you're ready. I know there's more to this than one simple dream."

Aodhán groaned and sat on the ground across from Ryan. "Ye remember how Ciarán and I could hear one another's thoughts when we went after Bradaigh?"

"Don't tell me you still can. I thought that ended with the dawn of a new day—or the setting, as it may have been."

"And so it did, but I think it must have sparked something else. I see Ciarán in me dreams from time to time."

"Well, he is your brother, and you've both been through a lot. There's nothing unusual in that."

"'Tis a bit more than that. He asked me to check these tombs. He's been having dreams o' his own. Well, more like visions, I guess ye'd call them."

"Ye mean like when he goes off into those trances of his . . . *dercad*, he called it."

Aodhán nodded. "He fears Ruadhán is alive and that he means to harm Fionn and Aisling."

"And he told you this in a dream?"

"I know it sounds daft, but we were trained—"

Ryan held up his hands in a calming gesture. "Yeah, I get it, and I respect his intuition. The thing is, it doesn't make any sense, not if Ruadhán was buried here. These guys were sort of dead on arrival, weren't they? As opposed to those in Tuamaí Dearmadta, I mean. So if you think Ruadhán's alive, why aren't we looking there?"

"I told ye. Ruadhán would never have betrayed—"

"Yeah, I know, we've had this conversation. What's the answer, then? Does Ciarán have any ideas?"

"No, I think he was hoping I'd just find his tomb and put an end to it." A smile pulled at his cheek. "Which is why that empty cave with the burnt wax bothered me so."

Ryan nodded. "I see your line of thinking, but there's no evidence to back it up. You're a scientist now, not a pagan priest, and we gather proof before forming conclusions. I think maybe Ciarán is experiencing the normal fears and anxieties of fatherhood. He's just transferring them to a tangible figure in Ruadhán."

"Had a good deal of experience at that yerself, have ye?"

Ryan chuckled. "No, but my brother has. It's not a unique occurence."

"Perhaps ye're right." Aodhán plucked a bright yellow tormentil from the ground beside him and held it to his nose, closing his eyes for a moment before looking back up at Ryan. "Ruadhán used to make a potion with this flower when we'd have an upset stomach. It worked well enough, I suppose, or maybe the malady just went away on its own. 'Tis hard to tell." He stood up and brushed his hands on his jeans. "I suppose we should be finishing up."

He hesitated a moment, looking back at the tomb of Éibhear. "Ye don't think Daniel will be wanting to open those tombs, do ye? Opening ours . . ." He shrugged. "We were accused o' crimes, but those buried here were good men and deserve to be left undisturbed."

"After all this time, chances are there'd be nothing left but a bit of dust and perhaps some grave wax, if that. Unlike you and Ciarán, they were already dead when they were placed in those tombs and didn't receive the special preparations you two did. Fifteen hundred years is a long time. In those caves, even natural mummification is extremely unlikely."

I know that, but how would ye feel about going and digging up yer grandparents' graves? I may not have known them all, but that's what they were to me."

"I get your meaning." Ryan stood and patted Aodhán on the back. "We are archaeologists. It's sort of what we do. Don't worry, though. I doubt Daniel will see any difference between this site and Tuamaí Dearmadta. You can be sure Fitzcairn won't."

****

"Good morning to ye, Mrs. Flynn." Ruadhán smiled as he placed his bicycle against the fence. Fionnuala was hanging out her wash, her children—Ciarán's descendants—running around her feet. But it wasn't them he was interested in. He had no time to wait for them to grow before starting a new priesthood. And she apparently had a number of sisters. All the better. Ciarán would be fathering the priesthood whether he wanted to or not, and he wouldn't be able to do a thing about it.

There was the issue of the Book of Carraig, though. He must be careful to find out where they'd hidden it and retrieve it before allowing himself the pleasure of dealing with his renegade priest. And this young woman might just be the one to help him do that.

"Oh, good morning to ye, Mr. McGuire. How are ye this fine day?"

"Just out getting a breath of air and a wee bit o' exercise. Yer husband's off to work, then, I suppose."

"He is that. Down in Castlebar. Have ye been?"

"I have. In fact, I stayed there a bit while deciding where it was I wanted to settle. Seems a good number o' those roundabout work down there, even that young fella . . . What was his name?"

"Aodhán?" She shoved a peg over a white *léine* and turned back to face him. "Oh no, he's one o' the archaeologists. I thought Niamh had mentioned that."

"So she did." He allowed himself to sound a bit apologetic. "I'm sad to say me memory's not what it used to be."

"Ah, well, it happens to us all soon enough, doesn't it? Aodhán will be working somewhere hereabout, wherever Professor Lambert has sent him for the day."

"Daniel Lambert, now he's the site director, is he not?"

She hung up the last pair of pants then looked at him out of the corner of her eye. "Ye'll be wanting someone to pass the time with, I suspect. Why don't ye go on down to Mrs. Byrne's. 'Tis on yer way home, just after the curve in the road, but before ye come to that grand stand o' gorse bushes that cover the old stone wall."

"Sure, I know it well." It was a good thing Aodhán and his associate had pointed the place out to him the day he'd asked about the hiking trails. The woman's directions were atrocious.

"Ye may find Daniel working there. Sometimes he spends his mornings doing one thing or another in that shed behind Mrs. B's." She looked around as if she were about to confide something of great secrecy to him, so he leaned in closer. "Between ye and me, I'm sure he's gone a bit sweet on the widow, and she on him, I'm thinking."

Ruadhán laughed. Did these people have nothing else on their minds? "Well then, I'd best not be bothering them. I'll be on me way, maybe catch up on a bit o' fishing. Me regards to Duffy."

He wanted to see what else he could find out about Ciarán, but he'd have to tread carefully. If she possessed a grain of her ancestor's skills, she might notice his intrusion. Staring off in the distance, as if to enjoy the scenery, he listened intently, though he soon realized that even if she did have his talent, her mind was too cluttered to notice him taking a peek. *Pick Kathleen up for dance class, and Timmy has football practice at five. Have Duffy pick up some milk and bread on his way home and a cake for Brigid's birthday.*

He shook his head, chuckling to himself. The goddess was wise to require her high priests and guardians to remain unwed. Ah, but there it was, tucked away in her memory. Ciarán's ring! Ruadhán's blood boiled. She'd shown it to Aodhán. So the arrogant little snipe had given it to his son, after all. A son who had clearly become a Christian. He would pay for that final sacrilege.

"Are ye all right, Mr. McGuire?" Fionnuala hesitated a moment, clasping the small oblong disc she wore around her neck, a medal of some sort, he thought.

He had to gather himself together, not reveal the fury that was bubbling in his gut, and hope he hadn't gone too far. "I am, just enjoying the countryside on this beautiful morning. I think I might be taking a hike before I stop to get me fishing rod. 'Tis a glorious day, is it not?"

"Sure, it is. I'll be telling Duffy ye were asking for him, then." She smiled again, a pleasant expression that lit up her sapphire eyes. If she had any sensation that he had entered her mind, the moment had passed, bogged down again by the trivial pursuits of her everyday life.

He'd best not press it, though, for it seemed she might hold a trace of her forefather's talent. "That would be grand. I'll be seeing ye in church on Sunday, no doubt."

Her smile broadened. "Oh, ye will that." She turned and grabbed her youngest daughter around the waist. "What is it ye're getting into now, darlin'?"

****

Ciarán jumped at the sound of clattering glass and turned to find his wife standing over the sink, rubbing her forehead. Checking the twins were secure, he walked over and took her in his arms. "Ye don't have to be getting up and making me breakfast every morning, ye know."

He led her back to one of the kitchen chairs and sat her down.

"It's not that." She closed her eyes, rubbing her temples, but continued to talk. "You remember how I told you I get visions sometimes, and how they usually come with these massive headaches?"

"I recall ye mentioning how ye were a wee bit psychic, or so ye thought."

"Well, I just had the weirdest vision, but then I don't think I've ever had one that wasn't strange. If I can just rest a bit, I can keep the headache from coming."

"Ye go lay down, then. I'll look after the wee hooligans."

"But ye have work."

"Me first class isn't until ten. Now off with ye."

Ciarán picked the twins up, one in each arm, and carried them to the nursery. "Now then, ye wee imps, yer *mamaí* isn't feeling well, so ye'll be taking a wee nap so I can tend to her. D'ye understand me?"

Aisling gave him a big smile, but Fionn grabbed his ear, then giggled when Ciarán frowned.

"All right, then, in ye go, both o' ye." He laid them in their cribs and watched over them a moment, but as they'd been up since four, they fell off to sleep almost as soon as they hit the mattress.

Caitlin was laying on the sofa, rubbing her temples, by the time he got back. "Get up a minute and lay on me lap," he said while he slipped beneath her head. A moment later, he was massaging her forehead, and he could feel the tension draining from her shoulders.

"So what was the vision about, then?"

"I'm not sure. I never am. Fionnuala was with a man, and a chill went through me, but I don't know why. I don't think she was frightened of him."

"What did he look like?"

"I can't say. Nothing was really clear. But she was gripping her medal."

"What medal was that?"

"The miraculous medal she wears around her neck. Like the one I have." She reached up and touched her own, sighing as she opened her eyes. "I'm feeling better now. You should become a masseuse."

"'Tis only yerself I want to be massaging, but we need to speak about these visions o' yers, *a chuisle*."

"It's nothing. They only happen once in a while." She went to sit up, but he pressed her back down on his lap, giving her a quick kiss on the lips. "Well, if you insist."

"I want to talk about this." She opened her mouth to speak, and this time he simply placed a finger over her lips. "Ye get the headaches because ye don't know how to deal with the visions. Ye're not strong enough yet, but I can teach ye to control them."

"The way you do yours, you mean," she said, a sarcastic tone to her voice. "At least I haven't fallen out of bed with mine."

"Those are dreams, not visions, so stop trying to change the subject. Visions come without warning, out of nowhere, and there are ways to handle them, exercises I can teach ye so ye're not bothered by headaches. 'Tis something I've had to deal with all me life."

"Did everyone in your priesthood have them?"

"Not everyone, no. There were others, though. Enough so that Ruadhán and Domnall saw fit to instruct us in how to deal with them and interpret them."

"And these exercises will stop the headaches?"

"For the most part, unless it's an extremely powerful vision."

"Okay, then, what do I have to do?"

"First of all, when one comes, don't run from it. Face it head on, delve into it even more."

"But won't that hurt all the more?"

"The first few times, but after that ye'll be the one in control, not the visions."

"And what about these exercises?"

"When ye think about one o' the visions ye've had, does it give ye a headache?"

"Some of them do. Just the ones I haven't figured out."

"Then bring them to mind and try to figure them out. It will hurt at first, but ride through it, like ye would one o' those waves o' yers. The more ye do it, the stronger ye'll get and the easier it will be."

"That's it?"

"There's one more thing, and 'tis probably the most important. Don't be afraid o' them. They're naught but visions. They don't tell us what is, only what was or what could be. We control the visions. Always remember that. Now think o' the vision ye saw this morning without being afraid o' what ye'll see. 'Tis only a shadow, remember, not a reality."

She groaned but closed her eyes and bit her lip. The tension returned to her shoulders, and her hand shook as she rubbed her forehead, but gradually her muscles relaxed, and the grimace dropped away from her face. When she opened her eyes again, she blinked a few times before speaking.

"I still don't know what it means."

"No, but ye're not afraid of it anymore, and 'tis no longer causing a headache, is it?"

"True, though I wish I could figure out why I got such a chill when it came. I was sure she was afraid, and yet I didn't see any fear in her eyes."

"Well, ye'll be able to think on it now whenever ye like without it giving ye a headache. It might come to you sooner or later, or it might not."

"You mean you don't always discover what they meant?"

"Truth be told, most o' the time I never do." He bent over, kissing her on the lips again. "Now if ye're feeling better, I'd best be getting ready for work."

CHAPTER 19

Ciarán hated going through customs. He was sure someone was bound to spot him as a fifteen-hundred-year-old artifact and either return him to his tomb or throw him in jail for breaking out of the museum. It was ridiculous. The logical side of his brain informed him of it in no uncertain terms. But after barely keeping his dinner down on the flight, that was not the side that held sway. Thank God he carried Fionn in his arms. The child had the uncanny ability of anchoring him to reality, which in this case meant keeping Ciarán's overactive imagination in check.

"There they are!" a voice shouted from the other side of the customs checkpoint. Fionnuala stood on her toes, waving at them, Mrs. Byrne beside her, jumping up and down like an unruly yo-yo.

"Anything to declare, sir?" the customs agent said.

"Just meself," Ciarán said with a silent groan. *Why don't you just tell him you're one of their ancient artifacts?* Fortunately, the man just laughed and patted Fionn on the head, causing the child to giggle before promptly burying his head in Ciarán's chest. "He's a wee bit shy, I'm afraid."

"They always are at that stage." The man laughed again and waved him through, and Ciarán could feel the tangled mass of knots in his stomach begin to loosen. He was safe with his Irish family again.

He'd barely nodded his thanks to the agent than Fionnula was plucking Fionn from his arms, singing the child's praises. His son was having none of it. The boy's bottom lip began to quiver, and his tiny arms reached out for Ciarán.

"Dear Lord, Fionnuala," Duffy said to his wife. He handed the boy back to Ciarán, and Fionn clung to his father's neck, whimpering. "The lad's not laid eyes on ye since he was a few weeks old, and here ye go ripping him from his *dadaí*'s arms."

"Sure, ye're right. What was I thinking? 'Tis just we're all so excited to see the wee things again. That picture ye sent is lovely, but it doesn't do them justice, now does it?"

Ciarán laughed and turned Fionn to look at the three women, for Niamh had now joined the other two, with Aodhán and Duffy standing off to the side. He kissed the child's head and whispered, "Say hello, to yer Auntie Fionnuala, darlin'." The small child let out a squeal and buried his head in his father's sweater once more.

"There, there, now leave the wee things alone," Mrs. Byrne said, "and give them a chance to get settled. Ciarán, ye and Fionn can go in the car with Aodhán and Niamh while Caitlin and wee Aisling come with us. I've got a nice room set up as a nursery right next to yers. Now let's be about getting yer luggage so we can be on our way. 'Twas all I could do to dissuade the professor and the lads from coming along as well, but where were we to sit them? On the roof?"

Ciarán and Caitlin looked at one another, barely able to contain their laughter. Mrs. Byrne could carry on when she was excited. She was like a sergeant major. He suspected she'd even test Ruadhán's authority.

When they got to the cars, Niamh sat up front with Aodhán. "I'd let you sit up here, but I don't think Fionn would be having it."

"He'll be warming up to everyone once he's been around ye a bit," Ciarán said.

"If he's anything like yerself and yer brother here, he'll have everyone wrapped round his tiny fingers," Niamh said. "'Tis clear he's already got them all falling over themselves to hold him."

"O' course, ye wouldn't be including yerself, now would ye?" Aodhán said with a snicker.

"Sure, I'll be the first in line. I fell for ye, didn't I?"

Fionn let out a happy squeal, and they all laughed. "Right," Ciarán said. "Let's see ye have the same response the next time yer Auntie Fionnuala looks to hold ye, ye wee hooligan."

Aodhán threw a quick glance at Niamh and cleared his throat. "About Fionnuala—she's got a wee bit o' a surprise for ye. D'ye think ye can be coming over to Duffy's round one this afternoon?"

What was this bunch up to? Ciarán narrowed his eyes. "I suppose we could. Can ye at least tell me what it's about?"

"'Twould be better if we waited."

"Is she having another wee one?"

"Not that she's mentioned," Niamh said, "but ye never can tell with them two. Ye'd think they were married only yesterday, the way they're always holding hands and such."

"And what's wrong with that?" Ciarán hugged his son, contemplating the fun they'd have making another.

"Not a thing!" Aodhán threw another glance in Niamh's direction. "I like to think we'll be doing the same."

"Ye may not be saying that when the little consequences are waking ye up in the wee hours o' the morning," Ciarán said. "Though I wouldn't trade them." He glanced down at his son again, his heart exploding with joy every time he looked at him. "Would I now, ye wee rug rat."

Fionn squealed in glee and stared into his father's eyes before leaning on his shoulder and giving a contented sigh. His eyelids fluttered a moment before closing, his fist stuck in his mouth.

Ciarán gave a contented sigh as well. He was never more at peace then when he was holding his children or locked in Caitlin's embrace. For all he had suffered, God had truly blessed him, and yet he still couldn't help but wonder why he'd been granted this new life. Was it truly just to put an end to Bradaigh's reign of terror?

Stop questioning the Lord and accept his gift graciously, Father Mike always said, and except for Domnall, Ciarán had never known anyone wiser than the canny old priest.

****

"It won't be doing ye any good to stare at me, brother," Aodhán said. "I'm well aware o' what ye're about, and I'll not be letting ye stroll through me mind unchecked. Ye'll discover what Fionnuala has to say when ye see her and not before."

The hint of a smile touched Ciarán's lips, and he switched his gaze to Niamh.

"Oh no!" she said. "I'm heading over there now. Caitlin and I can take the twins with us. 'Twill give yerself and Aodhán a chance to catch up on things." She reached down to take Aisling from Mrs. Byrne's lap, and the woman groaned.

"Ye can leave them here, ye know. Sure, Daniel and I don't mind watching the pair o' them."

"I know that," Caitlin said. She hoisted Fionn up on her hip, and the child wrapped his arms around her neck, snuggling against her sweater. "But they're just getting used to you. I'm afraid once we headed for the door, they might not be so happy."

"Caitlin is right, Mrs. B." Daniel rested one hand on the woman's shoulder while taking a pipe from his pocket with the other. "They'll be back for dinner, and you'll have plenty of time to play with the little tykes then."

"Right, we're off, then." Niamh grabbed Caitlin by the hand and hurried her along, causing Ciarán to frown.

"What are ye up to, brother?" he asked when they'd all gone. Even Mrs. B. and the professor had taken refuge in the living room.

"Ye'll find out soon enough. Right now I want to be talking to ye about that tomb I found. What d'ye think?" Aodhán poured them each a cup of tea and sat down at the kitchen table.

"I don't know what to think. 'Tis like ye said. Someone had to be laid to rest there. To begin with, Ruadhán would never use sacred candles in an empty tomb, let alone let them burn all the way down and all."

"Ryan suggested there might have been grave robbers, maybe years ago."

Ciarán shook his head. "I can see them making off with the jewelry and such, but taking the body as well is a bit far-fetched."

"And yet exactly what the world thinks happened to us."

"And they're wrong, now aren't they?"

Aodhán shrugged and placed a plate of biscuits on the table. "Sorry, I ate all the chocolate ones." He sat down, trying to sort it all out. "D'ye think maybe there was nothing left o' the body? After all, it could be over fifteen hundred years old."

"I've spoken to Steve about that. He said there still would have been something, even if 'twere naught more than a bit o' wax and teeth. Who'd want to be taking that?" He pushed the biscuits around on the plate. "All the chocolate ones?"

Aodhán couldn't help but laugh. "'Tis what I said, isn't it?"

Ciarán grumbled and picked up one with raisins in it. "But ye hinted there was something else that caused ye to question it, more than the candleholders, I mean?"

"There was, but don't be asking me what. I've not a clue. I was hoping maybe ye might be able to get something more."

"D'ye think it could have been Ruadhán's tomb?"

Aodhán sighed. "I get a sense o' him being there, but then as high priest he would have been no matter who was being interred, now wouldn't he? And if it were himself . . ."

"Sure, he'd be dead and no danger to anyone. But none o' it sits right with ye?"

"It doesn't, yet I've no explanation for it either. We've time to stop up there and have a quick look before heading over to Duffy's if ye've the mind to."

"I do, though I'm not sure how much help I'll be. Between the twins and the plane ride, me mind feels like there's a fog surrounding it."

"I thought that was yer usual state." Aodhán chuckled. "We'll have a look, and we can go back tomorrow if ye like as well. We'd best be about it, though. If we're late for lunch, Fionnuala will have me head."

****

A chill surged through Ciarán's muscles as they approached the cave. "Was it unsealed when ye found it?"

"The stone was in place, but only loosely, not wedged in like the others." Aodhán stood on one side and nodded for Ciarán to grab the other. "'Twas easy enough for Ryan and I to shimmy away from the opening."

"And ye expect me to be doing the same? In me good clothes?" Ciarán frowned at his brother. Was he forgetting all he'd been taught? "Why did ye not just give it a flick o' yer wrist?"

Aodhán's lips quivered into a smile. "I did, actually. Just pulling yer leg, as Dennis would say." He gave a wave of his hand, and the rock scraped away from the opening.

Ciarán tried to hide it, but he couldn't help laughing. It was good to see Aodhán so happy. Now if they could just figure out what was going on here. Warm air brushed his cheek as he entered the tomb, though a chill still permeated his body. Picking up the lantern he'd brought along, he held it up and looked around. Aodhán was right. He could get a sense of Ruadhán here.

"How long d'ye figure that fissure's been in the upper wall?" he asked.

"'Tis still damp, but that's because it rained last night. As to when it originally happened, there's no telling. It might have happened five years ago or five hundred."

Ciarán sat on the ground and let himself drift away, deep into a state of *dercad*.

"What is it you really want to ask, *a mhic*?" Domnall said. "You say I answer in riddles. Do you not ask in the same form?"

"All right, then: Is this Ruadhán's tomb?"

"That is not the question you truly wish to ask. You see, you take part in the same games you accuse me of playing."

"Does he live, then?"

"Why do you doubt your own intuition? Your heart has already given you the answer. If you believe that, what you do not comprehend is how."

"Riddles and more riddles."

"Then stop asking questions you cannot answer. I come to guide you, to help you use your intellect, not to spoon-feed the answers to you. You ask how. Use your knowledge to find the answer. It is there within your muddled mind. Until you clear it, the answer will elude you."

Domnall smiled at Ciarán. "Do not look so dejected. The answers are within your grasp. You have but to close your hand around them. First, though, you must return to your roots and all that has sprung from them."

Once again, the man faded from his sight, leaving him with more questions than answers. Ciarán blinked and looked to Aodhán, who was leaning up against the altar, waiting patiently.

"Well," his brother said. "Anything?"

"Only that I'm more convinced than ever the man comes to torment me."

"What did he say this time? Maybe if ye say it aloud, we can figure it out."

"He said I was the one speaking in riddles, not asking what I really wanted to know."

"What did ye ask, then?"

"If this was Ruadhán's tomb." Ciarán got up, brushing the dirt from his slacks.

"I gather he didn't tell ye."

"What d'ye think?" He headed outside, and Aodhán followed, snickering to himself. "Ye find it funny, do ye?"

"I find it perplexing how after all these years ye still don't understand our father. When did he ever give us the answers we sought?"

Ciarán frowned. "Never that I can remember."

"And yet ye found yer way somehow."

"Because he guided us to the answer."

Aodhán shrugged, waving his hand so that the boulder slid back into place. "And I'd wager 'tis what he's still doing. Ye're just too stubborn to see it, but then ye always did fight him on it."

Ciarán leaned against the stone. "What do ye mean by that?"

"Ye always pressed him to tell ye more, didn't ye, until ye got so aggravated ye figured it out yerself. Which was his aim in the first place, I might add."

Ciarán frowned. As much as he hated to admit it, his brother was right. They started back down the hill, and he let his mind mull over what Domnall had said. "He said me heart had the answer to whether or not Ruadhán was alive, and though I didn't understand how, the answer was within my grasp. I need only to look to my roots."

"So he is alive, then?"

"How should I know?" Ciarán walked on ahead so that Aodhán had to catch up.

"Domnall's right." Aodhán grabbed his arm to stop him for a moment. "Ye really don't listen, do ye?"

Without another word, Ciarán hurried down to the road and waited for Aodhán before heading back toward Mrs. Byrne's. "All right, I'm listening," he finally said.

"Ye know well enough what yer heart tells ye."

He stopped short. "In truth, 'tis that Ruadhán's alive, but how could that be?"

"Domnall gave ye the answer to that as well."

"It was within me grasp if I returned to me roots and cleared me head." He gave a frustrated growl and started down the road again. "And what's that supposed to mean? Caitlin says I can be so dense at times. I'm not certain what that means either, but sure I'm thinking it has to do with me not grasping things others can clearly see."

Aodhán tried to conceal a smile, but it crept out on his lips nonetheless. "She's not wrong there, but in this case a bit o' sleep might be helping, I suppose."

"Easier said than done."

"Or maybe ye just need to remember how to relax a bit. Ye're wound tighter than a fat man's girdle. Maybe that's what Domnall meant about returning to yer roots. No matter how hectic things got, we could always find serenity deep within ourselves."

A wave of shame washed over Ciarán. Once again, his brother was right. He'd been so worried about being the perfect husband, the perfect father, even the perfect teacher, that he'd lost touch with the part of himself that made him all those things.

"After we stop by Duffy's, I'll take a walk by meself, out along the quiet lanes. I do think he's alive somehow. Though I can't for the life of me see how it came about."

"Ye'll sort it out," Aodhán said, "but for now 'tis off to Duffy's before we're late and Fionnuala hangs us out to dry."

Ciarán chuckled. "Another o' Dennis's idioms?"

"No, this one is Mrs. Byrne's. She's threatened me with it on many occasions, and while I'm not exactly sure how she'd be carrying it out, I'm certain 'twould not be pleasant."

****

Ruadhán watched from the bushes as the two brothers walked down the lane. Domnall never should have revealed his identity to them, but what did it matter? In a way, it had worked to his advantage. Aodhán had unknowingly led him to Ciarán and to one of his descendants. The wayward priest's blood ran through her veins, and thus so did that of his goddess. If he could only get his hands on the sacred book, he would steal her away. Then what?

She could birth a new priesthood, but he was an old man. Who would be there to guide these new children in their ways? Surely the Book of Carraig would hold the answer. He need only find where the treacherous little thieves had hidden it. Which was why he must bide his time and lead their suspicions away from himself.

That would be easy enough to do. He chuckled as he sneaked around the side of Fionnuala's house. Diversion was an old trick, but it worked well. The cocksure little viper would be so worried about the little ones, his own and Fionnuala's, he'd not concern himself over her, nor would she. Especially now that Domnall was no longer there to watch over him.

"And who's to say I'm not?"

Ruadhán rolled his eyes. "Do not nettle me, *a chara*. You are long gone from this world."

"Ah, but am I?"

"Wherever you are, you will not interfere. It is not your way. Your God has given them free will, has he not?"

"Free will, yes, but he has also encouraged them to seek guidance where they may."

"And so, as I said, you can do nothing more than guide them."

Domnall ducked his head to the side, seemingly acknowledging Ruadhán's statement. "It seems it is all that was ever needed in the past."

"Guide them into Tuamaí Dearmadta, did you?"

Domnall smiled, still unruffled. It had never ceased to amaze Ruadhán how calm the man remained. "And yet they still survive," Domnall said, "in spite of your condemnation and that of the goddess."

"For now, they do."

"Tread carefully, *mo chara*. My sons may not be the fools you think. They have grown in intelligence and power."

"Even now I could bring them to their knees, as well you know, but I will not. I seek only to rebuild our priesthood."

"It is another world, Ruadhán. Do you hold on to the past out of love for the goddess or for the power she has bestowed upon you?"

"They never truly honored her, nor did you. If you had, you would be by my side now, not guiding your traitorous sons in their disbelief."

Without another word, Domnall bowed and disappeared into the glow of the afternoon sun, leaving Ruadhán more angry and more determined than before. His brother had a knack for making people reevaluate their decisions, but he would not be deterred from the path the goddess had forged for him. Not even Domnall could drive him from that course.

CHAPTER 20

Fionnuala sat Aisling on her lap, and tears started flowing down her cheeks. Ciarán bent down before the woman, puzzled as to why seeing his children would cause such a reaction. Though he started to say something, Aodhán motioned him into a seat at the table.

"Hush a moment, and give her a chance to tell ye what's on her mind."

Confused, he sat next to Caitlin and waited, his patience stretched to its limits. It never had been one of his virtues. Aodhán should know that, but instead of hurrying the woman along, he remained quiet while she blew her nose and composed herself. Finally, she took a deep breath and began to explain.

"D'ye not see the resemblance between us?"

Ciarán frowned. Where exactly was this going? He'd never really looked that closely at Fionnuala before. Duffy would probably have given him a fister to the nose if he did. But since she was asking him to . . . She had dimples and deep black hair, and her eyes were a dazzling cerulean blue, just like Aisling's and Fionn's and . . . his. But what did it mean?

He threw a glance at Aodhán before turning back to Fionnuala. "What does it mean?"

The words were barely out of his mouth when she handed him a ring, one he knew all too well, one he thought had been lost forever. "Where did ye come by this?" His words weren't accusatory, just questioning, and he looked back to her, praying she had a logical answer.

"It was passed down in me family, from eldest son to eldest son, but when it got to me father . . . well, I had no brothers, so me father passed it on to me."

He knew he should understand what she was saying, but none of it made any sense. Closing his eyes, he took a breath and let his mind drift away to another time, another place, long before.

****

Ciarán gazed down at the ring he wore on his left hand, on the finger the Romans believed held a vein that ran straight to the heart. Would he ever forgive himself for what he was about to do? He could still remember Domnall's words as he'd handed it to him on the day he'd become a cleric.

It is engraved with three letters, each one representing a noble quality: faith, loyalty, honor. Live by them, and you can be proud of the man you become.

Was he living by them? He did have faith in this new religion and was doing the honorable thing, but loyalty? Domnall would surely not think him loyal or even honorable for that matter. And yet Ciarán had to follow his heart. If he could only speak to Domnall of it, explain how his heart filled with love for Aisling.

He yanked the ring from his finger. What was the point? In marrying Aisling, he was betraying all he had been taught to honor. It was fitting that he left the ring behind. No longer could he believe in the goddess of his *túath*. And as far as honor and loyalty went, even Domnall would see him as a betrayer of both.

"Are you sure about this?" Aodhán came up next to him and looked around the empty dormitory. "If so, we'd best be about it before anyone returns."

Ciarán placed the gold ring, inlaid with marble, in his brother's hand. "Return this to Domnall. Tell him I am sorry that I could not be the student he deserved."

Aodhán hesitated before taking the ring. "Removing it is paramount to rejecting all he believes, all the priesthood believes. He will take it as a personal affront."

"Best he separates himself from me now. Aisling and I will not be able to remain here long. Once it is discovered what we have done, Ruadhán will demand accountability, both from Domnall and from yourself. Plead ignorance and, when asked, condemn my actions. I will not have the consequences fall on either of you."

"And your sons and daughter? What of them?"

Ciarán dared not confide any more of his plans. Aodhán's mind was strong, but in an unguarded moment . . . and Ruahán was not one to relent. "Care for them as I should have."

"Where will you go?"

"Please, *mo chara*, ask me no more. 'Tis bad enough I have asked what I have. You cannot guard your mind from sunset to sunset. And Ruadhán is not one to rest when the honor of the goddess is involved."

Aodhán nodded, but Ciarán could sense his friend trying to search his mind. Fortunately, he was able to block him. He should scold him for trying to do so, but he would have done no different had their positions been reversed, and it was not his place to reprimand his brother priest.

"Let us go now. The sun is nearly above the horizon, and all will be returning from the grove, their morning prayers finished."

"It is good that Ruadhán still expects you to be keeping track of Padraig's movements, lest he would wonder at your absence for so long."

"And what of yourself?"

"I went for a walk through the forest to check on a family of birds. As guardian of the air, it is within my purview."

Ciarán lifted an eyebrow. "You would tell an untruth, to Ruadhán of all people?"

"I will not be lying. There is a family of sparrows I plan to look in on. And if they ask where you are, I can honestly say I do not know, thanks to your stubbornness."

"And if he asks if you knew what I was about?"

"I'll tell him that I had some knowledge but had hoped to talk you out of it." Aodhán frowned. "He may not believe that I thought to succeed, but he will believe I tried, as I have. I will miss you, *mo chara*."

He looked in Aodhán's eyes, so like his own, so like Domnall's, so like his children's. "And I you, my friend." You have been a brother to me, and I shall never forget you, but you must distance yourself from me now. Curse my name if you must. I will not be offended."

Aodhán laughed, trying to lighten the moment, no doubt, but his eyes spoke of his pain. "I have done that on more than one occasion, *mo chara*. No one will be surprised."

Ciarán swallowed the ball of sorrow that had formed in his throat and closed Aodhán's fingers around the ring. "Let us be about it. Aisling will be waiting."

****

"What did you do with ring?" Ciarán opened his eyes and turned to Aodhán, his heart thumping a rapid rhythm against his ribs. Had his brother given it to Domnall, as he'd requested, or had he given it to Bréanainn after stealing him away? Could it be possible that he had married and passed it down through the generations? No, it was too much to hope for, and yet Fionnuala's eyes and hair . . . how had he never noticed before?

"I gave it to your eldest son, Bréanainn, before I left him on the road. It was my hope he would pass it on as I had asked, but he was a wee lad. As I was sealed in my own tomb not long after, I never . . ." He lifted a shoulder, knowing his meaning would be obvious.

"But how can we be sure?" He looked both to Fionnuala and to Timothy by her side. Why had he never noticed how much the child looked like his mother, how much he resembled his own son? Or maybe he had and found it too painful to consider.

"Well, there's more, isn't there?" Fionnuala was still crying, but he realized they were not tears of sorrow or pain. The smile on her face practically stretched to her ears, causing her dimples to deepen.

"Tell him, Mamaí." Timothy was bobbing up and down like a toy boat, his own smile dancing happily across his angelic face.

"Me maiden name was McKieran, and there's been a Fionn in our family for as far back as I can remember. Seems it went with the ring."

Ciarán's mouth dropped open, dozens of thoughts colliding in his head. Could any of this be real? "Fionn was me *seanathair*'s name. The one who raised Aodhán and me, until the priesthood came to retrieve us."

"Aodhán told us when he realized who I was."

"And how long have ye known, then?" He turned to his brother, and Aodhán held his hands up in surrender.

"We've known a few weeks, but it wasn't something to be telling ye over the phone, now was it?"

"We both agreed 'twould be best to wait till I could tell ye face-to-face."

"Ye're right, o' course. And 'tis not as if I could have come any sooner, what with the babes and me classes and all." He was still trying to wrap his head around all he'd just been told. "So ye're me granddaughter, then?"

"And me too." Unable to stay his excitement any longer, Timothy ran around the table and wrapped his arms around Ciarán's neck. "Wait till ye meet Seanathair Fionn."

Ciarán held tight to the boy, his words gradually creeping into his consciousness. Grandfather Fionn, he would be his descendent as well. And Fionnuala had something like six sisters, didn't she?

"Now just calm yerself down, Timothy," Duffy said. "We can't be saying anything about this to anyone else. Remember, we talked about this, about Ciarán and Aodhán's secret."

"I remember." Timothy slipped down onto Ciarán's lap and rested his head against his chest, the way Bréanainn might have, the way Fionn did, and Ciarán held him tight, a combination of emotions bubbling up in his chest. Joy at finding his family, pain at all the years he'd lost, frustration at the secret that would hinder their reunion.

"'Tis all right, lad. We can't be telling everyone, but surely we might be letting yer Seanathair Fionn in on our little secret. Let's wait a bit and see, though, eh."

Timothy's smile reappeared, as did his excitement, and he jumped from Ciarán's lap, clearly unable to sit in one place. "Uncle Ciarán said we could, Mamaí . . . I mean . . . Should I still be calling him Uncle Ciarán?"

"I think 'twould be for the best," Fionnuala said, the tenderness in her eyes spreading beyond her son to take Ciarán in as well. "And I believe he said we'd wait a bit and see, so ye're still not to say a word. Is that clear?"

"I would never break a sacred trust," Timothy said. "That's what it is, isn't it, Uncle?"

"I believe it is."

Fionnuala smiled, tousling her son's hair. "We haven't mentioned a thing to the rest o' them. Kathleen would be blurting it out before she could stop herself. This one wouldn't have known either . . ." Fionnuala cast a mock frown in her son's direction. "But he was eavesdropping, wasn't he?"

Timothy's cheeks darkened to a rosy pink. "Well, I'm glad I did, or I wouldn't know Uncle Ciarán was really my grandfather, would I?"

Ciarán smiled, leaning over so that he was staring into the boy's eyes. "I know ye'll keep our secret well. Uncle Aodhán and I are trusting ye with our lives."

"I won't tell anyone unless you say I should. I promise."

"Well then," Duffy said. "Should we be about eating? Sure, me stomach's certain me throat's been cut."

****

Caitlin had been unusually quiet the entire day. At first, Ciarán hadn't noticed it, but as the day wore on, it began to trouble him. There was only one thing he could think of that could be the cause of it.

"This won't make any difference as far as Fionn and Aisling are concerned, ye know. I love them more than me own life."

Caitlin had been folding some clothes, but on hearing him she stood up straight and turned around to face him. "I didn't think it would. Why would you ever—"

"Ye've been so quiet since we found out. I thought . . ." For once in his life, he couldn't find the words to say what he needed to. How his heart was so full of love for her and the twins, and yet there was room for Fionnuala and all the rest as well.

Caitlin dropped Aisling's little skirt on the bed and walked over to him, wrapping her arms around his waist and looking him in the eyes. "Let's get one thing straight, Ciarán Patrick Donnelly, I would never doubt your love for us or your capacity to share that love with others as well."

"Then why . . . ?"

"I figured maybe you needed some time to mull it over. I know I did. Don't get me wrong, it's fabulous, but . . ." She shook her head and laughed. "It is mind-blowing, isn't it? To think that you found not one descendant, but a whole slew of them. And better yet, it's Fionnuala. They're already like family. And Aodhán is marrying Duffy's sister."

She started to cry, though this time he could see they were happy tears, filled with love and excitement. He wrapped his arms tight around her, squeezing her to himself. The twins were fed and sleeping peacefully, and all he wanted was to take her to himself and show her how much he loved her.

Lifting her in his arms, he carried her to the bed, lowering himself above her.

"Why, Mr. Donnelly, are you about to ravish me?"

"I am, Mrs. Donnelly. Have ye any objection?"

"None whatsoever."

He bent over, his lips embracing hers, a soft, gentle caress that whispered the promise of more. And God, how he wanted more, wanted to feel his soul touch hers and assure him that it was all real. He slipped his hand beneath her blouse, grateful she was wearing one of her nursing bras that fastened at the front, for he had every intention of suckling there. Though he had a far more nefarious purpose in mind.

Ciarán sat up. Turning off the light and throwing his T-shirt to the side, he returned to his wife, one hand massaging her breast beneath the bra while the other undid the buttons of her cotton blouse. Within seconds, his chest was pressed against hers, flesh to flesh, their lips locked in a feverish dance of carnal delight.

Caitlin's fingers slipped between their bodies, creeping beneath the waistband of his jeans until they reached their destination, and Ciarán released a moan of anticipation. Sweet Brigid, her touch caused an ache of desire so intense it ran along his thighs and reached deep into his core.

Leaning on his side, his tongue still exploring the intricacies of her mouth, he slipped his pants down to his knees, using his legs to kick them off the rest of the way. Succeeding in that endeavor, he brushed his lips along her neck, coming to pause for a moment on her full breasts. His tongue caused the tips to rise, like tiny cherries, and he wanted to devour her sweet nectar.

Caitlin gasped, her fingers knotted in his hair, pressing against his neck and urging him on. Continuing to caress her hardened nipples with one hand, he slipped down to kiss the tender skin above her hip-hugging jeans. His fingers shook, fumbling with the button until he was able to shimmy them down to her knees. She did the rest from there, kicking them aside, her body arching to meet his lips, prodding him to venture farther.

And Ciarán obliged, his lips moving lower to caress the scar that had now paled into a thin white line. Shifting his body, he crept even lower, nudging her legs apart so he could suck the soft, supple skin high on her inner thigh, and she moaned in anticipation, her legs spreading wider, encouraging him to explore deeper and more intimately.

Sweet Brigid! How he loved this woman.

****

His fingers slipped within her, and Caitlin gasped. Every cell in her body tingled, the hint of ecstasy signaled in every move of his body. Each pass of his tongue inched farther up her thigh until at last his fingers parted to grant it entry. She gripped his hair, rich and luscious, the tip of his tongue sending a throbbing ache through her body, and she arched her back to press it deeper.

Her thighs trembled as he obliged, spreading them farther apart and sucking harder and faster. But she wanted more, wanted him pulsing inside her, his body melting into hers until they were one being, joined in a passionate embrace. He always knew when she had reached her limit, when her need for him was beyond bearable, for he slipped up her body, sliding within her, slow and gentle at first, his lips stopping to suckle at her breast until the tips ached with yearning.

She threw her head back on the pillow, savoring the sense of him deep within her, her body rising to meet his every movement. At her urging, Ciarán rose to engulf her lips once more, his breath warming her, filling her with his love. His body pressed against hers, each thrust sending shivers of delight to her core, and she gripped his muscular form, begging him to bring her to the precipice of desire.

Crying out in pleasure, she mounted the summit, his warmth and devotion filling her with the intense arousal only he could supply. A wave of ecstasy engulfed her, and she abandoned herself to his care, his life throbbing within her, his seed spent once more. She wondered if it too would find a home, the way Fionn and Aisling had, and the thought left her with a thrill of contentment.

Exhausted, his head resting against her chest, he whispered the words that filled her heart with even more joy, though she didn't know how it was possible. "Sweet Brigid, *a chuisle*, I love ye more than life itself."

CHAPTER 21

The house was dark and silent when Ciarán woke. Caitlin lay snuggled against him, a shaft of moonlight revealing the curve of her luscious lips. He sighed as he recalled the moments before he'd drifted off to sleep. But somewhere in his slumber that feeling of contentment had disappeared, leaving him tense with a sense of foreboding. Experience warned him that was not a sensation he should ignore.

Slipping out from under Caitlin's petite form, he sat on the edge of the bed and pulled on his pants and T-shirt. He closed his eyes, listening to the sounds of the night. A dog barked off in the distance, a frog croaked somewhere beneath his window, but there—the crunch of footsteps on gravel. Three o'clock, the small travel alarm on their nightstand said. Who would be out and about at this hour?

Best be ready for anything. After pulling on his socks and shoes, he slipped into the hallway and checked on the twins. Sleeping like little angels at the moment. The thought made him laugh, for he knew a bit of wood nymph slumbered in each of them, waiting to wreak havoc as soon as they woke. He kissed each of them on the forehead, then turned to gaze out the window.

His stomach clenched. There against the low stone fence across from the bed and breakfast rested the chief priest Ruadhán. Though more salt than pepper now, his long beard was well-groomed and rustled in the soft summer breeze, and his white robe shimmered in the moonlight. He gazed up at the window and nodded, causing Ciarán's blood to freeze even as it coursed through his veins.

No, he wouldn't let the man near his children. He wouldn't abandon them the way he'd abandoned Bréanainn and the others. Tearing down the stairs, he reached the front door and threw it open, his pulse pounding in his throat. Without thinking, he charged across the yard, toward the white-robed figure, but before he knew what was happening his foot caught in a bramble, and he cried out in pain as he landed facedown on the road.

The house lit up like the Christmas tree they'd had last December. He could hear footsteps thumping on the staircase and the chatter of alarmed voices. In desperation, he cast a gaze across the road, but although the dog still barked in the distance and the frog still croaked beneath his window, Ruadhán was nowhere to be seen. Had it all been a dream? Or had the chief priest been playing with him?

Ciarán was just sitting up, checking his ankle, when Caitlin came bursting through the open door. "What happened? Why are you wandering around at this time in the morning? Are you all right?"

Not wanting to alarm her, he smiled. "I couldn't sleep, so I thought a bit o' fresh air might do me some good. I must have tripped over that bramble."

"What bramble?" Mrs. Byrne brushed past Caitlin, Aisling in her arms. "I just had young Eoin over here clearing the yard. Wouldn't want the wee ones getting caught on a thorny bush, now would I?"

Ciarán gazed down at his throbbing ankle. If that was true, Ruahán had planted it there deliberately and lured him from the house. "Where's Fionn?"

"Right here," Daniel said. "You woke the poor things up."

"No, he didn't." Caitlin knelt by his side and looked at his ankle. "It was about time for them to be waking up anyway."

"Let me take a look." Steve joined Caitlin, a frown crossing his face as he checked Ciarán's ankle. "It's not broken, but you did a good job of spraining it, and I'll need some antiseptic to clean out the cuts from the bramble. Ryan, give me a hand getting him back upstairs."

"Why didn't you look where you were going?" Caitlin followed them up the steps with Mrs. Byrne and Daniel leading the way.

"Never mind that. Wait till I see that Eoin," the landlady said. "I'm going to give him an earful and all, leaving that bramble across the path like he did."

"No, Mrs. Byrne." Ciarán winced as he took the third and fourth steps. "Caitlin's right. I should have been looking where I was going. Besides, I saw the yard this afternoon, and it was neat as could be. The thorns must have been dragged in somehow or blown there. Maybe one o' the cars."

"Hmm." She stopped at the top of the stairs, frowning. "Well, if ye're sure 'twas nothing round after the lad finished up."

Ciarán reached the landing and nodded. "I'm sure. 'Twas not a twig in sight."

Fionn had started to fuss, so Caitlin took him into the small nursery Mrs. Byrne had prepared. "Will you be all right while I feed them?"

"O' course I will. Steve here's going to see me all cleaned and wrapped up like a shiny gift, aren't ye?"

"He'll be fine." As soon as Steve settled him on the bed with a basin of water and everything else he'd be needing, he closed the door and turned to face Ciarán. "You want to tell me what really happened?"

"I saw Ruadhán—staring up at the twins' bedroom, he was—so I went running out after him. That bramble wasn't left there by Eoin. Ruadhán set it out, knowing I'd come running when I saw him. He counted on me tripping over it, though he was probably hoping for a worse injury, unless . . ."

He stopped mid-sentence, and Steve looked up from where he'd bent over to tend Ciarán's ankle. "What is it?"

"No, Ruadhán wouldn't have resorted to such a thing. He was a pompous arse at times, but I never knew him to stoop to that."

"You're afraid something may have been on the thorns, a poison of some sort?"

"It crossed me mind, but 'twas not his way."

"This is the man you keep having dreams about? The one who wants to steal your children?"

"It is, but poison?" Ciarán shook his head. "If he meant to do me in that way, he'd have made sure I knew what he was about."

"That's comforting. Well, do you feel anything strange? There doesn't seem to be any infection or discoloration around the wounds other than the expected bruising from the sprain."

"No, I'm fine. Just sore. How long will I have to be staying off it?"

"For a day or two at least. The swelling will probably subside by tomorrow night, but I'd stay off it another day or so anyway, just to make sure it heals okay. As far as the cuts, they should heal in a week or so, barring any tainted thorns."

"Don't be saying anything about this to Caitlin, eh. She's so happy being here with everyone. And it may have been nothing more than a dream at any rate. They can be quite vivid at times. 'Tis a gift, me father used to say, but I'm not so sure about that."

"Because they're so vague, you mean."

"That's it! Vivid and vague at the same time. I can't always tell what they mean. Sometimes 'tis naught more than me own fears taking form."

"Have you mentioned anything about it to Aodhán?"

"I have. Why d'ye think he's had Ryan wandering around the Hills of ár Sinsear with him?"

"Yeah, Ryan did mention that. Have you spoken to Father Mike about it?"

"He thinks 'tis just me own fears about being a father and guilt over having to leave me fifth-century children."

Steve shrugged. "Maybe he's right. Try to get some rest. For now, everyone's safe. In the morning, I'll take a look out by the wall and see if there are any footprints."

Ciarán laughed. "There won't be. Ruadhán would never be so careless."

"Unless he wants to make sure you know it's not a dream."

Somehow that thought didn't do anything to ease Ciarán's mind.

****

"The clumsy oaf tripped over his own two feet, did he?"

Ciarán could hear Aodhán coming up the stairs and put down the book he was reading. *Airport.* Caitlin had a wicked sense of humor. And she expected him to get back on a plane, with his children to boot.

"Morning, brother," Aodhán said, a twinkle in his eye. "I hear ye had a bit of a rough night."

"Close the door and get in here. I need to be talking to ye."

The smile dropped from his face, and he pulled a chair up close to the bed. "What is it?"

"I saw Ruadhán last night. I'm sure o' it."

"D'ye think it could have been one o' yer dreams?"

Ciarán sighed and shook his head. "I can't say for sure, but one thing I am certain o': that yard was spic and span, as Dennis would say, when we got home last evening, but I tripped over a clump o' blackthorn that was nearly as big as I am."

"And ye didn't see it? The sky was lit like a bright lantern last night."

"I wasn't thinking about that, now was I? He was staring up at the twins' window."

"Sure, ye don't think . . . yer dream said 'twas not them ye needed to be worrying over."

"But me dreams come in riddles, don't they? I have to decipher them before they make any sense at all, which is usually at the last moment."

"Yer dream saved Caitlin from being ravaged by Bradaigh, didn't it?"

"Only just, but I didn't realize what it meant till the last minute. And I was too late to save Niamh from his perversions."

"Niamh's well, brother. Ye arrived in time to save her life and all the wee ones in that school. Ye're too hard on yerself. Ye get snippets o' the puzzle and expect to put them all together at once."

"All right, then. What could it mean? 'Tis the older ones I need fear for." Ciarán scrubbed the palms of hands against his eyes. "Me older children, but I have no older children . . . unless Fionnuala? Has Ruadhán found out about her somehow?"

"How could he? First, he'd actually have to be here, and regardless o' what ye saw last night, we can't actually be sure 'twas him."

"A lot o' old men in white robes running round here, are there?" Aodhán rolled his eyes, and Ciarán continued. "What ye mean is we can't be sure I actually saw anyone. 'Twould not be the first time me dreams seemed real."

"So what are we to do, then? We can't be watching over them all twenty-four hours a day. It could mean Timothy. He's older than the twins, or Fionnuala's father or one o' her sisters. The list is enormous. Ninety-nine percent o' which don't even know who we are, let alone what Ruadhán might be about."

"I don't know, but something lured me outside last night, and 'twas no dream that lay that clump o' blackthorn in me path. Blackthorn, Aodhán, o' all the bushes round."

"*Straif.*" Aodhán stared out the window. "If the wounds were to go septic. Perhaps 'tis yerself ye need to be looking out for. Maybe that's what Bréanainn meant by the older ones."

"I don't know, but we'll need to be on guard and keep an eye out for anyone that looks suspicious."

"He won't be walking round amongst us, not if he's still wearing his robes."

"Why not? Bradaigh did."

"But he'd dressed like everyone else, and even with that, ye'd have known him straightaway if ye'd seen him, now wouldn't ye? 'Twas only because he kept himself hidden from us that he could carry it off."

"Has there been anyone new to the village lately?"

"A few people, actually. An older woman inherited a cottage from her father. And a middle-aged couple with children moved into a place at the north end o' the lake. He's started a charter fishing company. And an older man, retired from teaching in Dublin."

"Have ye met him?"

"I have, and I'll admit 'twas something familiar about him. Before ye ask, I already checked him out. Niamh has a friend at the school he says he taught at, and her description o' the man fit him perfectly. Seems he's who he says he is. Name o' Cormac McGuire."

"But there was something familiar about him?"

"There was, and I thought hard about it. It finally came to me. Ruadhán was sure to have a few brothers, just as we did. And 'tis likely they produced some descendants. Chances are 'tis one o' them. Besides, Cormac doesn't have as much gray as Ruadhán did, and he wears glasses, not to mention he has no beard, or priestly mark for that matter."

"Appearances can be changed. Look at us. We look nothing like we once did."

"True enough, but if 'twas indeed Ruadhán ye saw last night, he's altered nothing. He looked much like he always did. If that's the case, it couldn't have been our Mr. McGuire, now could it?"

"Then we need to find out if 'twas just another o' me dreams or if Ruadhán truly is walking about."

"I don't think the Book o' Carraig will be able to help us this time."

"No, but maybe the Cave o' Rúin Ársa can. Steve said I should be back on me feet in a day or two. As soon as I am, we'll take a look round, see if anything's been disturbed. In the meantime, see if ye can find out anything more concerning this Cormac McGuire."

****

"Afternoon, Cormac," Aodhán said later that day as he headed down to one of the locals' favorite fishing spots. "D'ye ever do anything with the fish ye catch? Sure, ye must have landed a good deal by now."

"Ah, if only that were the truth o' it. Alas, I'm not a very good fisherman, it seems. I've caught a few, though. Terry O'Day taught me how to clean them, and they fried up rather nice, if I do say so meself."

Aodhán smiled and sat down by his side. "'Tis a grand day, isn't it?" He opened a small bag with a bologna sandwich in it, offering half to the old man.

"Oh no, I'm fine. Just stopped home a while ago to get a bite to eat. Ye're not working today, then?"

"We are, mostly classifying artifacts. I'm on me lunch break now." Aodhán took a bite of the sandwich and stared out across the water. How was he going to broach the subject without raising the man's suspicions?

"Ye're not from around here either, are ye?" Cormac asked.

It seemed the man had given him the opening he needed. "No, me brother was one o' the archaeologists on the site here. I came to visit him last year, met Niamh, and . . ." He shrugged.

"Decided to stay. A wise choice, I'd say. She's a lovely *cailín.*"

"She is that. What made ye decide to settle here, o' all places? Sure, 'tis a ways off the beaten path."

"Oh, I've been here before. I may not be much o' a fisherman, but I love it anyway. It's got quite a reputation for salmon and trout fishing. Me friend and I spent some time here one summer, years ago. I fell in love with it then and, after deciding to retire, made up me mind to return."

"Where's yer friend living now?"

"He's passed on, God rest him, as have many I once knew. There are a few that remain, but . . . well, ye lose touch over the years, don't ye? Now I'm making new friends here."

"Did ye never marry, then, have children?"

"There was a lass once, long ago, but I put me career above her, I'm afraid. She wed another, and I went off to follow me destiny."

"Ye're not from Dublin, then?"

"Not originally, no, but the opportunity arose, and so I took it. Let's just say the lass wasn't pleased about me decision. 'Twas more than that involved, but I'd rather not speak on it, if ye don't mind."

"Oh, o' course. I didn't mean to be prying. Just making conversation."

"I took no offense, lad. Sure, I've asked a few questions o' me own, haven't I? How else are ye to get to know people. 'Tis no secret. Why settle for a lowly teacher when ye could have a prince?"

"A prince, was it?"

Cormac laughed, his hazel eyes sparkling as he spoke. "Well, maybe not a prince, but he was a good bit better off then I was. And to be fair, I could have taken a job more to her liking, but I chose me passion over her. I suppose 'twas just not meant to be. Never found another to interest me either. And so now I sit here, content with the new friends I'm making and enjoying me retirement."

"I'm glad ye're happy, then. I'd best be getting back to me cataloguing."

"What kinds o' things do ye find up in those hills anyway?"

"We don't excavate in the hills much anymore. There was an accident last year, and they've deemed them too dangerous. We've been working at a few sites round the lake."

"Well, wherever it is, what kinds o' things do ye dig up?"

"Pots and other kitchenware, mostly. A few pieces o' jewelry, a bone here and there."

"Glorified grave robbers, then." Cormac laughed, his eyes twinkling once more. "I'd like to think if someone were to dig me up centuries from now, they might find a book or two, maybe one on fishing."

Aodhán's stomach clenched for a moment. *Don't be ridiculous. The man was a teacher. It's only natural he'd mention books.* "The prevailing theory is that nothing was written down from the period, that it was all passed down by word o' mouth. What d'ye think about it?"

"Me? Sure, I wouldn't know, but it seems odd that they wouldn't have found some way to make a record o' things."

Aodhán wasn't certain how he thought the man would react, but his question hadn't affected the man's pleasant demeanor in the least. "I'm thinking ye're right. Most likely 'tis just that time took its toll. Parchment, bark, whatever they wrote on would have disintegrated over the years, unless o' course, they'd happened upon a way to preserve it."

"D'ye think they might have done? Sure, I'd love to get a look at something like that. Imagine the history it holds."

Aodhán's heart was pounding. But what had the man really said? Nothing that anyone interested in history wouldn't say. "I'm sad to say Professor Lambert hasn't come across anything so marvelous." Still, perhaps he should add a little extra precaution. "'Twould go straight to Dublin if he did. Ye can be sure o' that. Such a grand discovery would need to be conserved immediately."

"Ah well, we can always dream."

"True enough. I'd best be getting back or the professor will be docking me pay. Best o' luck with yer fishing."

Aodhán headed back toward the lakeside grove where they were working on excavating what remained of a few standing stones. He had to stop being suspicious of everything the man said, of reading meanings into his statements that weren't there. And yet he couldn't keep his mind from drifting in that direction. Perhaps he was allowing Ciarán's dreams to influence him too much. Besides, how could Cormac be Ruadhán if the latter had appeared to Ciarán the night before in his high priest regalia, beard and all? No, Cormac might be a descendant of the chief priest's sibling, but nothing more. He didn't even want to entertain what it meant if he wasn't.

CHAPTER 22

Are ye sure ye should be gallivanting about on that ankle just yet?" Aodhán asked.

Ciarán put the kickstand down on his bike and grinned at his brother. "We've not done any walking as yet, now have we?" He turned to start up the hill before him, certain Aodhán was rolling his eyes.

"We will be now, though, won't we, and up a hill, no less."

"Taking over for yer future bride, are ye?"

"What d'ye mean by that?"

"It seems I remember ye complaining about Niamh saying the same to yerself."

"'Twas six months after I was injured, now wasn't it, not two days, and the doctor had already said I was fine."

"And Steve has given me the all-clear as well, not to mention 'twas only a sprained ankle to begin with, not a serious back injury."

"Are the wounds healing? You know how bad blackthorn can be."

"'Twas more than the thorns I was concerned about. There are potions in the Book o' Carraig that could affect the mind if it got into yer blood stream."

"Ye don't think Ruadhán would . . ."

"I don't know, but I can't help wonder why such concoctions were there in the first place." They had just reached the cave, and both he and Aodhán stopped short. The boulder had been moved aside, the dark entrance gaping wide. "Have ye been up here since we removed the Book o' Carraig?"

Aodhán barely shook his head, his eyes darting over the hillside. "It could be the wee hooligans, I suppose. We've had to chase them away from Tuamaí Dearmadta now and again."

"Or it could be Ruadhán."

"If he was here," Aodhán said, "sure, he's discovered the book is missing. He won't be at all pleased."

"We'd best go inside. Maybe he's left us a message." The cave was empty, just as they had left it almost a year before.

Aodhán walked toward the murky void at the rear of the cave. "We should have brought more than these little torches. 'Tis black as pitch back here." He let out a yell and staggered backward, the sound of his flashlight clattering against stone as it fell into what appeared to be a deep chasm.

"What happened?" Ciarán sprinted across the cave and knelt beside him.

"I think I almost slipped away to the otherworld. I felt a bit o' rock shift beneath me foot and grabbed that boulder there to keep meself from falling forward. Lost me torch, though."

Ciarán shifted forward on his hands and knees, Aodhán following with the utmost caution. When he felt the edge of the large fissure, he shined his light into the hole. "Sweet Brigid! I suppose the elders were right, then. This cave is the portal to the otherworld."

"What d'ye mean by that?"

"Sure, anyone who went over the edge is bound to end in Tír na nÓg or heaven or whatever else ye deem the afterlife to be."

"Sweet Mother!" Aodhán inched back and wiped a hand across his face. "That could have been me. Niamh would never forgive me if I went and fell into a gaping abyss."

Ciarán shot a glance at the boulder to Aodhán's left. "Ye would have if ye'd been but a wee bit to yer right. Sure, yer guardian angel was watching over ye and all."

Aodhán blessed himself and stood up. "That he was. We'd best be getting out o' here and seal this place up. God forbid a wee one wanders in here exploring."

Ciarán took a quick look around before nodding. "There's naught else to see here anyway. If Ruadhán was here, he left us no message."

"Or that was the message. He's sure to know 'twas us that took the book."

Ciarán didn't say a word, but followed his brother outside. Could Ruadhán have had a hand in Aodhán nearly going over the edge? Was he the elder one he needed to worry about? He winced as his foot shifted a little on the rocky ground. Maybe it was both of them.

"What made ye walk back that way in the first place?"

"I heard a shuffling sound, like feet moving across the ground."

"'Twas probably just a wee mouse or some other animal."

"Most likely, but I'm not going back to see if ye're right. The poor thing is probably a lump o' fur lying at the bottom by now anyway."

They shifted the boulder across the opening, wedging it tight in place. They needed all the energy they could muster to do it, drawing strength from the forces of nature that surrounded them. Aodhán sat against the boulder, resting his arms on his knees.

"Well, one thing is sure." Ciarán flopped down by his side. "If 'tis moved again, we'll be certain Ruadhán is alive and well."

"True enough. The way we've wedged that boulder in there, 'twill take more than brute strength to budge it." Aodhán stretched his back.

"Is it still bothering ye?" Ciarán asked, concerned about his brother's injury.

"Now and again, but don't look so worried. The doctor says 'tis normal and will get better in time."

Ciarán nodded, knowing Aodhán wouldn't try to conceal anything from him. He sighed and looked back up at the cave. Aodhán was right. Ruadhán would be furious if he had entered the cave. Not only would he have discovered the book missing, but he'd likely found out about them as well. Though they'd managed to keep their true nature confined to a select group of confidants, they couldn't conceal the fact that two archaeologists had fought it out with a serial killer the year before. Two archaeologists named Ciarán and Aodhán. Ruadhán would figure it out. Would he know where they'd sent the book as well?

"I'm thinking we may need to be taking a trip to Dublin," he said.

"Dublin?" Aodhán threw him a curious glance. "What on earth for?"

"To see he hasn't broken in and stolen the book."

"Sure, Brian Flaherty would have noticed if he had."

"He wouldn't make the scene we did, now would he? The book could be gone and no one the wiser. It won't be hurting to take a look, now will it?"

"Ye've a good point, what with it not being on display and all. We can't be telling Brian we've come to check on it, though. After me being stolen right from under his nose, he's a bit sensitive about it."

"Not to worry. We'll think o' something to put the man's mind at ease . . . and ours as well."

****

Ruadhán slipped out from behind the large stone pillar inside the cave, his hands balled at his sides. How dare those two traitorous clerics enter the sacred precincts of the Cave of Rúin Ársa yet again. He cast his eyes into the dark chasm at his side. 'Twould have been an odd justice if one of them had been swallowed by the abyss and sent to the otherworld. He still needed them, though. Without a doubt, they had removed the Book of Carraig.

He closed his eyes for a moment, trying to quell the anger that was building within him. How dare they touch the sacred book with their filthy hands. Worse yet, from the rumors around the village and the knowledge he'd gained from scanning Duffy Flynn's mind, they had even attempted to read the words it held. Though in that case, it might not have been such an unforgiveable transgression since it ridded the world of that wicked malcontent Bradaigh. Perhaps the goddess had even willed it so, but if that were the case . . .

He sat down on a large boulder. "How am I to take this, me lady? If ye truly did permit it, am I to continue along as I have or leave them at peace?" He got up and started pacing. "I do not understand. Why have I been reawakened?"

It should have been you who awoke to quell Bradaigh and his perversions. He could hear the sweet melody of the goddess's voice whispering in his ear. *Clearly, their god has more power than I thought. Fear not, my faithful son. Stay true to the path you have charted, but take care in your actions. We must not alert them too soon to your true objective.*

Ruadhán sat back down on the boulder and sighed, his mind and purpose joined as one once more. He would wait a bit longer before leaving. And perhaps not leave the entrance so wide open this time. Ciarán was right about one thing: they didn't want some innocent child falling into Tír na nÓg. Just a crack would be enough to alert the two miscreants of his presence in this world.

With a wave of his hand, the boulder moved enough for him to exit the cave, and a flick of his finger replaced it within an inch of complete closure. Enough for Ciarán or his brother to notice should they come up to investigate again. Such fools to think they could outwit him. They didn't even recognize their chief priest. He would see to it they never woke from their sleep this time, but first Ciarán would watch as the goddess took what was never rightfully his. With one child, a descendant of one that was taken, she would re-father her priesthood. Then Ciarán and his conniving brother would sleep an endless sleep, their fates at the hands of their goddessmother once more. This time he would make sure of it.

He growled beneath his breath as he hurried down the slope. Alas, first he had to locate the Book of Carraig.

While he recalled many of the potions and satires held within it, he was, after all, an old man. Even the goddess wouldn't expect him to remember every inscription. Besides, he dared not chance the possibility of the book falling into someone else's hands. Someone who truly had no notion of the power it held or someone who intended to use it for evil. At least Domnall's youngest sons, whatever their faults, did not seem intent on doing that. Perhaps the goddess would not make them suffer long, after all.

He smiled to himself as he slipped behind a gorse bush that stood across from Duffy Flynn's home. Fionnuala had gone inside, the three youngest children whining about their lunch, but Timothy remained outside playing with some sort of spinning toy. Now was his chance to move on to the next step in his plan.

Brushing off his suit, he walked up to the child. "Good afternoon to ye, Timothy."

"Oh, hello, Mr. McGuire. D'ye want to be speaking with me ma or da?"

"Actually, 'tis yerself I'd be speaking with. As ye're off from school on the Saturday, I was wondering if ye'd be joining me for a wee bit o' fishing. 'Tis supposed to be a grand day for it, but the lads are off on other pursuits, and I'd be grateful for the company. I've rented a wee boat and all. O' course, ye'd have to be up at the crack o' dawn and check that 'tis all right with yer mother and father. I could speak to them now if ye'd like."

The boy hesitated a moment. Ruadhán knew he'd been scolded and forbidden from leaving the confines of his own garden for the next week, so he let the wee scamp mull it over for a bit. If he was anything like his ancestor, he'd come up with an excuse to avoid allowing Ruadhán to speak to his parents and go anyway.

A cry went up from the house. The younger brother, Ruadhán thought. Followed by a scolding from his mother about playing with his food. Sure enough, the wee urchin jumped on the diversion. "Oh no, that's all right, Mr. McGuire. She's a wee bit occupied at the moment. I'll let them know and meet ye down by the dock in the morning. Sure, they won't mind a bit. 'Twill give me something to do and keep me out o' me ma's hair."

"Well, all right, then, but ye be sure to ask yer parents' permission. I wouldn't want to be worrying them any."

Timothy waved good-bye and went back to his spinning toy. Yes, he was just like his impudent ancestor. Ruadhán's plan was working perfectly.

****

"Now remember," Steve said as they drove along the N5, "we're just there to check out a few pages of the book. After Aodhán disappeared, Brian beefed up security, and he's a little touchy about it."

Ciarán could well imagine. Brian Flaherty was the museum director in Dublin, and he had no desire to upset the poor man any further. "Did no one tell him what really happened?"

"Do you really want to let someone else in on your secret? Aren't there enough already? One slip of a tongue, a casual remark, and you could find yourself back on a lab table or under supervision in some government facility."

"Only if they were believed. 'Tis a bit far-fetched, isn't it?"

"Do you want to take that chance? You've a family to think of now. Brian will get over it."

"I know ye're right," Aodhán said. "'Tis a shame, though. The poor man's taking me theft all on himself, just as Neil has in New York."

"They didn't suffer any real consequences because of it," Steve said. "The security was up to snuff in both instances, so they weren't held accountable."

"Up to snuff?" Aodhán said.

"It met the standard the museum required," Ciarán said.

Steve chuckled. "What are you two doing? Keeping a catalogue of idioms?"

Aodhán crumpled his brow. "Learning the language is hard enough, isn't it, without all the extra little bits."

"We had our own, ye know." Ciarán leaned back against the seat and closed his eyes. Little by little, he was getting used to traveling by automobile. Now if he could only conquer the plane flights. "Ye don't speak Irish, d'ye? Is there anything besides English ye do speak?"

"Yes, the physiology of the human body. While my friends were learning how to conjugate verbs in Spanish or French, I was studying the intricate workings of the digestive system."

"Fair enough." Aodhán leaned forward, resting his arm on the back of the front seat. "I'm sitting in the front on the way home."

"Ye're not," Ciarán said. "I've got to get used to it now that I'm driving."

"Ye've been driving for months now, and do it every day, I might add. I walk to work."

"How old are you two?" Steve shook his head, a grin spreading across his face.

"Too old to be acting like Duffy's wee ones, I'd say." Ciarán shrugged, ashamed of his childish behavior. "Sorry, brother. Ye're right as usual."

A guilty smile crept across Aodhán's lips. "I've been driving into Dublin twice a week, haven't I? 'Tis just I never get to sit in the front and simply enjoy the scenery."

"Doesn't Niamh ever drive? Caitlin's always getting behind the wheel."

"She does, but she's usually got grades to mark or something, so 'tis easier for me to do it."

"Well, I tell you what," Steve said, "you can both sit up here on the way back, and I'll take a nap on the backseat."

"Now wait one minute," Ciarán and Aodhán said simultaneously before they all broke out in laughter.

Ciarán was happy to get his mind off Ruadhán and what danger his children might be in, but the conversation seemed to have run its course, so inevitably it turned back to the issue at hand.

"Brian knows to expect us, does he?" he said in an effort to divert his attention for a bit longer.

"Daniel called him yesterday." Steve put his blinker on and changed lanes. "Mind you, Brian wasn't thrilled. He's not even going to leave us alone with it."

"Do ye think he suspects us, then?" Ciarán said. "I mean, we were there when Aodhán went missing."

"I think he does," Aodhán said. "The man's friendly enough, but he always gets this wee tic in the corner o' his right eye when I'm around. His head may not be able to explain it, but somewhere in the nooks and crannies o' his brain, he knows it."

"Nooks and crannies," Ciarán said, "like the English muffins?"

"Exactly, but Niamh says ye can be using it this way as well."

"Seriously?" Steve said. "We're discussing the possibility that Brian Flaherty might, somewhere in his subconscious mind, know that you're his missing Celtic priest, and you two are debating the usages of idioms."

"'Tis a serious business," Ciarán said. "Besides, I think Aodhán might be right. Neil Dwyer does the same with me, doesn't he? Not a tic exactly, but he's walked away scratching his head on more than one occasion."

"And you're sure there's nothing else causing him to do that?"

Ciarán narrowed his eyes at Steve. He knew the man was just making a joke, but it seemed an appropriate response. Caitlin used it on him all the time.

"All right, this is it." Steve turned the car off. "Remember, don't make the poor guy feel like we're checking up on him."

They decided to go in the front door so it appeared no more than a friendly visit. Brian was there waiting for them, wringing his hands. "It's still there."

"We didn't think it wouldn't be," Steve said. "Didn't Professor Lambert mention why we were coming?"

"Sure, he did, but . . ." Brian's cheeks tinted a deep fuchsia. "When I heard ye'd want to be seeing the book, I was too busy running the reasons through me head to hear another word he was saying, now wasn't I?"

"There's nothing to worry yerself over, Brian," Aodhán said. "We want to copy down a few o' the inscriptions, see if we can't be translating them."

"'Twill keep Caitlin occupied," Ciarán said, "her just having the babes and all."

"That's right." A broad smile broke out on the director's face. "I hear congratulations are in order. A boy and a girl. Yer brother never stops bragging about them, and rightfully so."

"They are grand. Aisling and Fionn. I never thought two little creatures could fill me heart with so much wonder."

"Amazing that, isn't it? I have a few o' me own. Wait till they get a wee bit bigger, though. They'll be turning that hair o' yers gray soon enough." He smiled, patting Ciarán on the back. "I reckon we'd best be getting that book for ye. I've set it up in one o' the private rooms, and if ye wouldn't be minding, I'm keeping a few guards in there with ye. 'Tis not that I don't trust ye, but those thieves that stole the Celt were canny sods, weren't they? Took him right from under our noses. Better safe than sorry."

"'Tis no problem at all, Brian." Aodhán flashed the man one of his most charming smiles. "We shouldn't be more than an hour or so. Just lead the way."

The man smiled back and led them to the book. He'd no sooner left then Aodhán leaned over to whisper. "Did ye see the corner o' his eye twitch? It happens every time."

Steve frowned. "I suppose we should tell the poor man one of these days."

"I think we should as well," Aodhán said. "Every time it happens, I want to take him aside and let the cat out of the bag."

"That's one of Dennis's, isn't it?" Aodhán nodded and Ciarán smiled, thinking fondly of his friend back in New York. "Well, I agree with ye both, but now's not the time to be doing it, especially when there might be another rogue priest running round looking to steal it."

"Don't even suggest that," Steve said. "At the moment, it's no more than speculation. No offense, Ciarán, but it could be nothing more than your overactive imagination."

"I agree with ye there as well, but until we know for sure 'tis best we continue to keep them in the dark, eh." He sighed and rested his hand on the ancient volume. At least for today it was safe and hadn't fallen into the wrong hands . . . or the right, depending on one's point of view.

CHAPTER 23

Ciarán jumped out of bed the next morning to the sound of someone banging on the front door, followed by muffled voices at the bottom of the stairs. A woman was crying. One thought sprang to his mind, and he dashed into the hall to find Caitlin standing at the top of the stairs, Aisling in her arms. He gave a sigh of relief at the sight and the sound of Fionn's gurgling coming from the nursery. The feeling was short-lived, for the look on Caitlin's face belied the scene of tranquility that reigned outside their bedroom door.

"Timothy Flynn is missing," she said. "Fionnuala's beside herself."

Ciarán's breath caught in his throat, the words from his dreams resounding in his ears. "Fear for the older ones."

Caitlin must have sensed the sheer panic surging through his soul, for she simply squeezed his arm and uttered one word, "Go!"

Taking the steps two at a time, in nothing but his jeans and T-shirt, he stood in front of Fionnuala, struggling to control his own emotions while trying to calm hers. "Tell me what happened. When was the last time ye saw the lad?"

"Last night, when I gave him his bedtime kiss. He thinks he's getting too old for it, but . . ." She started to cry again, and he pressed her against his chest as he would his daughter, for in essence was that not what she was? When she seemed to have her tears under control again, he pulled back and asked her another question.

"And when did ye notice he was missing?"

"Just a few minutes ago. I called him down for breakfast. When he didn't come, I went up to see what was keeping him. 'Tis not like him to miss a meal, especially o' late. He's eating us out o' house and home now he's growing so . . ." The tears started again, and Ciarán steered her into the parlor and sat her on the love seat before sitting next to her.

"He's a lad, Fionnuala, probably off on some adventure, 'tis all." He said it to calm her, but he suspected her fears were all too real. Perhaps he should have told them to keep watch, should have warned them, but they could debate that later. Right now he had to find his grandson.

"If that's what he's done, I'll tan his hide so he won't be sitting down for a week."

"Well, maybe not quite that long," Ciarán said, trying to hide the desperation building in his stomach, "but sure, I'll be giving him a good tongue-lashing to go with it. For right now, though, we need to be finding the wee hooligan. Have ye told Duffy?"

"Sure, he's off to work, isn't he? With a client in Castlebar."

"All right, 'tis just as well, then. Ye'd probably be worrying him for nothing. The lad will be back and well scolded by the time he gets home."

Fionnuala nodded and blew her nose. "'Tis just that he was already being punished, ye see. It seems like such a foolish thing now, but he has to learn. What if he ran off because o' it, though?"

"Then he'll be home before lunchtime," Mrs. Byrne said. "Me eldest lad, Declan, was always running away, wasn't he? After a wee bit, he'd come scurrying home, none the worse for wear."

That brought Ciarán up short. He didn't know Mrs. Byrne had any children. In spite of the intensity of the situation, he had to voice his surprise. "I wasn't aware ye had children."

"I do, just the three, but they're scattered all over the globe, they are. But 'tis no time for that now. Ye best be about looking for wee Timothy."

"Could he be with one o' his friends," Ciarán said, "or is there a secret spot he likes to go?"

"If it was secret, his mother wouldn't know about it, now would she?" Ryan rubbed his eyes as he came down the stairs dressed much the same as Ciarán.

"Ye'll be surprised what mothers know, ye cheeky thing," Mrs. Byrne said, one eyebrow lifted.

"I do know a few places," Fionnuala said.

"Let's be getting to it, then." Ciarán smiled and stood up.

"You're going like that, are you?" Steve came down the stairs fully dressed, and though his words were lighthearted enough, Ciarán could see the concern in his eyes.

"I suppose I'd best get me shoes and socks on."

"And a sweater," Fionnuala said. "'Tis a wee bit nippy this morn." She began to cry again. "And me wee lad out there without . . . No, he has his jacket. 'Twas gone from the rack when I got the others dressed to come over here."

"Ye see," Ciarán said, the tightness in his chest easing a bit, "so he has gone off on some adventure and didn't want say anything because he knew he wasn't supposed to, being in trouble and all."

"Or he's run away." Fionnuala's lips quivered again, and Ciarán squeezed her shoulders.

"Either way, we'll find him and bring him home. I'll be back down in a minute."

Before he could get to the hallway, Chris stopped him and handed him his shoes, socks, and a good warm sweater. "Cait said you'd be needing these."

"Thank ye, darlin'," he called up the stairs, grateful that at least two of his children were safe and sound. Though his nerves were a ragged mess, afraid that Ruadhán had taken his grandson, he took solace in one fact. The chief priest was not a wicked man at heart. He wouldn't harm the child just to get back at Ciarán. Take him away, yes, but harm him, no. At least he didn't think he would.

****

"Niamh and Caitlin have gone off with Fionnuala," Aodhán said, though he could see Ciarán's mind was elsewhere. "Ye're thinking to look up around the caves, then, are ye?"

"'Tis as good a place as any, I suppose, and I don't know where else we'd look. Fionnuala's checking with his friends and his favorite hiding spots, and Steve and Ryan are heading toward the sacred grove to see if he went nosing around over there."

"He's probably just angry with his *mamaí*. He was grounded for the week for cutting Kathleen's hair while she was sleeping. Just a wee bit, but still."

Ciarán laughed. "Why on earth would he be doing that?"

"Fionnuala cut his hair the day before, and it didn't come out as well as it could have. Kathleen couldn't stop giggling, said it looked like someone put a bowl on his head. To make matters worse, she did it in front o' his mates."

"Kathleen! That doesn't sound like her at all."

"Oh, she's sweet as an angel around ye and Caitlin, but she's a bit o' a pixie when she wants to be. And yet if anyone else had done the same thing, she'd have given them a fister." Aodhán shrugged. "I suppose that's what sisters and brothers do. D'ye think we had any sisters?"

"More than likely, I suppose, though I've no idea who they would have been. Married off to some tribal prince, no doubt."

"'Twould have been nice to know, though."

"It would." They started walking up the path to the caves, and a wistful look crossed Ciarán's face.

"Go on, then," Aodhán said. "What's on yer mind?"

"I was just thinking how grand it is that Fionnuala knows Timothy's favorite hiding places. 'Twould have been nice to have a *mamaí* that watched out for us like that."

"Ruadhán would say we did, though I'd beg to differ with him. Domnall did his best, I suppose."

"I believe he did." Ciarán stopped for a moment and stared up at the Tombs of the Ancient Ones. "Ye never did come across Ruadhán's tomb, did ye? Or Domnall's for that matter?"

"No, but that doesn't mean they aren't here. We only found a few, and I know there are more than that up here."

"I was just wondering . . ." He shook his head, bending down to pick a few milkwort flowers and handing one to

Aodhán. "'Tis silly, I suppose, but Caitlin said a lot o' the priests became Christian monks and such. Ye don't think Domnall could have? I mean, if he did, he wouldn't be buried here, now would he?"

Aodhán rubbed a finger across his upper lip. The minty smell of the flower reminded him of a gum Niamh chewed from time to time, and both always tickled his nose. "Ye have a point there, but I don't know how we'd ever find out. One thing is certain: Ruadhán would never have become a Christian. He'd have died before he abandoned the goddess."

Ciarán spun around and grabbed Aodhán by the shoulders, his face lighting with some unknown comprehension. "That's it! That's how Ruadhán survived."

"What are ye talking about? First o' all, we don't really know for sure that he did, now do we?"

"I know what I saw, brother. And 'twas no dream that put that blackthorn across the garden path. He was sending me a message. And now I'm afraid he's taken Timothy."

"All right, I don't doubt yer word, but how did he survive? Sure, he'd never have betrayed the goddess."

"No, but he'd give his life to protect her, to preserve her honor, now wouldn't he?"

"I'm still not getting yer meaning."

"With so many o' the priesthood becoming Christians, he may have sealed himself in that tomb we found, believing the goddess would watch over him, maybe even take him to Tír na nÓg with her."

"So he entombed himself because he couldn't face seeing her cast aside. But why not just drink some poison? There was always mistletoe around. If he longed to be with her . . ."

"Because he was loyal to the end. 'Twas not his choice to decide his fate, and so he left his life in her hands, the way he had ours."

The light finally dawned. "Only being a loyal son, he'd be sure she wouldn't make him suffer. But we didn't just wake up on our own. The tombs were opened and the shrouds removed. So how did he manage it?"

Ciarán frowned. "One epiphany at a time, eh, brother. I don't know how it came about, but I do believe it did. Maybe there are other potions in the Book o' Carraig."

"Oh, ye mean ones that let ye sleep for say, fifteen hundred years or so, then wake up all on yer own." Aodhán rolled his eyes.

"Well, I don't know, now do I? Perhaps the answer will be in those pages ye copied when we were up in Dublin."

"I thought we only copied them down to convince Brian 'twas why we needed to see the tome in the first place."

"It was, but since we already have them, you might as well translate them. Caitlin will be glad to help ye. Besides, it may hold other answers as well. Like how to locate a lost lad."

"And what are ye going to be doing while I'm doing that?"

"Keep looking for me grandson. If Ruadhán has him, he'll be wanting to make a priest o' him. He'll drug him, the way he did us. Once he gets in the lad's mind . . ."

"He'll be lost to us for sure."

Ciarán pinched the bridge of his nose and gave one quick nod. "I'm sure he'll be planning to rebuild his priesthood. Who better to do it with than the descendant o' a guardian?"

"But that means he'll have to be kidnapping a *cailín* or two as well, and ye know what will happen to the wee things when he does."

They'd arrived at the cave where Aodhán had come across the mysterious wax-covered candleholders. Ciarán gave a wave of his hand, and the boulder moved aside. "He'll not be taking anyone else just yet, not till he's trained Timothy."

"Sure, he's got to be close to seventy by now. Even he can't imagine he'll go on forever."

"He'll think he has a mandate from the goddess, won't he? And if he has that . . . it won't matter. Besides, he'll train the lad to do what he must."

Aodhán stood staring around the empty cave. He'd hoped to find the boy there, but it was as still and quiet as a tomb . . . Ruadhán's tomb. "Where to now? The Cave o' Rúin Ársa?"

"Ruadhán will believe it's the entrance to the otherworld."

"It may well have been for me if I hadn't grabbed on to that ledge. Ye don't think he'll throw the lad over, do ye? As a sacrifice to the goddess?"

Fear infused Ciarán's expression, but then he shook his head. "No, he'll be wanting to rebuild the priesthood, not destroy all vestiges o' me. Ye took me children from him, so he'll want to take them back."

"Ye're sure o' that?"

Ciarán didn't answer. He didn't have to. The answer was still written all over his face. No one could be sure what the old man was about, least of all two renegade priests.

****

Sealing the tomb back up with a flick of his arm, Ciarán and his brother headed for the Cave of Rúin Ársa. Ciarán didn't dare voice the fears that pierced his heart like pricks of the tattoo picks. He tried to look at it reasonably. It all made sense, didn't it? But then not even he could understand the machinations of Ruadhán's mind. Surely he wouldn't harm the boy, though. If Timothy was Ciarán's child, then it followed that Ruadhán would see him as the child o' the goddess as well. Of course, Ciarán had no idea what that meant for Timothy.

If all had gone as Ruadhán had expected, Bréanainn would have followed in Ciarán's footsteps, likely becoming a guardian one day, just as he and Aodhán had. But they had betrayed the goddess—would Ruadhán seek to appease her by making an offering of Ciarán's tainted spawn? Yet how could he know who the boy was? They'd spoken nothing of it outside their own small circle.

"He couldn't know," Aodhán said out of the blue, causing Ciarán to jump.

Ciarán had been so deep within his own thoughts he'd forgotten his brother was beside him. "Sneaking into me mind again, are ye, brother? I must remember to guard me thoughts more closely."

"There's no need to peek into that cluttered head o' yers. The thoughts spill out all on their own. Besides, I know well how ye think. How would Ruadhán have known who Timothy was?"

"What if he's been watching us all along, sneaking about, perhaps disguised as some newcomer to the village?"

"We checked out Cormac's story, remember. He's been teaching at a small school in Dublin for the last forty years or more, so unless he awoke long before us, 'tis not likely he's Ruadhán. And even if it were, did ye see him lurking about that day we told ye who Fionnuala was?"

"If he was lurking, I wouldn't have seen him, now would I?"

"Sure, yer Spidey-senses would have perked up." Aodhán shrugged and walked on ahead.

Ciarán scratched his head. What in the name of Brigid were Spidey-senses? He'd have to ask Caitlin or Father Dennis about that when things calmed down a bit. He sprinted up to where Aodhán was standing outside the cave. "I suppose ye mean I would have sensed . . ."

He'd been following his brother's gaze as he spoke and stopped short at the sight he beheld. The stone sealing the cave had been moved, just enough to make it obvious. Throwing a gaze in Aodhán's direction, he shifted the stone, preparing himself for whatever awaited them, but much to his surprise, the cavernous space was still empty.

"He's been here, though," Ciarán said. "Ye can be sure o' that."

Aodhán frowned, for even he couldn't come up with an argument against it, though he did try. "Someone else could have . . ." He let out a long sigh. "I suppose ye're right, but where is he keeping himself?"

"He knows these hills far better than we ever did, and I'm sure we could slip away unnoticed if we thought on it a bit."

Aodhán searched the hillside. "What is it ye think he really wants, then? If he did this, left it open a bit, 'twas no mistake."

"No, he wanted us to know he's here, but more than that, he was making sure we knew he was still the chief priest."

"We need to find Timothy."

Another thought crowded Ciarán's mind. What if Ruadhán simply wanted to see Ciarán and his brother entombed again? He might use the boy to lure them in. And if that was the case . . . He needed to clear his head, organize his thoughts so that they made some sense.

"I'll leave ye alone a bit, then," Aodhán said, a smile brushing his lips. "I didn't need to enter yer mind to see ye're wanting to slip into *dercad* either. I'll meet ye at the foot o' the path, but don't be long about it. We still need to find Timothy."

Ciarán nodded as he watched his brother head down the hillside. When he was alone, he sat on the ground and stared straight ahead, willing the fear and tension to drain from his body. As usual, his father appeared, his robe still the garb of the high priest . . . or was it a monk?

"Did ye become a Christian?" Ciarán asked, though he wasn't sure why that should be the first thing on his mind with everything else that was happening.

Domnall laughed. "You always did let your mind wander. How many times did I scold you about it?"

"Not enough, it appears."

"Hmm," his father nodded and went over to rest against a rocky outcrop. "Perhaps Ruadhán was right, and I was far too lenient with the pair of you."

Though Ciarán was tempted to debate the subject, he brought his mind back to his real concern. "Where does he have Timothy?"

"You know I cannot tell you that, but I will say that while your fears are justified, they are at the same time quite unnecessary."

"More riddles, it seems. The pot is hot and yet 'tis cold."

"Return to your Gaelic please. I have no desire to decipher your new language. Though you have done well in learning it."

Ciarán grumbled but did as his elder asked and switched back to the ancient dialect. "Does nothing ever change, Father? You praise me and yet scold me, all at once. They call that a backhanded compliment here."

Domnall nodded, scratching his bearded chin. "I can see the correlation."

Ciarán grumbled again, for his father was stirring him off course, as usual. "Where is he hiding Timothy?"

"The boy is in plain sight. All you need do is look."

"Where am I to do that, a Athair? You would talk in riddles when a child is at risk."

"The child is in no danger, *a leanbh*. You never were a very good fisherman."

"What does fishing have to do with anything?"

"You have no patience, *a mhic*, but plod into the stream, thinking the fish will not scatter. Pick your bait and learn to sit quietly and listen, or you will lose that which you have just gained."

"And what is that? My newborn children, Caitlin, Aodhán, Uncle Mike, Fionnuala's family? I've gained so much in the last two years."

"You have, but you still have not managed to find any discipline. Would it matter which of those you named was in danger? No, it would not. So do not worry over who, so much as how."

"That is what I'm trying to find out, a Athair, but, as usual, you give me only riddles."

Domnall shrugged, the hint of a smile flashing across his lips. "Then why do you come? You have all the answers you need, *a mhic*, but you must train your mind to see clearly. The riddles are within your own head."

"Is that what ye are, then? Just a figment o' me imagination?"

Domnall frowned. "Gaelic, please!" He sighed and shook his head. "I have indulged you too much. Clear your mind, and you will see what lurks hidden in the corners. Once you do, you will have your answers . . . well, most of them anyway. What would life be without new things to discover? *Dia leat, a mhic.*" With that, he was gone.

Ciarán let out a growl and scrubbed his hands up and down his face. Why did he always do that, dangle the solution before him, cloaked in mystery, then walk away into the mists of time? *Because he's not going to give ye the answers, fool. He wants ye to discover them for yerself.* And how was he to do that? He hurried down the hillside to find Aodhán sitting on a low stone wall.

"Didn't tell ye anything, did he?"

"What's new? I don't know why I even bother."

"Maybe because ye know he'll force ye to look within?"

"What are ye talking about?" Ciarán wasn't in the mood for Aodhán's calm appraisal. "All he ever leaves me with are his riddles."

"Because ye already have the answers. We've been through this before, brother." Ciarán opened his mouth to protest, but his brother raised his hand, staying his objections. "All right, maybe ye don't know where Timothy is exactly, but ye know more than ye think about the whole thing. Ye just let yer emotions cause yer thoughts to run into one another so ye can't see it."

"Ye're right, I know, but I just can't . . ." Ciarán sank down on the wall next to his brother. "I feel like I've known the lad all me life. He reminds me so o' Bréanainn. I know it's been generations, but . . . he is me grandson."

"Let's get back to Duffy's. Maybe he's already come home, and we're fretting over nothing. Mrs. Byrne could be right, ye know. Lads run off from time to time, but they usually come home right enough when the sun starts to set."

"We never did."

"Didn't we, though?" Aodhán chuckled. "Maybe not the way Fionnuala thinks Timothy might have, but we did sure enough in our own way. Or have ye forgotten about yer secret grove?"

Ciarán grinned at the memory. "That was different. 'Twas the whole lot o' ye I was trying to get away from, and I was searching for naught more than a bit o' peace and quiet."

"Maybe 'tis all Timothy was looking for as well, or maybe his feelings were just hurt. Ye must recall how unfair life can seem to a nine-year-old."

"Ye're right yet again. He'll most likely be waiting for us at the gate. One thing is sure: we've searched all through these hills, and there's naught more we can do here. Maybe Steve or Caitlin have discovered something. At any rate, Duffy should be coming home soon. Best we be there when he does."

Ciarán's expectations were soon crushed as they walked up to Duffy's cottage. Fionnula came running out the door at the sight of them, the hope melting from her face like icicles in the midday sun.

"Ye've not found him, then?"

Ciarán could only shake his head. Clearly, no one else had succeeded either. "I'm thinking we'd best be calling the garda in. Sure, he's fine and all, but just as a precaution."

She leaned against him, tears streaming down her face, and a vise tightened around his heart. He'd never felt so helpless or so lost. Had his past once again returned to haunt him and the ones he loved?

CHAPTER 24

Mamaí?" a voice called from down the road. "What's wrong?"

Ciarán looked up, the vise squeezing the life from his heart dropping away. Timothy came running toward his mother, the fishing pole he was carrying thrown on the pavement.

"Timothy!" Fionnuala pulled away from Ciarán, hurrying toward her son while everyone else stood still, staring at the sight, relief etched on every face.

"Where have ye been?" Fionnuala said. "Sure, ye've had us all worried sick."

The boy hung his head, speaking too low for anyone else to hear. Not that it mattered, for Ciarán's blood had begun to boil. Heat raced into his face, and he dashed down the road, his heart playing a raging symphony against his ribs. Without a word, he grabbed the man Timothy had been walking with by the collar, shoving him up against a tree and nearly causing the elderly fisherman to stumble backward over the low stone wall. Only Ciarán's grasp on the man's collar stopped him falling into a gorse bush.

He heard someone calling his name, but it was drowned out but the rush of fury surging through his ears as he punched the man in the face. Blood spewed everywhere, but he didn't care. He pinned the man against the tree.

"What were ye doing with the lad? So help me, if ye harmed a hair on his head, I'll make ye regret it."

"I don't know what ye're talking about." Cormac grabbed a handkerchief from his pocket and held it up against his nose. "Why would I want to be harming the wee lad?"

The voices called his name again, but he didn't listen. He tightened his grip on the man's collar, shaking him. "Tell me what ye were about."

"Fishing," Cormac said, "nothing more." The man's voice was shaking, a look of horror contorting his face as Ciarán pulled back his arm to hit him again.

Something caught him by the elbow, something else gripped his shoulder, and there was that voice again. Fionnuala? He blinked away the rage and turned his head to look at her.

"Stop hitting the poor man," she said. "He did naught. 'Twas all Timothy's doing."

Ciarán's hands shook as the fury drained from his body, but he still didn't release Cormac's collar. "What was Timothy's doing?"

"Go on!" Fionnuala said, a cross between anger and relief tinging her voice. "Tell yer uncle what ye did."

Though his mother pushed him in Ciarán's direction, the boy didn't look up, and he mumbled so that Ciarán couldn't hear a word he was saying.

"Speak up," Fionnuala said, "afore yer uncle does poor Mr. McGuire any more harm."

"Mr. McGuire said he'd take me fishing, but only if me *mamaí* said yes."

"But yer *mamaí* knew naught o' it, and he took ye anyway?"

Timothy shook his head. "I told him Mamaí said I could go."

Ciarán glared at Cormac. "And ye just took the lad's word for it?"

"In retrospect, I'll admit 'twas foolish o' me, but I had no reason to doubt the lad."

"Don't be ridiculous, Ciarán," Fionnuala said. "I'm always telling the wee ones they can do something as long as their parents say yes. Ye'll see yerself when yer babes get older. Now, Timothy, tell yer uncle why Mr. McGuire might o' been thinking I knew about it."

"I told him she did, and when he wanted to go in to say hello, I told him she'd been awake with Bridie last night, and 'twould be better to let her sleep."

"Ye out-and-out lied to the man?"

"Yes, sir." Tears were streaming down the boy's cheeks, but he hurried to explain himself between sobbing hiccups. "'Tis just that I wanted to go, but Mamaí and Dadaí told me I wasn't to be going anywhere for a week on account o' what I did to Kathleen's hair, so I knew they'd say no."

Ciarán knelt down by his grandson's side. How many times had he confessed just such antics to Domnall? "And ye didn't think yer *mamaí* would notice ye were gone?"

The boy's face squished up into another tearful outburst, and Ciarán squeezed him against his chest until the sobbing subsided some. He sat him on the stone wall, next to Mr. McGuire, who was still nursing his sore nose, though at least the bleeding had stopped.

"Ye know what ye did was wrong," Ciarán said. "I thought the worst o' Mr. McGuire here, and I think we both owe him an apology."

Timothy nodded. "I'm sorry, Mr. McGuire. I didn't think about me getting yerself in trouble as well."

"Mr. McGuire's not in trouble," Fionnuala said, "but he might have been harmed if I couldn't stop yer uncle from beating him to a pulp. Which he'll be apologizing for as well. Won't he, now?"

From the heat in Ciarán's cheeks, he was sure he must be a bright crimson. "I do apologize for any harm I caused ye. I'll be more than happy to pay for any medical bills and a new sweater. I suppose I shouldn't have jumped to conclusions."

"Think nothing o' it. Ye were looking out for yer nephew there. I may have done the same meself if I thought someone had taken a lad in me charge."

Something in the man's voice tugged at Ciarán's memory, but the man smiled, and it was lost. Perhaps Aodhán was right and he simply resembled someone from their past.

"I don't blame ye if ye never want to be taking me fishing again," Timothy said through the sniffling.

"Don't be silly, lad. The truth is ye're the best fishing partner I ever had. Ye can be sure I'll be checking with yer parents before I do, though. Ye've broken me trust, and 'twill be hard to earn it back. I don't take kindly to those who betray me."

There it was again, the unreachable itch that tickled Ciarán's memory. He had to stop this. Ruadhán may be out there somewhere, but this couldn't be him. This man had been teaching in Dublin. They had proof of it, or so Aodhán claimed. A wave of exhaustion came over him.

"Would ye stay for dinner?" Fionnuala asked Cormac.

"Oh, thank ye, but another time, perhaps. Right now I'd like to get home and clean up. Besides, I'll be cooking a nice salmon dinner for me supper tonight. Speaking o' which." He opened the basket he carried around his waist and took out two decent-sized salmon. "I believe these are Timothy's."

"Maybe ye should keep them, sir. I don't deserve them."

"Nonsense, 'twas hard work reeling them in, and I'm sure yer *mamaí* will enjoy them."

"I will, thank ye," Fionnuala said. "Can Ciarán be giving ye a ride home, then?"

"No, thank ye kindly. After sitting on that boat all day, I need to be stretching these old muscles o' mine. *Slan.*"

"*Slan abhaile,*" Fionnuala said. She watched the man walk down the road and then turned on Timothy and Ciarán. "I don't know who I'm more furious at. Ye for running off without telling me, or ye for not letting the man explain before giving him a fister."

Before Ciarán could say anything in his defense, Duffy pulled up and jumped out of the car, taking in Ciarán's blood-covered sweater. "What's happened? Is everyone all right? Have ye called for an ambulance?"

Timothy was still staring at the ground, and Ciarán had a sudden flashback to his childhood. He felt for the poor child and, resting a hand on his shoulder, knelt down before him. Lifting the boy's chin with his finger, he gave him the most encouraging smile he could muster.

"Why don't ye dry yer eyes and get yerself up to yer room? Ye know yer *mamaí* and *dadaí* love ye. They just need a wee bit o' time to let their tempers cool. Off with ye now."

Timothy looked to Fionnuala, but when she nodded, he flew into the house and up the stairs. Duffy watched the boy go before bringing his attention back to his wife and Ciarán.

"Now do ye want to be telling me what's going on? Clearly, no one's seriously hurt."

Fionnuala frowned at Ciarán. "No one except poor Mr. McGuire."

"He's not seriously hurt," Ciarán said, protesting perhaps a bit too vehemently.

Fionnuala flashed Ciarán a stern frown, though her expression softened when she turned to her husband. "We've been out looking for Timothy all day. Seems Mr. McGuire took him fishing, thinking the wee scoundrel had our permission and all."

"Which o' course he didn't since he was being punished." Duffy cast a quick look in Ciarán's direction, clearly not sure whether to scold him as well as his son or break out laughing. "And let me guess, Ciarán here punched first and asked questions later."

Fionnuala placed her hands on her hips. "Hmpf, he didn't ask any questions at all, did he? He would have beaten the daylights out o' Cormac if I hadn't stepped in. The poor man was mortified when he found out what happened, and quite understanding."

"I'll admit I might have overreacted a bit, but I thought . . . There's more to it than any o' ye know."

Steve and Ryan had managed to slink away in the midst of it all, but Aodhán had been standing off to the side with Caitlin and Niamh, watching it unfold. "Perhaps 'tis time we told them, eh, brother. They've a right to know."

"Glory to God," Fionnuala said, "what's this really all about?"

"Let's be going inside," Duffy said. "I need a nice cup o' tea . . . perhaps with a shot o' whiskey in it if the expression on Ciarán's face is anything to go by."

This wasn't how Ciarán wanted to tell them. In fact, he still wasn't sure it was the right thing to do. He might be worrying them over nothing. But then he remembered the open tomb and the ancient figure he'd seen standing across the road from Mrs. Byrne's. Aodhán was right. They needed to be warned, and if he didn't explain his irrational reaction to Cormac McGuire's appearance, Fionnuala might never forgive him.

Caitlin squeezed his arm, standing on her toes to kiss his cheek. "I'd better get back to Mrs. B's. Just speak from your heart. Fionnuala will understand."

****

Ciarán sat staring down into his tea. Even with the addition of whiskey, he couldn't dull the feeling of dread that suffused his soul. He'd have to tell them everything. What would they think of him once they knew?

"Ye know, o' course, we're ancient Celtic priests," Aodhán said, "but 'tis a bit more to it than that." He looked over his shoulder to make sure none of the children were listening. "We were born children o' the goddess herself and chosen as guardians. I was to care for the creatures o' the sky, and Ciarán was to father the priesthood."

"Well, he must have done the job well enough since we're all here." Fionnuala let a smile creep across her lips at last, but there was a hesitancy in her eyes.

"'Tis not the fathering that I dread telling ye about," Ciarán said, "but the how o' it. Each Beltane I'd choose a lass from the village to . . . stand in for the goddess. Then after the child was born, the wee *cailín* I'd chosen would receive her reward."

"And what reward was that?" There was a quiver in Fionnuala's voice now, and Ciarán's stomach clenched. Would she hate him for what he'd done?

"She was sacrificed and sent to Tír na nÓg," Aodhán answered, clearly aware of Ciarán's inability to say the words.

"Ye killed the mother o' yer child?" Fionnuala sat back in her chair, a stunned expression transforming her lovely face.

"How many o' these women were there?" Duffy asked. Ciarán could see he was trying to refrain from judgment, but it couldn't be easy.

"I had three children: Bréanainn, Áine, and Daibheid."

"And which one was Aisling the mother to?" Fionnuala's voice broke as she spoke.

"None. After falling in love with Aisling, I could no longer partake in such a ceremony. I became a Christian, and we wed, planning to take the children away from there, but I was betrayed and condemned to the tomb."

Fionnuala reached out and placed her hand over his. "Because ye'd taken someone to yerself ye had no intention o' sacrificing, ye mean."

"'Twas almost Beltane. I could have chosen her, but . . . she begged me not to give up me new faith. She was at peace . . . dying." Ciarán couldn't speak anymore. His throat felt as though it were closing up. Duffy shoved a shot glass of whiskey in front of him, and he downed it in one gulp. Though it burned going down, it did the trick.

"So they sacrificed her anyway and put ye in that tomb while ye were still breathing." Fionnuala squeezed his hand,

and the tension slipped from his body. Whatever revulsion she felt must have dissipated on seeing his distress. "And then Aodhán stole yer children away, and me ancestor was raised as a Christian. Without ye two, I wouldn't be here today."

"'Twas Ruadhán's own fault, really. If he hadn't sent me to spy on Padraig, I never would have met Aisling or come to believe in Christ."

"Well, there ye are. Sure, ye didn't know any better afore ye heard this Padraig speaking . . ." Her eyes widened. "Ye can't mean St. Padraig himself?"

"He wasn't a saint then, now was he?" Aodhán said.

"Glory to God! Me ancestors spoke to the saint himself." She blessed herself, placing her hand on her chest to catch her breath.

Duffy smiled at his wife's reaction, kissing her cheek before pouring himself a shot of whiskey and downing it in one go. "So . . . what does all this have to do with Ciarán's reaction to Mr. McGuire?"

"He . . . We . . ." Aodhán shrugged, not exactly sure how to explain it, so Ciarán took a deep breath and continued.

"The chief priest Ruadhán . . ."

"The one that entombed ye," Duffy said.

"He's alive . . . here. . . now. Mr. McGuire's new to the area, and there was something so familiar about him. Then Timothy went missing and turned up with the old man . . ."

"Ye thought he was this Ruadhán o' yers." Fionnuala laughed. "Sure, ye're daft, the two o' ye. Niamh spoke to her friend at the school in Dublin, and he described Cormac to a tee, even said how he'd retired recently. But Niamh's told ye all this." She threw a disapproving glance in Aodhán's direction.

"'Tis not Aodhán, but meself." Ciarán took a drink of his fortified tea and forged on. "I have these dreams, ye see. They're not always clear, but I've learned to pay attention to them. They warned me Ruadhán was coming for me children, though 'tis not Fionn and Aisling I should be concerned over, but the elder ones. Timothy . . ."

"Ye think we should be watching for this Ruadhán," Duffy said.

"To tell the truth, I don't know. I told ye, me dreams aren't always clear. It might mean Fionnuala or maybe even her sisters. Or I might have it all muddled up and it means the babes in spite o' what Bréanainn said."

"Ye saw Fionnuala's ancestor in yer dream?" Duffy looked to his wife before continuing. "Ye're sure 'tis not just yer own insecurities . . . or regrets?"

"I thought it might be until I saw Ruadhán watching the twins' nursery the night I twisted me ankle."

"And ye're sure ye weren't just walking in yer sleep?" Duffy frowned, hesitating a moment before speaking again. "Ye know I have a great respect for these dream o' yers, but . . ."

"I know what ye're thinking. Trust me when I tell ye 'tis possible he did survive."

Fionnuala cast a questioning gaze in Aodhán's direction. "And ye've had these dreams as well, seen this man?"

"I don't dream quite as vividly as Ciarán, nor have I seen the man in the flesh, but . . ." He nodded. "I do believe he's alive, and if he's managed to discover who ye are, 'twould be his way to think ye and the children belonged to the goddess."

"Well, what are we to do, then?"

"Just keep an eye out for strangers," Aodhán said, "especially those with beards who may seem a wee bit too friendly."

Fionnuala leaned back in her chair, chewing on her bottom lip for a moment before speaking again. "There's still something I don't understand. If that's what he looks like, why on earth did ye think he was Cormac McGuire? Saints preserve us, ye can't suspect every stranger that comes to the village. Fishermen come all the time. Am I to suspect every one o' them? This is all too ridiculous. We clearly haven't met the man, so how would he even know we were yer descendants? Have ye gone about telling everyone? For sure it is, we haven't."

"O' course we haven't," Ciarán said, "but we wouldn't necessarily have to. He can scan yer mind. Much better than I or Aodhán can."

"Ye can read our minds, can ye?" Fionnuala pressed her lips together.

Ciarán suppressed a groan. There was no need to enter her mind; her thoughts were coming in loud and clear. So much for the woman's sympathetic understanding. But then what did he think was going to happen? Granted she and Duffy had experienced what Bradaigh could do, but it had been almost too much for them to accept. This was bound to be beyond the realm of even their open-mindedness.

"Not read it, exactly," he said. "'Tis hard to explain."

"Hmmm, well, we'd need to be meeting the man for him to do that, now wouldn't we?"

"No, ye wouldn't. He'd just need be in yer vicinity."

"Well, I've seen no one lurking about aside from ye lot. Besides, that still doesn't excuse ye for giving it to poor Mr. McGuire. We met him at church in mid-August, and ye said it yerself, ye saw this Ruadhán o' yers not even a week ago. And didn't he look just the way ye remembered him? Unless ye're thinking Cormac's one o' them quick-change artists. Perhaps ye'd like to be going and searching the poor man's house."

Ciarán pondered the notion for a moment, but the look on Fionnuala's face warned him against it. Instead, he stood and smiled an apology. No sense pressing the issue at the moment, not until he had absolute proof that Ruadhán was alive and well. "No, ye're right there. Just be careful and promise ye'll be letting me know if ye do come across anyone that fills his description. Now I'd best be getting back to Mrs. Byrne's. The twins probably have Caitlin about ready to tear the hair from her head."

"And why would she be doing that?" Aodhán asked. "Or is it another o' Father Dennis's sayings?"

"It is. I'm thinking it means she'll be a wee bit stressed and probably not in the best o' moods."

"Niamh and I will be leaving ye at the door, then," Aodhán said, a huge grin breaking out on his face.

CHAPTER 25

Caitlin looked up as Ciarán walked in the door, his sweater spattered with blood. She was well aware of his fears about Ruadhán, but Mr. McGuire looked nothing like the chief priest Ciarán had described. And he'd never even given the man a chance to explain. He'd just overpowered him like a schoolyard bully. On top of that, Fionn had been fussing from the moment she walked in the door, his sister joining in just when Caitlin thought he was settling down. The last thing she needed to deal with was a third child.

"What were you thinking, manhandling that poor old man. If you'd taken a moment to ask Timothy, he would have told you he was just off on a fishing trip with Mr. McGuire."

"He wasn't supposed to be going anywhere, now was he? If McGuire had seen to it Fionnuala knew. . ."

Caitlin laughed out loud. "From what I understand, the little rascal said he had her permission."

"He still should have asked."

"And was that the reason you attacked that poor old man, or is there something more?"

"He's fine, and I apologized, didn't I?" He started for the stairs, but Caitlin grabbed his arm.

"Don't you dare wake them up. They haven't had a nap all afternoon and were in rare form when I got back. It's a bit early, but I think they might be teething."

He frowned and looked down at his sweater. "I just want to be changing me sweater. Ye'll have me head if the stain sets in."

"It's already done that, and if Fionn or Aisling hear you, there'll be no getting them back to sleep."

"I'll stay with them, then."

"Ciarán, no! You've got to stop this. They can sense your anxiety."

"Don't be ridiculous."

"Three nights in a row I've found you on the floor, sleeping between their cribs. I can't even take them for a walk unless you're with me."

"Ruadhán is here! D'ye not know what that means?"

She reached up and touched his cheek. "No one else has seen him, Ciarán, not even Aodhán."

"Aodhán saw the stone moved from the Cave o' Rúin Ársa, and there were the candles . . ."

Caitlin rolled her eyes. She hated to upset him, but he needed to know the truth. "He won't say it to you, but he's not so sure you're right about Ruadhán surviving."

"He told ye that, did he?"

"Don't be upset with him. He trusts your instincts, but you're getting everyone upset. And now you've gone and attacked poor Mr. McGuire. Did it even occur to you to ask him what was going on before you started using him for a punching bag? No, of course it didn't, because you're so obsessed with Ruadhán coming for your children you can't see any other possibility. You need to stop it before you drive us all crazy, especially yourself."

"Ye're right." He grabbed the car keys from the hall table and headed for the door.

"Where are you going? Supper's almost ready."

"I need to get off by meself and think a bit."

"You're going to drift away into *dercad* again, aren't you?" Caitlin wasn't sure how she felt about that anymore. What if they were just hallucinations? They were certainly making his obsession worse. She wished Uncle Mike would get here and talk to him.

"Does that bother ye?"

"I'm not sure anymore." She couldn't hold the tears back. After the afternoon she'd had, her nerves were already pulled taut. This was just straining them all the more. "We can't live like this. I dread you going to sleep because I don't know what new worry you're going to wake up with. And now you're punching random men without even hearing them out."

Ciarán wrapped his arm around her and pulled her to himself, blood-spattered sweater and all. "I'm sorry, *a chuisle*. I didn't mean to be worrying ye. Ye're right. I can't let me dreams be controlling me life or yers. I'm just going to run over and have a talk with Aodhán."

She shouldn't have said anything. What if she came between him and his brother? "Ciarán, all he said was he didn't know how it could be possible. Don't be angry with him."

"I'm not, *a ghrá*. I just need to talk to someone who has the same background as I do. 'Twill help me sort things out."

"You won't be late, will you?"

"I'll call if I see it's getting too late, but I'll be with Aodhán, so no need to be worrying yerself. Even if I get completely pissed, Aodhán will keep his head and get me home or let me sleep on his floor. Either way, I'll be safe enough.

He kissed her on the lips, then pulled back and smiled. But she knew him too well. His past was coming between them again, dragging him away from her and weighing heavily on his mind. Until this was sorted out, until the dreams stopped, he would have no peace, and she could do nothing about it—or could she?

****

Ciarán drove the short distance to Aodhán's cottage and sat in the car for a moment. Was Caitlin right? She was afraid he was losing his mind. He was sure of it. But he'd had dreams all his life, and many had been troubling. Never had they filled him with such an overwhelming terror, though. Sorrow, pain, and regret, yes, but not terror.

The car door opened and Aodhán got in, answering his unspoken question before the words had left his lips. "'Tis because the dreams have never involved yer own flesh and blood before. Duffy told me once that he loved Fionnuala more than life itself, but that love paled in comparison to what he felt for his children."

"Ye could have told me ye didn't truly think Ruadhán was alive."

Aodhán shrugged and handed Ciarán a ham-and-cheese sandwich. "That was before we found that boulder moved at the Cave o' Rúin Ársa. To tell ye the truth, I'm not sure what to believe. 'Twould not be the first time ye thought something ye saw in a dream was real, even after ye woke." He lifted a shoulder again and took a bite of his sandwich.

"When was that?" Ciarán lifted the bread and looked at the ham and cheese. "No tomatoes?"

"I didn't have much time to throw them together, now did I, ye ungrateful sod."

Ciarán bit into the sandwich and took the bottle of soda his brother handed him. "So when did I ever think me dreams were real before?"

Aodhán lifted an eyebrow, a smile tugging at the corner of his mouth. "Let's see, there was the time you woke convinced Domnall had come in and given us permission to go fishing."

Heat rushed into Ciarán's cheeks. "I just said that so he wouldn't be angry when he caught us at it."

"That worked grand, now didn't it? We still spent the next two weeks cleaning out every animal stall in the village."

"In all fairness, it might have been worse if I didn't tell him that."

"Ye truly still think he believed ye. Sweet Brigid, ye can be thick sometimes. Why don't ye ask him about that next time you slip into *dercad*? Then there was the time ye told poor wee Coinneach he was needed in the village." Ciarán shrugged. "Ye made that up as well?"

"If I didn't, we'd have been stuck with him all day. Ye should be thanking me for that one."

"I suppose ye're right, but did it ever occur to ye that ye were out-and-out lying?"

"It wasn't. I did have a dream that Domnall told us we should go fishing and another that someone wanted Coinneach in the village."

"But ye knew they were dreams."

"When I woke, but no one ever asked me about that."

"No wonder ye and Father Mike hit it off so well. Ye're kindred spirits."

"I never hurt anyone . . . except for yerself from time to time, I suppose. I am sorry for that, brother, but this is different. Even if me dreams did linger after I woke, 'twas never long before I saw them for what they were."

Aodhán opened his soda and took a drink. "Well, I believe ye now. That's all that matters."

"Do ye?" How could he even question his brother? He'd never been anything but loyal to him. Had even given his own life for Ciarán's children.

"I never pretended I did when I didn't. If ye recall, I told ye I doubted Ruadhán was alive on more than one occasion, so when Caitlin asked me, I told her the same. The more I thought about the blackthorn, though, and the candleholders and the boulder being shifted, the more I thought ye might be right. Ruadhán always did like blackthorn. I'm thinking he may have used it from time to time to punish his enemies."

Ciarán threw the last bit of his sandwich back in its wax-paper wrapper. He'd lost his appetite. "I need ye beside me on this, brother. Caitlin's right, I am obsessing over it, and 'tis not only herself I'm upsetting. The babes are fussing more than usual. D'ye think they can sense me worrying or that Ruadhán is close?"

"I'm thinking 'tis more likely being in a new place or gas or . . . I don't know, what else bothers the wee things?"

"Caitlin says she thinks they might have already started teething, but . . . I don't know what to do. Every time I think o' that dream, o' Ruadhán ripping me babes from Caitlin's arms, I can hardly breathe. They don't only hold me heart, Aodhán. They *are* me heart."

"Then there's naught else for it, I suppose. We have to find Ruadhán and see what he's really about."

For all his caution, Aodhán had more courage and strength than any man Ciarán knew, save for Domnall and Father Mike, perhaps. "Easier said than done, I'm afraid."

"Maybe not. Call for him and see what happens. He's just arrogant enough to come."

Aodhán never ceased to amaze him, but what was it Father Mike used to say? The most obvious answer was usually the most effective. "Caitlin will be upset, but I'll need to sleep in the twins' room again tonight."

"Ye've been doing that?"

"I have, and ye don't need to be scolding me for it. She's already taken care o' that. But if he comes, he'll be looking to their room. I want to see him coming."

"Ye've no plan on sleeping at all, then?"

"No. If I can see where he's coming from, perhaps we can figure out where he's been keeping himself."

"Niamh won't be happy about it either, but I'm thinking I'll sleep in the archaeology shed. That way I can watch to the southeast as well."

"So ye won't be sleeping either?"

Aodhán grinned. "'Twill not be the first time we've gone the night without sleeping. At least it won't be on our knees this time."

******

Ciarán slipped out of bed, certain Caitlin was asleep, but he hadn't even checked the twins when he turned to find her standing by their bedroom door, her arms crossed over her chest and her eyes flashing a deep ivy. "What are you doing?"

"I thought I heard Aisling crying?"

"Stop it, Ciarán! Don't even think about lying. You're horrible at it."

"I thought I was getting rather good."

Her eyes narrowed. Father Mike said they were like reptilian slits when she got angry and her bite was just as deadly.

"All right, then, but ye're not going to be liking it."

She didn't say a thing, but he could almost hear the growl squeezing past her tightly closed lips. Better get it over with.

"I'm tired o' the dreams, so I've . . . called for Ruadhán. We need to talk this out."

Her eyes widened this time, almost as much as her mouth. She clearly couldn't believe what she'd just heard. It could have been worse, he supposed. After a moment, she seemed to recover herself. She released a long, hard breath, then spoke, her voice dangerously soft.

"Are you telling me you're having these nightmares, warning you this chief priest is going to come steal our children, and you . . . you . . . invited the fox into the henhouse?"

"The what?" Good Lord, he'd have to be asking Dennis about that one.

"He wants to steal our children, and you just opened the door and invited him in."

"Don't be ridiculous. 'Tis not like that. I complained to Aodhán about being so tired I was certain to sleep like a rock tonight. If Ruadhán's been watching us, sure, he'll think it a good opportunity to come round. When he does, I'll confront him."

"And what do you think you'll be able to do? Bradaigh nearly killed you, and this one's a chief priest. You'll have no chance against him."

"Ruadhán's not Bradaigh. I doubt he's any thought to killing me. If anything, he'll want to be seeing me back in the tomb."

"Oh, that makes me feel so much better."

"I'm not going to let him. He'll not have his underlings with him this time. If I can talk to him, he might see sense. He's not a completely unreasonable man."

"Ciarán, please! There's been no sign of this Ruadhán or anybody else from your past. Daniel said no tombs have been found open, and there's been no one hanging around or asking about the children. Now come to bed and stop obsessing over nothing more than a dream."

"Let me do this, just for a night or two. If he doesn't show up after a week or so, I'll stop."

"A week or so." She closed her eyes and blew out another long breath before opening them again. "You're going to do it whether I want you to or not, aren't you?"

"I'm sorry, Cait. 'Tis something I need to do."

"You know what? Don't bother coming back at all. In fact, why don't you just have Mrs. Byrne set up a cot in here for you? Do you think the kids don't sense something is wrong? They may not be able to talk, but they can hear the stress in your voice, feel the tension in your touch. Ruadhán's not going to have to take them, you'll drive them away all by yourself if you keep this up."

"They're just babes."

"For now, but what are you going to do when they grow? I'm sure some ridiculous dream will warn you about something, and you'll forbid them to go out or see their friends."

"Now ye're the one who's talking nonsense."

"Am I, Ciarán? Because you're scaring me. You've had dreams before, but they've never caused you to lose touch with reality. I'm done. I can't spend my life worrying about things that might never come to pass."

"Caitlin . . ."

"No, the twins are fine, Fionnuala is fine, and her children are fine. We're going shopping in Castlebar Monday morning, Niamh, Fionnuala, and I. And no, you're not coming. You're going to go to the airport and pick up my uncle, Dennis, and Mary. Then you're going to tell Uncle Mike what you've been up to and have a long talk with him."

"I'm not a child to be told what I need to be doing."

"Fine, then you can spend tomorrow night in the archaeology shed with your brother."

How on earth did she know Aodhán was in the shed? Maybe she'd been doing some surveillance of her own.

"Yes, I know he's there. What I don't know is why he keeps going along with your asinine antics. You'd think he would have learned by now."

"What d'ye mean by that?"

"He was entombed alive because of you, then he comes here and you nearly get him killed, and Niamh told me it was you who asked him to go digging around the hills for open tombs. What if he'd found Ruadhán all by himself and his legs barely healed?"

It was as if she'd plunged a knife through his heart. That's what she thought of him. Nothing more than a self-centered troublemaker who had lost all sense of reality. He grabbed a blanket from the rocking chair and headed down to the shed. He'd send Aodhán home. No sense in causing an argument between him and Niamh as well.

****

Aodhán didn't put up much of an argument, and Ciarán could see why. The bench in the shed was hard and uncomfortable, but it provided a perfect view of the road across from the twins' bedroom. He tried to relax, think of other things, but he couldn't get Caitlin's words out of his mind. Was he really that selfish? She wasn't wrong. Aodhán wouldn't have been put in the position he was if he hadn't acted so irresponsibly. He should have thought it through more, planned their escape, but he had been so in love with Aisling. Or had it just been lust, the yearning to feel her body next to his?

He shifted on the bench, unable to find a comfortable position. Maybe he didn't deserve one. But Aodhán hadn't needed to whisk his children away like he did. *O' course he did. You can lie to yerself, but ye know he never would have abandoned them. When ye chose yer path, ye forged his as well.*

Groaning, he got up and stared out the window. Ruadhán wasn't coming. He'd know it was a trap. Aodhán had known that too, and still he'd humored him. *I don't deserve a brother like him.*

And here I was thinking I didn't deserve one like yerself.

"Aodhán? I thought ye went home."

His brother shrugged, a smile slipping across his face. *I did. 'Tis just a dream ye're having.*

"If that's so, I can't be believing anything ye say, now can I?"

Quite the contrary, brother. Ye're far more honest here. Ye know in yer heart it would have made no difference how much ye planned. Dáire meant to betray ye. If anyone's to blame for me interment, 'tis him. Besides, I never would have found Niamh if ye hadn't wed Aisling. I can't thank ye enough for that.

Ciarán chuckled. "I do a good job o' convincing meself I'm to blame for nothing."

Ye're not doing the talking here, now are ye?

"I thought ye were a dream."

I said ye were dreaming. That doesn't mean me words are a part o' it.

"So the connection between us does still exist. I wasn't certain ye'd realized."

I went and searched yer tombs, now didn't I? Sure, it wasn't for me health.

"I never have given ye enough credit for sorting things out, have I?"

'Twas better that way, brother. Sure, ye have an inner strength that comes easy to ye. A conviction I lack.

Ciarán frowned. "How can ye say that? Ye saved me children, knowing what it would mean, and faced Bradaigh with me, using yer last ounce o' strength to do him in, even though ye knew 'twould likely mean yer death."

Domnall was right. Ye never have listened. I didn't say I had no courage, but I wait for the danger to come to me. Whereas ye run toward it, head on.

"And what has that got me? All I ever did was cause trouble for ye, and now I'm hurting Caitlin as well."

Rest easy, brother. Ye've done me no wrong, though ye can be a disagreeable sort when ye're worrying yerself over it. Now sleep. Caitlin is fine, but she'll be needing some o' that strength o' yers any minute now. Oíche maith, a dheartháir.

Before Ciarán could reply, a scream broke his sleep, and he woke up, tumbling off the bench. It was Caitlin, crying out his name, terror in her voice. He darted across the yard, through the back door, and up the stairs. His heart was drumming against his ribs so hard they were in danger of breaking.

He heard the twins crying first, just before he spotted Daniel and Mrs. Byrne holding them at the top of the stairs.

"Calm yourself, son," Daniel said, resting a hand on his shoulder. "She's just had a nightmare. Steve's in with her, making sure she's all right. What she needs now is someone to calm her fears, so no more talk of this Ruadhán stalking these little ones." He frowned at him, then nodded toward the bedroom door.

He had to stop obsessing. It was hurting his wife and his children, not to mention driving everyone else crazy. Unsure of the reception he'd receive, he stuck his head through the doorway and held his breath.

Caitlin immediately ran into his arms, tears cascading down her cheeks. "I saw Ruadhán holding a knife to your throat, standing over some sort of abyss. And then you fell. I screamed out, but . . . It's just a dream, though, isn't it? Ruadhán's not back. He's not going to take you away from me."

"Hush, *a chuisle*, 'tis naught more than a dream, and I'm afraid I'm to blame for it." He wiped the tears from her cheeks, brushing back her hair and kissing her forehead before tightening his embrace and resting her head against his chest. "I've no reason at all to think Ruadhán's returned. 'Tis just me own insecurities dredging up unfounded fears."

"Ye'll come back to bed, then? No more sleeping on the floor in the twins' room or out in the shed?"

He could hear Father Mike counseling him. *Sometimes 'tis permitted to tell a small lie when 'tis for the health and welfare o' another. The key is not to be doing it for yer own gain.* Ciarán knew he could no longer cause Caitlin to worry, or anyone else for that matter. Not unless he had some real proof of

Ruadhán's intent. Though he would share his dreams with Aodhán, he would minimize their meaning when he woke in the night . . . at least until Ruadhán made his move.

CHAPTER 26

Ciarán wiped the sweat from the back of his neck as he looked toward the customs gate. He still had an overwhelming sensation that he was being eyed up as the artifact he was. *Don't be an idiot. Ye're just a man like any other.* He tried to keep his mind on spotting Father Mike and the others, and the tension eased some.

Even though it was just over a week since he'd left New York, he longed to talk to Father Mike and hear Mary tell him he was acting the fool. He chuckled to himself. If the old priest had lived in the fifth century and learned the skills of their priesthood, he would have been a match for Ruadhán. He doubted he'd be afraid of the chief priest even now. It was a sobering thought, and he reminded himself to ensure that confrontation never happened.

A high-pitched voice called his name, and he looked to see Mary's head sticking out from behind one very tall Irishman with a red nose and plaid jacket. He couldn't keep the smile from breaking out on his face, unbidden tears wetting his eyes. This was just what he needed to free him from the clasp of his dreams.

Mary came running at him, grabbing his head on either side and planting a huge kiss on his cheek. A frown crossed her forehead as she pulled back. "You don't look like you've been sleeping much. Are those babies keeping you up? Teething, I expect, though it is a bit early."

"'Tis good to see yerself as well, a Mathair."

She slapped his arm and pointed to her bag. "Well, are you just going to stand there, grinning at everyone like the cat who swallowed a mouse, or are we going to get going?"

"Why would I be smiling if I ate a mouse?"

"I'll explain later," Dennis said. He gave Ciarán a fraternal slap on the back and took Mary by the arm, heading toward the exit.

"I expect ye'd best be doing as she asks." Michael grabbed his shoulder in greeting and nodded toward Mary's suitcase.

"I expect ye're right." Ciarán laughed and grabbed the woman's bag before guiding the priest toward the door.

"Now what is it that's troubling ye so?"

"How did ye—"

"I've known ye long enough to recognize the worry in yer eyes. Besides, Mary's right. Ye don't look like ye've been getting much sleep, though I doubt it has much to do with those wee babes. Ye've been having more dreams, have ye?"

"'Tis worse than that. I've seen him, Michael. Everyone except Aodhán thinks I imagined it, but I know the difference between a dream and what I saw."

"Are the twins safe, then?"

"I don't know, but the stress o' it all is causing a strain between Caitlin and meself. The last straw, as Dennis would say, was when I took to sleeping on the floor between the twins' cribs." Ciarán shook his head. "Ye were right to be worried about me getting close to Caitlin. Ye said me past would keep causing trouble in me life."

"Now, lad, I believe what I said was our past had a way o' catching up with us, but I was referring to the fact ye hadn't even told the lass about yerself yet. We all have a bit o' history, lad." Ciarán lifted an eyebrow, and the priest laughed. "Even meself. 'Tis only a problem when we don't confide the truth in those we love, and ye've done that. Beyond that, ye've no control over what may appear."

"Then what am I to do about it? I have told her, but she thinks 'tis no more than a dream, the manifestations o' me fears over being a father." This time it was Father Mike who raised his eyebrow, and Ciarán was quick to respond. "'Tis not. I saw the man, and there have been other signs as well. Even Aodhán thinks I'm right now."

Michael took a deep breath of the crisp morning air. "Are you two coming?" Mary shouted back in their direction before letting them take the lead.

"Have a bit o' faith, me son. The twins are no less safe with ye sleeping in the next room, and all the worrying in the world won't protect them. Ye're doing all ye can to find him, are ye not?"

"I am, but I don't know where else to look."

"Then there's nothing else for it than to put it in God's hands. 'Tis always darkest before the dawn."

A smile tugged at Ciarán's lips, and he gave in to it, a wave of relief and hope washing over him, flushing the stress away. "That's one o' Dennis's, isn't it?"

"Well, ye can't be around the man without picking out one o' his idioms here and there. This one is true, though. Just when things seem their darkest, 'tis then the Lord lets his glorious light shine through."

Ciarán let out a cleansing sigh, sending a whispered prayer up to heaven. Perhaps Michael was right and he should let the Lord's voice guide him a bit more. He hadn't been doing that lately. "'Tis not that I don't believe, Michael. But I worry that the Lord and I might not agree on what's best."

Michael laughed and patted him on the back. "He may not, 'tis true, but I'll still be putting me faith in his hands and pray that we're in agreement. Regardless, fretting about it won't be changing the outcome one bit, now will it? The only thing that's likely to do is cause trouble between yerself and those ye love. Now let's be getting to Mrs. Byrne's before I pass out from lack o' sustenance."

"They fed ye on the plane, Father."

"That wee bit they put before me? Sure, 'twas not enough there to feed a bird."

Ciarán smiled again and opened the car door. It was always good to talk to Michael.

****

"D'ye want to be telling us about it?" Niamh asked as she and Fionnuala accompanied Caitlin down to Castlebar.

Caitlin hadn't exactly been a cheerful companion, and they were almost there. All she wanted to do was cry and feel Ciarán's muscular arms around her. But that wasn't going to happen, was it? Not after Saturday night. He'd promised her he would stop obsessing over Ruadhán, and granted, he hadn't gone to sleep in the twins' bedroom the night before, but she could sense the tension in his muscles, see the wariness in his haunting blue eyes.

It worried her, and she reacted by snapping out at him. She couldn't help it, though. His dreams had never troubled him to such an extent before, and there had been some doozies. He almost seemed detached from reality, not able to tell the difference between the shadows of the night and the light of day.

"Ciarán and I had an argument Saturday night. I found him sleeping in the twins' room for the fourth night in a row, waiting for Ruadhán to appear, as if the man was going to rise from the ground."

"I know," Niamh said. "Aodhán mentioned it. "I can't say I was too pleased with him meself."

"I said some awful things. Hurtful things. I just didn't know what else to do, how to make him see what he was doing to us all. He stormed off to sleep in the archeology shed, but then I had this horrible nightmare, most likely caused by all this talk of Ruadhán, still . . . it left me trembling."

"What was the dream about, then?" Fionnuala said.

"You're going to think I'm just as bad as Ciarán. Ruadhán was there, though how I knew it was him, I can't say. I just did. He was holding a jeweled knife to Ciarán's throat, pulling him toward this dark abyss, and then Ciarán fell."

"What d'ye think it means?" Fionnuala said.

"Probably that she's worried sick about Ciarán. It's the thought o' Ruadhán that's pulling him toward a deep hole o' obsession, and Cait's afraid she's going to lose him completely."

"I suppose you're right. I am terribly worried about him. He's had dreams before, but never this bad."

"Are ye still rowing with him?" Fionnuala asked.

"No, we made up after my nightmare, and he promised he was going to stop. He hasn't returned to sleep in the nursery since, so that's a good sign. The thing is, even though he's putting up a casual front, I can sense the tension in his muscles, see the worry in his eyes. I've gotten to know him too well for him to hide his emotions from me, yet how can I say anything when he's making so much of an effort?"

"I hate to say it, but Aodhán's not so sure Ruadhán won't be showing himself." Niamh cast a quick glance in her rearview mirror.

Caitlin wiped a dribble from Fionn's mouth. "But Aodhán said he thought Ciarán had just dreamed seeing him. He said he'd done that before."

"Oh, he did at first, but then they came across some curious things, and . . ." She put her blinker on and headed off the highway, "Well, he's not so sure anymore."

Caitlin's gaze shifted back to the twins. "Maybe we shouldn't be going off to Castlebar on our own, then?"

"We're not alone, are we?" Fionnula said. "As long as the three o' us stay together, sure, no old cleric is going to harm us, now is he?" They'd pulled into a parking spot, and she opened the door for Caitlin, resting a hand on her shoulder as she did. "Maybe I shouldn't have been so hard on him Saturday afternoon though. I did give him a bit o' what for. I'm thinking I'll buy him a few o' them candy bars he likes so much. Sure, that'll make it all right again."

"He's not a child," Caitlin said. "I think it will take more than a few sweets to take his mind off everything. Funny, though, that's exactly what he said to me Saturday night, that he wasn't a child, but I blew him off, completely ignoring his concerns. I suppose I didn't want to think any of it could be possible."

"I know what ye mean," Fionnula said. "The thought o' some old man lurking down a country lane waiting to pounce on ye is enough to make anyone's flesh crawl.

Imagine the creature thinking Ciarán's children would belong to that goddess o' his."

Niamh turned the engine off and picked up her handbag. "'Tis because Aodhán saw to it Ciarán's fifth-century children escaped his clutches. He wants revenge, I suppose."

"But what does he plan on doing with them?" Fionnuala said. "Sure, he can't be thinking o' starting up that priesthood o' his again."

"That's one theory," Niamh said.

"He might want to make sure Ciarán's buried alive again as well," Caitlin said. "Maybe permanently this time."

"And he'll be wanting that book o' theirs." Fionnuala shivered, like she'd just walked through a cold puddle. "But we'll not be thinking about that today. I'm going to go in that shop and get those candy bars for Ciarán. Why don't ye and Niamh go into the pub and get settled? I shouldn't be a minute."

****

Fionnula starred at the candy counter. *Now what was it Ciarán called them? Snickers, I'm thinking, but 'tis not what we call them here.*

"Good day to ye," a voice said. "What brings ye to Castlebar?"

Fionnuala jumped and looked around. "Oh, 'tis just ye, Mr. McGuire."

"Ye were expecting someone else?" He smiled and picked up a Marathon bar.

"Marathon! That's the name o' it. I've been trying to remember what they call the Snickers bar here in Ireland. Ciarán loves them, and well, after Saturday . . . I'm afraid he's been in the doghouse with everyone, so I thought I'd bring him a few sweets to smooth things over."

"That's kind o' ye, but sure, the lad did nothing wrong. I might have reacted much the same meself 'twere the situation reversed."

"Well, he should have given ye a chance to speak, but I reckon his heart was in the right place." She smiled and picked up a few of the candy bars. "I see ye like the sweets as well."

"Not particularly, but I had a sudden urge for one. Though I'm thinking it must have been fate, me coming in here like this and meeting yerself. I've an old war wound, ye see, and it just started acting up again. I was going to ask one o' the clerks here to help me out to the car, but now ye're here. If I could just lean on ye a bit, 'tis right round the corner."

"'Twould be no trouble at all. Make up a bit for Ciarán going off on ye like he did without even taking a moment to ask ye about it."

"Now I told ye, I don't want ye to be troubling yerself over that." They started walking around the corner toward his car. "Sure, ye were all worried sick over the lad."

"We were that, and ye can rest assured the wee scoundrel won't be going anywhere for a month. Just let us know if ye've any work needs doing round yer place. He'll be over to help ye with it."

"Sure, 'tis right kind o' ye. I'll be keeping it in mind." Opening the back car door, he put his packages in. "Have ye ever seen one o' these, lass?" He held up a small box, lifting the lid as she bent over to get a better look.

Spots began to flash before her eyes, and she grabbed on to his arm to keep from falling. Her knees collapsed beneath her. She was drifting away, falling through a long mist-filled tunnel, the wind hissing past her ears. And all she wanted to do was sleep.

****

"Shouldn't Fionnuala be back by now?" Caitlin adjusted the collar of Fionn's thin jacket. Being early September, the warmth of summer was fading, and there was a distinct nip in the air that Monday morning. "She was just stopping in next door to get Ciarán a few Snickers bars."

"Snickers?" Niamh put down the menu. "What are they?"

"Marathon bars here, I think. He doesn't care what they're called. He loves them. It was the first candy bar Mary gave him after he woke up." She brushed a wisp of Aisling's hair from her eyes. "It all seems so long ago now, but it's been just a little over two years."

Niamh smiled, a faraway look in her eyes. "I remember the day Aodhán and I met, a year ago last Thursday, it was. Duffy and I were out for a ride, and there he was walking with Ciarán. Sure, didn't I think me heart stopped right there and then? Told me he studied birds. I don't think he knew what else to say."

Caitlin smiled. "And now in two weeks you'll be married."

"Does it change things?" Niamh asked. "I hope it doesn't because 'tis grand the way it is."

"A little, I suppose, but not in a bad way." Caitlin sighed, thinking about the argument she and Ciarán had engaged in on Saturday night. Then again, they'd argued before they were married as well, usually when his past started elbowing its way into their lives. "I think maybe you get more comfortable with each other."

"So he slacked off on doing the sweet little things ye loved so much about him."

Caitlin laughed. "A bit I suppose, but . . . there are better things. Though we still argue, he's always there, waiting for me when I get home, even if he might not be talking to me. It never lasts with him. He can't stay quiet that long."

"That's true." Niamh laughed as well, then cast a look toward the doorway. "Perhaps I ought go see what's keeping her, eh. Just order me the colcannon and a Guinness when the waitress comes."

Caitlin did just that and asked for a shepherd's pie for herself. She frowned down at the twins. "Sorry, sweeties, but in a few more months you can start tasting all kinds of wonderful things. I'm sure your *dadaí* will have you spoiled in no time."

She did love the man so much, but these dreams had her worried. Aside from the obvious threat, they were taking a toll on him. He hadn't slept right in nights, and his eyes had dark circles under them. Maybe Father Mike could help. He always knew what to say when it came to Ciarán, and just about anything else when it came to it.

The waitress had just put the food down on the table when Niamh returned, her eyes flashing with worry, her brow crinkled. "Pay the bill. We need to be going."

Caitlin cast a look down at the luscious shepherd's pie, then back to Niamh. "What is it? What's happened?"

"I'll tell ye on the way." She picked Aisling up from the high chair and nodded for Caitlin to grab Fionn.

"All right, just give me a minute to pay." She grabbed the waitress and apologized for their sudden departure and, after handing her the money, bent over and picked up her son.

"Now do you want to tell me what's going on?" She strapped Fionn and Aisling in the little chair-like contraptions that were strapped to the backseat before sitting in the front seat herself.

"Fionnuala went off with some man." Niamh flipped the blinker to head out into traffic, her hand trembling on the wheel. "The clerk in the candy store didn't remember much about what he looked like, but he said she seemed to know him. White hair, he thought, or maybe more salt and pepper, and he had a bit o' a limp. He couldn't be sure. It was busy, and she'd already made her purchase."

A bolt of fear shot through Caitlin. Ciarán had been warned about the older ones being in danger. Could the man have been Ruadhán? But no, Fionnuala wouldn't know him. Would she?

"Well, where did they go?"

"Out the back door 'tis all they could tell me. I walked out that way and searched the street in both directions before coming back round to the pub. There wasn't a hint o' them in sight."

"Shouldn't we stay and look for them a bit, maybe even notify the police?"

"I suppose we should at least tell the *garda*, though I know what they'll say. 'Tis too soon to be jumping to conclusions, especially as the woman seemed to go without a fuss. Still, what if it was that Ruadhán? I'm thinking we should be getting home and telling the lads."

"I suppose you're right, and we could call DI Travis from there. At least he'll understand the urgency of the situation, being he knows what really went on up at the hillfort last year."

"True enough, but what if he's taken the lads as well?"

"No, Ciarán and Aodhán will know him. It won't be that easy with them, but I don't understand. Why did she go with him?"

"The clerk said the man was limping a bit. Maybe he was just a stranger looking for help. Fionnuala's kind like that."

"She might have helped him to the car, but if it was anything more, she would have come back and told us or at least asked the clerk to let us know. None of this feels right."

The look of panic in Niamh's eyes only confirmed Caitlin's fears. She sat quiet for the rest of the ride, her mind racing. Had Ciarán been right to worry the way he had? And if so, was Fionnuala just the beginning? Would Duffy's children and her own be prey for the ancient priest as well?

Her stomach tied into a huge knot. How was she ever going to tell him his friend—no, more than that, a woman who was essentially his granddaughter—had gone missing?

CHAPTER 27

Ciarán smiled as Caitlin and the others drove up. After the talk he'd had with Father Mike that morning, he was in a much better state of mind. Whether Ruadhán was lurking about or not, it did no one any good if he lost his perspective. The man would come regardless, and it was best if he faced him with a clear head. Besides, all he was doing was upsetting Caitlin, and if she was right, maybe even the twins.

He walked up to the car, broadening his smile, and opened the door, ready to give his mea culpas. Before he could say a word, though, Caitlin jumped into his arms, her eyes a deep mistletoe green, but it wasn't anger he saw there.

"What is it?" He gave a quick glance in the car. Aisling and Fionn slept peacefully in the backseat. But where was Fionnuala? She was to go with them, wasn't she? Unless they'd already dropped her at home. "What's happened?"

"Fionnuala's gone missing," Caitlin said, her voice trembling. She fought to hold back the tears. "I'm so sorry. We should have listened. They said she went off with a man who had graying hair, but they couldn't be sure. She knew him, though, or so they thought."

"All right, calm yerself, *a chuisle*. Who's this *they* ye keep talking about?"

"She stopped into the shop next to the pub to get . . ." Niamh hesitated. "Well, I don't suppose it'll be mattering what she went in after. The fact is she left with someone and never returned. They did say he had a limp, though."

Cormac McGuire flashed to mind. Why did he distrust that man so? *Because there's something about him that's just a bit too familiar, that's why.* "Graying hair, they said." It certainly fit McGuire, though he didn't have a limp the last time Ciarán saw him. Still, limps could be faked. "Like Mr. McGuire, perhaps?"

"Sure, ye can't be thinking it was Cormac?" Niamh frowned. "Ye're not planning on going to beat on the poor old man again, now are ye?"

"'Twas hardly a beating." Ciarán headed down the road, suppressing his suspicion of the man. "Just a quick jab in the nose 'twas all it was."

Caitlin caught up and took him by the arm, giving a slight tug so he'd stop. "Ciarán, have you any real reason to think it was Cormac?"

He leaned over and kissed her forehead. "Don't be worrying yerself so. I have no intention o' laying a hand on the man, but he might have seen her this afternoon. Maybe he has an idea where she's gotten off to."

Niamh and Caitlin nodded, following him down the road, each with a twin on their hip. After what happened on Saturday, Ciarán supposed they had good reason for being a bit skeptical of his motives. Truth be told, they weren't far off. In spite of the lack of evidence to support his suspicions, he didn't trust the man.

Cutting across a field or two, they arrived at Cormac's house just in time to catch him bringing what must have been the last of his groceries into the house.

"Good afternoon to ye, Mr. McGuire." Ciarán walked up the path and smiled, though he could feel his lips trembling. "Let me give ye a hand with them."

The man flinched slightly but let go of his bag. "Thank ye, 'tis right kindly o' ye."

With what I did the other day, ye mean. "'Tis the least I can do after giving ye a sore nose and all. Did I cause ye to be limping so as well?"

Caitlin rested a hand on his arm once more, afraid he was going to haul off and cuff the man again, no doubt. He patted her hand and smiled.

"No, not at all, not at all," Cormac said. "Don't be fussing yerself over this. Just a victim o' me own clumsiness. Missed the last step coming down me own stairs, didn't I, fool that I am."

"I see ye've been shopping down in Castlebar." The man opened his mouth, probably to question how he knew where he'd been shopping, but Ciarán pointed to the store name on a jar of jam.

"That I have. Saw Fionnuala down there as well, I did. She was kind enough to help me out to the car."

"Did you see where she went after she left you?" Caitlin asked. Fionn was fussing for his lunch, and she kissed him on the head.

"Why, back to the pub, I presumed. Weren't ye to have a bit o' lunch together?"

"We were," Niamh said. "But she never came back."

Cormac frowned. "Sure, she just stopped to help someone else, kind as she is. Probably looking round for ye even now. She'll be finding her way back soon enough, I expect."

"I'm sure ye're right," Ciarán said. "We'll be notifying the *garda* to keep an eye out for her, just in case." Without taking his eyes off the man, he smiled. "Ye have a good day and watch where ye're stepping."

The man gave an awkward nod, clearly understanding Ciarán's double meaning. "Ye'll be letting me know when ye find her, won't ye? I'd hate to think me asking her to give me a hand to the car may have brought her to harm."

"We will, good day to ye now." Ciarán walked away, alarms going off in his head. But what was he going to do, thrash the man within an inch of his life for nothing more than a niggling at the back of his head? Caitlin would never forgive him, and if it turned out Fionnuala really did just stop to help someone else, neither would she.

He had to find Ruadhán. Regardless of his promise to stop obsessing over it, whether it caused another argument or not, he had every intention of spending the night in the nursery. If Ruadhán had taken Fionnuala, it may have been nothing more than a distraction to shift their attention from the twins. If so, Ciarán would be ready for him.

Thanks to Father Mike, his head was clear now, not clouded with worry. He'd explain it all to Caitlin, with a calm and logical argument, not the rantings of a sleep-deprived madman.

****

Ciarán stood off to the side while Inspector Travis took all the information he needed from Niamh and Caitlin, assuring them that he'd get his men on it right away. Though his tenor was confident, Ciarán could see the doubt in his eyes. *Probably wondering if I'm the one he needs to be speaking to.*

They were finishing up, so Ciarán walked outside and sat on the low stone wall across the way from Mrs. Byrne's bed and breakfast.

Moments later, Travis came to join him. "What's really going on here, lad? Not another o' yer perverted high priests, I hope."

"I wouldn't be calling Ruadhán a pervert, more like a faithful servant, determined to make things right in the eyes o' his goddess."

"There is another priest walking around, then?"

"I can't be saying for sure, but I believe there might be."

"But how? Sure, I thought there was to be no more excavation up in the hills."

"There's not." Ciarán tilted his head in a half shrug. "I'm thinking this one managed to wake all on his own."

"Glory to God! Have we come to that now?" He took off his hat for a moment and wiped his brow. "But why would he be feeling the need to take Fionnuala? Sure, she's nothing to do with yer goddess." He sat down on the wall and pulled out a cigarette. "Would ye like one?"

"No, thank ye. How much more d'ye want to be privy to?"

Travis laughed. "Sure, I didn't want to be dragged into any o' it, did I, but I'm here now, like it or not. 'Tis best I know all I can if I've any hope o' finding Fionnuala Flynn."

"She's me descendant, and Ruadhán . . . When I was entombed, Aodhán made sure to get me children away to a Christian enclave down in Cork."

"That must have gone over well with this chief priest o' yers." He took a drag on his cigarette and blew out the smoke. "I'll assume that's what got Aodhán entombed."

Ciarán chewed on his thumbnail and nodded.

"Holy Mother! And what does this Ruadhán want now? All yer descendants?"

"I don't suppose he knows who all o' them are, does he? I'm not even sure how he found out about Fionnuala, though I'm afraid she may just be the start o' it. And then there's the Book o' Carraig as well."

"That's the book that helped ye defeat Bradaigh, isn't it? No doubt he'll be after that."

"He will, and once he gets it, ye can be sure he'll be wanting to see Aodhán and I entombed alive once more, for good this time. Sure, he'll be livid when he's discovered we entered the Cave o' Rúin Ársa and removed it. That is, if he hasn't already. 'Twas a sacred book, not to be touched by anyone but those on the high council."

"And poor Fionnuala's got herself caught up in all o' this." He took another puff of his cigarette, blowing the smoke out the side of his mouth. "Will ye be able to handle this one?"

Ciarán frowned. "Mother o' God, don't be telling me he's more powerful than the last."

"I'll give him meself before I let him hurt anyone else, but the truth o' it is he's a threat to no one but me own."

"What can I do to help, then?" He threw his cigarette on the ground and stamped it out. "Though I have to ask, were ye all a bunch o' troublemakers?"

Ciarán huffed a sarcastic laugh, his fears clear in his tone. "Ruadhán's no troublemaker. He's anything but. 'Tis why he's here. He believes he's doing the will of his goddess."

"Any chance ye might be convincing him otherwise?"

"I'm thinking he buried himself alive to keep from betraying her, so no . . . I don't think I'll be changing his mind."

"What are ye going to do if we do find him, then?"

"Offer meself up in Fionnuala's place. I might be able to convince him that such a prize would please the goddess far more than a wee *cailín*. After all, he's sure to think 'tis all me fault to begin with. He's not a wicked man, not like Bradaigh, but he is vengeful. I just need to find him."

"And what if he takes yer babes after he's sealed ye up in that tomb?"

"He won't, not if he's given his word. Breaking yer oath is frowned on by the goddess."

Travis nodded. "If I had me way, I'd dynamite every one of those caves and make sure no one ever came out o' them again."

"There are good men up there as well, men like me father, Domnall. I'm sure he must be buried in the hills somewhere."

"I suppose ye're right." Travis stood and stretched his back. "Right then, I'd best be about it. 'Tis going to be a long night, I fear." He rested his hand on Ciarán's shoulder. "We'll do our best to find her. Just watch yerself, eh."

****

It was after dark, the moon shining bright, when Ruadhán slipped up to the Cave of Rúin Ársa with Fionnuala slung over his shoulder. He was getting too old for this, but surely the goddess knew that. Soon it would all be over. The seeds of a new priesthood would be planted, the Book of Carraig back in his possession, and Domnall's rebellious son returned to his tomb. Only this time, he'd make sure he never saw the light of day again.

As for Aodhán, with Ciarán out of the way, his spirit should be far more malleable. He didn't have the rebellious streak his brother did. In fact, he may even be able to bring him back into the fold and, with the goddess's guidance, perhaps mold him for leadership of the priesthood one day.

CHAPTER 28

"Ciarán?" Caitlin stood in the doorway to the darkened nursery.

Ciarán cast a glance in her direction before looking back out the window. What could he say to calm her fears? The moonlight reflected off the dark green of her eyes, a beam of its light accenting her trembling lips. How he wanted to kiss that mouth, to let the warmth of her breath fill him for all eternity.

"Are the twins safe and sound?" he asked.

"They're fussing a bit." She strode over to his side, tugging him by the shoulder until he turned to face her. "They want their father."

"And what would ye have me do, Cait?" He brushed the hair off her shoulder. "Leave Fionnuala to him?"

"Ye said he wasn't a wicked man. Surely he'll release her as soon as he realizes he's not going to get what he wants."

"That's just it. He believes what he's doing is just and righteous. I was to live in eternal torment, half-living and half-dead, but I was awakened. Sure, he'll be thinking a god he doesn't understand released me to live again, against the goddess's will, and in doing so denied her justice. And then, to make matters worse, me children, her children, were taken from her. He won't give in till he sees justice done or dies trying."

"But what if he comes for Fionn and Aisling anyway? How can we stop him if you're not here?"

Ciarán touched her cheek, damp now with tears. "Hush, *a chuisle*. I will make him swear on the goddess herself. He will not betray those words."

"You can't be sure of that."

"That is the one thing I can be sure o'. Unlike meself, he values his oaths."

"And what of the oath you made to me? To love and to honor, in good times and in bad . . ."

"Till death us do part. Whatever Ruadhán has planned for me, God will not let me linger long. Have faith in that, *a chuisle*." He kissed her forehead and stared out the window again. How he wanted to explain it all to her, but he mustn't. Ruadhán might steal into her mind and see their plan. Besides, what if it didn't work? No, better this way.

She sighed and sat in the rocking chair, slipping one leg beneath her. "You were with Aodhán and Steve all afternoon, right through supper. What were you talking about?"

"What Ruadhán might ask o' me or Aodhán and what, if anything, we could do to deter him. We also went over those bits o' the Book o' Carraig ye translated for us to see if 'twas anything there to help us." She looked up at him, hope lighting her eyes. "No, *a ghrá*, there was nothing."

He hated lying to her, hated what this was doing to her, but it was for the best. Even Father Mike would approve of this small lie. Besides, their plan wouldn't work unless Ruadhán demanded what Ciarán suspected he would.

The moon had shifted, and he heard Caitlin gasp. "What is Mr. McGuire doing down there? We should warn him." She went to yell out the window, and Ciarán put his hand over her mouth, dragging her away.

"That's Ruadhán!" He should have known better, should have paid more attention to that niggling little prickling he'd felt in his head every time he saw the man. Of course the man had transformed himself. Hadn't Ciarán done the same after waking so that even Caitlin hadn't known him? All his fear and anxiety had dulled his senses and allowed Ruadhán to manipulate him.

Ciarán fisted his hands at his sides, determined not to let the chief priest get the better of him. This would take all the concentration he could muster. He couldn't allow Ruadhán to break into his mind, couldn't allow him to intercept his thoughts.

"Are ye ready, brother?" Aodhán crept up next to him and gazed out the window. "How did I not see this?"

"None of us did," Ciarán said.

"Ye did, at least something about the man bothered ye. I should have paid ye more mind."

"It would have made no difference. I couldn't tell ye what it was about him that troubled me. I had a wee bit o' an itch in the back o' me brain, but I couldn't scratch it. 'Twas him slithering in whenever I got close, I suspect, but me nerves were so frayed I never noticed."

"I wonder what he did with the real Mr. McGuire?"

Ciarán let out an ironic chuckle. "Knowing Ruadhán, the man's probably sitting on a tropic isle somewhere, thinking he's won the jackpot."

"True enough." Aodhán frowned and pulled him over by one of the cribs, speaking so Caitlin couldn't hear. "What if this doesn't work?"

"It has to. I'll not have another living soul die for me sins."

Aodhán scrubbed a hand across his mouth. "I don't have yer skill, brother."

"Yes, ye do." Ciarán grabbed his brother's shoulder, staring deep into his eyes, those eyes so like his own, so like his children's. They were Domnall's eyes, and Ciarán knew they concealed a powerful talent.

"Ciarán!" Caitlin had risen and walked to where they were standing. She wrapped her arm around him and rested her head against his chest. "Will I at least see you again?"

"O' course ye will. He's sure to want the Book o' Carraig and won't do anything until he gets it. He'll have to give us time to retrieve it. Now stay here with our children. And no matter what ye hear, don't leave. Please promise me this."

"But, Ciarán . . ."

He turned her so that they were standing face-to-face, his arms wrapped around her waist. "I'll always be with ye, *a chuisle*, no matter what." She opened her mouth to speak, but he pressed his lips over hers, etching the feel of her deep into his memory. Then without another word, he pulled away and headed downstairs.

****

"Well, have you decided to face your responsibilities?" Ruadhán said, easily slipping into the ancient Gaelic he knew so well.

"Where is Fionnuala?" Ciarán said, his voice catching.

"Sleeping peacefully, but don't worry. I haven't given her anything as potent as I intend to give you."

"And you think I'll drink it?"

"Oh, you'll drink it. You're far too noble to refuse, given the consequences if you don't. Domnall did manage to instill a bit of honor in you. If only he had bred as much loyalty to your goddess."

"She's not my goddess."

Ruadhán clutched his hands at his sides and breathed out a long breath. "I will not be drawn in by your skill with words. It is petty and useless. You will drink the potion I give you and accept your punishment. I have taken extra precautions to see you don't escape the grip of the goddess this time."

Ciarán's stomach clutched. Had they missed something? No, he couldn't think about it. Couldn't chance letting Ruadhán slither into his mind.

"And when you have done so, your granddaughter will help me start a renewed priesthood."

"No! You can have me to do with as you will, but I must have your oath that you will demand nothing from anyone else."

Ruadhán barked a laugh. "You have no bargaining power here."

"Haven't I? You do not wish to retrieve the Book of Carraig, then?"

Fury flashed in Ruadhán's eyes, a rumble of thunder sounding off in the distance. "You dared to touch the sacred book! But then it was not the first time, was it? I should never have let Domnall convince me to pardon you so easily."

"What became of my father?" In spite of the dire situation, Ciarán found he wanted to know what had happened to the man who'd nurtured him and Aodhán in their youth and even now appeared in his meditation.

335

Ruadhán's lip turned up in a snarl. "It is no wonder you turned your back on the goddess, for did he not do the same? In her time of need, he abandoned her for your new god, just like the rest of them."

"He became a Christian?"

"If that's what you call yourselves, then yes." A nasty laugh rang from his lips. "Your brother looked for him in the Tombs of the Ancient Ones, but he will not find him there.

I've no doubt he was buried like all the rest, in the dirt with a cross stuck in the ground above him."

Somehow that knowledge warmed Ciarán's heart and gave him the strength to go on. "Do we have a deal, then? You will leave my family alone, all of them, and in return I will give you the book and drink your potion."

Another rumble of thunder shook the air. "You will be at the Cave of Rúin Ársa as the dawn lights the sky. Dress appropriately for a child of the goddess."

"But I don't have . . ."

"Then you'd best find some. You will not disgrace your mother even more by appearing before her in your Christian attire. Perhaps your brother can help with it since he will be powerless to do anything else."

"You wear these clothes."

"Only to move amongst you undetected until my plan was in place."

"And what was that plan?"

"I'd have thought it was obvious. As your—what, forty-fifth—great-granddaughter, Fionnuala is blessed, as were you. You can see it in her eyes. I had intended to use her to father a new priesthood. Gradually, I would have taken your children. But once again, you have forced the hand of our goddess. I cannot abandon the sacred book to the hands of Christians, nor can I break my oath once given, unlike yourself."

The thought of that old man lying with his granddaughter turned his stomach. But he needed Ruadhán's word before he gave up anything. "And do I have that oath? Swear it on the goddess of our *túath*."

"You will drink the potion I have prepared and return the book."

"I will."

"Then I concede to your demands and swear upon the goddess of our *túath*. Now go to your priest and prepare yourself, though little good it will do you. Our goddess will not allow your god to interfere again."

****

Duffy darted for the door, but Aodhán grabbed him by the arm and held him back. "Give us a hand here, would ye?" he shouted to Steve and Ryan. Together, they managed to drag the man into the parlor, pressing him down on the love seat.

"Now sit there, will ye, and let Ciarán handle it."

"I should have let Ciarán knock his pan in the other day. Dear God, I can't believe we defended the bastard. He had me Timothy as well. Maybe if I'd let Ciarán give him a good beating then, me Fionnuala would be safe at home instead o' God knows where." He struggled to stand, but Steve and Ryan held him down.

Aodhán knelt before him. How could he get Duffy to trust them without telling him everything? Even allowing Steve in on their plan was chancy but a necessary risk. Duffy shoved him aside, but Ryan was a large man and yanked him back down as if he held a rubber band around Duffy's waist.

"Now sit still, will you?" Ryan said. "I don't want to get rough with you."

Aodhán took Duffy by the shoulders. "D'ye want those wee young ones to be missing their da as well as their ma? Have a little faith, eh. Ciarán knows what he's doing. He saved Niamh, didn't he?"

"Only just, and nearly got himself done as well, not to mention yerself."

"But he didn't, now did he?"

Duffy was fighting to hold back the tears, his chin trembling. "She holds me heart, Aodhán. If I lose her . . ." He shook his head, pinching his fingers against his eyes.

"Then we'll have to make sure not to lose her, won't we?"

"Perhaps we should say a prayer or two," Father Michael said, "to give us strength for whatever lies ahead. First, though, I'll be needing a wee word with Aodhán." The priest lifted him by the collar and led him over to the corner, away from everyone else. "Now d'ye want to tell me what that lad is doing out there all by himself?"

Aodhán hung his head. "He's making a deal with Ruadhán."

"What kind o' deal?" Father Mike's voice held an edge that belied the gentle man's character. Granted, Aodhán hadn't spent much time with him, but from what Ciarán and Caitlin said, he never even raised his voice.

Aodhán dared not look up to meet the man's eyes. Even Steve said the priest had a way of wriggling secrets out of a person, but Ciarán was like a son to him. He must think Aodhán a coward. He had to say something.

"Ciarán insisted he go alone."

"I know how thickheaded the lad can be, but 'tis not what I asked ye."

"He has something in mind . . . that's all I know."

"In the pig's arse," Michael said, his cheeks red, whether from anger or embarrassment, he couldn't tell. "Ye two visit each other's heads like other people stroll through the park." He took a deep breath. "Is it dangerous, this plan o' his?"

Aodhán gave a quick nod. Neither he nor Ciarán was really sure it would work, but what other option did they have?

Michael scrubbed his hand across the stubble that was sprouting on his usually clean-shaven jaw. "He'll see me before he puts this plan into play, then, will he?"

"He will, Father. I'm sure o' it."

"But he won't be telling me anymore than ye did?"

"No, Father, I'm afraid not. It would mean putting yerself in danger as well."

"Ye'll be coming with him, then, for the blessing. I have an idea ye're not exactly exempt from Ruadhán's wrath either." He sat down in a chair next to the fireplace. "I'm afraid I'm a wee bit late to this party, as it were. Why has the man taken Fionnuala, o' all people?"

"Because she's Ciarán's descendant."

"His what?" The priest blessed himself. "Sweet Mother in heaven. How did ye find that out?"

Aodhán leaned against the windowsill. The priest had just arrived that morning. Ciarán never even had a chance to tell him. "I gave Ciarán's son Bréanainn his ring. The lad apparently passed it on to his children, and . . ."

"Saints preserve us . . . Fionnuala is his granddaughter o' sorts." He thought for a moment before looking up again. "Oh dear, but ye and Niamh . . . will ye be able to wed?"

"Niamh is Duffy's sister, not Fionnuala's."

He breathed a sigh of relief. "Oh, that's good, then. Though I'm not sure it would really matter. I mean, after all, 'tis far more than the third degree, now isn't it?"

Aodhán couldn't help but let a chuckle rumble in his chest. "So it is, Father."

"Well, that explains why the lad's willing to risk his own life, then, doesn't it?" Aodhán's head popped up, and the priest smiled. "I just hope yer plan works, whatever it is. Sure 'twould be a shame if those two wee tykes never got to know their da."

He couldn't just let the priest go without easing his mind. Even if he couldn't tell him exactly what the plan was, he could confide some information at least. "Father, we do have a plan, but 'tis risky. We can't even be sure if 'twill work at all."

"Well, 'tis good ye have a plan at any rate." He stood up and squeezed Aodhán's arm. "'Tis always darkest before the dawn, lad."

"What's going on here, Father?" Ciarán walked into the parlor and shot a glance in Aodhán's direction.

"He didn't tell me a thing, so calm yerself down. Now kneel, the two o' ye. Just in case I don't get another chance to see ye both together." They hesitated for an instant, the reality of the situation hitting Aodhán right between his eyes, like a stone from a slingshot. "Well, get to it," Father Michael said, "and bow yer heads."

They did as he asked, and he placed a hand on both their heads, just as he'd done before they set off to face Bradaigh. How often could they test fate and survive? The priest's lips were moving, but Aodhán couldn't hear the words, nor could he distinguish the thoughts that raced through his head, except for one. *Dear heavenly Father, protect them.*

****

Caitlin found Ciarán standing over his children, watching them sleep. There would be no sleep for him that night, though.

"What did you promise him?" she asked.

He didn't answer. There was no need. She knew what Ruadhán wanted. "You're going to let him do it to you again, aren't you? Only this time he'll make sure you can't wake up." She sank down into the rocking chair, her heart ripping in two, the breath caught in her throat, and he bent down beside her. Wiping the tears from her cheeks, he leaned over and captured her lips with his own. She wrapped her arms around his neck, wanting to believe that if she held him there, he would be safe.

"I love ye so, Cait, but he'll take them all, one by one, unless I turn meself over." He lifted her from the chair, pressing her to himself, the warmth of his body piercing the thin material of her short nightie. "Leave me with something to take to the tomb."

Unzipping his jeans, he sat in the rocking chair, pulling her down on his lap. He tugged on her nightie, shifting it up, and the tingle of his flesh sent a yearning through her soul. She gasped as he entered her, the gentle rock of the chair pressing him deeper, sending waves of excitement down along her thighs. Their lips met once more, his tongue searching for hers, the taste and smell of him filling her senses.

They moved slowly, lovingly, allowing the tension to build. His hands pressed against her back, nudging her closer, and she obliged eagerly. But she wouldn't rush it. This memory might need to last her for the rest of her life. His hands slipped beneath her nightie, caressing her breasts, his thumbs circling their tips. He was leading her to the edge of a precipice, and she followed without question, praying they would go over the edge together, locked in each other's arms. And so they did, falling together, the thrill of their souls touching leaving pure joy in its wake.

She didn't rise right away, but lay against his chest, damp and content, sealing the memory securely with her other treasures: the day he opened the rectory door, the first time they made love, the moment their children were born. The next thing she knew, he was whispering in her ear.

"I've got to go, Cait. 'Twill be dawn soon."

She stood up, the feel of him still deep within her. "How long have we been sitting here?"

He smiled as he rose and brushed the hair off her shoulder. "A few hours, I should think. I sat there listening to yer breath, to the babe's breaths. 'Tis that I'll hold in me heart, whatever me fate may be."

"Don't go, Ciarán. There has to be another way. Inspector Travis is looking for her."

"He won't find her." Whispered voices drifted up the staircase, and he kissed her forehead. "I have to prepare meself."

"What do you mean?"

"I'm to dress in me *léine*."

"But it's at home.

"I'll wear Aodhán's. There's naught much difference in them."

Caitlin's tears had started again, and he pulled her to himself, cupping her head against his chest. "Hush, *a chuisle*. No matter what, I'll always be with ye. Remember that. I want ye to stay here with Fionn and Aisling. I don't want ye to remember me . . ." He took a deep breath, shaking his head. "Let the last memory ye have o' me be o' last night."

He kissed her once more before walking out into the hall to meet Aodhán. Caitlin sank back down in the rocking chair, an emptiness seeping into her heart. No, she wasn't about to stay home while he went off to face his death. She wouldn't let him die alone. She couldn't.

CHAPTER 29

Brought reinforcements with you, I see," Ruadhán said, still refusing to speak English, even though Ciarán knew he'd learned it well. "I expected Aodhán and perhaps poor Duffy there, but not a pair of archaeologists and a priest as well. To give you a last blessing, I suppose."

Ciarán held his tongue. Ruadhán was just baiting him, taking pleasure in what he likely viewed as his victory. "Let's get on with it, shall we? I'd hate you to waste the day."

"Waste the day!" Ruadhán barked a laugh. "The day is already midway through, or have you forgotten that as well?"

"I have not forgotten, but that was another time. In this world, the dawn heralds the new day, not the setting sun."

"You would do well to remember what Domnall taught you. Your fate will soon be in your goddess's hands." He bent down and opened a suitcase, a smile slithering across his face. "Surprised to see our sacred items?"

Indeed Ciarán was, though he wasn't about to admit that to the chief priest. He must have brought them into the cave with him when he prepared himself for the long sleep. "Nothing you do surprises me. Tell me, though, why did you allow the candles to burn down? The goddess must not have been pleased with such wastefulness."

The Celt's smile fell away, and he stood, anger clear in his eyes. "So you located my tomb, after all. I intended to snuff them out before the tonic took its hold, but it worked faster than I had expected. The goddess of our *túath* understood that and forgave."

"I would expect no less, especially for such a loyal follower." A wave of fear surged through him. No, she was not his goddess. He cast a quick look in Father Michael's direction and said a prayer. *St. Michael the Archangel, defend me in battle.*

"You will not experience such kindness, I fear," Ruadhán said, the sneer returning to his face. "If you had done as you were asked and reported the preacher's words, we could have stemmed his influence before it could spread. The goddess will not forget how you have forsaken her."

"I would love to take credit for the rise of Christianity, but I held no such influence. There were already enclaves springing up down in Mumhan and over in Ulaidh, even near Tara itself. Our priesthood was destined to die out. Not even you could prevent that."

"You are indeed your father's son. He spoke similar words as he betrayed the goddess, pleading with me to *see the light*. Yet I am still here, but he is gone."

"True, but so am I. How do you explain that?"

"Your god stole you from the goddess, but she will take you back now. Out of kindness, she welcomed this new god, and he turned against her, taking what was not his to take. She will not be caught unawares again."

"I may die at her hand, but it will not be her who wins my soul."

Ruadhán rose, a thermos in one hand, a silver cup in the other. "We shall see." He poured a thick syrupy liquid into the goblet, stirring it with a *sabhaircín* bloom.

Ciarán's bowels clenched. He knew what lay ahead, knew once he drank he would be able to do nothing to stop the flow of its poison through his body. "Where is Fionnula?"

"She is here, safe and unharmed. First, however, you must drink."

Ciarán shook his head. "Do you think me a fool? I'll see my granddaughter safe and sound, or I'll force the liquid down your throat."

"And do you think I am so naive as to hand her to you and believe that you will drink? Many years ago, you proved you cannot be trusted."

"I will not waiver on this. I will see her safe, or I'll not drink an ounce."

"And I will seal this cave and leave my seed deep within her womb. It makes no difference to me. Either way, it will please the goddess."

"You know her, know her family, and yet you'd do such a thing, you disgusting old pervert."

"You think it is for pleasure that I would do this? I only wish to rebuild the priesthood. Three children are owed to the goddess, three children your brother took from her. What would you do to regain your children?"

"Fionnuala was not taken from her."

"No, but as the others are not here, we must improvise. Of course, if you drink of the cup, offering yourself in recompense, she may relent."

"You gave your word they would be safe if I drank your potion. It is you who are now playing word games. Do I need secure the goddess's pledge as well?"

Ruadhán let out a bitter laugh. "Very good, *a leanbh*. You have grown in wisdom. But no, the goddess will be satisfied with you."

"Then prove it. Let us at least see Fionnuala is safe."

"Alas, your word is not as trustworthy as the lady's, but I will compromise. You may see her, but not until I have the Book of Carraig. I will release her then; however, if you refuse to drink, I will cut her down where she stands."

"And if I drink, you and your goddess will leave everyone alone."

"Everyone?" Ruadhán lifted an eyebrow.

"Yes, everyone. She will have me. You said that would satisfy her, so there is no need for you to harm anyone else."

Ruadhán frowned, deep in thought. At last, he nodded. "I will force no one, but should they choose to join me, they shall be free to do so."

"Under your influence? No, if it is their will, their own free will, they may, but you may not manipulate their minds."

"Domnall did indeed teach you well, but I will agree to that. I will see you returned to your mother's bosom. That will be enough. Now where is the Book of Carraig?"

Ciarán turned to his brother, giving the slightest nod. If their plan failed, if something went wrong, he would never see his wife or children again, any of them. Aodhán stepped forward, laying the book on the ground, and a wave of hesitation surged through Ciarán. He clutched his fists, flashes of his first entombment playing through his mind.

Ruadhán went to pick up the tome, but Ciarán grasped his arm, shaking his head. "The book stays at Aodhán's feet until I see Fionnuala safe and sound."

Ruadhán growled and handed him the cup. "And you will drink before you do. Your brother retains the book should I not do as we've agreed."

Ciarán nodded and took the cup, taking a long drink. The elixir was thick and gagged him, the small amount already clouding his mind and slurring his speech. His arms and legs became numb, and his heart slowed so that he could feel but a flutter in his chest. The cold pierced through his bones; his breath frosted in his throat. And there were the hallucinations that slipped into his fog-addled brain. It was death, and yet he lived. He swallowed hard, praying he'd have the courage to face it again.

****

Ruadhán let a sigh of relief pass his lips and bent down to touch the cover of the sacred book. Though Ciarán's unworthy hands had touched it, it showed no sign of disrespect, save that of the years it had lain untended in the cave. He should have gone for it, taken it with him. Another area he had failed the goddess.

I was so concerned, my lady. So intent on preserving the priesthood. If I had lingered any longer, Domnall would surely have prevented me from doing what I knew I must.

Still, the book was safe in his care now. The goddess would surely forgive him. He reached over to open it, to see its sacred words once more, but Ciarán stepped forward and grabbed his arm, his strength still formidable in spite of the elixir's effects.

"I believe we had an arrangement. You have seen the book. Now where is my granddaughter?"

Pulling his arm from Ciarán's grip, Ruadhán stood, scowling at his wayward priest. "Do you doubt my word?"

His speech was slurred, but he still spoke clear enough for him to understand, albeit growing more labored by the moment. "I doubt the nuances of it. You have a way of embedding loopholes into your vows."

"And you do not, *a leanbh*?"

The fallen priest had the audacity to shrug off his accusation. Ruadhán gazed down at the book, but he was sure it was the Book of Carraig. The cover had secret codes inscribed in the bronze and gold inlay, inscriptions Ciarán would know nothing of.

"Very well, then. You shall have your Fionnuala, but I shall not wake her until you finish the elixir."

Ciarán nodded. "I'll finish your poisonous potion. Where will you lay my body?"

"Why do you care? Do you think your friends will wake you as they did before? I assure you, priest, no one will rouse you from this sleep. The goddess will be alert to their machinations."

"My wife will want to visit from time to time, lay flowers and pray for my soul."

Ruadhán shrugged. "What does it matter? Once I secure the tomb, they will never break its seal. You will be laid here in the Cave of Rúin Ársa. Did you not see the long narrow hollows in the stone walls, two to each side of the book?"

"No, what were they?"

"It was first thought that Carraig and the original council of elders would be laid to rest there, but when the first elder died, Carraig decided it would be unseemly, burying their bodies with the sacred book. After all, they were mere men."

"And yet you'll bury me there? The elders would not be pleased."

"The Book of Carraig will no longer be there, so there will be no irreverence involved. In truth, I believe the goddess will be pleased at the turn of events." *More pleased than you know, my traitorous priest.* He walked into the cave to find Fionnuala sleeping peacefully in the alcove where he had placed her earlier.

"Come now, my dear. Your family wants you back." He bent down and lifted her in his arms. For a man in his seventieth year, he was still quite fit, even after his fifteen-hundred-year sleep. Pausing for a moment, he stopped to thank his goddess and tell her what was to come.

"I swear to you, my lady, Ciarán shall be with you again before the dawning of the new day. The potion I have mixed is potent. No one but you shall be able to wake him. Not even his god."

Sighing, he gazed down at Fionnuala. "It would have been wonderful to learn what it felt like to lay with you, my dear, but I cannot let such carnal curiosity distract me." He walked outside, resting Fionnuala on the grass by the cave's entrance.

Duffy ran forward, kneeling by his wife's side, but Ruadhán held up his hand and knocked him away with a bolt of energy. "Leave her. First, Ciarán must finish the elixir." He stood and turned to his rebellious priest. "Remember, priest, should you fail to drain the cup, I can put her back into a deep sleep as easily as I wake her. Now drink, and I shall revive her."

****

Ciarán lifted the cup to his lips, swallowing a wave of nausea. For a moment, it was as if he and Ruadhán were the only ones there, cut off from the rest of the world. "Do you hate me this much, master?"

"I have never hated you, *a leanbh*, but you must return to the goddess what is hers. I am a chief priest of the *túath*, sworn to keep the law. You could have taken my place one day, but you let emotions cloud your judgment. It is regrettable but right that you should end this way."

Ciarán stared down into the crimson syrup and wiped the back of his hand across his lips. Before he could take another drink, a voice echoed up the hillside.

"Ciarán, no, stop!" Caitlin came charging up the hill, her cheeks wet with tears. She ran to his side, nearly knocking the cup from his hand, but Ruadhán grabbed it in time.

"What are ye doing, Cait? Ye know I have to do this."

"No, I don't." She glanced at Fionnuala, lying on the grass and gasped. "Is she . . . ?"

"Not yet, but I've no doubt she will be if I don't drink o' this cup." He brushed back her hair and leaned over to kiss her dampened lips, imprinting the feel of them in his mind. After a moment, he pulled back, trying to smile as he spoke. "I thought I told ye to stay with the wee ones."

"And since when do I do what you tell me?" Her lips quivered into a shaky smile. "What am I going to do without you?"

"Hush, *a chuisle*. Ye'll see me every time ye look at Fionn. Sure, he's me spitting image, as Denis would say."

"They'll never even get to know you."

"Then ye'll tell them about me and likely make me sound grander than I ever was." He wiped away the tears that streamed down her cheeks before nodding for Aodhán to take her. She went without protesting, which wasn't like her at all. The fire in her eyes was doused, telling him she knew she was powerless to stop what was about to happen. His heart ached. How he wanted to tell her of their plan, but what if it didn't work? Would that not be even crueler? Besides, if Ruadhán caught a whisper of it, there would be no chance.

Instead, he turned to Father Michael. "Will ye say a blessing over me, Father?"

"Of course, my son. Kneel down, then. Dear heavenly Father, be with this lad as he goes forth with courage and determination . . ."

The words seemed to fade away as he glanced at Caitlin. Aodhán's arm was wrapped around her trembling shoulders, her own hand clasped over her mouth, though it did little to quell the sobs. He wanted to speak to her, to say something to calm her, but the only thing that came to mind were the words Aisling had once said to him.

"Faith, my love. I live in Christ."

"Enough of this sentimentality!" Ruadhán thrust the cup back to Ciarán's lips. "Finish it now, or I shall drag her back into this cave, and trust me, should I seal the entrance, no man will enter again."

Ciarán stared down into the syrupy liquid, then, closing his eyes, lifted the cup to his lips and took another sip. The world spun around him, and he gripped a large boulder beside the cave's entrance. Though his stomach protested, an overwhelming urge to throw up the putrid liquid clenching his guts, he knew it would never happen. The thick syrup coated his insides, clinging to it like barnacles on a sunken ship.

"Wake her," he said. "You swore."

"You have failed to finish the elixir."

"Do you think I would have the strength to stop you from forcing the remainder down my throat? Please, master, let me see her safe before I leave this world."

The words seemed to touch Ruadhán, and he nodded. Bending beside Fionnuala, he waved a small package beneath her nose, and she woke, blinking in the early morning sun.

"What happened? Did I pass out? I was helping Mr. Maguire . . ." She looked around. "What are we doing up here?"

Duffy ran to her side, lifting her and leading her a few steps away. She was safe; Rhuadhán had kept his word. Now Ciarán must keep his and drink the remainder of the liquid. His eyes met the chief priest's, and he nodded before raising the cup to his lips once more and draining it. Though he gagged as it made its way down his throat, not a drop was spilled. The world around him began to blur. Frigid fingers clutched at his arms while long-dead voices whispered in his ears. Still, somehow he managed to stand.

Through the fog in his brain, he saw Ruadhán bend down to retrieve the book. If he opened it . . . Before he could finish the thought, Ruadhán rose, his eyes flashing with rage.

"You treacherous creature! Where are the pages that belong in the book?"

Ciarán chuckled. "You'll never find them."

The high priest turned and grabbed Aodhán by the arm. "We'll see about that. This one never was as strong as you."

"He's stronger than you ever imagined, but it won't matter. Only I know where they are. And my mind is so clouded now you won't be able to make any sense of what you find there."

Ruadhán balled his hands together, a flush of crimson rising in his cheeks, his eyes glowing with fury. A bolt of lightning lit the sky, followed by a peal of thunder. As the ground shook, Ciarán slipped down along the boulder, his legs no longer able to hold him aloft, but a claw-like grip raised him up and dragged him into the cave.

He felt the blade against his neck before the sight of it registered in his head. They hadn't counted on Ruadhán resorting to physical force.

"Tell me where the pages are, or I will end your life here and now."

"You can't physically harm a chosen child of the goddess. See, I remember some things Domnall taught me. Or was it you that told me that?" His mind was getting duller by the moment, and yet he felt the need to taunt the pompous priest.

"Ah, but you are no longer a chosen child."

Crap. He hadn't thought of that. They were moving deeper into the cave, beyond the altar, toward the ledge Aodhán had almost fallen off. Did he mean to throw his body over after he slit his throat? Either action would be enough to end his life by itself. No need to be so dramatic. He shook his head, trying to clear away the cobwebs. What was wrong with him? He was about to die, and he was making stupid quips.

"Since your memory is so sharp, you must also remember this cave holds the entrance to Tír na nÓg. What faster way to send you to your goddess mother and rid the earth of your treachery?"

Ciarán closed his eyes, expecting to feel the sharp blade of the knife cut into his throat, but instead a blow knocked him to the side. He was falling, but Ruadhán had released him. With every last ounce of strength, he reached up to grab the edge of the ledge, his fingers barely holding on. A blur of white and silver plummeted past him, followed by the clatter of metal against stone. His fingers were growing weaker, slipping from the ledge as the numbness spread out through his limbs, his muscles growing weaker by the second.

He looked down into the darkness, certain he was about to die. His brain so muddled he could barely think, he whispered a quick prayer. "Dear God, forgive me my transgressions and deliver me to heaven."

CHAPTER 30

Caitlin stood staring at her hands, unsure what had just happened, unable to move. She heard voices buzzing around her. Fionnuala stood staring at her own hands, disbelief etched on her face.

"What have I done?" Caitlin heard her say, but nothing was registering in Caitlin's mind just yet. It was as if she were in some sort of bubble, the world around her distant and apart.

Father Mike was talking to her, but what was he saying? She couldn't hear him. Aodhán and Steve were rushing toward the back of the cave, toward the dark abyss where Ciarán had just fallen.

It all came back at once: the sounds, the sights, and the memory of what she'd just done, but no, not her alone. She looked toward Fionnuala again, their eyes meeting in a horrific realization. They'd done it together, reached out toward Ruadhán, sending some sort of invisible blast of energy in his direction, so powerful it sent him over the edge into the darkness. But he had taken Ciarán with him.

"No! Ciarán!" She darted forward, but her uncle pulled her back, speaking to her in the soft yet stern voice he used to calm someone down. It was the voice he used when speaking to those who had recently lost a loved one. No, not Ciarán.

"Let Aodhán and Steve try to reach him," Uncle Mike said.

Try to reach him. The words reverberated in her head, though she couldn't seem to form a response. She was numb and drained, emotionally and physically. Fionnuala came over to her, tears flooding her cheeks. "What happened? I was reaching out for Ciarán, confused about why Mr. McGuire was holding a knife to his throat. I wanted to stop him, is all."

"It wasn't Mr. McGuire," Caitlin said, her own hands still trembling. "It was Ruadhán."

"So Ciarán was right about him all along, and now I've gone and . . ." She looked to Caitlin, confusion filling her dazzling blue eyes. "I couldn't stop it. I wanted to push the old man away from Ciarán, make him drop the knife, and the next thing I knew . . ."

"Some kind of force, not electric, more like a powerful blast of air . . ."

Fionnuala nodded. "Ye felt it too. Coming right from me fingertips as if I'd drawn the energy from the world around me and concentrated it on that old man. But Ciarán . . ."

She started to cry again, and Duffy wrapped his arm around her. "Hush, lass. It looks like Aodhán may have ahold o' him."

Caitlin's heart raced. What was it Ciarán had said to her? The memory was faded, for it was only said in passing. Something about her not being strong enough . . . yet. Strong enough for what? She gazed down at her hands again. If she had been the cause of Ciarán's death, she would never forgive herself. What had she done? And Fionnuala . . . Of, course! She was Ciarán's descendant, but if it passed down through the generations, then why her?

I know ye've said ye're a bit psychic . . . She heard Ciarán's voice, and pain engulfed her heart. None of it mattered if he wasn't there with her, with Fionn and Aisling. She sent up a silent prayer to her guardian angel. *Angel of God, please help him.*

****

Ciarán's fingers slipped a bit more—at least he thought they did. He could feel nothing at this point, for his limbs were numb and weak. Ruadhán had given him a potent dose indeed. Certain the blood was freezing in his veins, he let his eyelids closed. Maybe sleep would bring warmth and peace. Fighting it was only delaying the inevitable.

"Do not succumb, a Athair." A sweet, lilting voice spoke in his ear, and he forced his eyes open.

"Aisling?" Could this be his beautiful daughter, already grown?

The sweetest smile he ever saw lit her face. "Do not be daft, my sister is still a wee babe. You must find the strength to fight. She and my brother will need you to show them the way."

"Áine? Forgive me for abandoning you. I did not think."

"You did not abandon us, a Athair. Our uncle carried us to safety."

"I should have seen you safely away myself, long before I wed Aisling, but I allowed my desires to control my actions, without a thought for you and your brothers."

"You acted impulsively, 'tis true, but not with malice or lack of love for us. Did you not recall us as you lay with your new bride and make plans to come for us?"

"How could you know of that? Are you of the *aos sidhe* or simply a ghost that fills my addled mind?"

Áine shook her head, her deep blue eyes sparkling. "You still cling to bits of the old beliefs, do you not? Trust in yer Lord and God, a Athair."

Two strong hands slipped beneath his arms, and he swore he saw the tip of a wing. Had angels truly come for him? But was it to save him from death or carry him to heaven? Or was it all just a figment of his unbridled imagination?

"They cannot save you from death alone, a Athair. You must help them. My uncle is reaching for you, but you must raise your other arm and allow him to get a better grip, or he will not be able to hold you."

Ciarán's eyes had closed again, his chin resting on his chest. With great effort, he forced himself to look up, prying his lids open. A blurry visage swam above him, grasping his left wrist. Was it indeed Aodhán?

"You must raise your other arm, a Athair. Do it now. You never abandoned us, but if you do not do this, you *will* be abandoning wee Aisling and Fionn. Fight to be there for them."

Somewhere deep in his core, a strength flared up, and he forced his arm above him, even as the sweat froze on his face. His fingers trembled, pain shooting through the limbs that had moments ago been numb, but he forced it up, praying for salvation, whether in this world or the next, until he drifted into unconsciousness.

****

"Grab his other arm," Aodhán said, and Steve rushed forward, reaching over the edge of the cliff.

"Where's Ruadhán?" Steve asked.

Aodhán shook his head and gazed down into the murky void that lay below them. "Tír na nÓg by now, I expect. This is an entrance to the otherworld, or so we were told. I doubt he survived the fall." Steve grimaced, and they lifted Ciarán up onto solid ground.

Good Lord, he was heavy. *Dead weight,* an unbidden voice echoed in Aodhán's head, and he pushed the thought away. He looked over to Steve, but the man was intent on trying to feel for Ciarán's pulse. What if they'd waited too long?

Caitlin rushed over, sinking to the ground and resting Ciarán's head on her lap. His eyes flickered for a brief moment, and she called his name, but he drifted off again.

"Why is he so cold?" Though she may have been succeeding in holding back tears, she couldn't keep her voice from cracking.

As cold as death, the voice whispered once more from the depths of Aodhán's mind. No, it was the elixir, nothing more. He looked to Steve again.

"There, I felt a beat, just one, and it was faint, but . . ." He grabbed the needle he'd helped Aodhán prepare and searched for a vein.

"Ruadhán's elixir would slow the heartbeat. I remember thinking that me heart had stopped completely, yet somehow I lived."

Steve gave a nod before wrapping the blood pressure sleeve around Ciarán's arm. Aodhán didn't like the creases that formed in his forehead. He could see in Caitlin's eyes that she didn't either.

"What's wrong?" she asked. "What did you give him? It's not working, is it?"

"We have to give it a few moments," Steve said, though the look he threw in Aodhán's direction did not bode well. He stood and walked to the side of the cave, motioning for Aodhán to follow. "I can't even pick up a steady pulse. There are ten seconds or more between each beat. Are you sure about this antidote? I've never seen anyone survive with a pressure that low before."

"No, I'm not. Ciarán thought it was the one, but . . . Isn't there anything else you can do?"

"How? I don't even know what I'm dealing with here. Don't you have any idea what was in it?"

"Mistletoe, I'm sure, but more than that, I can't say."

"Well, that could explain the slowing of the heartbeat and drowsiness, but I'm surprised it didn't upset his stomach."

"Oh, it does, feels like something's clawing at your insides. Yet ye can't purge yerself o' it."

"Something keeps you from vomiting?"

"I suppose. Ruadhán wouldn't want the elixir coming back up, now would he?"

"I felt a beat," Caitlin said, her eyes pleading for Steve to confirm it.

Steve nodded and flashed a tentative smile. "It'll take a few minutes, but that's a good sign."

Aodhán looked to Steve, hopeful, but the doctor shook his head. "If that's the first since I took his pulse, they're getting even farther apart. His temperature is near freezing, hypothermia is sure to set in, and there's nothing I can do. It doesn't seem to be working."

"Maybe it has to be administered right away."

"I've no idea." Pain filled the man's eyes as he gazed down on Ciarán's pale face, his lips turning a bluish color. "There's no sense in prolonging it."

They walked back over and Steve picked up his stethoscope. His expression didn't appear promising. "Father, perhaps you'd better . . ."

"No," Caitlin said, the tears escaping their tremulous barriers once more. "He's going to be fine. He survived fifteen hundred years after drinking it. He just needs a bit of time to wake up."

"It won't hurt for me to say a prayer or two, darlin'," Father Mike said. "Just to be on the safe side."

Caitlin nodded, though Aodhán noticed she kept her hand over Ciarán's neck while the priest prepared himself to administer the last rites. Could she be right? If they'd only studied the book more before sending it off to Dublin instead of relying on a few scribbled inscriptions, they might have been sure of the remedy, and Ciarán wouldn't be lying here on the brink of death. They'd both just wanted to keep it safe, out of the wrong hands. But more than that, they'd wanted to put the past behind them. And now Ciarán was paying the price for their negligence.

"Per istam sanctam unctionem," Father Michael began, but the words had no sooner passed his lips than Caitlin gasped.

"There, I felt it again."

"Cait . . ." Steve rested his hand over hers. "He's gone."

"No, he's not. Just take his blood pressure."

Steve pumped the small bulb again, pressing his stethoscope against Ciarán's arm, but this time he looked up, a seed of hope flashing in his eyes. He sat for what seemed forever, pressing the stethoscope against Ciarán's neck, though it probably wasn't more than a minute. No one spoke, no one even dared move. "There, I've got a pulse. It's weak and erratic, but it's definitely there."

Father Michael knelt on the other side of Ciarán, whispering a silent prayer while Steve took his blood pressure once more, then listened to his heart and took his temperature. To Aodhán's relief, the lines etched in Steve's forehead eased a bit. "His blood pressure is rising, and his body seems to be warming."

"Glory to God," Father Michael said.

The screech of an ambulance siren could be heard in the distance. "Aodhán, could you bring me a blanket? There's one just outside the cave's entrance."

Caitlin was gazing out the opening, her eyes a deep moss green. "Is that ambulance for Ciarán?"

Aodhán handed the woolen covering to Steve and sat down beside her, squeezing her hand. "We told Ryan to call for it if we weren't back within the hour. It's just a precaution."

Caitlin brushed the hair off Ciarán's pale forehead, her fingers shaking as she looked to Steve. "But why does he need to go to a hospital? You said everything was getting better."

The concern in Steve's eyes was palpable. "It is, but that doesn't mean he's going to wake up right away. I'd rather have him somewhere we can keep an eye on him . . ."

"I'd watch."

"I know you would, Cait, but we can put him on an IV there, make sure he's getting liquids while he's asleep. It may take a while before everything's back to normal. And if his pressure should start to drop or he has a seizure or anything . . ."

Caitlin's eyes widened. From Steve's expression, he realized too late what he'd just said.

"Don't get upset. I'm not expecting him to, but Aodhán said the potion Ruadhán gave him had mistletoe in it, so it could happen. Chances are it would have already done so by now if it was going to, but . . ."

"Listen to the doctor." Father Mike rested his hand on Caitlin's shoulder and used his thumb to wipe a tear from her chin. "'Twill be better for him to get some rest, and sure, he wouldn't be getting any o' that at Mrs. Byrne's, now would he?"

Ryan came in with two men from the ambulance, and Steve wrapped the blanket tight around Ciarán's limp form. Aodhán breathed a tentative sigh of relief. Though he knew Ciarán wasn't out of danger yet, at least things were looking better. He walked down the hill with Steve, watching as the attendants carried Ciarán to the ambulance.

"There's more to it than that, isn't there?" he asked.

Steve rubbed a palm across his stubble. None of them had taken the time to shave that morning. "I don't know. I'll need to run some tests, make sure everything's all right. But the truth is I believe he's in a coma. He could sit up five minutes from now, none the worse for wear, or he could sleep like he's under some enchanted spell for years. I just don't know."

"Maybe all he needs is true love's kiss."

Steve looked back toward the ambulance at Caitlin sitting over Ciarán's prone form. "I'm sure she'll try it at some point, but I'm hoping his body gets the message on its own, just in case it doesn't work." The stethoscope still hung around his neck, and he took it off, folding it in his hands.

"Ye've done all ye can," Aodhán said. "'Tis in God's hands now."

"The last time he drank that stuff he slept for fifteen hundred years."

"But we were wrapped in the shrouds then and left in ice-cold tombs. Sure, he'll not sleep that long this time. Not when he's warm and breathing fresh air. Besides, he's had an antidote, hasn't he?"

"Yes, one you're not really convinced will work."

"I have to believe it will, for I don't think I can bear to lose me brother a second time, not this soon after finding him."

"What's so special about those shrouds anyway? Ciarán's managed to do away with them all, much to Daniel's annoyance. He's led us to believe he's destroyed them, though knowing him, I can't believe he hasn't got one of stowed away somewhere."

Aodhán couldn't help but smile. Indeed he had, but he wasn't about to let Steve know that, even if he didn't agree with Ciarán's sentiments about the possible use of the shroud. He didn't understand how it worked anyway.

"I can't say, but sure, there must be something about them. After all, none o' us woke until they were removed." He thought for a moment and looked back up toward the cave. "Except for Ruadhán, that is."

"Do you think he managed to survive that fall?" Steve asked, following the direction of Aodhán's gaze.

"No, I think he's gone to the otherworld. Even Ruadhán's powers couldn't manage to save him from that drop. I could hear the Scian na Lúin bouncing off the walls as it fell. If Ruadhán followed the same path . . ." He shrugged. "We never suspected he had it. If he'd so much as given Ciarán a wee cut with it . . . 'twould be nothing we could have done to save him."

"Why is that?" Steve ran his hand through his hair and stared down the road.

"D'ye not know the legend?"

"Of the knife, you mean? No, I've never heard of it."

"Ye've heard of Fionn mac Cumhaill, have ye not?"

"Yes, of course, but I don't recall him having such a weapon. Then again, Irish mythology is not my forte. I'm more interested in the flesh-and-blood aspects of history."

"It makes sense, doesn't it? Ye being a doctor, and all." They'd reached the bottom of the hill, and Aodhán sat on the low stone wall at its base. "Fionn had a weapon known as Mac an Lúin. A mere cut from it would inevitably prove fatal. The goddess o' our *túath* aided him in one o' his endeavors, and as payment she asked for a wee bit o' his sword."

"The Scian an Lúin?"

"I've seen a man die after he did naught but prick his finger on it. We should have thought this out better. Should have realized he'd be taking it all to the tomb with him."

"Why not take the Book of Carraig, then?"

"I suppose because 'twas never to be removed from the Cave o' Rúin Arsa. 'Tis watched over by the goddess herself, ye see, and an entrance to Tír na nÓg."

A siren wailed, signaling they were ready to go, and Aodhán watched Steve climb in next to Caitlin. He'd feel better once Ciarán was in the hospital and on the mend. He only prayed the antidote didn't take fifteen hundred years to work.

CHAPTER 31

Caitlin sat by Ciarán's side, holding his hand and making idle conversation. Whether Ciarán heard her or not, she couldn't be sure, but she told herself he could. All she knew for certain was that she wanted to talk about their future together. Saying it out loud somehow made her believe it would all work out, that Ciarán would wake and be none the worse for wear.

"I don't want to do it until the twins are a bit older, but I think we should put a pool in, don't you? We can build a nice patio around it, with a table and chairs, and you can teach them to swim. Of course, we'll still go to the beach. They should experience that as well.

"They'll be getting big enough to put in their own rooms soon. I think we should keep the nursery for a while, though. We're sure to have another child or two. I wonder if they'll be twins as well. Steve might know what the percentage of us having more than one set of twins is. You'll have to remind me to ask him.

"I think we should definitely paint Fionn's room blue, but I'm not crazy about pink for Aisling. What about green or yellow or maybe even lavender?"

"Discussing colors for the twin's rooms?" Steve picked up the chart on the end of Ciarán's bed and checked it before pulling the blood pressure sleeve out of his pocket and checking it himself. "I thought you already painted them?"

"We did, but I can change my mind, can't I? Besides, I'm not sure Ciarán cared for the mint green." Caitlin bit her lip while he took her husband's pressure. "Well?"

"Well, what?" He grinned. "It's normal, one fifteen over seventy." He stuck a thermometer between Ciarán's lips and lifted his wrist.

"Have they put you on staff here now?"

"Not quite, but I've gotten to know the head of staff pretty well, and he gives me a wide birth." He looked at the thermometer before shaking it. "Before you ask, it's normal."

"Then why isn't he waking up? Don't lie to me, Steve." She could feel the tears welling in her eyes, reacting to her unspoken thoughts, and she blinked them away.

Steve sighed. Walking around the bed, he sat down next to her and put his arm around her shoulders. "I don't want the word to scare you, but he's in a coma."

"A coma? But I thought you gave him an antidote? I don't understand."

"I told you not to let the word scare you. In Ciarán's case, it might simply be an extremely deep sleep. The antidote needs time to counteract the poison, but it is working. His blood pressure, pulse rate, and temperature are all normal. Dr. O'Brien wants to do an EEG just to be on the safe side, but I don't think he'll find anything."

"Hopefully, I'll find a brain." The doctor walked in the room and smiled. "Visits to hospital are becoming a habit with yer husband. Next time tell him if he'd like to see me, he can just walk in the front door, and we'll have lunch."

Caitlin returned his smile. He was a pleasant man with wheat-colored hair and blue-gray eyes, and she felt secure knowing he and Steve would be taking care of Ciarán.

Two orderlies came in and started wheeling the bed out of the room. Alarm must have shown in her expression, for the doctor's smile dropped away, replaced by a more somber expression. "Has Steve not explained that this is just a precaution?"

If she spoke, the words would turn into sobs, so she simply nodded. Dr. O'Brien glanced at Steve before pulling up a chair and sitting down.

"Steve's told me quite a story about yer husband there. It explains a lot, hard to believe as it is."

"He did?" She cast a look in Steve's direction.

"Yes, about Cormac McGuire stealing some pages from that ancient book we discovered last year, and how he'd planned to test one of its potions on Fionnuala—until Ciarán stepped up to the plate, that is."

"Oh yes, we still don't know how he managed to gain access to the book."

Dr. O'Brien shook his head. "And he truly thought he was some sort o' ancient priest, tasked with carrying out a sacrificial ceremony?"

"I'm afraid so," Steve said. "He'd even stolen someone else's identification so that he could hide his *true identity*."

"Ye don't know who he really was, then?" the doctor said.

"No, I'm afraid not, but DI Travis is looking into it."

"Well, 'tis a good thing ye'd been studying that book o' yers and knew what to give yer friend there, else I'm afraid we'd be holding a funeral for him now." The doctor started to walk away, then stopped for a moment. "How did ye know anyway?"

"Ciarán and I had just read about the ceremony," Caitlin said, "and I recognized it. The antidote was listed alongside it."

"It was easy enough to make, so I was able to get it up to Ciarán in time."

"Well, 'tis sure the angels were with ye. It'll take a while for it to work, but it seems to be doing its job. Ciarán's body has been through a lot, though. More than likely he needs a good night's sleep and nothing more. Come the morn, I feel sure he'll be right as rain."

Caitlin couldn't hold the tears back anymore. She rested her head against Dr. O'Brien's shoulder and let the tears flow. To their credit, neither he nor Steve mocked her for her foolishness, but allowed her to release all the anxiety and stress of the last twenty-four hours.

"What's happened?" Father Mike walked in the room, cheerful as usual, but a cloud dropped over his expression when he spotted Caitlin in tears. "Where's Ciarán? Why wasn't I called for?"

"It's all right, Michael," Steve said. "He's just gone for an EEG, as a precaution, nothing more. His vital signs are all normal, but since he isn't awake yet, we want to make sure it's nothing serious."

"Ah well, as long as that's all it is. Saints preserve us. 'Twas a good thing I persuaded Mary to stay with the wee ones, then. She would have had a right scare if she'd been with me." Steve stood and Michael sat in his chair, handing Caitlin a handkerchief. "Now blow yer nose and we'll say a prayer together."

Caitlin did as he instructed. Her uncle could always brighten her spirits, no matter how low they got. "How did you ever convince Mary not to come?"

"Ye're thinking she'd be leaving Mrs. B to have all the fun with the wee ones. 'Tis a good thing ye had twins, that's all I'll say, lest they'd be fighting over who got to spend more time with the poor thing. Now bow yer heads, the lot o' ye. After the day we've had, we could all spend a bit o' time with the Lord."

****

Aodhán stopped by later that evening, looking as though he could use a bit of a sleep himself. "You look almost as bad as Ciarán," Caitlin said.

He shrugged his shoulder and sat down next to her. "We are twins."

Caitlin let a smile touch her lips for the first time since the night before. "That does sound like something Ciarán would say. When was the last time you slept?"

"Probably about the same time you did." He grinned, reaching over to squeeze her hand. "But I am going to lay back in this chair and take a good long nap now, and ye're going to let Steve take ye home and get some rest. Sure, the babes are fussing, aren't they? Fionn takes the bottle well enough, but getting Aisling to is a right battle. They want their *mamaí*. So go kiss the wee things for him and tell them their *dadaí* loves them. I'll call ye if there's any change."

"You're right, and I do miss them, but I'm afraid if I leave him . . ."

"He's not going to die while ye're gone, *a deirfiúr*. He wouldn't dare risk yer wrath. I know 'tis hard to believe, but he hears ye, even in his sleep."

371

"Then all the more reason I need to stay."

"No, all the more ye need to go and take care o' yerself and those wee ones. He nearly died to make sure ye were all safe. What d'ye think he'd be saying if he knew ye were running yerself down so?"

Caitlin couldn't stifle another tiny smile. She knew exactly what Ciarán would have to say and stood, albeit reluctantly. "Well, he'd better wake up and say it, then."

"He will, after he's slept a good bit. 'Tis just like him, finding a way to get out o' work. Ye should see the list Niamh and Fionnuala have."

Caitlin let out an aborted gasp. With all that was happening, she'd forgotten Niamh and Aodhán were to be married in a little over a week's time. "The wedding! Oh, Aodhán, you need to go help Niamh. I'll be fine here."

"Thank ye for the offer, but if ye don't mind, I'd rather not. It's been a long day, what with the business up at the cave and all, and I need the rest. Besides, 'twill do Fionnuala good to be keeping busy."

She started for the door but stopped a moment, not quite sure now was the time to ask. The events of that morning had been lost in all the commotion, but now that it had quieted down some, she needed to know what exactly had happened. Whatever it was that had knocked Ruadhán into that abyss, she and Fionnuala had been behind it, and the result had almost cost Ciarán his life.

Aodhán peeked up at her through his thick lashes before sitting forward and resting his forearms on his knees. "Go on, then, say what's on yer mind. How's a man to get any sleep with all that shouting going on?"

"I didn't say a word."

"No, but yer thoughts are causing the mother o' all rackets."

"Are you reading my mind?"

A dimple appeared in his right cheek, the spark in his blue eyes brightening with humor. "There's no need, *a chara*. I can see it in yer face."

"All right, then. How is Fionnuala?"

Aodhán seemed to understand her twofold question, for he scrubbed his hand across his face and blew out a long, weary breath. "She's fine. Both Dr. O'Brien and Steve checked her out. Seems it was naught more than a strong sleeping draught that Ruadhán gave her."

"But she woke so quickly?"

"Steve's thinking 'twas some sort o' strong odor that pierced through the fog o' sleep."

"Like smelling salts?"

Aodhán frowned. "I think 'twould be a bit more powerful than salt."

She suppressed a snicker, causing Aodhán to smile. He was such a kind soul. "I'm sorry. I didn't mean to laugh. Smelling salts are a lot more pungent than table salt."

"Ah, well then, I suppose so, but that's not all ye're wanting to talk about, is it?"

"Fionnuala's already asked, hasn't she?"

"She might have mentioned it. Though I have to say, I've been wondering about it meself. Not about the possibility o' such a thing happening, mind ye. Ye've seen Ciarán and I use such power against Bradaigh. But . . ."

"But how did Fionnuala and I manage it. All I wanted to do was stop Ruadhán from hurting Ciarán. I reached out and . . . my fingers were tingling, all the way up to my elbows."

He lifted his eyebrows. "That's a lot o' power. And ye've never experienced anything like it before?"

"No . . . Well, not exactly . . . No, never." What could her visions or headaches possibly have to do with anything?

"Which is it, Cait?"

"I have these visions sometimes. They're of things I've never seen before, usually upsetting things. And they give me killer headaches, but Ciarán showed me how to work through them."

"He knows about them, then?"

"Yes, and he said something about me not being strong enough . . . yet. I didn't think anything about it at the time, but now . . . What happened, Aodhán?"

"All right, then, sit yerself down and I'll try to explain it, but with two conditions."

Caitlin lowered herself in the chair and narrowed her eyes. "What conditions would they be?"

"First, as soon as I've finished, ye'll go home and get some sleep."

She let out an annoyed sigh, leaning over to take Ciarán's hand. "Did he tell you to say that?"

"It doesn't work like that, but I'm sure if it did, 'twould be his exact words."

"Fine, then, and what's the second thing?"

"Let me get some rest. I've been awake for as long as Ciarán, but as usual, 'tis himself who's getting the sleep."

Caitlin got up and brushed back her husband's hair, kissing his forehead. "What does that mean?"

Aodhán chuckled. "Sure, I've caught him sleeping with his eyes wide open, haven't I? He says he's not, but I know better. 'Tis probably why he was so adventurous. He'd just sleep through most o' the punishments we received, and no one was the wiser." He shrugged. "Well, almost no one."

Caitlin smiled, though she couldn't keep the worry from her voice. "Well, his eyes aren't open now."

"They will be soon, lass. Now as to what happened this morning. 'Twas just yerself harnessing the energy from the world around ye."

"Is that all?" Caitlin got up and started walking back and forth in front of Ciarán's bed. "Well, I didn't like it. How do I make sure it doesn't happen again?"

Aodhán stood in her path and took her by the shoulders. "'Tis not some curse to be feared, *a chara*. Ye control it."

Tears filled her eyes once more, but she held them at bay. "But I didn't. Don't you see? I could have killed Ciarán. He went over that cliff because of what I did."

"Is that what ye think happened? No, Cait, yer shot hit Ruadhán dead on. If Ciarán had been himself, he would have been able to throw himself clear."

"But he wasn't, and my . . . shot . . . or whatever it was caused him to go over as well."

"If ye and Fionnuala hadn't done it, I would have. Ruadhán wasn't only holding a knife to Ciarán's neck, he was holding the Scian an Lúin."

Caitlin searched her memory, trying to uncover any mention of such an item in the file cabinet that was her brain. Her expression must have given her away because Aodhán laughed.

"Ye don't know what that is, do ye?"

She folded her arms across her chest and scowled at her brother-in-law, though it was all in jest. "No, smarty pants. What is it?"

"Sure, ye've hear o' the Mac an Lúin?"

"Yes, of course, but it's only a myth."

"Is it, though?" Aodhán leaned back in the chair again, lifting an eyebrow.

Catilin grabbed on to the chair as tiny spots danced before her eyes. "Are you telling me one scratch from that knife . . ." She darted to the head of Ciarán's bed, rubbing her fingers over his neck. Could that be why he hadn't awakened yet? This could be worse than she thought. What if Ruadhán had nicked him as he fell?

The room began to darken, and she felt Aodhán grabbing her by the shoulders.

****

"Are you all right?" Aodhán asked. Sitting her down on a chair, he perched on the edge of the bed and gazed deep into her eyes. "I thought ye were going to faint on me."

She swallowed, taking a deep breath before nodding. "I'm okay now, but Ciarán . . ." Tears glistened in her eyes.

"He wasn't cut. Steve and I already checked." Aodhán handed her a glass of water and nodded for her to drink.

She took a sip before handing it back, a shaky smile crossing her lips. "Then it's not just a myth, and this knife or *scian* holds some sort of treacherous magic?"

"I don't know if 'tis magic. More likely just dipped in a deadly poison before use. The point I'm trying to make is that ye may have saved Ciarán's life."

"We don't know that yet." She took hold of Ciarán's hand, squeezing it tight. "I still don't understand, though. I can see why Fionnuala might have such powers, being descended from Ciarán and all, but how did I get them?"

"Sure, I don't know that, now do I? Any more than I know why Paul McCartney can write songs that seem to touch so many or why Mary's scones taste better than Mrs. Byrne's—and don't be telling them I said that. 'Tis a gift, a talent that needs to be nurtured and honed."

"A talent! I knocked a man off a cliff with a flick of my hand. It's not exactly something you can pick up in school."

Aodhán tried not to laugh, but that's exactly how he had learned to manage his gifts. "Ye're looking at this all wrong, lass. 'Tis a gift from above, just like any other. How ye use it will determine its value."

"But I don't know how to control it. I don't even understand it."

"Perhaps that's why the good Lord sent ye Ciarán."

She rested back in the chair, tiny creases appearing between her eyebrows. "Does that mean Ciarán's my ancestor too?"

This time Aodhán couldn't hold the laugh in. "I can't be telling ye that either, not with any certainty. We are talking about fifteen centuries, but there is one thing I do know for sure. Being Ciarán's descendant is not a prerequisite for having such talents. In our time, there were many who possessed the gifts. All who came to our priesthood held talents much like our own, some to a greater extent than others."

"Will the twins . . . ?"

"Must ye keep asking me questions I've no answers for?" He smiled and rested his hand over hers. "I can't tell ye that either, *a chara*, any more than ye can tell me if they'll be interested in archaeology."

"Oh, they will be," she said, a full-blown smile finally touching her lips.

"Well, either way, ye and Ciarán will be there to guide them together. Now off home with ye, and try to get some rest. He'll wake soon enough. The lazy lout's most likely just using it as an excuse to take a few days off."

He led Caitlin to the door, and she turned and kissed him on the cheek. "Thank you for always being there to watch his back."

"He's had mine on more than one occasion as well."

Caitlin laughed, and the sound warmed Aodhán's heart. Perhaps something he said had eased her mind, if only a bit.

"I'd love to hear those stories sometime." She stifled a yawn. "But not just now. You will call . . ."

"I will. Now off with ye, or Mary will be taking me to task for not seeing ye get some sleep. And there's a force o' nature neither o' us wants to contend with, not even Ciarán."

She nodded and headed down the hallway to where Steve was waiting. He watched her for a moment, the quiet hallway calming his spirit, before returning to Ciarán's bedside and taking a seat. "I know yer games, brother. Ye're just using this as an excuse to get out o' explaining it all to Cait and Fionnuala. Well, I've done it now, so ye can wake any time. But ye'll be owing me for this one."

He suppressed a yawn and sat back in the chair, stretching his feet out before him. *"Oiche mhaith, a dheartháir. Codladh go maith."*

CHAPTER 32

The early morning sun caused Ciarán to blink, skewing his vision for a moment. Was he dead? He squinted into the bright light. He was surrounded by white clouds, and an angel kept watch by his side. Well, at least he'd gone to heaven.

He snuggled back down into the soft clouds, still incredibly tired. *I wonder where we went wrong with the antidote?* To be fair, Ruadhán had clearly upped the dosage. They should have expected that. He wouldn't want to chance him waking up again in another fifteen hundred years or so. But it wasn't just the elixir. There was something more.

A knife to his throat. That's right, Ruadhán had realized the pages that been removed from the Book of Carraig. Ciarán remembered something, an invisible hand—no a blast of energy . . . from Caitlin. No, there were two . . . Caitlin and Fionnuala. He blinked again. Why was he so surprised? Hadn't he suspected Caitlin had talents? Untapped, but there nonetheless. And Fionnuala was his descendant. He should have expected it would have been hereditary in some. They must have instinctively unleashed them when Ruadhán held the dagger to his throat.

His hand flew up to his throat. Was that what killed him? Were the legends of Scian na Lúin true? No, he could feel himself falling off the ledge and into the blackness of the abyss. He'd caught hold of the edge. What had happened to Ruadhán? Recalling a flash of white tumbling past him and the echo of metal hitting stone, he had his answer.

Áine, his beautiful fair-haired daughter, so like her mother, had stood beside him, floating on air. She had come to him when Bradaigh had wounded him as well, encouraging him to hold on to life. There had been angels, as well, holding him up, and somehow he'd raised his arm toward Aodhán. No, he couldn't be dead, could he? They'd laid him on the cave floor, his head resting in the lap of another angel. She was so beautiful, the same one standing guard over him now, so he must be dead. Perhaps the antidote didn't work, after all.

Who would watch over his children? Surely they would possess some of his and Caitlin's talents. But Caitlin didn't understand them herself, so how could she teach them? Aodhán would care for them, teach them all he needed to know. His mind drifted back to the scene of his death.

Even as lay he in the cave, unable to move, he could feel himself drifting away. But a prick was digging into his arm. Why were they giving him another tattoo? He lifted one eyelid and gazed down at his right arm, his brain clearing a bit as he saw the IV. No, not a tattoo. Steve was giving him the antidote. But wait. Why did he need an IV in heaven? The angel to his left stirred, and he looked toward her. Caitlin, his beautiful wife, his earthly angel, smiled. He wasn't dead, after all.

But where was he? Too tired to think, he returned her smile and drifted back off to sleep.

****

"What are you smiling about?" Steve said. He and Dr. O'Brien had just walked into the room. Caitlin nearly jumped up and hugged both of them.

"He opened his eyes and smiled at me," she said, unable to contain her enthusiasm. Why didn't they seem as excited as she was? Surely that meant he was waking up. A bolt of fear struck at her very core. Or had he just awoken for a moment to say good-bye?

"Are you sure you didn't just dream it?" Dr. O'Brien threw a glance in Ciarán's direction.

Caitlin wanted to state a firm denial, but in truth she couldn't. He did still look like he was sleeping peacefully.

Steve stepped forward and shook Ciarán by the shoulder. "Let's just check it out the old-fashioned way, shall we? Ciarán? Ciarán! Can you hear me?"

His eyes fluttered open a bit, and he groaned, snuggling down under the covers. "Just a few more minutes, Master Domnall," he uttered in ancient Gaelic.

"It sounded a bit like he was asking someone named Domnall if he could have a few more minutes." The corner of Dr. O'Brien's mouth quirked up. "It wasn't Irish exactly, but I think that was the gist o' it."

"Yes, it was," Caitlin said. "He must be dreaming he's back in the fifth century." Oh no! What had she said? Her concern must have shown on her face, because Dr. O'Brien broke into a broad grin.

"'Tis naught to worry yerself over, lass. Being he spends so much time studying the fifth century, 'tis not unusual that he might find himself wandering around there in his sleep from time to time. I had a dream once about a very large heart assisting me in an operation, but stranger yet, it was wearing pink lipstick." He laughed, a rich, deep laugh that calmed Caitlin's nerves.

A gentle wave of relief floated over her. "What do you think it meant?"

"I've no idea. Perhaps it's best not to analyze them too closely as long as they don't affect our sleep . . . or our waking hours. If Ciarán starts to believe he's a pagan priest, however . . ." He laughed again and made a note on the clipboard at the end of the bed.

She shot a quick look in Steve's direction before clearing her throat. "So does that mean he's going to be all right?

Steve lifted one of Ciarán's eyelids, shining a small flashlight in it, and Ciarán groaned again, shoving his friend's arm away. "I would say he is. He's still working off the effects of the potion, though."

Dr. O'Brien had moved over to take his blood pressure and nodded. "He's coming out of it, and if his reaction is any indication, he'll be good as new in a day or two."

"Good," Ciarán grumbled from under the covers. "Now will ye stop all yer poking and prodding and let me sleep the rest o' it off?"

He reached out and clutched Caitlin's hand. She couldn't explain why, but tears started flooding her cheeks, like the shaky dam holding her emotions at bay had finally broken. She pulled her chair up close to the bed and rested her head next to his. And he responded, brushing back her hair and craning his neck to kiss her forehead.

He blinked again, clearing he throat. "When d'ye think I can get all these tubes out o' me?"

As soon as ye're able to sit up and eat a proper meal," the doctor said.

Ciarán rubbed a hand across his face and pushed himself up. "Some hash browns and bacon with a side o' toast, I'm thinking. No eggs. I still can't abide eating the wee things."

Dr. O'Brien shook his head, a laugh on his lips. "Fair enough, but ye'll have a nap right after. Ye need to rest and let the poison get well out o' yer system."

"It's a deal," Ciarán said. "And if I can see me babes after lunch, I'll nap again if need be. Otherwise, I'll be taking meself out o' here. As I've not died, I'm free to do so, am I not?"

"Ye are," the doctor said, "but ye'd be a fool to do so."

"And you won't be!" Caitlin said. "You've given me more than enough stress these last few days. You're going to stay right where you are until Dr. O'Brien says you're well enough to go home."

"Ye have me conditions. Now about that breakfast?" He grinned broadly, and Caitlin couldn't help but laugh. She was so happy to have him back, alive and well.

✳✳✳✳✳✳✳

Ciarán got his breakfast, though to be perfectly honest, he didn't think he would have been able to hold firm on his threat even if he hadn't. As it was, he enjoyed his hash browns and bacon before obediently slipping back beneath the covers, thoughts of seeing Fionn and Aisling utmost in his mind.

He drifted off into his dreams, like he always did. Domnall was walking beside him, tall and straight, his salt-and-pepper hair ruffled by the gentle spring breeze, more salt than pepper now.

"But am I not permitted to see him, master?" Ciarán asked. "I know I am to serve at the goddess's pleasure, to give her the children she so desires, but am I still not his father?"

Domnall sighed, a sad smile touching his lips. "You are, but you must never speak of it. The goddess would not be pleased. Bréanainn must have no conflict as to where his loyalties lie. You shall be his teacher, nothing more. If all goes well, and you hold true to the goddesss's wishes, she may allow you to be his mentor as well."

"So he is my son, and yet he is not?"

"It is the goddess's right as his mother. You are but her consort, but 'tis she who birthed him."

"'Tis Orfthlaith who birthed him," Ciarán said, forgetting himself.

Domnall's reaction was swift and firm. He turned, grabbing Ciarán by the shoulders. "To even whisper such a thought is a betrayal of your goddess. Orfthlaith was naught but a vessel to carry the goddess's child. She served our mother well. Do not demean her sacrifice by lowering it to naught more than a physical act."

"Forgive me, master, I am troubled that I can never truly be a father to Bréanainn."

Domnall cupped the back of his head, his lips softening into a smile. "Just because the lad cannot know that you fathered him does not mean you cannot be one to him. Is it for the child you feel pity or yourself?"

Ciarán nodded, a warmth suffusing his cheeks. Domnall always knew him so well. "Myself, I suppose. I am so proud of him, and yet I can never express that pride."

"Of course you can." Domnall let go of him and nodded that they should continue down the road. "You will be his teacher. Do the job well, and I shall see you are his mentor as well. As such, you will be well within your rights to feel pride in his achievements, just as I do in yours."

"Do you have any children of your own, master?"

Domnall shook his head, a chuckle rumbling from his chest. "Have you learned nothing under my tutelage, *a leanbh*? I am a high priest. I may not marry."

"But you might have been a guardian, chosen to father the priesthood."

Domnall frowned. "When the honor was bestowed upon you, the names of all former guardians were wiped from our records."

"But I remember those who served before me."

Domnall chuckled again, though there was a hint of warning in his words. "Then you would do well to forget them. The children they fathered are not their own, but those of the goddess, loyal to her above all others. Those priests served to please her, just as Orfthlaith did, nothing more. Do you understand that, Ciarán?"

"I cannot say I do, master, but I will obey your command and forget who they were."

"And forget as well that you fathered Bréanainn?"

"How can I forget that, master?"

"Then you must never speak of it again or give him reason to suspect it. Such a betrayal would greatly displease the goddess and bring her anger down around the entire *túath*. Do not disobey me in this."

"I will not, master, but I cannot keep my heart from rejoicing each time I see him. It pains me to think that seven years shall pass before I may spend time with him again. He will not even know me."

"He will know you as his teacher when the time comes. You must satisfy yourself with that, or you will lose all."

"You would take him from under my care?"

"If Ruadhán even suspects you might reveal that knowledge, he will see to it you never see the child again. Do not be so foolish as to risk all to satisfy your own selfish needs."

"I will not, master."

"Good, now let us speak of other things. I weary of this conversation and your continuous questioning of the priesthood's precepts."

"I will try to do better, master.

Domnall chuckled again, though lighter this time. "You will try. I have no doubt of that. It is whether or not you succeed that troubles me. Let us get back to the compound. It is nearly time for supper, and my grumbling stomach will tolerate no more controversial discussion."

"Ciarán! Ciarán!"

"I am coming, master," he said in his ancient tongue before realizing it was Caitlin's voice he heard.

She laughed, and as she bent over to kiss his forehead, a tiny hand poked his cheek. "We've brought you some visitors. The second term in your negotiations, I believe."

Ciarán pushed himself up, his heart filled with love for the tiny creatures who stared down at him. He took Aisling from Caitlin's arms and reached up for Fionn, who was currently in the protective grip of none other than Mary Monaghan.

"Don't you think one at a time is enough for now?"

"No, I don't," he said, though Mary's scowl caused him to drop his arms and rephrase his answer. "I'm fine, a Mhathair, really, and I've missed them something fierce."

"Well, I suppose if I sit on one side of you and Caitlin on the other, they'll be safe enough."

"I'd never risk their welfare, no matter how much I wanted to see them."

Mary's expression softened, and she sat down in the seat on his right side, handing Fionn over. "I know that. It's just sometimes you don't realize your limitations."

Was that a reprimand? Ciarán could never be sure with Mary. She had a subtle way of scolding you and making it sound like a pat on the back. Either way, she always got her point across.

"I'll only hold them for a few minutes, till I start to feel drowsy again." He took Fionn in his right arm and Aisling in his left, rejoicing in the sound of their happy gurgling. Squeezing them tight in his arms, he hugged them to his chest. It made no matter that Aisling was nearly ripping his lower lip off while Fionn had stuck a finger up his nose, tugging hard on the nostril.

"We'll have to be giving his hand a good wash," Mary said, feigning disapproval.

Ciarán and Caitlin laughed, causing the twins to squeal in glee, and Ciarán held them tighter. If he could hold that moment in time forever, he would. He had never felt happier.

****

Three days later, Ciarán arrived back at Mrs. Byrne's as good as new. The muscles in his left arm were still a bit sore from wrenching it to hold on to the ledge, but that would heal in time. At least he didn't feel the need to doze off every half hour anymore. A chill ran through him as he thought of the dagger Ruadhán had held to his throat, the Scian an Lúin. One scratch and his life would have been over, elixir or not. He had not counted on that, and that miscalculation could have cost him everything.

It wasn't until a while later, when he was sitting in the garden, watching the sun go down, that he thought of it again. Aodhán came to sit beside him, his brow marred by deep furrows.

"We have to find it, ye know," his brother said.

He was so content, so happy, he hated the thought of leaving the warm cocoon of Mrs. Byrne's home. "Scian an Lúin, ye mean?"

"If a child should stumble across it . . ."

"I know, but maybe 'tis naught more than a legend. How can a piece o' metal kill that easily?"

"We've seen it happen, *a dheartháir*. D'ye not remember the cleric Colm? And all he did was try to sell the sacred chalice."

"Granted, but Ruadhán may have dipped it in some potent poison. Sure, it would have worn off over the years. 'Tis certain to wear away again."

"And do ye want to take that chance? What if it were Aisling or Fionn that stumbled across it?"

Ciarán sighed. Did Aodhán always have to be so sensible? "Ye're right as usual, a dheartháir. Though I have to warn ye, Caitlin will not be happy about me wandering round the countryside, not even a day out o' hospital."

"We won't be alone; Inspector Travis and some o' his men will be with us. They found Ruadhán's body this morning and agree they should continue to search until they can locate the dagger."

"He believes ye, then, about it being deadly, I mean?"

Aodhán chuckled. "O' course he does. After all he's seen in the last year or so, he doesn't doubt our word. He's a good man and keeps our secret well. Except for his sergeant, he only tells his men what he deems absolutely necessary."

"And what did he tell them about the knife, then?"

"That it had been dipped in a deadly poison that got into the bloodstream through contact. They're all wearing heavy gloves."

"Let's be going, then. We can still get a few hours' searching in before it grows too dark. I'll need to be telling Caitlin what I'm about, though. She may read me the riot act, as Dennis would say, but she'd have me head if I didn't tell her."

"Two o' Dennis's idioms in one sentence." Aodhán laughed. "I'm impressed, brother." His laughter died off, and he squeezed Ciarán's shoulder. "I thought we'd lost ye for a bit, *a chara*. Try not to be doing that again."

"I'll do me best, ye wee eejit. As if I planned the whole thing."

"Actually, ye did," Aodhán said, a grin back on his face as he headed down the path. "Ye'd best be about telling Caitlin, then. Ye can catch me up after ye do."

His brother was right. He had planned it and done a poor job of it. In the future, he'd have to be more careful and consider all the possibilities. Though it wasn't his nature, he'd have to learn not to be so impulsive.

He shook his head. What was he talking about, in the future? Sure, this was the end of it. Yet as much as he tried to convince himself of it, he had this sinking feeling in his stomach that there would always be some new adventure around the bend. For now, though, all were safe and content. Well, except for Caitlin, perhaps. She was not going to be happy about his gallivanting about the countryside.

Taking a deep breath, he headed inside. "Caitlin, darlin'."

CHAPTER 33

Three days later, Ciarán and Aodhán stood outside the cave where Ruadhán had once entombed himself. Niamh had washed Aodhán's *léine*, and Mary had managed to whip up a new one for Ciarán. It only seemed right that they give the chief priest the burial service he would have wanted.

"Shouldn't we go in as well?" Caitlin asked.

"No, *a chuisle*, it would not have been permitted. We won't be long about it."

"We should go, brother." Aodhán carried a bag of items they intended to leave in the tomb with Ruadhán. "I've a wedding to be preparing for, ye know."

Ciarán kissed Caitlin on the cheek and walked into the dark cave. They'd replaced the candles that stood at each corner of the altar, and Ciarán used a long match to light the new ones. He stood for a moment, looking down at Ruadhán's bruised and broken body.

"What d'ye think will happen to him? Sure, the Lord must know he was an honorable man . . . in his own way, that is."

"Father Michael would say 'tis not for us to judge, now wouldn't he?"

Ciarán laughed. "He would that." Leaning over, he placed the elaborate silver collar around the chief priest's neck and the circlet on his head. "The undertaker did a grand job with him, considering."

Aodhán picked up a ceramic cup and handed it to Ciarán. "He did. I got a peek at him right after they found him. 'Twas not a pleasant sight."

"Why don't ye anoint him?" Ciarán said. "I'll finish putting these things round."

Aodhán frowned. "'Tis yer place, and ye know it. As the guardian of the goddess, ye outrank me."

Ciarán supposed he owed the man that much, even if he had tried to kill him. "I'm not sure I'll remember the words."

"'Twill come back to ye. Tell me, brother, d'ye ever dream o' that time, o' sitting listening to Domnall instruct us?"

"O' course I do. 'Tis a part o' our lives, and it wasn't all bad. Domnall became a Christian, ye know."

"How would ye be knowing that?"

He nodded in Ruadhán's direction. "When we met that night to discuss what I needed to do to get Fionnuala back, he told me how it all came about. So many o' them were turning to the Lord; he felt 'twas the only way to protect the goddess."

"I'm glad for Domnall." Aodhán picked up the shroud and spread it over the chief priest's body. "This was meant for yerself, ye know. He had it all folded in that satchel o' his."

Ciarán lifted a shoulder in a half shrug. "I suppose it was. He always did think ahead."

"There's one thing I don't understand, though."

"Just one?" Ciarán smiled. "What is it, then?"

Aodhán tucked the edges of the shroud under the chief priest's body. "Oh, I've many, but an answer to this one will do for now. Why didn't he take the Book o' Carraig with him? He seems to have gathered most o' the other sacred items."

"The book was never to be removed from the Cave o' Rúin Ársa. Few knew the cave even existed, and as it was the portal to the otherworld, he likely believed the goddess would protect it herself."

"I suspected as much. He must have been furious when he found it missing."

"I can only imagine. I don't believe he would have harmed Fionnuala, though. 'Twas me he wanted, me he blamed for everything."

"'Twas not yer fault the priesthood dissolved."

"In his mind, it was. If I hadn't betrayed the goddess . . ." Ciarán shrugged as he finished anointing the priest's head with the mixture of mistletoe, primrose, and cowslip. "I think he believed she rained her anger down upon the priesthood because o' me betrayal."

"Well, no matter, he's at peace now. Sure, the Lord will consider what was in his heart."

Ciarán put the small pot down. "Right, then. We've done all we can here. Ryan's carved his name into the stone, under Caitlin's supervision, o' course—Ruadhán, chief priest o' Túatha de Ui Fiachrach Muaide, loyal son o' his goddess mother."

"I haven't heard that in a while." Aodhán nodded as they left the cave. "He'd like it, I'm thinking."

****

"It seems like we just did this," Ciarán said that next Saturday. Aodhán and Niamh's wedding was a few hours away, and they were getting ready. "Only we'll not be running off at the last minute to locate the Book o' Carraig this time."

"No, that's certain," Aodhán said. "'Tis back at the museum in Dublin, along with the Scian na Lúin. I've stressed the danger to Brian Flaherty. He placed it in a sealed, transparent box and wore a thick pair o' gloves doing it, I might add."

Ciarán laughed. "How did ye explain that?"

"Sure, I didn't have to. I just told him we nearly lost one o' our archaeologists and that Daniel thinks it must be some sort o' poison ground into the blade. He didn't need to hear anymore."

"Ye didn't lie. I've never seen anything like it. More than that, Steve says he hasn't either, and he's peered at it under that microscope o' his. I'm wondering, though, if maybe we should have destroyed it altogether."

"I was thinking the same thing. If anyone ever manages to steal it . . ."

"They'll pay the ultimate price for their crime, that's sure. Ruadhán would think they deserved it."

Aodhán looked in the mirror to knot his tie. "D'ye think he would have truly used it on ye?"

Ciarán touched his neck absentmindedly. "I think he would have done anything if he thought it was honoring his goddess. But he didn't succeed, and ye've got a goddess o' yer own waiting for ye down in the church."

A knock sounded on the door, and Ciarán opened it to see Father Michael standing on the other side. "Are ye ready, then?" He looked at Ciarán and frowned. "Ye've not got any last-minute errands to be running or anything, now have ye?"

Ciarán understood the man's trepidation. Just one year before, he and Aodhán had taken off in search of the Book of Carraig, barely making it back in time to be waiting at the altar for Caitlin. He rested his hand on the priest's shoulder. "Ye've no need to worry, a Athair. I think we're ready to go."

The priest exhaled. "Ah, that's grand. Niamh is radiant, and Father Seamus is waiting for the two o' ye."

****

Ciarán couldn't help glancing at Caitlin as he stood beside his brother at the altar. She was as beautiful as ever, even after giving birth to two children. The sun's rays danced off her hair, the stained-glass windows tinting the deep auburn with a hint of blue and green, and her flawless skin sparkled in the early morning light. Fionn, in his little sailor suit, wriggled in her arms. Mary held Aisling, who was clad in a powder-blue dress that brought out the color in her eyes.

He didn't think he had ever been happier. They were his family, his wife and children, to love and protect. Pride swelled in his chest, causing a lump to grow in his throat, and he coughed to swallow it. Caitlin smiled at him, causing another part of his body to swell. He bit his lip. Not now, but tonight, when the wee ones were asleep and she lay naked in his arms.

Taking a deep breath, he returned her smile and glanced at his brother. He had to get his mind on something else. This was Aodhán's wedding day. Who would have ever thought either of them would be allowed such happiness? He looked back out toward the pews. Fathers Michael and

Dennis sat beside Mary on the groom's side, along with Mrs. Byrne and most of the archaeologists. This was his extended family. Mary, his adopted mother, who'd taken him under her wing, scolding him and fussing over him as if she'd birthed him herself. Father Michael, closer to a father than his own had ever been, and Father Dennis, who'd become like an older brother to him.

The lump was back in his throat, but he had no time to think about it, for at that moment the music began, and Niamh and her father stood at the church doors. Wee Brigid and Kathleen walked down the aisle, strewing pink-and-white rose petals along the red carpet, followed by Fionnuala, his own granddaughter, looking renewed and beautiful after her recent ordeal.

Ciarán heard Father Seamus speaking. "Do you, Niamh Áine Flynn, take this Aodhán Michael Donnelly . . ." But Ciarán's mind was a year in the past, standing at the altar with his own radiant bride.

****

Aodhán's heart skipped as he repeated the words Father Seamus spoke. "I, Aodhán Michael, take you, Niamh Áine, to be my wife. I promise to be faithful to you, in good times and in bad, in sickness and in health, to love you and to honor you, all the days of my life."

Then the priest turned to Niamh, and she repeated his words. "I, Niamh Áine, take you, Aodhán Michael, to be my husband. . ."

Aodhán couldn't help but think—hadn't they already done all those things? They'd been through a lot in the short time they'd known each other, and she'd stood by him steadfastly, cared for him as he recovered with a tenderness he could never have imagined. For his part, he recalled the pain that gripped his heart when he thought Bradaigh had killed her last year. He would have given his own life to save hers—and still would. He gazed into her eyes, sparkling now with happy tears, and smiled.

The priest asked for the ring, but much to Aodhán's chagrin, his brother seemed to be miles away. Reliving his own wedding, no doubt. The thought warmed his heart and quelled his annoyance. Still, he did need the rings. He poked Ciarán's arm, causing him to jump.

"The rings, brother?"

"Oh, sorry." An awkward smile crossed Ciarán's lips, his cheeks flushing a healthy pink, and he reached into his pocket to retrieve the two golden bands.

Aodhán's hand trembled as he placed the tiny golden circlet on her finger, a symbol that she was his wife. Fionn and Aisling picked that moment to cry out in glee, causing everyone to laugh. Any tension Aodhán felt flew from his body. He and Niamh were husband and wife. Nothing but death could separate them now.

The rest of the Mass seemed to pass in a flurry of incense and prayers. Before he knew it, he was whisking his bride to the front steps of the church and receiving congratulations from friends and family.

Ciarán shook his hand, then hesitated a moment before pulling him into a bear hug. "I'm so happy for ye, *a chara*. Forgive me for all the suffering I've caused ye, but I can't regret it's brought ye to me here now."

"'Twas well worth it. I'm glad ye're me brother, Ciarán, as well as me friend."

"Come on, you two." Caitlin nudged Ciarán to the side, handing him Fionn so that she could give Aodhán a hug as well. "There's a line of people waiting to congratulate you."

Mary was next in line. She held a tissue to her nose, Aisling planted firmly on her left hip. "Oh, you make such a lovely couple." Blinking away the tears, she gave him a big kiss on the cheek. "I'll be expecting a few grandbabies from you as well come this time next year."

"Now, Mary," Father Michael said, "they've only just wed. Give them some time to settle in."

Aodhán had to bite his lip to keep from laughing. He was fairly sure they were well settled in already, but he wasn't about to tell anyone that, especially Duffy Flynn, who was next in line.

He sniffed a bit and blew his nose. "Ye take good care o' her now, ye hear, or 'tis meself ye'll be answering to."

****

Ciarán sat down next to Fionnuala at the reception and sighed. Fionn had finally fallen asleep on his shoulder, his little sailor suit crumpled up beneath Ciarán's arm. "I'm so sorry for all ye had to go through. Me dreams were telling me 'twas not the twins I needed to worry over."

"Don't be silly," Fionnuala said. "I barely even knew anything happened. One minute I was helping a kindly old gentleman to his car and the next I was waking on the floor o' that cave." She reached over and touched Ciarán's hand. "I truly don't think he would have hurt me."

"Nor do I, still . . . I should have seen ye safe. Ye are me granddaughter, after all."

Fionnuala reached for the ring that now hung around her neck on a chain next to her miraculous medal. "Are ye sure ye don't want it back to give to Fionn?"

"No, 'twas meant for Bréanainn, and you're his descendant."

"'Tis a grand wedding, is it not?" A man about Ciarán's age came around and sat on the other side of Fionnuala, causing her to roll her eyes.

"That it is, Donnabhán. Enjoying yerself, then?"

"I am that, and who are these two fine-looking gentlemen?" he said, nodding toward Ciarán and his son.

Ciarán didn't like the look of the man. There was something devious about him. Maybe it was the way he kept flitting his eyes back and forth between him and Fionnuala or the subtle tic that pulled at the corner of his left eye, but Ciarán didn't trust him. He tried to smile and put his preconceptions out of his head. After all, the man couldn't help what he looked like.

"This is the groom's brother, Ciarán, and his son, Fionn."

"Fionn is it? The same as meself."

Fionnuala seemed to suppress a silent groan. "Your name is Donnabhán, and ye know it, so stop the nonsense." She turned to Ciarán, rolling her eyes once more. "This is me cousin Donnabhán McKieran."

"I prefer to be called Fionn. Nuala here just doesn't like it because she knows I have a stronger claim to our ancestor's ring than she does."

"The ring?" Ciarán said, feigning ignorance.

She stood and headed across the room, dragging Ciarán and Fionn with her. "Ye enjoy yerself now, Donnabhán, but we've got to see about the food."

"The food?" Ciarán said, just as glad to be away from the disconcerting man. When they'd found a quiet corner, Fionnuala sat and yanked him down beside her. "I thought we were to be seeing about the food?" His stomach grumbled, and she let a smile put the sparkle back in her eyes.

"We will in a minute. I just want to be telling ye about me cousin first. He's one o' yers as well, though he's what ye might be calling the black sheep o' the family."

"What does the color o' a sheep have to do with anything?"

Fionnuala's smile broadened. "'Tis just one o' those sayings ye keep adding to that little book o' yers. It means he's not like the rest o' us, or I should say most o' us haven't the time o' day for the man."

"What did he do?"

"He's just a sleezy little man, always looking to see what he can wheedle out o' someone else. 'Tis from his mother's side, we're thinking, though Lord knows she was a darlin' herself. Some o' her brothers, though . . . They're the ones that put the notion in his head, I'm thinking."

Ciarán frowned. Maybe it was just him, but she seemed to be talking in circles. His arm was going a bit numb, so he shifted Fionn to his other shoulder. Though the child stirred for a moment, he soon put his thumb in his mouth and settled down once more.

Fionnuala smiled. "They've had a busy day, poor things."

"That they have, but they'll sleep well tonight, so I'll not be complaining. Now what notion is it they put in Donnabhán's head?"

"Oh!" Fionnuala grinned, clearly realizing she was indeed rambling on. "'Tis about the ring, ye see."

"Me ring?"

"'Twas to be passed down to the eldest son in each family, who was to be named Fionn. As I told ye, me da being the eldest received the ring as soon as he came o' age. But then he never had any sons. Only having one brother himself and the rest all sisters, I'm thinking he thought he might not have a son, so being the pragmatic man he is, he named me Fionnuala."

Ciarán nodded. "The feminine form of Fionn."

"'Twas a good thing too, for he never did have a son, so when I came o' age, he passed the ring on to me. Me uncle Colm never had a problem with it, but me cousin Donnabhán—he's Colm's eldest ye see—he thought the ring should rightfully go to him, being me da had no male descendants to pass it on to."

"So that's why he wants to be called Fionn."

"'Tis his middle name, so I suppose 'tis not that unheard o', but 'tis the reasoning behind it that's off. He thinks because he's calls himself Fionn that proves the ring should be his."

"Well, 'tis not his choice, now is it? The ring was mine to pass on, and I say it belongs to yerself and wee Timothy when he's grown."

The smile dropped from Fionnuala's face. "He's there again, watching us. Ye don't suppose he's been trying to hear what we've been saying?"

Ciarán frowned. That was the last thing they needed. Still, he had no proof, and they could always say he'd heard them wrong. "If he is, it will do him no good, now will it? Who's going to believe a word o' such a tale?"

"True enough, I suppose. I'm thinking 'twould be better for us to be changing the subject, though. Just in case. Besides, from the sound o' yer stomach, ye're about to join Fionn there and chew on yer own hand if ye don't get something to eat." She laughed again, and they headed toward the buffet table. Ciarán cast a final look in Donnabhán's direction but decided not to let it ruin his day.

****

It was close to midnight when Ciarán lay down next to his wife. The twins had gone to bed without any trouble, and Caitlin snuggled up against him.

"Aodhán and Niamh looked so happy. I hope they have what we do."

"D'ye now?" Ciarán slipped his hand under her nightie and pulled her close in his embrace. "And what would that be?"

"A love so deep I feel you're a part of me. You're not only in my heart. You are my heart."

"And what o' the wee ones?"

Caitlin laughed and slapped his chest, snuggling in deeper, her words but a whisper. "They're in there as well. After all, they're a part of you and of me. Every time I look at them, I'm filled with awe. Two beautiful little new lives formed from love."

"They are that, so what do ye say we see if can do it again, eh?" He looked down when she didn't answer and chuckled. Making a brother or sister for Fionn and Aisling was going to have to wait a bit. Caitlin was sound asleep, a soft smile caressing her lips.

Ciarán let out a contented sigh. *"Codail go sámh, a ghrá.* Ye are me heart as well." Then he closed his eyes and drifted off into a peaceful sleep.

TO BE CONTINUED IN

Book Four in The Cross of Ciarán Series

The Ring of Eagna

www.andrea-matthews.com

On Facebook at Andrea Matthews Historical Romance
On Twitter at Andrea Matthews Author
@AMatthewsAuthor

Ciarán's Favorite Shepherd's Pie

Ingredients

1 pound ground beef
5 large potatoes
2 cups mixed vegetables (previously cooked: peas, carrots, and corn preferrable)
½ cup yellow onion, chopped
1 tbsp. prepared mustard
½ cup catsup or steak sauce
½ cup beef broth
¼ cup flour
butter

Instructions

Brown beef in pan. In the meantime, boil potatoes in a separate pot. After beef is browned, drain fat and mix in beef broth, mustard, and catsup or steak sauce, adding flour to thicken the gravy. Add chopped onions. Move mixture to casserole dish. Add previously cooked vegetables to mixture in casserole dish and blend together with spoon. Check to see potatoes can be pierced with fork easily. In the pot with potatoes, drain water, add milk, and mash. Add mashed potatoes to top of meat mixture in casserole dish, making sure potatoes seal the edge of dish. Top with pats of butter. Bake at 350 degrees for about 45 minutes and serve.

Mary Monaghan's Famous Chili Soup

Ingredients

1 pound ground beef
2 cans crushed tomatoes
2 cans dark red kidney beans
1 cup rice
2 small yellow onions, chopped
Chili powder to taste

Instructions

Brown ground beef in frying pan, drain fat, and put beef in large pot. Add crushed tomatoes and stir. Drain kidney beans and add to pot. Add rice and onions. Stir. Add chili powder to taste. Cook over medium heat, stirring often for about one hour. Serve with saltine crackers. Even better the second night.

Mrs. Byrne's Bed & Breakfast Colcannon

Ingredients

8 russet potatoes
1 head cabbage
1 cup bacon or ham (previously cooked)
4 scallions
1 stick margarine
1–1 ¼ cups milk
Salt and pepper to taste

Instructions

Boil potatoes in pot of water until they can be pierced easily with a fork. Cut the head of cabbage into strips. When potatoes are cooked, remove them from water and replace with cabbage and scallions. Cook until cabbage begins to soften, but do not overcook. In the meantime, add milk and butter to potatoes and mash. When cabbage is ready, drain the remaining water and add the mashed potatoes to pot and gently mix with cabbage and scallions. Crumble bacon or chop ham and add to pot. Mix gently once more and serve.

GLOSSARY

Irish:

Aiteann – gorse bush

A Athair – father

Aos sidhe – people of the mounds, fairy folk

Bhí mé bródúil asat i gcónai, a mhic – I was always proud of you, son

Brog / broga – shoe / shoes

Cailín – lass, girl

Cave of Rúin Ársa – Cave of Ancient Secrets

A chara / a chairde – friend / friends

A chéadsearc – dearest love (literally, my first love)

A chuisle – darling, dear (technically, pulse)

A chuisle mo chroí – pulse of my heart / beat of my heart

Claíomh of Ailbe – Sword of Ailbe

Codail go sámh – Sleep tight

Conmaicne Mara – Connemara, a region in the west of Ireland

Cup of Cheartais – Cup of Justice

Dadaí – Daddy

A deirfiur – sister

Dercad – a deep form of meditation

A dheartháir – brother (as in sibling)

Dia duit – hello (technically, God to you)

Dia is Muire duit – Hello to you too (technically, God and Mary to you)

Elixir of Suain Cráite – Elixir of Tormented Sleep

Ériu – ancient name for Ireland

Fáinne na Eagna – Ring of Wisdom

Filidh – professional class of poets who practiced divination. In Ciarán's priesthood, it is a seven-year period immediately before full priesthood.

Garda – the Guard, the Irish police force

Geis – a taboo or vow

A ghrá – love (as a term of endearment)

Hills of ár Sinsear – Hills of our Ancestors

In ainm an Athar, agus an Mhic, agus an Spiorad Naoimh – In the name of the Father, and of the Son, and of the Holy Spirit

Is chuisle mo chroí thú – You are the beat of my heart

Lann na Leorghnimh – Blade of Atonement

A leanbh – child, baby

Léine / léinte – a tunic, shirt / tunics, shirts

Mamaí – Mommy

A Mháthair – mother

A mhic – son

A mhuirnín – darling, my beloved

Mo mhic dílis – my loyal son

Mumhan – ancient name for Munster

Oiche mhaith, a dheartháir. Codladh go maith – Good night, brother. Sleep well.

Ollamh – the highest rank of the *filidh* or any group. In Ciarán's priesthood, it is the highest rank of cleric or a major cleric.

Sabhaircín – primrose

Satire – a poetic curse that could vary in effect from mild insult to death

Scian an Lúin – Dagger of Lúin

A seanathair – grandfather

A seanchara – old friend

A shagart – priest

Straif- fourteenth letter of the ogham alphabet, associated with the blackthorn, a tree known for its dark secrets

A shíorghrá – my eternal love

Slan – good-bye

Slan abhaile – safe home

A stórín – little treasure, little darling

A tiarnán – my lord

Ta mo chroí istigh ionat – my heart is within you / I love you
Tír na Haislinge – Land of Dreams
Tír na nÓg – Land of Youth, the otherworld
Triubhas – trews or trousers
Tuamaí Dearmadta – Forgotten Tombs
Túatha de Uí Fiachrach Muaide – Ciarán's *túath* or clan
Ulaidh – Ulster
Veil of Cinniúna – Veil of Fate

<u>*Celtic Celebrations:*</u>
Golden Year – every nineteen years; the guardianship ceremonies were held during this year
Imbolc – festival marking the beginning of spring
Ostara – spring equinox
Beltane – fire festival celebrating the coming of summer and fertility for the coming year *Lughnasa* – harvest festival
Samhain – festival marking the separation of the light and dark seasons on the calendar, when the division between the land of the living and the land of the dead can be breached